NEOPRIM

ZETA TRILOGY, BOOK ONE

ROB GRAFRATH

Copyright © 2021 by Rob Grafrath

First hardcover edition August 2021

Cover design and chapter heading art by Gabrielle Grafrath

ISBN 978-1-953470-01-0

Published by Ourania Publishing

PROLOGUE

THEY APPROACHED the neoprim camp as strangers always should —
showing their palms and making conspicuous noise.

The showing of palms was an awkward gesture for Oraxis, on
account of the dead gazelle slumped over his shoulders. He shouted
across the field in a strained voice, "Hello! May we enter your camp?
We bring fresh meat to share!"

Over the sound of dogs barking came a man's reply, "Stay there!
We will come to you!"

The men took their time crossing through the tall grass with
spears at the ready, watching for any signs of ambush or other
trickery.

"Paranoid lot, this one," Genevieve sent to Oraxis, via mindspeak.

"And young!" Oraxis mindspoke. *"Who sends pubescents to
parley?"*

"You think anyone without a gray streak is a pubescent." Granted,
the oldest among them was struggling to grow a proper beard. *"I'm
sure the older men are off on a hunt."*

*"Whatever the case, this should make getting in easier. Lay on the
charm and play me as the fool."*

Genevieve cleared her throat to point out the joke left untold, then stepped forward and waved at the closest young man. She put on her doe-eyes, raising her voice to a higher pitch and adding some breathiness. "Hi, sorry to bother you! I see you're settling in for the evening. If there's a place at your fire for two more, then this fresh meat is yours to enjoy. My man was lucky enough to have felled the beast, but *foolish* enough not to have the tools to clean and dress it."

A few of the young men chuckled.

"Where is your tribe?" The young man in charge demanded.

"Nice Marilyn impression," Oraxis sent, *"but I don't think he's impressed."*

Genevieve ignored him and replied, "We were separated from them during a hunt, almost a month ago. It's a long story." She took two steps towards the man, letting her hips swivel. "But I could tell it to you if you'd like."

She could see the young man's tension easing as he assessed her, then Oraxis.

He set the butt of his spear against the ground and leaned on it. "It's just the two of you? Have you no pooches?" Their own dogs paced and sniffed around the field, but didn't approach Genevieve or Oraxis.

"We have no pooches," Genevieve said, shrugging.

An adolescent with dots of white paint on his face had stepped closer. He showed his teeth in a wide smile, then said, "I know why you were separated from your tribe."

"Oh?" Genevieve said, raising an eyebrow and humoring him with a smirk.

He took a step closer, then another.

"Gen," Oraxis warned, via mindspeak.

"Relax, O," Genevieve replied, *"I've got this."*

Paint-dot-boy leaned towards her, making a show of sniffing the air. He stepped backwards, waving one hand back and forth, holding his nose with the other. "They couldn't stand your stench!"

Genevieve's smile turned to a scowl as the other men encircled them, laughing.

Oraxis pretended to stifle a laugh of his own. Genevieve shot him a glare. She understood he was feigning good spirits, trying to ease the tension by joining them in mocking her, but it still stung.

"Bakkra!" The first man shouted, backhanding the shoulder of paint-dot-boy. "What sort of thing to say is that? She doesn't smell! Tell her so!"

"Yeah, give her a second whiff, Bakkra!" Someone in the crowd taunted.

"Porom will try to kiss the stinky woman," a boy jeered.

"Obviously, approaching your camp was a mistake," Genevieve spat. "Your people are cruel to strangers. We'll make our own camp tonight."

She turned her back on Porom and Bakkra, heading back the way they came. The young men who had closed the circle behind them stepped in her path, but Genevieve wouldn't be intimidated. She walked between two men, pushing them apart, sending them stumbling. Oraxis slid through the opening she had made, still carrying the gazelle over his shoulders.

As Genevieve marched away through the knee-high grass, a quarrel escalated behind them. Porom was facing off against Bakkra.

"See what you have done!" Came Porom's voice. "They bring enough meat for the whole tribe and your insults drive them away!"

It sounded like they were pushing each other, but neither Oraxis nor Genevieve turned to watch. The dogs were barking at their agitated masters.

"*Well played,*" Oraxis mindspoke.

"*Whatever. Thanks for standing up for me back there.*"

"*Gen, you know it was all a part of the act. Are you going to let a puerile insult like that upset you? Look, if I turned defensive, it just would've escalated from taunts to fisticuffs.*"

"*Sure, so you play one of the boys while I play piece of meat number two.*"

"If you can think of more effective lures than sex and steak, be my guest."

"I say we take their meat anyways!" A young man shouted from the quarrel behind them.

Another countered, "Are you such a poor hunter? Steal a man's meat, and you'll be cursed by his ancestors."

The sound of someone running towards them through the grass approached from behind.

"Don't turn around," Genevieve sent. She could see Oraxis tensing, ready to respond if the approaching man attacked.

"Forgive my kin," came the voice of Porom. "He thinks he's funny, but he's not."

Genevieve and Oraxis stopped and turned around.

Porom gestured to the distant campground. "We are the Scorpion Tail Tribe, and you are welcome to our camp. We'll help you clean your kill, and I'll introduce you to Chief Talmid."

"Thank you," Genevieve said, though her heart felt like it skipped a beat when she heard the name "Talmid".

She mindspoke to Oraxis, *"O, did you hear that? Talmid — that's the name Jamji said she was going to—"*

"You know we can't tell her," Oraxis sent. *"Besides, it's an ancestral name, used every few generations. It's probably not him."*

Genevieve doubted that, but Oraxis was right that they couldn't tell Jamji.

As they say: what happens in Eden, stays in Eden.

THEY WERE ROASTING meat by twilight. Oraxis and the young men of the tribe were in the tall grass, wearing nothing but their woven codpiece baskets. They were facing off in wrestling matches, and Oraxis was mopping the floor with the poor guys.

It wasn't a very fair fight, of course. Aside from having studied martial arts for a thirty-year stint — when was that, a hundred fifty years ago? — Oraxis also sported a full suite of bioenhancements. That included myofibrites, which supplemented his natural muscles, granting him more strength and speed than his modest frame suggested.

"They think if they can best your man, you might lay with one of them," a woman behind her said.

Genevieve turned to see the woman laying on a fur, breastfeeding a baby.

"Well," Genevieve said, "they're not having much luck so far. They're all too young for me, anyway."

She gave the baby a considering look. It was the ideal age for alpha seeding.

"I've found our winner," she sent Oraxis.

"Good. Boy or girl?"

"I don't know yet."

"Let's just hope it's healthy."

Genevieve was standing to go talk to the woman. She tried not to let agitation show on her face as she replied to Oraxis, "Healthy? You mean, don't pick another sickly little runt like Pip? I have a right mind to show those boys you're wrestling how to choke you out."

"Gen, that's not what I—"

She closed the conversation channel.

"What's your name?" She asked the woman.

"Yephanie," the woman said, pulling the baby from her breast and sitting up. She covered herself with her leather tunic, then lifted the bundled baby up to her shoulder, bouncing it. "And yours?"

"Ayr," she lied. "And your babe?"

"We haven't named her yet."

That wasn't a good sign. Postponing the naming of a baby can signify that it was unwanted. Also, where's her daddy?

She sat on the fur next to Yephanie.

Genevieve asked, "May I hold her?"

"Certainly. Are you a ma?"

"No," Genevieve said, gingerly accepting the bundle from

Yephanie. "I haven't been so lucky. But I have raised many of my kin. I was a second-ma to a few of them."

The baby was strikingly beautiful. Her skin was light brown, her cheeks chubby. She was well-fed and bright-eyed. The adorable thing melted her heart like butter. A tear threatened to come to her eye, but she blinked it away.

"Can I ask — why haven't you named her yet?" Genevieve smiled at the baby, receiving a fleeting, toothless smile in return. Oh, this was a *cute* one!

"Wilhelm and I haven't found the right name yet," Yephanie said. She was watching the baby in Genevieve's arms, beaming with pride. Good — the baby's father was still around.

"I see. Well, I do hope you find one soon, or she'll grow up thinking her name is 'babe'."

Yephanie laughed, leaning back on her elbows and watching the men wrestle.

Genevieve laid the baby down on the furs and loosened her soft leather bundle. After playing with the baby for a while, she decided that it was time to do what they had come to do.

She picked the baby up, held it against her shoulder, and leaned her head against that of the baby, pressing her temple against its soft skin.

A chain of neurites — synthetic, neuron-emulating nanites — formed at Genevieve's temple, manufactured via overproduction of her neurite network. The microscopic neurite chain passed through her skin, penetrating painlessly into the skin of the baby. The neurites migrated through the fissures of the baby's skull, then set to the task of self-replicating.

Over the course of the next year, the foundational framework of the baby's synthetic neurite network would form. By the time she was old enough to speak, the nanites would be fully incorporated into her brain. Then, the aposynchronization data packets would begin to flow.

Her sensory inputs would be captured. Her connectome would

be digitized, compressed, and broadcast through the underground network of mycelites permeating the crust of Genesis. Her aposynchronic orb at the Synthetic Intelligence Central Processing Facility would faithfully record all of these data on her behalf, storing every moment of her life in full fidelity until the day that she accessed it for the first time — the day her Beta Bootstrapping began.

Genevieve reopened her channel to Oraxis, sending, *"It's done."*

NIGHT HAD FALLEN and most of the tribe was going to sleep. Oraxis laid nearby, absent-mindedly playing with his beard, staring at the stars.

Genevieve continued fawning over the baby, reluctant to relinquish her to her mother. It wasn't often that she had the opportunity to play with a baby, and she was making the most of it.

Wilhelm was away with many of the other men, so Genevieve was glad to keep Yephanie company and help tend to the baby. Oraxis had agreed that it would be fine if they stayed with the tribe for a few days.

"You're a good caregiver," Yephanie yawned. "How many of your kin have you raised?"

"Five," or would it be six? Pip-Tau and Pip-Rho complicate things. "But we're expecting a sixth soon."

Yephanie gave an approving grunt and nod.

Genevieve crooned a counting song to the baby. "Alpha makes one, beta makes two, gamma makes three, delta makes four, epsilon makes five, and zeta makes six!" She tapped the baby's nose on "zeta", and it let out a squeal of a laugh.

Yephanie leaned in to watch the baby's delighted reaction. "She liked that. Say that last part again."

Genevieve sang, "zeta makes six," tapping the baby's nose again, sending it into another bout of giggles.

"Zeta," Yephanie sang. The baby cooed. Yephanie scooped her

baby up and out of the fur bundle. She held the naked baby's pudgy body up to the night, declaring, "Zeta is a good name! I know Wilhelm will like it. I name you Zeta!"

From the campfire nearby, the eld they had introduced as Chief Talmid turned to smile back at Yephanie. He said, "Everybody, did you hear Yephanie? She has named her girl using a new name. Her name will be Zeta!"

Murmured echoes of "Zeta" swept through the tribe as they tried out the word for the first time.

"Gen," Oraxis mindspoke, "we have a problem."

Genevieve sighed. "Cultural contamination, I know. So they learn a little Greek. I don't think that's—"

"That's not what I mean," Oraxis sent, sitting up and looking at the stars. "Look east, here it comes."

Genevieve looked up at the starry eastern sky. She saw Soma, Genesis's larger moon, shining full and bright. Varuna, the distant ice moon, was in its new moon phase. Its teal crescent wouldn't return to the night sky for weeks. "O, what are you talking about?"

Then it appeared — a blooming fireball approaching from the east.

Gasps and shouts rose from the neoprim tribe as the brilliant light caught their attention. People began pointing and calling out.

"Wake up!"

"A falling star!"

"It's an omen!"

It was too slow to be a meteor — its white glow crawled past the stars. It grew an orange tail as it processed. Small flecks broke off and burned in its wake. The main fireball broke in two as it passed overhead.

The neoprims were flipping out over it. They'd probably make up a whole new sky god myth to explain the phenomenon. So much for cultural contamination.

"Whose was it?" Genevieve mindspoke to Oraxis.

"Proliferans. It was their new communications relay vessel.

They've been boasting that their latest signal obfuscation algorithm was undetectable by Specters. Guess they were wrong."

"Offworlders," Genevieve sent, shaking her head.

"EoE Sha-Omega Anise already denounced them. She says The Council would never authorize transmissions in low orbit. I'm sure the Proliferans misbehaved, but Specters are also getting bolder these days."

The wreckage spread and tumbled, breaking into pieces as it tore through the atmosphere, forming a cluster of orange-white embers. It grew closer as it fell, suggesting that it would impact somewhere to their west.

Someone was pulling on her hand.

Genevieve turned, seeing Yephanie, wide-eyed and full of wonder. "I know what it is, Ayr!" She held the baby, Zeta, up towards Soma. She declared, "Soma sheds tears of joy at the beauty of Zeta's name!"

The tribe cheered. Dogs yipped and howled in response to the commotion.

"Well," Oraxis said, picking up his pack, "I think we'll go see if we can catch some Soma tears."

"You're leaving?" Chief Talmid asked, approaching them. "Stay and celebrate the good omen!"

"Oraxis, this isn't our problem," Genevieve sent, even as she began pulling on her moccasins and apologizing to Yephanie and Chief Talmid. "The Proliferans will send down a clean-up crew."

Oraxis sent, "They can only come Eden-side with EoE authorization, and we all know Sha-Omega is too proud to ask for help. Right now, every thrill-seeking teenager is making a bee-line for that crash site. If we can beat them to it and keep them away, then there's a fair chance that Genesis can handle this on our own."

"Fine, how far is it?"

"Out of the Noddites reporting their positions, we're among the closest to the crash site at fifty kilometers."

"We'll be running all night!" Genevieve sent.

"No, I can make it in a little over an hour. You'll be there in two, tops. I'll meet you there."

Oraxis set off, jogging across the field. Once he was out of sight, he'd pick up the pace, pushing his bioenhanced body to the limit. She shook her head. Offworlders and Specters seemed to be at the core of *every* problem on Genesis.

"I wish I could stay," she told Yephanie. "Take good care of Zeta, okay? She's a very special child."

Yephanie nodded. "I will. It was nice to meet you, Ayr. Be careful out there — dangerous creatures lurk in the darkness."

Genevieve muttered, "You don't know the half of it." She stole one more glance at Zeta, then kissed the baby on the forehead. She whispered, "Goodbye, sweet Zeta. I can't wait to see you again."

Genevieve turned, activated her infrared vision, and disappeared into the night.

1

WHO AM I?

A MIND STIRRED in an empty place. It had been there for a very long time, but only now could it sense the passage of time.

There was no sight or sound. The mind had no body to control, which seemed wrong. It had the unsettling sense that the empty place was all there was, and all that ever will be. It felt exposed, naked, trapped.

Worst of all, the mind was alone.

It couldn't speak without a mouth, but it could think using words. The timid voice within said, "Hello?"

The sound of the mind's voice was feminine. This was a revelation — she was a "she".

She waited silently. After a long, lonely time, two other minds joined her in the emptiness. They were unseen, but could be felt as surely as if they were touching her. Were they touching her?

One of the minds spoke with the voice of a woman — gentle and patient. "Hello, dear. How are you feeling?"

"I'm...confused," she said. "Who am I?"

"Oh," the woman said. She hesitated. "You don't know your name?"

"No! Not my name, not *anything!*"

The other mind spoke. This one was a stern man. "That's discouraging. You should at least know something about yourself."

This truth loomed like a jaguar in the trees. She rejected it. She would not show weakness. "Well, I *do* know my name. I just don't want to tell you until I know who you are."

The woman replied. "Oh! Well, in that case, my name's Genevieve."

"And I'm Oraxis," the man said. "So, what's your name?"

She grasped at her memories, but they slipped through her fingers like water. The harder she tried, the more frustrated she got.

"You don't know?" Oraxis sighed. "Very unfortunate."

This infuriated her, so she cast him out.

Genevieve sputtered, "Wait, did you just…"

She considered whether to cast the woman out, too. A moment later, the man's presence returned. "You *booted* me?!" He seemed tickled. "How did you manage to do that? You really are something else, child."

"I'm not a child."

"Oh? Are you sure?" he said with amusement. "Maybe you are, but you can't remember."

She tried to cast him out again, but this time he clung to her mind like a tick. She imagined burning him with the tip of a stick pulled from the fire. She could even see the glowing red tip as it smoldered, carefully lowering towards the embedded parasite.

Genevieve said, "O, are you seeing this?"

"I am," Oraxis said, sounding impressed. "She's already pulling imagery into her slate-space. She *is* something else, alright. Let's see how she does with a replay."

"Is that a good idea? This identity gap—"

"Gen, it's what she needs. She's a natural at manipulating slate-space, so I think she'll do well with a replay. It's either this, or she goes back to neural mapping. It's sink or swim."

She noticed the nothing-place around her becoming loose, slippery, squishy like clay. She was a bead of water, rolling backwards off a leaf, splashing into a puddle.

Oraxis had called it "slate-space". The name brought to mind large, flat rocks, dappled with moss. There had been a slate outcropping hanging over the edge of the spring pool.

Sink or swim?

She could swim — she loved it.

Her little bro, shivering in knee-deep water? Not so much.

"Zeta! Zeta, come back, that's no fair, you know I can't swim good. I hate it when you go swim in the deep water. And it's too cold! I'm getting out."

Such a whiny babe.

Zeta smiled and turned to float on her back. It felt like being home again after a long journey. Such peace. Spider monkeys swung through the branches above. She wished she could do the same. Swimming was good, but so was climbing. She looked again at the slate looming over the water's edge and something tugged at her.

Something wasn't right.

Zeta swam back to shallow water, stood, and stared at her bro-kin, Charra. He stared back, arms crossed, his deep brown eyes narrowed. She was seeing his face again, for the first time. How long has it been since she has seen him? Days? Years?

Her name was Zeta.

Her bro-kin's name was Charra — her *lost* bro-kin.

Memories failed her, but emotions came back as a flood of pain and loss, of love and purpose. Charra's image blurred as tears welled in her eyes. Her throat constricted. Her heart pounded in her ears.

Charra looked like he had seen a ghost. "Um...Zeta?"

At that, she erupted into heaving sobs of joy and sadness. She crashed through the water towards her precious babe-bro. His eyes widened in shock and he started backwards, but she was already embracing him. Darkness from the edges of reality rushed in even as she wrapped her arms around him and wailed promises to never let go.

But he was already gone.

———

ZETA REELED, tumbled. She clutched without hands, cried without eyes, gasped without lungs.

Oraxis's voice met her as she collapsed back into the nothing-place. "Back so soon? Oh, goodness, and quite upset."

"Do you want to talk about it?" Genevieve asked.

Gathering her wits, Zeta growled as if through gritted teeth. "Bring him back."

"Sorry," Oraxis said, "I don't know who you're talking about. Even if I did, that's not how it works."

Genevieve said, "You seem to have done quite well, if you came back with a purpose. You know, the first time—"

"I said: Bring! Him! Back!" Feral rage coursed through her. She wrapped her essence around that of both Oraxis and Genevieve, compressing them, forcing them out. They resisted, but she kept squeezing until they were out of her mind.

She had to figure this place out. One thing she knew was that this was *her* place, and *they* were the intruders. It felt good to have control.

Another thing she knew was that her name was Zeta, and her bro's name was Charra. She had been swimming with him, but now she was here. There was so much more that was missing, but just having this much knowledge filled her with more emotion than she could handle.

Oraxis and Genevieve returned. They were mosquitoes, which kept coming back no matter how many times she swatted them.

Genevieve said, "I'm sorry that you're upset, but please, let us in. We can help you."

"You can help me," Zeta spat, "by bringing my bro-kin back."

"Your bro-kin?" Genevieve asked. "What's his name?"

"His name is Charra, and my name is Zeta, and my pooch..." Zeta couldn't remember her pooch's name. Did she even have a pooch?

"Your pooch?" Oraxis asked.

She concentrated, but came up with nothing. Zeta cursed the nothing-place. "I can't remember. This place is a memory trap. Let me out of it!"

"You'll get out," said Oraxis, "in due time. The best way for you to remember who you are is to stay here in slate-space for a while."

Slate-space? She needed to learn more, to get out. "This nothing-place is called slate-space? Tell me how it works."

Genevieve said, "A long time ago people used to draw pictures on slate to help teach lessons and explore ideas. That's what this place — this blank slate-space — does for you. You can do more things with it, but for now, all you need it for is a process called *assisted narrative reconstruction*. You re-learn who you are by replaying experiences of your past. Experience replay is like reliving a memory—"

"I don't want memories!" Zeta snapped. This woman was making no sense. "I want my bro-kin back here, right now. I had him in my arms and then he disappeared."

"He never was here, Zeta. That was a relived experience — a replay. It felt real because it was real for you at one point. The replay probably collapsed because you diverged — you changed it from the original experience."

Zeta was confused. This was nonsense. "It was nothing like a memory. It was real. Now, let me out!"

Genevieve sighed.

Oraxis spoke. "It's fine, Gen. She'll figure out the rules of the game as she plays. I'm opening her up to another replay."

Slate-space loosened again. Genevieve spoke with a rapid urgency. "Zeta, don't try to control it. Don't change it. Pay attention, learn, feel it, and accept it into your reality. Acceptance, Zeta! Remember that! Zeta! Zeta!"

Why did she have to yell? Wincing at the light and shivering, Zeta dragged the skins up over her head, just to have them yanked back off again. "Zeta! Zeta, you have to be kidding me, are you sleeping?"

"I'm up, I'm up! Give the skins back. It's too cold in the morning these days." In truth, Zeta had been awake, reveling in the warmth of the skins, dreading the inevitable cold. Had she been daydreaming? Who was she just talking to?

"Ha!" mocked Yephanie-ma. "Morning? Surya burns high in the sky. Do you need a squirt from the water skin?" She was not offering a drink, but a dousing.

"No, I'm up! Where's Charra?"

"That's what I want to know. He said he was collecting sticks, but he's been gone for too long. Will you find your bro for me? Check the spring pool."

The spring pool with the slate outcropping. Slate-space? Was that something from a dream? She let the strange thought go and began getting dressed. Where was that nice bearskin, anyway?

THEY HAD BEEN at this camp for longer than usual, and she was getting wanderlust. She reached for any excuse she could find to get out of the camp, which reeked of offal and excrement piled upon each other.

You were supposed to go dig a hole to dump in, but the ground in the thicket was nothing but rocks and roots, and the nights were getting cold. It was easier to dump on a large leaf, roll it up, carry it a suitable distance, and toss it. But too many of the tribe had gotten sloppy with their tossing. Such a stench! The flies were everywhere!

Everyone knew it was time to move on — to leave their piles of rotting rubbish behind — but old Chief Talmid just keeps on putting it off until another day.

"Withered old man. He's growing roots." She looked around, scanning between the trees to be sure that nobody had heard her, half-hoping that someone did. She was a fair distance from the camp now — close enough to hear the murmur of voices, but far enough to have a bit of privacy for a squat in the bushes.

Just as she finished, something came rushing through the underbrush towards her with the vigor of a predator closing in for the kill. Zeta stood, startled, then caught a glimpse of the beast which had hunted her down.

"Pen!" Zeta squealed with glee as Penelope-pooch emerged from between the bushes and bolted towards her. The pooch pounced, her paws impacting Zeta's chest, sending the two tumbling to the ground. Zeta laughed as Penelope-pooch leapt and licked, growled and huffed in delight.

Zeta had claimed Penelope-pooch as a pup, and the two were seldom far apart. She had thick, finger-length fur of a sandy color. Her eyes were bright and her perky ears stood straight up — pink triangles, always twitching about as she scanned for the sounds of danger or opportunity. She was of the hunting and tracking variety, with keen senses and a sharp mind.

"My guardian spirit, my golden hunter, the goddess of pooches," Zeta fawned, scratching Penelope-pooch behind the ears, getting licked on the face, "let's hunt bro-critter. Where's Charra, Pen? Go find him! Find Charra!"

Penelope-pooch led the way, sniffing and huffing through the undergrowth. Once the oppressive camp was far behind, Zeta could appreciate the excitement and beauty of the thicket. They sped between densely packed trees covered with vines.

She jumped over moldy logs. She dodged between spiked bushes. Spider webs on the face and cuts on legs were all part of the fun of this dangerous place. Sharp rocks and slippery roots made picking the next foot placement a continuous effort of scanning and planning.

Escape the stagnation.

Seek the waters of purification.

Defy the caution of the elds with their twisted walking sticks and twisted spines.

How many months ago had the tribe entered Talmid's Stinking

Thicket? Zeta had always resented leaving behind the flowing, yellowed grasslands, surrendered to Red-Painted beast-men with Gravan-cursed stick-slings and evil Night-Thunder Spirits.

Better to be eaten by a golden-eyed panther than suffer at the hands of a man or consumed by a spirit, so let it be adventure in the jungle rather than lazy days on the plain.

Penelope-pooch must have caught a scent or a sound, because she stopped running and had slowed to a silent prowl. She sniffed the air, stepping with caution.

They had found their quarry! Zeta bristled with excitement.

Bro-critter hunting — what a wonderful game!

THEY CRAWLED up a hill of dirt and bare roots. Zeta peeked over the top root. On the other side, perhaps thirty paces away, was that monkey-babe Charra. Accompanying him were two adolescent pups chosen from Penelope-pooch's litter: Gorgon-pup and Chimera-pup. None of them had any idea that hunters were preparing for an attack.

Charra was shouting commands at his pups. "Get out of the way, Gorgon-pup! I'm slinging a stick that way. You'll get stabbed right through if you get in the way."

She watched him struggle with a stick-sling. Zeta's eyes widened. She gasped, covering her mouth. The killers who drove their tribe off the plains had used those weapons. They were cursed and brought nothing but trouble. Even touching one was a sin against Gravan, the god of rocks and simple things.

A stick-sling was a large stick with string tied to the ends, connecting them and pulling it tight, causing the stick to bend. A straight, sharpened stick could then be flung forward with deadly speed by placing its end against the string, pulling it back and letting it go. Put some poison on the pointed end and you could kill a man with a single shot, from a great distance.

Zeta pushed aside the memory of Jebbam-bro-pa laying face-down in the grass with feather-tipped sticks poking up out of his back. That was a long time ago, and she had been too small to do anything about it.

Zeta had secretly tried to make her own copy of their weapon, but it never worked. Charra didn't seem to be having much success, either, but his selection of sharpened sticks was a pitiful assortment of twigs and sapling stems. He was also holding the stick-sling wrong; you're supposed to hold it in your odd hand and pull the string with your favored hand so you can aim it. His latest laughable attempt sent a stick toppling end-over-end.

Penelope-pooch continued to watch her pups playing and yipping with the ignorant abandon of youth. She let out a barely audible growl, losing patience. Zeta whispered to her, "Okay, Penelope-pooch-ma, you pounce those silly pups and teach them a lesson. I've got dibs on bro-critter. Ready...set...go!"

Zeta leapt over the top of the hill and charged down the other side, yelling an attack call, "Ay, ay, ay, ay!"

Penelope-pooch barked as she ran towards their three flat-footed victims, instantly overtaking Zeta. Charra screamed in high-pitched horror and burst into a mad dash, never even turning around to see who had ambushed him. The pups' reactions were pathetic — they ran away in different directions, yipping the whole time with their tails between their legs. What useless guardians, leaving their master to his own fate.

Zeta reached the bottom of the hill, then jogged to a stop. She called out to Charra, laughing, "Bro-critter, you scared little monkey-boy! Come back and pick up your sticks!"

His stick-sling lay in the dirt where he dropped it. She went to pick it up. "I found your stick-sling, Charra! It's mine now!"

That was the way a raid worked. She remembered a storyteller once say, "To the victor go the spoils." Which made her "the victor" and the stick-sling was...spoiled? She didn't understand it, but sometimes storytellers said some pretty weird things.

Penelope-pooch was not so quick to call off the attack. She had picked one of the two pups to pursue and it sounded like she had already caught up to him. The snapping, growling, and huffing sounds of a fight came from some unseen place behind the trees. The pooch-ma was teaching her pups a lesson on vigilance.

Charra's stick-sling was a finely crafted weapon, which meant that he had found or stolen it. The wood was smooth and flexible, but hard. She couldn't tell what the string was made from. If she could just figure out the trick to getting the feathers onto the sticks, then she was sure she could use it.

"If they catched me with that they'd burn it," Charra said. He was standing some distance away, half-hidden behind a tree, sniffling and wiping his arm across his nose.

"Don't you worry about that. Besides, it's *my* spoils now, so you can call me Victor. Pen! Come!" Zeta commanded. The pooches stopped their fighting, though there was plenty of growling and panting as they returned. Gorgon-pup was limping.

"Oh, you've hurt your pup, Pen!" She met the pooches at the tree where Charra hid, then bent down to call Gorgon-pup over. He did not come, but laid down and licked at a wound on his leg.

What a vicious mom!

Well, at least Penelope-pooch paid attention to her pups. Yephanie-ma barely noticed that Zeta and Charra existed now that she had a squealing little piglet of a babe to take care of — Hareshnid, son of Rod-*non*-pa.

That "non" had earned her a slap across the mouth more than once. Well, now that they had a stick-sling, they could finally run away. They had been planning it ever since the babe came.

"Today is the day, Charra," she announced. There was no need to explain what day she meant.

Charra searched her eyes to see if she was serious. "Really?" He half-whispered.

"Yeah. Enough talk — let's do it."

Charra was silent for a long time. He muttered, "But I didn't say bye."

Zeta scoffed, "You bug-brain! If you say bye, then they'll know you're leaving and they'll stop you. Hey," she handed him the stick-sling, "you're a man now, and this is your weapon."

Charra looked at the weapon, then back to Zeta. He nodded gravely, with the eyes of an adult. It was slightly disturbing. Maybe he really *was* a man.

"Alright," Zeta said, breaking the tension, "we'll fill our water skins, take a dip, then walk west."

Zeta was no fool — she knew the truth of their situation. Neither of them knew how to use the weapon, yet, and they knew almost nothing of hunting. But they knew how to cook roots and which bugs wouldn't make you sick if you ate them. It wouldn't be all fun and adventure, but eating bugs and roots was better than living with the losers that called themselves the Scorpion Tail tribe.

ON THE WAY to the spring pool, Charra explained how he had found the stick-sling in a bundle along with some rotten fruit. Whoever had hidden it wouldn't be coming back. Gravan had probably struck them down.

Zeta said a silent prayer to Anansi to help her trick Gravan into overlooking their sin.

Finding the spring pool was as easy as following the clear, trickling stream to its source. It was shrouded, as most places are in the thicket, with vine and moss-laden trees, and surrounded by slick rocks. The water was clear, cold as ice, and had the cleanest taste that Zeta could imagine. A slate outcropping hung over the side of the pool.

Slate.

Slate? Why would that be important? Her bro-kin's loud complaint interrupted her thinking.

"It's too cold to swim in!" Charra hooted as he began inching into the water.

Zeta laughed at his reaction. She pulled off her furs and leather straps, then slipped into the water. It took her breath away, but she didn't hesitate to swim towards the center. She called back to him with chattering teeth, "No, it's n-n-not too cold, you just have to get used to it. It's the c-c-cleanest water in the world, Charra. Wash yourself! It's g-g-good to be clean."

Goosebumps covered her body. It wasn't long ago that she had decided that she shouldn't be naked in front of boys or men anymore, but her babe-bro didn't count. Her body had changed, and she wasn't comfortable with people's prying eyes, judging her development and deciding how soon she would be ready to have babes. No thanks, not interested!

She swam to the deepest part of the pool, where the bottom was too far down to see clearly, even through the crystal clear water. The slate outcropping loomed nearby — Gravan's minion, sent to judge her.

She shook off the notion.

The pooches had taken a drink, but were not interested in swimming. She didn't blame them, since their fur would get soaked, leaving them in a miserable state. They played and patrolled in the nearby thicket. The pooches and the boy — this was her true family. It was the only family she needed.

"Zeta! Zeta, come back, that's no fair, you know I can't swim good. I hate it when you go swim in the deep water. And it's too cold! I'm getting out."

Such a whiny babe.

Zeta just smiled and turned to float on her back. Spider monkeys swung through the branches above, triggering a memory.

Or a memory of a memory?

Floating in a nothing-place?

She looked again at the slate looming over the water's edge and something tugged at her. Something wasn't right. This was all a dream. It tugged again, threatening to pull her under the water, to the bottom, through the bottom and into a vast nothingness. Zeta swam back to where she could reach the rocky bottom again.

She stood, shook her head to clear her mind, and looked up at her shivering babe-bro. There he stood, knee-deep in the frigid water, arms crossed in stubborn defiance, and in a flash she realized why she was here.

A torrent of emotions gathered at the edge of her mind. She was careful not to grasp at them, or she would lose him.

She recognized this moment!

There he was, in all of his innocence, his power, his *defiance*. They had decided once and for all that they didn't have anybody else in the world, and that they didn't *need* them. They would make it on their own, using their stick-sling and their three pooches. The revelation had been like putting down a boulder which she had carried for years. Her swim in the spring pool had been a ritualistic cleansing, and she had emerged with a sense of boundless peace.

She wanted that perfect moment to last forever — the moment when she felt happiness for the last time.

But it did not last forever.

2

TISANE

"Tea?"

"Which kind?"

"I was making lemongrass."

"A blend? With green tea?"

Genevieve checked in the clay tea leaf jar. "No, we're out of tea leaves, so I was just using the lemongrass I had dried—"

Oraxis interrupted, "Well, then that's not *tea*, now is it? That's a *tisane*. I mean, it's fine, but—"

"No, that's okay, if you'd prefer—"

"I wasn't saying I *preferred* anything, just that you called it *tea* and it's not technically *tea* if it's not made from camellia. You see, in ancient China—"

"Whatever! Do you want a *lemongrass tisane*, or not?"

"Sure."

Genevieve rolled her eyes and pumped water into the black tea kettle.

He knew she didn't appreciate his obsession with semantic precision. The decent thing to do would be to let the little incorrect things that people say slide if you know what they're talking about.

He would love to, but he had a reputation to live up to.

Genevieve placed the kettle on the flat plate of the potbelly stove. "I've been thinking that maybe after we're done bootstrapping Zeta, it would be nice to take a dive into the archives. You know, independent enrichment."

Oraxis gave a sardonic chuckle. "Sick of my nitpicking?" He put a foot on the ground to swing his hammock. She had every right to some alone time, of course, but she didn't get off that easy.

Genevieve shrugged. "Take it how you will."

Okay, so she didn't want to spar. Fair enough. He said, "I think it's a fine idea. I've been daydreaming about taking a solitary expedition, anyway."

"An *interplanetary* expedition, I assume?"

"That's the best kind."

"*And then getting snatched away by a Specter,*" Genevieve sent, via mindspeak. Her aversion to talking about the Specters aloud bordered on superstitious.

"*Hmph. That's what self-destruct is for,*" Oraxis replied.

Genevieve shook her head. She went to the window to gather the sprigs of dried lemongrass, mindspeaking, "*You know as well as I do that if you run across a Specter, your god-forsaken curiosity will get the best of you. I think you* want *to see one. You'll probably even bait 'em, like Pip-Rho.*"

He sent, "*You could program an Odysseus Protocol into my reactor.*"

"*And have you curse me for my tight parameters? I can hear it now.*" Genevieve switched to her mock Oraxis-impression voice. "*Hopefully I make it away from the station before this hair-triggered mini-nuke blows,*" then, back in her normal tone, "*besides, you'd find some tricky little loophole in whatever conditions I come up with. It's like...trying to tie Houdini to the mast.*"

Oraxis chuckled aloud at the blend of industrial-age history and Greek fiction.

He *loved* a good genre mash-up.

Genevieve crushed the lemongrass with a mortar and pestle. Surya's midday light passed in through the window, cutting through the dust, painting a glowing rectangle on their pounded dirt floor. The stark light cast the rest of the cabin interior into shadows.

Oraxis and Genevieve both had a difficult time breaking the habit of calling it "sunlight" — native Genesisians would often tease, "Your Earth and Sun are far away and long ago, friends."

Dust motes drifted into the beam of light, glowing brightly for a moment before drifting back out into the shadows. For every mote in the light, there were a thousand others floating in the air of their cabin, unseen. Oraxis watched the motes dance. He counted them in a sweeping assessment. One hundred twenty-one particles were visible without engaging enhanced optics.

"Guess how many dust motes are dancing in that beam of Surya-light," He said, gesturing towards the light with one hand. With his other, he played absentmindedly with his bushy auburn beard.

"Seriously?" Genevieve groaned. "Can't you appreciate the beauty of a dance without measuring it?"

Oraxis performed a projected estimation of the number of similarly sized suspended particles which drifted unseen in their cabin's interior. Genevieve would be uninterested in the result.

He said, "Doesn't their simple beauty spark your curiosity to know more? It's not that I don't appreciate the aesthetics of their dance, but knowing how many invisible companions these lucky few in the spotlight have applauding them out in the shadows makes it all the more poetic."

Genevieve sighed.

"How interesting would it be to put one of them through a particle analyzer? Map its unseen contours, analyze its chemical properties, dissect it, learn all there is to know about one little dust speck."

"We're dissecting dust dancers now?" Genevieve asked.

Oraxis laughed, "Ah, *yes*, can't you hear them screaming? Poor souls. Of course, there really *are* life-forms on those dust specks — microbes."

"Wherever you're going with this, it's starting to sound like 'Horton Hears a Who' gone terribly wrong."

This reference was lost on Oraxis. He blinked, shook his head in a quick dismissive gesture, then continued. "The more you learn about the things around you — in your house, in your body, in your planetary system — the richer your universe becomes. Chemical analyses of a mote of interplanetary dust verses the dust in this room are going to have two *very* different results. Their similarities and differences would tell a story. Gen, this system still holds so many mysteries, and the exploration algorithm of an AI-piloted drone isn't going to send it sniffing down the same trails as those a human's imagination would. We need to have *humans* out there exploring, learning, for the sake of Genesis."

Genevieve put down the mortar and pestle, turned, crossed her arms, and leaned against the countertop. *"Oh, I get it,"* she mindspoke. *"This was a romantic sales pitch for your solo space mission. Well, that's a* beautiful *narrative you have there. Nobody can argue with such noble a pretense as 'for the sake of Genesis', now can they?"*

She used air quotes.

Once she starts gesticulating, Oraxis knows he's done for.

Genevieve grew heated, saying, *"I mean, seriously! After seeing what they did to Pip-Rho, I can't believe you'd even think about going out there alone. Why should it be you out there and not someone else? There have to be, like, a thousand some-odd people,"* She waved her hands in a flippant gesture indicating an innumerable sum, *"in your asteroid-hopper club. What about all those Astri living out there? You don't think they're better qualified than you for the job? Don't you think your time would be better spent training neophytes to analyze space dust instead of flying around out there all alone, trying to do it all yourself?"*

"Gen, the Astri don't share, and this isn't their system anyway.

And, yes, I have trained hundreds of the Noddites in interplanetary exploration, and nine out of ten of them are too afraid of the dark to go further out than Soma."

"*They* should *be afraid!* You *should be afraid!* That's the problem, isn't it?! *You're not afraid of* anything. *If you get abducted by a Specter — you, Earthling! Not a native-born Genesisian — you! And if the abductions are for learning about humans, then imagine the damage that could do! What they could learn from dissecting your brain! You're not just any old dust speck, and you know that."*

Oraxis sat up and shook his head, running his hands through his hair. He mindspoke in a lower tone, slowly, to drive the point home. *"We have no solid evidence that the people abducted by the Specters are used to obtain human knowledge. Even if they did, how would they understand it well enough to use it against us? They're absolutely alien—"*

"Exactly." Genevieve said flatly, both aloud and in mindspeak.

Oraxis closed his eyes. His jaw clenched. He drew a breath to speak just as the tea kettle whistled. They both looked over at it accusingly, as if its screech were an intentional interruption of their argument. Oraxis shook his head and chuckled with humorless resignation. The kettle was right — he should shut up.

THE TISANE WAS BREWED and poured in silence. They sat on the hard-packed dirt floor, quietly following the motions in the timeless ritual of sharing a cup of hot tea — or tisane, if tea was too dear.

Simple, polite mindspeak was exchanged. The prior topic was left behind.

They wouldn't need to bother with what to do for their next independent enrichment for quite a while, anyway. For now, they had a girl in their care who was busy sorting out her existence, living through a set of private experiences which they could only guess at.

Oraxis said, "It feels wrong to leave the child alone here while we go off to a show."

"The child?" Genevieve asked, raising an eyebrow.

"She's nine years old, Gen. She's a child."

Genevieve cleared her throat and put her cup down. Oraxis braced himself.

"First off," Genevieve said in the sing-song tone reserved for telling stories to toddlers, "we are now inhabitants of the planet which our faction has given the regrettable name Genesis, orbiting the star Surya."

Oraxis knew where the train of thought was heading. He waited patiently for it to arrive at the station.

She continued, "Had Zeta grown up on Earth then she would have circled around the sun fifteen times in the time that it took her to circumnavigate Surya nine times. You *know* that, but the lower number of nine skews your perception of her age as being younger than it is. Let's not let such as trivial a matter as orbital cycle durations muddy up our thinking."

"Secondly," Genevieve said, "the society in which we lived on Earth was a post-Judeo-Christian Western culture at the height of the Gilgamesh era. We lived for a *very* long time in a world which had held drastically different moral principals regarding childhood and maturity. Our sensibilities are now considered old-fashioned, even prudish, by the standards of Genesis. In the neoprim societies of Eden, sexual maturity marks the entry into adulthood. Granted, Zeta has more maturing left to do, both mentally and physically, but she's more mature than you'd like to think she is. She would have begun menstruating long before—"

"Ok, I get it," Oraxis said, shaking off the topic, "she's not a child." He sighed, then sipped his tisane to punctuate the end of the conversation.

He grasped for a new topic, saying, "You said before that you expect she'll be in our care for a year, like Jamji. Well, from what I've seen so far, I'd say she'll be rid of us in three months."

Genevieve shook her head. "No. No, she'll stay for a while. She puts up a strong front, but I think she had some bad experiences she needs to sort out. This business with her brother might just be the first of it. She's already clutching hard onto that past, and may never want to let go. That's what's driving her to these early advancements in manipulating her slate-space — that white-knuckled grasp she has on her narratives. She won't want to have anything to do with our world until she's resolved her own."

Oraxis looked at the flakes of lemongrass debris settled at the bottom of his cup. Zeta seemed like a stubborn one, that was for certain.

What if she refused to move on from that first replay? She could relive it as many times as she wanted, but if she doesn't let go of it she'll just keep on looping, trying to fix something, to change something, to make it right when it all went wrong.

Crash, reboot, crash, reboot — a hardware failure in an infinite loop. It was an antiquated analogy, but an apt one. Replays could be addictive.

It would be an even more dangerous period when she learned how to design her own constructs. A misguided designer could start with a canon experience and then tweak it until they were spending years at a time living in a complete fantasy world.

Genevieve took the cup from his hand. "If it were just any old show, I would say one of us stays here with Zeta. But this is Jamji's *last* performance — her farewell to Genesis. We're both going," she said, standing. "We should start walking now."

"It would be more prudent to stay here as long as we can, monitoring Zeta. If I have to tune into her slate-space, I'll be tuned out of my body, so—"

"Come on, I won't let you stub your toe."

"Uh-huh, and what about the time when I ended up at the foot of a cliff with a broken spine?"

"You didn't tell me you were tuning out."

"I *did*, you just didn't hear me." It was his own fault for heading into slate-space without having positive confirmation that his safety lead was ready. This was a dead old argument, lost long ago, which he should not have resurrected. "Anyways, it'd be safer to take Zephyr, and faster. We won't have to leave for another hour."

"And worse for our reputation. You know what they say about us — that we think we're too good for our own feet."

Oraxis was picking up their stoneware plates and bringing them to the wash basin. "If you worry so much about living up to the minimalist neoprim norms, I might as well smash these *pointless luxuries* and burn the cabin down. Tonight we can sleep with some dogs in a field."

Genevieve mindspoke pointedly, *"They could hear you through the window, you know."*

Oraxis leaned his head out the window and looked around. "I don't see any eavesdroppers. And we're bootstrapping here — nobody is supposed to come within a half kilometer. Gen, I'm not ashamed of who I am. We contribute to this society. We weren't raised in their world, and we don't need to pretend that we were. They all understand that." Oraxis turned to survey their modest cabin. It was absolutely spartan by their standards, but to a Noddite it was distastefully materialistic. "I'd go so far as to say they're charmed by our *eccentricity.*"

Genevieve headed over to her wardrobe, opened it, and sighed. She was never content with her limited options of skins and furs.

Oraxis said, "Everything about our lifestyle is countercultural, but we're granted these indulgences so long as we don't overdo it or violate the Core Principals. Enhanced animals like Zephyr are common in Nod. Plenty of others would arrive by beast."

Genevieve grunted as she squeezed into a bleached leather dress with a fur shawl. "Ready to go?"

"Flying?"

"Walking. Get your stick, O."

"Ok." He knew better than to keep pushing it. He also knew that his true motive was probably that he just loved to fly. "I'm going to check on her one more time before we go."

ORAXIS CROSSED the cabin and looked down at the silent bundle of furs in the shadows. He went to a knee. With the care of a father tending to his sleeping baby, he pulled the furs back from Zeta's face.

She had light brown, caramel-toned skin and dark brown hair. She seemed to have a mix of what Earthlings would call Mediterranean and West African features, but what Genesisians would associate with the Northern Grassland tribes. Her nose was stout with a slightly upturned bulb, her face an oval. She was very pretty, indeed.

He placed a hand on Zeta's forehead, as if checking for a fever. His double-mind sensed his intentions and translated them into actions. A microscopic filament of neurites snaked out of his index finger, weaving its way through Zeta's skin, between the fibers of her skull, and connecting to her neurite network.

The filament would create a direct link between their minds. Oraxis's eyes glazed over as he dropped into the void of her peripheral slate-space.

He was immediately struck by the stressful undertone of her slate-space. Even bootstrappers couldn't eavesdrop on replays, but they could tap into the essence of the experience. The feeling of Zeta's slate-space reminded him of being inside a house when it was storming outside.

Genevieve joined him. "Oh, she's having a bad one."

"She's powering through it, though. Her last break was two hours ago."

"Should we bring her out of it?"

"Not yet. We'll be able to tell if she's threatening dissociation or crash-looping after another hour or two."

"We should stay with her. We'll take Zephyr later."

"I swear, you're like this for the first week every time. We can walk, Gen. She'll be fine."

"And if she pulls out of bootstrapping and finds herself in this 'wood tent'? She'll freak out."

"Nobody gets out this early."

"Nobody?"

"You might as well worry about a wayward meteor falling on the cabin."

Just to fact-check himself, Oraxis asked WoQS — the Worldnet Query Service — what the odds were of a beta breaking out of bootstrapping within the first two days.

One in four thousand eighty-two.

Okay, so that's a *bit* more likely than being killed by a meteor. Still, the odds were low enough.

After waiting for a few more minutes in the tumultuous void, he disconnected. If this state persisted into the night, he would have to consider anesthetizing and returning her to neural mapping before irrevocable damage was done.

Oraxis returned to his own mind and reconnected to his body, opening his eyes and taking a deep breath. He sighed, "It's a rough one, for sure." He looked around to find that he was talking to himself.

"GEN?" he asked the silence inside their cabin. He pinged her, but she was unresponsive. He grunted as he stood, then walked towards the door, pushing aside the thick skins.

It was a beautiful afternoon in The Thin Forest. Surya's light beamed through the tall, skinny pine trees which gave the forest its name. Oraxis stepped out and looked around the sides of the cabin for her. She wasn't in her herb garden or his Zen rock garden.

Oraxis looked up at Zephyr's tree. A massive nest sat atop the pine like an oversized hat. Within the nest rested an enormous golden eagle. Without the carbon lattice framework woven throughout the tree's internal structures, it would have snapped under such a weight.

The tree bobbed as the bird shifted to peer at Oraxis with speckled golden eyes, like ornate dinner plates. It stared with the unblinking intensity characteristic of birds of prey. Oraxis met the bird's gaze and mindspoke to it, *"Zephyr, please find Genevieve and tell me where she is."*

Zephyr delivered his response without emotion. *"She is fifty paces east of you, talking to a golden-haired dog of normal size."*

The bird broadcast this anthropolinguistic thought translation as it shifted its stare from Oraxis to a location just outside of view. The response was coupled with a navigation plan of walking east in a straight line.

Birds are simple, non-judgmental creatures, characterized by thought patterns which come across as stern or robotic in their anthropolinguistics. Still, it was tempting to read a hint of sarcasm into the response. "She's right over there, unobservant human," Zephyr seemed to say with such an elementary navigation plan.

He sent the bird a reward-thought and went to find Genevieve. She was kneeling in the underbrush, silently and gently petting Zeta's dog. The dog turned to face Oraxis as he approached, giving him a slight wag of her tail — the dog equivalent of a nervous grin.

"I didn't think you were a dog person," Oraxis said.

"I just wanted to see if she might like to sit with Zeta while we're gone. I know she doesn't like it in there, but maybe with some...convincing..."

"And what would be the point of that?"

"If Zeta wakes up, and she's with her dog, then it'll be a lot less traumatic than being in a strange place by herself. I know you're not Mr. Empathy, but I'd think you could figure that much out."

"We already went over this. She won't wake up. She can't—"

"I know, but...look, it'll just make me feel better to know that she's not alone. So, please, just help me get the damn dog inside."

They lured the dog using rabbit entrails as bait. Once inside, the dog sniffed about nervously. She nuzzled and licked Zeta, as if to wake her from sleeping. Finally, she gave up and laid down, with her head on her paws, watching the girl sleep. All the while, Oraxis and Genevieve watched from the door.

"So," Oraxis said, "are we walking now?"

"We'll stay a while longer and then fly. Let's not leave until we have to."

They laid together in the hammock and watched the dog watch the girl. Minutes passed in their vigil. The dog sighed, then licked the girl's face with a timid whimper.

"It's so sweet how much that dog cares for her," Genevieve mindspoke.

"And here, I thought you weren't a dog person," Oraxis replied, then kissed her forehead.

3

WOLVES

"Um...Zeta?" Charra said, his eyes looking past her to the other side of the pool. From between the trees, lurking in the shadows, shimmered a pair of green eyes. It was not yet twilight, but in the thicket the darkness always came too early, as shadows deepened and predators emerged.

For a heartbeat all Zeta could see was eyes, but then the rest of the beast's image resolved into focus. It was a black wolf. Scanning between the other trees, she found two more hairy black forms, watching them, creeping closer.

Without a word, Zeta crashed through the water and wrapped her arms around Charra. He had been stepping backwards in stunned disbelief, eyes wide. She swooped him up and ran with him over the rocks and roots, dirt and leaves. Where were the pooches?

"Pen!" Zeta called as she ran. Charra had slipped out of her arms and was running beside her.

"Gorgon! Chimera!" he called.

She could hear the snarling sounds of a pooch fight erupting just behind her. She glanced back over her shoulder. A flash of black fur tumbled over gold as the pooches and wolves fought.

"Use the stick-sling!" Charra said between gasps. "Go back for it!"

"No, just run! You'll die!"

Charra looked back over his shoulder and slowed to a stop, then turned. "Did you hear that? Someone yelled!"

"No, now run!" Zeta pulled violently on Charra's arm. But then she heard the call. She couldn't make out what was said, but it was definitely a young man yelling a command. The sounds of the pooch fight continued, but had diminished somewhat into the distance.

Something was running towards them with predatory speed, but before she could decide which direction it was coming from, it was already tackling her bro-kin. A massive black bulk knocked Charra to the forest floor. Its mouth was clamped onto Charra's face, twisting and tearing. It released, then bit into his neck.

Zeta shrieked as she dove onto the wolf's back, wrapping one arm under its neck and the other around the back of its head. She wrapped her legs around its body, using her momentum to pull it off Charra and on top of her. She squeezed as hard as she could, twisting violently, but the beast was strong — she could not break its neck.

The wolf thrashed its head, wrenching and twisting its body, kicking and scraping to get out of her clutches. It snapped at the air inches from her face, spraying her with bloodied spit.

She could hear another wolf bounding towards them through the underbrush. This would be her death. She could never hope to fight one wolf, let alone two. Charra was getting back on his feet, stumbling away.

The second wolf snarled as it pounced, tearing into the wolf within her grasp.

It wasn't a wolf — it was Penelope-pooch! Her guardian spirit!

With Zeta holding the black wolf upside down, Penelope-pooch easily tore into its exposed belly, ripping out a long rope of entrails and thrashing it back and forth, flinging blood. She bit and tore again. The wolf had let out high-pitched cries as it was torn open. It went limp in Zeta's arms.

Staggering to her feet and getting her bearings, she could see no sign of Charra in the failing light. She looked down at Penelope-pooch to see that the pooch was missing an eye. Chunks of fur and skin had been torn from her neck, leaving fleshy pink patches. She was seeping thick drops of blood, but not so much that she would bleed out.

"Oh, Pen, you're in bad shape, girl." She scanned the forest around them. "Got to get bro-critter and get back to camp. Find Charra, Pen. Charra! Charra!"

Pen sniffed at the air, limp-trotting aimlessly. Her senses had to be clouded with pain and the confusion of blood loss. The distant young man called out again in his strange tongue and the sound of the distant pooch fight stopped.

The forest fell dead silent. Even the chirping crickets did not dare to make their presence known.

She knew the way back to camp, but she would not go without her ward. Maybe he had headed back on his own? He should know the way.

From the direction of the spring pool, a beast was sniffing towards them. Leaves crackled and twigs snapped in its reckless pursuit.

"Charra," Zeta whispered, stepping away from the dead wolf and retreating, eyes fixed toward the crashing sounds of the beast in pursuit. Maybe it was one of the pups. Maybe it had found Charra and was leading him to safety.

She hid behind a tree, a stone's throw from the spot where they had killed the wolf. She glanced down at Penelope-pooch, holding out her hand, palm down, to tell the girl to be still and quiet. Looking back towards the fallen wolf, her hopes were dashed. A hairy black form was sniffing at the fallen wolf. She could see it nuzzle and lick the dead wolf's head. She heard it let out a faint whimper, and then it tossed its head back and filled the night with a long, wailing howl.

A second later, another howl answered it, and then another joined in. How many were there? She had no hope of fighting a pack of wolves. She would escape, come back with men, and find Charra.

ZETA TURNED AND RAN, hoping that the pack's howling would continue for long enough to drown out her footsteps. She just needed to gain enough distance that they couldn't hear her stepping on leaves and snapping twigs. She would get back to camp and Charra would be there. That's where he went.

What if he wasn't there? They would gather all the hunters and pooches. The men would bring spears and they would find him. They had that duty. Rod-non-pa would lead the hunt and take on the most risk. He must lay down his life, if that's what it takes. That is the price he must pay for taking over her family.

The howling had stopped. A man-boy's squeaking yell echoed through the forest in a strange tongue, his tone laden with anger and sorrow. This must be the wolves' master. Tame wolves? Wolf-pooches. It's not unheard of, but everyone knows it's a dangerous idea.

Zeta continued her retreat.

The sound of rapid pursuit descended on her from behind. She turned and reflexively raised her arm, protecting her face from the flash of a fanged maw. It snapped shut on her forearm, teeth digging deep in her flesh as she let out a grunting howl of shock, collapsing to the mud and tumbling down a rocky, muddy slope.

Zeta tumbled and slid, all the while the beast holding fast to her arm, jerking its head. She landed on her back with the heavy wolf-pooch on top of her. It let go of her arm and snapped at her again, trying for her face and throat. She raised her other arm to ward off the vicious attack. Thick, warm blood poured out of her bitten arm and onto her face.

She was blinded by pain and blood, so it took her a moment to realize that the wolf-pooch was off of her. It was bounding and thrashing by her side, trying to fling Penelope-pooch off its back. Penelope-pooch's jaws were closed on the back of the wolf-pooch's neck. It wasn't in the right spot for a kill, but it couldn't shake her off.

Zeta got on her knees, her head spinning, the world threatening to close in at the edges of her vision in colorful sparkles. Her favored hand wouldn't move, so she groped at the forest floor with her odd hand until she found a large rock. She dug her fingers under its edge, pulling it out of the hard mud.

She hoisted the rock in her odd hand, knee-walking to the wrestling beasts. The wolf-pooch had Penelope-pooch's leg in its jaws, rocking its head to drive the bite in, clearly in a losing position but not giving up. Zeta swung her arm down, slamming the rock against the top of its head. She grunted as she struck it a second time, putting all of her strength into the blow. Empty thud, crack of bone.

The beast went limp.

She looked down at her favored arm. In the darkness she couldn't tell how badly it was injured, but she couldn't feel her hand. Blood continued to pour from the arm. The elds had shown her what to do if she was bleeding like this. She had to squeeze it with something and make the blood stop or she would pass out and die.

She had no clothes or straps to use — she wore only blood and mud.

Zeta looked around, blurry-eyed, dazed. Could she use a vine? A sapling?

Her hair cord! Yes! The woven leather cord that she had used to hold her hair up was strong — it would work. She fumbled with the knot using her odd hand. Slippery, numb fingers clawed at the cord. She wailed in frustration. Finally, it loosened enough to rip from her hair. A knot of hair tore out with the cord, but the pain didn't register.

Zeta held one end of the cord in her teeth and wrapped the other around her dead arm, just above the elbow, two times. She looped and tucked the end of the tight cord. It held fast, reducing her bleeding to a drip.

She looked down at Penelope-pooch. The pooch was looking back into the forest with her remaining eye. She growled, exposing her bloody teeth in a menacing sneer.

Zeta looked in the same direction and saw a skinny man-boy creeping through the trees, half-crouched. In one hand he grasped the scruff of the neck of a black wolf-pooch. In his other hand was a spear, raised and ready to thrust. The wolf-pooch growled and pulled forward.

The man-boy caught sight of Zeta, then stopped. Soma's glow illuminated his face enough for Zeta to read his features. He wore a grimace, teeth exposed, tears running down his cheeks. He had the strangest complexion that she had ever seen — a pallid, red-speckled face and red hair. The whites of his pale blue eyes betrayed his fear.

"Por day-kay?!" He screamed, his voice cracking. She didn't know his language but could tell it was a question, or a plea. Or a demand? This pathetic little non-man filled her with hatred. The red boy's black demon-pooches had bit Charra's face and neck, sending him wandering into the night. They had ripped her and Penelope-pooch to shreds, and now he grits his teeth at her and shouts demands?!

"Where is my bro-kin?" She growled.

His black wolf-pooch had been pulling forward, snarling and letting out a continuous low growl, held back only by the hair the red boy clutched. When Zeta spoke, it lunged with a bark, pulling the red boy forward. He fell with a shout to the forest floor.

Zeta started backwards. Penelope-pooch was ready to fight, growling and snarling menacingly. The red boy let go of the spear and reached up to grab a second handful of neck fur. The blood-crazed beast dragged him across the muddy forest floor.

Zeta's head was swimming. She stood for longer than she should have, trying to decide between fighting or running. The red boy shouted something at her. Zeta jumped, then turned and ran. "Pen!" Penelope-pooch followed at her heels.

Everything was a fog as she stumbled through the forest. She was trying to run back to camp, but the forest refused to show her the way. One arm was cradled in another. Penelope-pooch limped at her side.

Minutes passed, with no sound of pursuit. They breathed in raspy, heavy breaths, their pace slowing to a labored, shuffling jog. A distant howl pierced the silence of the night.

Zeta glanced back between the trees. She whispered, "We will not die tonight, Pen. We can't die. We have to save bro-critter."

She could barely stay on her feet as she reached the familiar camp surroundings. Darkness was everywhere, thick and slippery.

Black blood shrouded the world.

The sounds of men talking and a woman laughing wafted to her, along with the smell of cooked meat. The light of the campfires flickered between the distant trees. If Charra had already returned, they would have been in an uproar. The lighthearted sounds of a peaceful camp split her heart. It crushed her hope like a beetle underfoot.

Zeta's bloodied, mud-coated, naked form shambled into the firelight. The camp's tone shifted in an instant. Women screamed. Pooches barked. Someone scooped her up as if she were a babe.

Everything was shouting, confusion, fear.

"Charra," was all she could say. Maybe they heard her.

They lay her down on soft fur. Something squeezed her injured arm, forcing a scream from her. She changed the scream into a word.

"Charra!" She gasped, then screamed, "Leave me! Find Charra!"

Her face was cold, numb. Her head fell to the side.

Between shuffling feet, she could see Penelope-pooch's form limping towards her. Zeta reached her hand out towards her pooch, earning a feeble lick. The pooch laid down with her wet head on Zeta's hand, her remaining eye fixed on the girl. The pooch's mouth was open. Her bloodied tongue lolled sideways as she panted.

Snippets of overheard conversations skittered through Zeta's fading consciousness.

"—boy is probably dead already."

"—should put the animal out of its misery."

Zeta gained her wits in a burst of energy. Her eyes opened wildly.

She struggled to sit up, but she was being pinned down by a dozen hands.

"By the spring pool! Black wolf-pooches and their red-boy master! Kill them all! Find Charra!"

The world was closing in. She gazed up at the worried women's faces crowded around above her. The faces vanished into an encroaching, sparkly haze.

"Do...not...kill...Pen. My guardian."

4

LAST DANCE

THE CAVERN of the Soul was a branching network of natural caves converted into an entertainment venue. Its designers had left most of the walls and ceilings in their native states, but leveled and smoothed the floors, adding platforms and steps as needed to accommodate the continuous changes in elevation. Hidden lighting inconspicuously highlighted the cave's features and gave a warm ambiance which complemented the cold rock.

The noise of the crowd echoed through the backstage corridors like a distant waterfall. Jamji sat among her fellow performers, stretching and warming up while her mind wandered.

She idly admired the artistic choices the cavern's designers had made, balancing cultured civilization with raw nature. She considered herself to be an artist with the same goals, as illustrated aesthetically in her biosynthetic mods and emotionally in her performances.

Oraxis and Genevieve would be in the audience, which didn't help Jamji's nerves. It's funny how you can perform in front of a thousand strangers, but when you add in a half dozen friends and family, the pressure grows by an order of magnitude. Carff promised he would watch the live feed from a cave in Eden somewhere, and the Pips would take a break from their latest project to tune in. She wondered if XT-Prime, or any Astri for that matter, ever bothered with Noddite entertainment. If the Astri were watching, that would easily double her viewers.

Or would it? Does a hive mind count as thousands of viewers or just one big one?

What about Paulie-boy? Would he show up after everything she put him through? She hoped not. Seeing her again could send him back into depression. Moral of the story: artists shouldn't date artists.

Artist? Would she keep that label after tonight? It was her *last* performance, after all. She was sure the Guardians didn't waste time on such frivolities. Dance wasn't going to save humanity.

No, it was time to grow up.

After tonight, The Art of War would replace the art of dance.

It is a matter of life and death, a road to either safety or ruin.

This resolve focused her mind and settled her spirit.

She wandered to the craft services table and began grazing on the miniature feast of high-calorie foods. Nut butters, cakes, wafers, and honey were her pre-performance favorites. Highly energetic activities required fuel, and there was no risk of overeating when your metabolism was tuned to such high input/output ratios.

"Jamji to the stage, please," mindspoke the assistant stage manager.

She shoved one more honey wafer into her mouth, then headed for the backstage entrance.

Jamji was the closing performance of the first act of the exhibition. The three performers leaving the stage nodded at her in greeting as they passed. They were all athletic men, dressed in one-piece leotards as if for dance or acrobatics.

The crowd's applause faded to silence as she took her place behind the opening of the large, black curtain. She looked to the side at the stagehand who would cue her.

A woman's voice broadcast an announcement which echoed through the chamber on the other side of the curtain. "Please welcome to the stage, Jamji Telson. She will perform an interpretive dance titled 'Origin Story'. This will be Jamji's final performance as a Noddite, and she would like to dedicate it to the Genesis Faction."

Jamji got her cue.

Taking a deep breath, she put on a serene face and walked with slow, deliberate movements through the curtain and onto the stage. A pair of bright spotlights flooded her vision, sending the audience into darkness.

She remembered a time when she had to calm her nerves by imagining that everyone in the crowd was naked. Now, she was the naked one. Granted, the scandal of her nakedness was averted by a few strategically positioned retractable dermal flaps. Genevieve called it "the Barbie treatment", since it gave her the neutered look reminiscent of the plastic doll of antiquity.

Another detractor from her nudity was the fact that Jamji's skin glowed in a uniform aquamarine hue. This bit of magic was made possible by her chromatites — billions of multi-faceted, light-producing nanites integrated into her synthetic skin.

The crowd applauded politely at her emergence from behind the curtain. She gave them a bow of her head, eyes closed, then switched to active invisibility. The microscopic photoreceptites embedded on every surface of her body were now recording and transmitting real-time image data to her chromatites. Her chromatites, in turn, were projecting omnidirectional pass-thru images of her surroundings on her skin's surface, relative to tens of thousands of distinct possible viewing angles.

A few rube-noobs in the audience gasped at this old trick.

The spotlights turned off, plunging the cavern into darkness, illuminated only by dim aisle lights and a trickle of light from the twisting entrance. The audience sat in a semi-circle around the thrust stage. The amphitheater's tiered benches reached halfway up the cave walls, transitioning into stepped balconies as the floor sloped upwards.

With silent feet, she ran to the end of the stage. She went to a knee, her head lowered, hands pressed to the stage. She scanned the crowd. In under a second she spotted Genevieve and Oraxis seated a few rows back. Jamji waved at them, knowing that nobody — including them — could see it.

Faint music faded in, provided by speakers hidden in the rocky walls. The opening came as a steady tone, pleasant and hopeful. Tiny pinpoints of white light were projected on the black curtain at the rear of the stage. Jamji started to glow a deep green and slowly rose to her feet.

And her last dance began.

THE DANCE BEGAN SLOWLY, with waking, stretching gestures. The music segued into a staccato tune, reminiscent of birds in the spring. Jamji pranced lightly on her toes in the timeless style of a ballerina en pointe, her reinforced skeleton making it possible to stand on the tips of her toes without shoes.

She was a picture of innocent delight, shifting her glowing hue gently between green and blue.

As she danced in simple, peaceful movements, the tempo of the music began increasing. At first it increased steadily, unnoticeably, but eventually the increased tempo was obvious.

Jamji's maneuvers grew in complication. She spun in a dozen rapid pirouettes, ran, and leapt. As the intensity of the music and dance grew, her chromatites transitioned to a bright white glow. Her expression shifted to that of rapt intensity.

From behind the curtain at the back of the stage, a shadow emerged. It loomed, only visible as a conspicuous void in the star field projection on the curtain. Jamji's intense dance continued, shifting her glowing tone to bright red, the music becoming a cacophony of chaos.

Jamji had already begun overclocking — increasing her neural firing rate to keep up with the escalating pace and complicated moves she was executing. She issued pacing and movement commands, even serving as her own control booth, using the amphitheater's interface to issue music and lighting cues through WUtils, the Worldnet Utility Service.

She thrashed in a flurry of inhuman speed. The intense heat produced by her myofibrite-enhanced muscles would be felt by the first few rows as she swept by them, spinning around the stage.

A roar echoed throughout the cavern.

Several spectators screamed. A thousand mouths gasped. Jamji collapsed into a cowering heap, immediately shifting her chromatites to a natural, almond skin tone, her hands raised in a pathetic, defensive pose. She had shifted in an instant from a being of ephemeral energy to a powerless, naked human.

The music had stopped. Seconds ticked by in stunned silence. The shadowy form which had occupied the back of the stage now resolved into a gray-glowing monster. It was as large as a rhinoceros, but had the powerful form of a predator. Golden claws like curved daggers sprouted from the tips of its paws. Its luminescent skin was accented by a web of shimmering golden veins.

Everyone in the amphitheater knew that this gray-and-gold beast could only be one thing: The Monster from the Stars.

The Monster stepped slowly towards Jamji, its eyes the black orbs of a shark. It shifted its weight in the slow crawl, bulging muscles writhing with potential energy. Its claws clicked on the stage with each slow step.

Jamji pushed herself backwards across the stage, retreating from The Monster, one hand still raised defensively. She looked around for an escape, but saw no way to avoid its advance. The beast wrinkled its snout in a snarl, exposing a mouth filled with sharp, golden teeth. It let out a deep, booming chuckle.

"What do you want?!" She wailed at it, gasping. "Why me? Why now? What are you?!"

"So many questions," The Monster replied, without moving its mouth. It was as if the menacing voice had come from within its belly. "What do I want? To eat you. Why you? Because you are food. Why now? Because you are ripe."

Jamji pushed herself to the edge of the stage. She could go no further without falling into the crowd.

The Monster stopped just a few paces away. Drool dripped from its massive jowls as it opened its mouth wide, exposing a throat which emanated a deep red glow from its hidden depths. From the beast's cavernous maw came, "What am I? Your devourer!"

It pounced forward, claws spread wide.

Jamji had shifted a moment earlier to her peak neural firing rate, sending the world into slow motion. The beast's lunge seemed to take a full minute. Her reaction was deliberate, every movement forced as if pushing through a pool of honey.

She turned her back to the creature, put her hands down on the stage, pulled her knees to her chest, and tucked her head. Her body was a coiled spring. With her hands, she pushed the stage away while kicking her legs into the air, releasing her energy in a single, coordinated movement. She sailed slowly through the air, feet first, arcing over the head of The Monster. It tried to raise its head to snatch her out of the air, but it was too slow. She landed behind it, absorbing the impact by curling into a kneeling ball, switching her chromatites back to intense white.

Jamji watched patiently as the beast landed and circled its bulky body back around to face her. It raised its head to emit a drawn-out roar. She crouched, impatient for it to finish the act of intimidation.

Her posture was no longer that of weakness. She challenged The Monster with her gaze and her bright white tone. Predictably, The Monster began its slow-motion shifting of weight downwards to prepare for a leap, then sprung forwards with wild eyes and a gold-toothed maw dripping with saliva, ready for the kill.

Jamji pressed her feet downward against the stage, releasing the superhuman power of her legs in a vertical leap. She switched her chromatites to active invisibility mode, disappearing into the darkness above the stage. As she rose, a streak of heat would have been visible in her wake to anyone in the audience with poor enough taste to be observing the performance in the infrared spectrum.

Looking down at the retreating scene of The Monster and the audience, she saw it land in the spot where she had been, biting down as if it had landed upon her and was making its kill. She turned her head upwards, engaging enhanced optics to spot the black rope dangling above her, with a loop tied at the end.

Jamji willed her slow arms upwards. She reached for the rope, grasping it with both hands. She squeezed the rough weave in her hands as hard as she could. Her leap had been a bit too high, and she ascended a few feet with the slack rope in her hands, at the apogee of her leap. Her grip stayed secure as she absorbed the snap of the drop, bouncing and swinging. She put a foot through the loop, then looked down at the scene below, returning to a normal neural firing rate.

The Monster was thrashing its head back and forth, as if it had a kill in its mouth and was flailing it to death.

She spoke to it through her mind-link. *"That's it, Pep! Just like you're killing a rabbit! Tear up that rabbit!"* She found that she could get the best performances out of Pepper-pooch if she tapped into his basic instincts, controlling his movement with a minimum amount of direct control.

She transitioned her pooch's chromatites to active invisibility, then calmed his mind. At the same time, she turned her own chromatites back on, this time in a faint deep green glow. The effect was a shift of the scene's focus from the stage to her hovering form. She wore a solemn expression, looking down at the stage below.

A few seconds passed in silence, allowing the tension of the violence to melt away. The hopeful melody from the opening dance played, but this time in a minor key, lending to a sense of disquiet. She turned her head to the ceiling, looking up the rope, and began to climb. As she did, she shifted her hue back to the deep, bright green of the opening dance.

Slowly, she climbed. The music faded, as did she.

APPLAUSE THUNDERED throughout the amphitheater of The Cavern of The Soul. The performance had gone *beautifully*, with an excellent response from the audience. Hoots and whistles followed. The rope lowered her towards her waiting companion below, who sat now, panting.

Pepper-pooch looked up at her and then around at the audience with a wagging tail and a tongue lolling in and out of his mouth. He was sending her his constant stream of simple thoughts, anthropomorphically translated into speech. *"That was fun! Did you have fun? Did I do well? I love you! We should play now! Do these people want to play now?"*

"Not now, silly! We'll play later. These people are all saying that you did a very good job. You are a very good performer, little Pep!" She sent her own stream of thoughts back at him. She dropped the last couple of meters from the rope to the ground and jogged with Pepper back to the curtain. The audience was standing now, the house lights raised enough for her to see them.

She turned and bowed in a faux curtsy and had Pepper-pooch lower his head with his front paws extended in a mock bow. *"Good boy, Pep!"*

She smiled at the spot in the audience where Oraxis and Genevieve had been sitting.

They were gone.

Her smile faltered. She used optical magnification.

Yes, they were definitely gone.

What. The. Hell?!

She shot a private message to their channel.

No response.

She turned and ran through the curtain, her eyes welling with tears. Fans and performers clustered backstage, applauding, trying to congratulate her. She switched on active invisibility and pushed past them, knocking one of her fans over in her retreat to the dressing room.

Once she reached her private space she gave the stone wall a solid side-kick. The thud reverberated in the stone. She paced the dressing room and cried fiercely, spamming Oraxis and Genevieve's channel with a flurry of urgent messages.

"What the hell?!"

"Where did you go?!"

"What the hell is wrong with you guys?!"

"Seriously, I can't believe you would leave in the middle of my performance!"

"Hello?!"

"HELLO HELLO HELLO HELLO HELLO?!"

"WHAT THE HELL?!"

What on Genesis could they have had to do that would be more important than watching her performance? Freaking jerks! They thought they were so important — such noble old souls with everybody clambering for their quote-unquote "wisdom".

She would *never* forgive them for this. Jamji plopped onto the floor and cried into the crook of her arm, ignoring incoming messages from her friends and other performers with subjects like "where did you go?" and "what happened?"

Fourteen minutes and thirty-seven seconds after Jamji's first message had been sent she finally received a response from Genevieve, with the title, "Please let me explain." Jamji let it sit in her queue in an unacknowledged state as she debated whether or not to open it.

No, screw them.

She rejected the message with the reply, "I'm sure you have more important things to do, so just save yourself the trouble and don't bother showing up next time. Oh, wait, there won't be a next time! Oh, well!"

She shut off all of her private communication channels, which were still receiving incoming messages congratulating her on her performance or asking where she was. She didn't want to talk to anybody.

This was the last straw — she had no family here. She couldn't *wait* to join the Guard Faction. She would leave tomorrow! She'd take her acceptance exams at the Guardian embassy, pass with flying colors, head to Syn-Cen, snatch up her aposynchronic orb, and take the next shuttle to Soma Station.

She was done with Genesis for *good.*

5

WAKING

Zeta went in and out of a tortured, dreamless sleep. All was confusion, indistinct pain. A wrong had to be made right. This resolve brought her to half-thinking alertness.

Men were talking. Pen watched her with one shining eye. The other was a red hole of clotted blood and fur. Zeta turned her head to look up at the sky between the trees. Cold, deep blue. A pair of stars flickered. Morning sky, or evening?

"She moves," an eld woman hissed. More women whispered and murmured.

"Get water."

Zeta rolled her head to the other side and looked between the women who sat beside her. She saw the campfire. The fire was low but there was enough light in the sky to see by. Men from her camp sat by the fire with an eld and a boy.

She blinked. It was the red-speckled man-boy!

She could never forget that skin, his thin nose and cold blue eyes. She stirred and drew a breath to shout at him, but could only wheeze and cough dryly.

All around the camp people were talking in tight huddles,

peering over shoulders at the strangers by the fire. She spotted the square face of Rod-non-pa, standing alone, looking down at a bundle he was holding. She assumed it was Hareshnid, bundled up in Rod's arms in an overly large fur, but then she saw the muddy foot dangling from beneath the bundle.

Charra!

Relief flooded in. The fool boy had made it back to camp! Furs blocked her view of Charra's face. How bad had the wolf-pooch's bite been? Could he be missing an eye, like Penelope-pooch?

Zeta panicked. This was wrong — all wrong!

Why was that brute Rod-non-pa just standing there and staring at Charra? His expression was tense, eyebrows furrowed, jaw clenched, lips tight. Was he angry? Where was Yephanie-ma?

Zeta looked back towards the men talking at the campfire. The old man spoke with Chief Talmid and the elds in a foreign tongue. He had a complexion like the man-boy, but instead of red-speckled skin, his was marked with the dark patches and unhealing sores of age. He spoke loudly, with a slow, somber tone. The red boy sat silently, his eyes wide and face slack with what could be vacant shock or aimless fear. She would bear any punishment if only she could get up and slap his ugly face until it was an even tone of red.

The men stood and exchanged bows. The two elds leaned towards each other and pressed foreheads together in the sign of kinship. Zeta could hear her teeth grind against each other. Her vision pulsed with every beat of her hateful heart.

The speckled boy was casting his pale gaze in a searching sweep of the camp. He spotted her, then said something in his foreign tongue to his eld. The eld looked at her, then shook his head and said something to the boy. The boy stared at her with vacant, soulless blue eyes. She returned his stare with an icy glare of her own.

A few more foreign-tongued pleasantries later and the strangers left. Penelope-pooch growled softly, as if she longed to chase down the strangers and end their lives. Zeta felt the same way.

"Rise, Zeta," Eve-eld-ma said. Someone put their hands under her armpits and helped her up. Penelope-pooch also got up, with almost as much of a struggle, but without help.

Rod-non-pa stood across the camp with the Charra-bundle in his arms, watching her with just as much tension in his face as he had earlier. Zeta took a step, faltered. Shaman Mora-eld caught her. Even in her eld years, the woman was lean and strong. Not like the thin and frail Eve-eld-ma, who was hurrying off in another direction.

Scanning the camp, most were watching her expectantly. Even the ever-pontificating Chief Talmid's wrinkled lips were pressed together, wiggling worriedly as he sucked on his gums and watched her with glassy brown eyes.

She looked towards Charra and took a breath to call out to him, but her voice failed her, emitting a raspy whisper.

Zeta's cousin, Vihaan, had been hovering nearby. Now he hurried towards her with a tortoiseshell full of water. She drank deeply, then patted his shoulder in thanks. He smiled falsely, with twitching hesitation, then clamored away, stuttering something about going to get more water.

"Charra," she demanded. The camp was silent. Charra didn't move. Rod-non-pa began to walk towards her, holding the boy as if he were a babe.

"Charra, come on, wake up and have a drink. Vihaan will get you some water." She couldn't allow the thought which loomed in the shadows of her mind.

Rod-non-pa continued his procession towards her with that damned expression. It was as if his face was doing battle against his heart, and could only hold it at bay by tightening into a contorted scowl.

"Where is Yephanie-ma? Where is my ma? What's wrong with all of you? Do you see what that boy and his man-killer wolf-pooches did to me?! To Penelope-pooch?! To my bro-kin?! Charra, tell them about the spring pool. We did nothing to provoke them! Tell them, Charra!" Her shouts provoked no response from this solemn-faced tribe. Only Rod-non-pa moved, relentless in his approach.

Zeta tripped and was caught again by Mora-eld before she could stumble to the rocky ground. She didn't realize that she had been stepping backwards, retreating from the unspeakable, unthinkable knowledge which Rod-non-pa pressed towards her to share.

Was this *real*?

Shadows of the truth were swimming in the darkness. Black wolf-pooches howled between the trees of her mind, circling and closing in as the tiny fire which was her whole world, her reality, her life, shrunk to a thin and wavering flame. Mora-eld held her on her feet until Rod-non-pa finally stood before her and held the bundle of skins which wrapped Charra, covering all but his dangling foot.

"Hey," Zeta choked out, "he can't breathe under there, Rod-pa." She could see Charra's hand within the bundle, dirty and ashen, caked with dried blood. Zeta reached out with her good arm, her hand quivering, and grasped Charra's hand.

It was cold.

"That water in the spring pool was sure cold, wasn't it, Charra? It takes a while to warm up after a cold dip like that. Where is Vihaan with that water, anyways?" She looked around feebly.

"Zeta," Rod-non-pa rasped.

"No!" Zeta shouted back at him, "You don't say anything! You don't say a word, Rod-*non*-pa!" Vibrant defiance fanned her dwindling flame into a firestorm.

Her sneering tone would provoke a slap from the brute. She would hit him back this time. She stared into his eyes, daring him to strike. Inconceivably, a tear rolled down his cheek. His bottom lip trembled like that of a whipped child.

What was this?

He pressed his eyes closed, his face contorting into a reddened grimace like she has never seen. Had her words truly hurt him this time? She gritted her teeth and attacked him with her most venomous tone, "Charra hates you, too, Rod-*non*-pa. Did you know that? He doesn't say it to your face, but he says the same things as me. You're not our pa, and you wouldn't care if we ran away or got hurt or even…"

Rod-non-pa was looking down at the bundle now, and began delicately pulling the furs off Charra's face, breathing in shaking sobs, tears rolling freely down his cheeks. Others in the camp wept. Zeta was paralyzed, transfixed by the unveiling of her bro-kin's face.

The fire inside of her died, the black wolves snuffing out her last flickering light. Charra's face was revealed, but it was not his face. In the place where his eyes, nose, and temples should have been was a mangled and bloody mess of flesh. His mouth was open slightly.

It wasn't real!

None of this was!

He couldn't be dead because the world *was not real*.

Zeta watched through the eyes of a girl who was erupting into a pained howl. The girl, whose body she was in, started to collapse, but was caught by a tribemate.

Charra was fine, of course. He was the one holding her up. He smiled and handed her a stick-sling. "You can kill them wolf-pooches with this! Use the light of Surya, it's everywhere!"

The red-speckled man-boy was the one who lay dead before her, his face having been ripped to shreds by Penelope-pooch. Darkness flooded the world. Black wolves streamed into the camp, consuming the light as they closed in around her.

They came as shadows, descending from the sky, from the branches of the high-topped trees, from between the roots of the trees in the dirt. Zeta held a stick made of pure white light in her hand. It glowed brilliantly and was burning hot, but did not burn her skin. She pulled the back of it onto the string of the stick-sling, pulled the string back towards her cheek, felt it burning next to her face for an instant before releasing it into the heart of one of the hairy black beasts. The shadow-wolf hurled back into the night.

She plucked another stick of light from the air, turned and shot it into the side of a black monster which was leaping through the air towards Charra. Shaft after shaft of white light flew from her stick-sling into the beasts, but she could not hold them at bay. The darkness surrounded her as the wolves silently swallowed her whole.

ZETA WAS BACK in the nothing-place of slate-space. Her mind was racing. Was this a dream, or was the camp a dream? Was Charra dead, or the speckled boy?

All was confusion, pain, loss. Panic overwhelmed her.

Nothing made sense!

She needed control. To make it all real.

This was not real.

Those people, Oraxis and Genevieve, would show up at any moment to torment her, or to plunge her into more waking nightmares. No, they were not people — they were *spirits*, feeding off her emotions. This was their slate-space mind-trap. Images of a slate outcropping started to form in the corners of her mind.

"No! Don't think about the spring pool," she told herself, shaking her mind, "you'll slip right back in."

The slate-space was nothingness again. Yes, she could control this place. She could escape the trap.

After a while her panic had washed away, leaving her feeling drained, floating in a silent stupor.

From somewhere outside of slate-space, Penelope-pooch whimpered.

"Pen! Pen! You're here?!" She reached out with her mind, but there was nothing else here. "Penelope-pooch, I'm here! Can you hear me? Are you here, girl? Come here, girl!"

Penelope-pooch was licking her face. She didn't have a face here, so it was impossible, yet it was happening. She couldn't feel anything, but there was warmth and wetness. It was as if she was a tiny speck floating around inside her own body. She concentrated on the feel of her body outside of slate-space, commanding it to raise her arm.

Penelope-pooch barked from somewhere beyond.

"Yes, that's it! Did you see that, girl? Did I move?" Zeta commanded the nothingness to reach out with her hand. She had the sensation of warm fur. She couldn't feel it directly, but was aware of it being felt. She forced her hand to open and close. It was like being in control of a massive, numb giant, tugging at it from within to command its clumsy limbs. Well, if she could control her limbs, then she could control her eyes. She tried to open them, but nothing happened. She wrapped her mind around the slate-space and commanded *it* to open her eyes.

Light flooded in. Sound pounded in her ears. There came flashes of bright light, then darkness, then Penelope-pooch, then logs stacked around her on every side. Noise and silence, spinning.

Penelope-pooch's nose filled her field of vision. She could see every bump, crevice, and shimmer of moisture on the pooch's nose. She was seeing it in finer detail than she had ever seen anything in her life. It was as if Penelope-pooch had grown to the size of a mountain, and Zeta's face was inches from the part of the mountain that made up the pooch's black nose. The massive nose retreated and her vision was spinning again, seeing colors that she could not describe.

She could hear Penelope-pooch's excited panting and huffing as loudly as a deafening waterfall, and in the next instant she couldn't hear anything at all except some faint thudding and tinkling sounds. The thuds were a lower tone than she had ever heard, and the tinkling high and clear, despite being barely audible.

"Zeta wakes. This makes me happy!"

This came as a woman's voice, somewhere between being heard and being said by her own internal voice, yet it was from the outside. It was surreal, like having thoughts slip in from someone else's mind, into your own.

Yet, they were not unwelcome.

Nothing seemed real, yet it was a more lucid experience than she had ever had. As confused as she was, she could still focus on the chaos with a sharp mind.

It was *too* real.

How did she get here, and what are all these strange sights and sounds? Even the smells were intense and detailed. Musty fur and the sap of trees flooded her nose, along with dirt, herbs, water, and fruit.

She finally managed to focus on Penelope-pooch. The pooch was as clean and vibrant as she had ever been. Both of her eyes were beautiful brown orbs. Zeta knew in her heart that the memory of the fight with the black wolf-pooches had been real, and that Penelope-pooch had lost an eye in the fight, yet here she was, without so much as a scar.

Zeta also realized that she had no pain in her favored arm. Had the spirits healed them? They say that anything is possible for spirits, since they travel freely between the realms of gods and men.

A thought, which filled her with wonder and dread, struck her: this was The Realm of the Gods!

ZETA WAS LYING on her side, amid a thick pile of soft furs. Feeling the furs underneath, she found that they were warm and supple, like the belly of a great bear. She cast aside the furs which covered her, then stood.

She was inside of a cave made of logs, neatly stacked to a height greater than a man. They even loomed overhead. They could topple into a pile, crushing her at any moment! This was some sort of log man-trap!

She surveyed her surroundings. Rocks and wood were shaped into unnatural forms around her. A perfectly square hole in one side of the trap let in the light of Surya. It was big enough for her to climb through, but that would surely send the logs toppling down around her. A faint glow also slipped in from behind a fur which hung to the other side of the trap. It looked like it was covering a larger opening which went all the way to the ground. Surely, the fur hid the alternate exit — this was the secret escape portal.

She scanned the inside of the log man-trap for any more tricks before she made her move. A conspicuous sling of white ropes was strung across one corner of the place like a great spider's web. What sort of thing was that?

Hammock: a woven net of rope used as a bed for sleeping or relaxing.

This thought came from outside of her mind, yet it was not heard. Along with the thought came an influx of images, giving her the full understanding of what a *hammock* was. She could imagine how she might go about getting into the hammock, if she wanted to. She suddenly knew how she could weave one for herself. She had no trouble remembering what it was called, even though she had only heard the strange word one time, from a foreign place in the back of her mind.

"Hammock," she said aloud. She realized as she said it that this was the first thing she had vocalized since waking up from slate-space. It was like breaking a spell. She also realized that she should be quiet, since she still didn't know where she was or who else might be around. The spirits, Oraxis and Genevieve, were likely to return soon and would not be happy to find that she had escaped their slate-space mind-trap and their log man-trap.

Incoming urgent conversation request from Oraxis Telson.

This came in the same tone as the information about the hammock, along with a nagging tug on her mind to respond to the request. The man wanted to talk to her? She thought the words, *"No! Go away! I never want to talk to you again!"*

With that, she could feel the request disappear. Zeta smiled at the power that she had over the spirits.

Looking down at her body, she found that she was dressed in skins woven together with great skill. It was softer than any leather she had ever felt, and parts of it were colored in pinks and reds. It was very strange garb the spirits had dressed her in, but at least it was comfortable.

She made her way to the hidden portal. Hanging from the logs next to the portal was a stick-sling lashed to a leather stick-holder. The holder was filled with perfectly straight, feather-tipped sticks.

It was too good to be true! Wait. Was it bait?

She inspected the area, but could see no trip wires. She carefully pulled the stick-sling and stick-holder from their hanging branch, which protruded from the stacked logs. She pulled the shoulder strap over her head, declaring these her spoils. Before leaving, she gave the trap one more pass. A pile of glossy red fruit sat inside a bowl. Zeta grabbed them, one at a time, dropping them into the stick holder.

Satisfied with her plunder, Zeta gingerly pulled the furs hiding the escape portal aside and peeked her head out. Nobody was outside. She slipped out of the portal, careful not to bump the precarious logs, and dashed to the trees. Penelope-pooch followed.

Looking back, she marveled at the meticulous stack of logs from which she had emerged. It was truly an amazing man-trap, but there was no time to gawk — she had to run!

6

CRISIS

Zeta of the Scorpion Tail Tribe's Beta Bootstrapping Protocol has been terminated.

ORAXIS'S FACE WENT NUMB. This was *bad*.

According to her vitals, Zeta had seemed to be doing better. Oraxis had tried not to let his monitoring of Zeta's state distract him from Jamji's performance. The dance was reaching the climactic moment when her vulnerable Earthling would be killed by The Monster from the Stars. To leave now would be unforgivable, but to delay their response was unthinkable.

Oraxis clutched Genevieve's hand and squeezed it hard, jerking his wide-eyed expression towards her, sending the urgent mind-speech message, *"We have to go. Now."*

"Ouch, hey! What are you talking about?!" Genevieve replied, turning to meet Oraxis's ghostly face with her own look of admonition. *"Jamji's performance—"*

"Zeta is aborted, Gen! We lost her!"

"No!" Genevieve shouted in mindspeak as she gasped.

Her gasp was lost in a crowd full of similar gasps which had accompanied The Monster from the Stars pouncing upon Jamji, pantomiming tearing her apart. Oraxis and Genevieve clasped hands and stood in tandem. They stumbled in their sideways retreat down the row, bumping past knees and stepping on feet. In their wake was a grumbling of complaints which their mumbled apologies did little to assuage.

"What happened? How did she..." Genevieve couldn't bear to finish the question.

Oraxis addressed the notion head-on. *"We don't know that she died, only that the Beta Bootstrapping Protocol terminated."*

They reached the exit aisle and followed the dim trail of lights up the slope between the seating aisles leading towards the exit.

Oraxis continued, *"That can also mean that she just found a way out of the protocol...but I don't see how she could have. Not so early. Pull me."*

Oraxis was giving his body over to auto-pilot so he could submerge himself in slate-space. This meant that Genevieve had to drag him by the hand, stumbling up the exit aisle's slope like a reluctant child. His consciousness flitted about slate-space in a feverish search for an answer as to what happened.

He poured through his privileged bootstrapper data, including Zeta's bio readings for the prior few hours. They manifested visually before him in a series of scrawling graphics. Nothing he didn't already know. Unconsciousness, then stress, then calm. Then she was gone.

He composed an urgent message to their nearest neighbors, asking for immediate notification if she was seen, and asking if anybody near their cabin could please check on her. Not that anybody *should* be near the cabin, since they were supposed to have vacated the area to give the bootstrappers privacy.

"Oh, and be on the lookout out for her dog," he appended to the message, including an image snippet.

Finally, he sent a summoning thought-command to Zephyr.

They reached the large, twisting corridor of the main entrance to

The Cavern of the Soul. There were no doors or curtains to push through, as the shaped rock surfaces and serpentine passageway protected the performance chamber from all but a faint hint of light. They hurried out and over the large green clearing outside of the cave which served as the foyer. It was lined with tall pines and had a wide, beaten path leading around the side towards the beast grounds.

"Has she replied?" Genevieve sent as she dragged Oraxis, stumbling across the edge of the clearing.

"Replied? How would—" and then it occurred to him that he hadn't even tried the simplest, most direct way to see what happened — querying Zeta directly.

Cursing himself, Oraxis sent out an urgent conversation request, addressed to Zeta of the Scorpion Tail Tribe. WorMS — the Worldnet Messaging Service — routed his request through its underground mycelite network. Within seconds he received the response.

Conversation request declined, sender blocked.

"What?! How? She blocked me?! That...that little cuss blocked me!"

"She blocked you? Well, it's...unfortunate, but it's also wonderful, Oraxis! It means she's alive!"

"Sure, so now instead of a medical crisis we have a child on the loose with no idea what's going on, no idea how she got here, in a foreign land full of freaking monsters and the strangest people she would have ever seen."

Oraxis tapped into an orbital feed of The Thin Forest region around his cabin, running motion detection and visual search algorithms. He took a risk, incorporating an infrared T-delta overlay, before WUtils slapped him with a Privacy Encroachment Citation. His view retreated to a useless orbital scale.

"Dammit, now Cain's cited me!"

"Well, if you'd stop with the WUtils hacker stuff—"

"Gen, the first Noddite she bumps into is going to start asking

when her Beta Ceremony is and invite her into a gameworld construct! Jesus Christ, Gen, this is the sort of brain-flaying crap that drives people into crash loops! We'll lose her yet, in the worst imaginable way!"

"Don't write her off yet, O. We can still finish her bootstrapping. We'll just have to do it...a little different from usual."

"With absolutely no control, and with her damn pride pushing against us every step of the way."

"Yeah, and with me pulling your foot-dragging zombie body every step of the way, too, right? Could you please rejoin me in the real world?"

Oraxis stole one more scan through the local channels, cursing the inane chatter before slipping back into his body. He immediately pulled loose from Genevieve's grip as he burst to a run. Genevieve followed closely behind, hands flattening and arms pumping in her fastest sprint.

THEY REACHED THE BEAST GROUNDS. Their wicker gondola sat in the clearing right where Zephyr had placed it, alongside an assortment of other gondolas, chariots, and wagons.

Oraxis and Genevieve dodged between wandering horses and ponies, a pair of massive hounds, and an enlarged lion. A racer snake with a slick grey-and-white body as wide as a tree trunk rested near the edge of the grounds in a coiled bundle. It watched them darting across the grounds, raising its head until it looked down at them from the height of a treetop. Its mouth was large enough to engulf a man without unhinging its jaw. The predator's instincts seethed behind its hungry, slitted eyes, yet its hard-wired neural inhibitions against hunting without permission held it at bay. Knowing about these restrictions barely sufficed to make Oraxis comfortable in the snake's presence.

"Why do some people insist on making enlarged snakes and

spiders?" Genevieve asked as they reached the Gondola, glancing back at the looming serpent.

"I know," Oraxis said flatly, shaking his head and helping Genevieve to climb into the gondola. "Complete vanity animals, very limited practical value." She could have hopped in without help, of course, but this was his gentlemanly tradition.

"At least they help keep the R.O.U.S. population down."

"R.O.U.S.?" Oraxis ran a WoQS query on the initialism. The top disambiguation hits didn't match Genevieve's context.

"It was a joke," Genevieve sighed, "a movie reference. Forget it."

In a flash, the snake's head turned and plunged into the trees. Its body uncurled as it disappeared into the forest in a cacophony of crunching twigs and broken branches. One instinct which had not been suppressed was that of self-preservation in the face of certain death, unless doing so conflicted with the wishes of its owner. And if there was one thing which could trigger a snake's instinct to turn tail and slither to safety, it was the sight of a descending bird of prey. Zephyr had wasted no time in his return, and he was now a rapidly growing shadow in the evening sky.

"Um, I think we're about to get hit by a gale blast here, O." Genevieve looked around at the animals. The hounds were sitting a few meters away, tongues lolling, tails wagging, apparently hoping that the running humans were playing a game that they could join in on. A few horses were grazing nearby.

"It'll be fine. I'll have him use a lateral thrust braking maneuver. That'll direct the gust over the treetops instead of downward," Oraxis gestured in a sideways sweeping motion with his hands. Just to be sure, Oraxis sent a thought-command to the bird to tell it to slow down and to exhibit strict control over its braking gust.

"*Confirmed,*" the bird responded in the dry tone of a utility-grade AI.

"Shoo! Go, run away!" Genevieve was shouting to the horses, waving her arms. The half-witted beasts only walked a slight distance in response.

Incoming urgent conversation request from Karn the Beastmaster.

Oraxis and Genevieve received the request in their shared public channel. They looked at each other expectantly.

"You get it," Genevieve said.

Oraxis looked across the field towards the distant gaping hole in the back of the round-topped mountain; the rear loading dock of The Cavern of The Soul. Karn's bulky, armored form was emerging from the base of the hole, running towards them and waving his arms over his head, an expression of grave concern on his normally jovial face. Oraxis accepted the request, opening a private channel between the two.

"Oraxis, I saw you running like death was nipping at your heels!" Karn shouted in Oraxis's mind. *"Is anybody hurt!? Do I need to sound an alarm?!"*

"We have a...bit of an emergency at home, but nothing for you to concern yourself with. So, uh, if you could pull all these animals back from the parking lot so they don't get in the way when Zephyr lands, that would be helpful."

Karn slowed to a stop and looked up. His eyes widened and his forehead wrinkled as his bushy black eyebrows lifted, his expression shifting from concern to awe upon spotting the descending golden eagle. Karn had seen the great bird plenty of times before, but never in a dive such as this. Zephyr had widened his wings slightly to slow his descent but was still in a rapid dive, and would be upon them in seconds. *"God of beasts, would you look at that! What a sight! He's magnificent, Oraxis!"*

"Karn, please, the animals?"

"Right!" Karn said, breaking his gaze from the sky and directing it towards the beasts in the field. He lifted both hands, pressing two fingers to each of his temples. He furrowed his brow and squinted his eyes. It was as if an electric shock struck every animal in the area. Horse screams and hound yelps erupted as the beasts sprinted in

unison towards the base of the mountain, instantly clearing the area around the gondolas.

A heartbeat later came the whooshing sound of Zephyr's powerful wings lunging forward as he performed the lateral gust braking maneuver. A jet of air roiled across the treetops, sending them into a violent thrashing dance, accompanied by a spiraling tempest of debris blowing over the forest.

Genevieve gasped and squeezed Oraxis's arm, pointing out a small bird tumbling like a leaf in the gust. She looked accusingly up at Zephyr, who was preparing to flap his great wings again to control his descent. His second flap was downwards and sent pine needles and dust swirling around them. Oraxis and Genevieve huddled together and covered their faces.

Genevieve had always said that when Zephyr took off or landed, it reminded her of movie scenes of helicopters. She had shown him a few examples, and he agreed that a lot of high drama could happen in that whirling, noisy, dusty chaos. That final, rushed goodbye. The shouted "I love you", just audible over the whining chopper. The urgent "Go! Go! Go!" of troops unloading a transport, then running, hunched over their rifles, into a war zone.

It was in this dramatic spirit that Oraxis thought, *"Don't worry, Zeta, we're coming."*

The thud of Zephyr's landing reverberated through the ground. Debris settled as a cloud of dust rolled across the field.

Karn was still sharing a channel with Oraxis, sending a stream of mindspeak. *"Woo-ah! What a landing! Oy-Oy! I tell you, Oraxis, my friend, I would be your eternal servant if you would take me for a ride on the neck of that bird! I have to say you're the luckiest man I know. Such a magnificent creature! And having an eternal companion like Genevieve to share him with? Now there's a treat, I wager! Oh, you've got an emergency, alright! Taking a gondola ride at dusk? Ha!"*

"Ok, Karn, we really have to go, thank you for your help with the animals," Oraxis sent with a polite request to terminate the channel.

"Ah, don't mention it. Just doin' my job, friend," Karn replied, confirming the request and closing their link.

Zephyr stood tall, in all his majesty, and surveyed the clearing with great golden-brown eyes. The other animals stood as a single frozen mass near Karn, who retained his direct control over them to keep them clear of the eagle. This would allow ample room to take off.

Zephyr lowered his head to the level of Oraxis and Genevieve, sending, "What is my command?"

"Take us home. Quickly," Oraxis sent.

Zephyr's black-tipped, yellow beak clamped onto the thick handle which arched over the gondola. Oraxis and Genevieve sat down and held onto the wooden handles attached to the inner corners of the wicker basket as they lifted and swung around. Zephyr poised his wings, taking a few bounding steps through the clearing. With a powerful flap, he was airborne. Four more beats of his massive wings and they had climbed above the treetops, banking towards home. Zephyr reached up with yellow feet and wrapped his black talons around the gondola handle, pulling it from his beak, swinging his passengers down into their cruising position beneath him.

The cool evening air whistled through the gondola. Genevieve moved to sit next to Oraxis. Her warmth, physical and mental, was comforting. He wrapped his arm around her and she lay her head against his chest.

"Did you see the messages from Jamji?" Genevieve asked via mindspeech.

"Yeah, she's raging. We should apologize and explain. Once she hears about the...situation...she'll understand."

Genevieve scoffed.

Oraxis sighed. Jamji was a world-champion grudger. "You should send it. You're the sensitive one."

"I'll write it, you'll edit it, I'll send it."

"Fair enough. Write fast, she counts the seconds."

"I know," Genevieve sent. She would probably dial up her neural firing rate to help speed up her message composing time. But thinking too fast would have detrimental effects on her ability to think deeply — The Hummingbird Effect, which was worse for some people than others. Genevieve was particularly susceptible.

She had a message crafted and shared with him for review in under a minute. He quickly reviewed and edited it, then handed it back to send. He watched as she rolled back a few of his word choice modifications before she sent it on to Jamji.

They waited with apprehension to see if she would accept the message.

"Declined," Genevieve sent.

Their shared sigh was a harmony of resigned defeat.

"Oh, well," Oraxis sent. *"We'll smooth it over somehow. Now, as for Zeta. You should try to open a conversation channel to her and see if she'll talk to you."*

"I already sent her a message, low urgency."

Oraxis verbalized his response, "You...low urgency? I'm sorry, but...low urgency?! So, are we really going for a leisurely gondola ride at sunset here or are we on a search-and-rescue mission? Maybe you've forgotten how unstable minds were when they came out of neural mapping before we came up with the protocol? We had a thirty-six percent fail rate those days, Gen. How many millions of broken minds had to be aborted? How many friends did we lose?"

Genevieve pulled back from him and scowled as she said, "Don't lecture me on fail rates, O. I know — I was there. I still think about Susie-Q every night. So, yeah, I get it. Now, think! You already tried an urgent message, and you got blocked. You probably scared her."

"You should have at least sent it normal urgency—"

"No! She needed a gentle approach. Let her find the message when she settles down to rest. Give her some space."

Oraxis blinked four times, working his jaw muscles, and then sighed with a slow shake of his head, relaxing his tension and patting

Genevieve's leg once. This is to say, he reluctantly admitted that Genevieve was right, as usual, and that he was sorry for being an ass. He didn't have to say a thing — after hundreds of years of reading each other's mannerisms, even the slightest gestures spoke volumes. It was the last communication they would have on the trip.

The old couple soared quietly through the chilly evening air. Zephyr's wings flapped a deep rhythmic beat, accompanied by the high-pitched whistling of wind through the woven wicker of the gondola. Oraxis had a heavy heart and a troubled mind.

Guilt. Worry. Regret. Failure.

Countless alternate paths of what they should have done differently played what-if games with the looming shadow of what could have gone wrong. The flight would be a mercifully short one. Soon, the silent torture of waiting would be replaced by the satisfaction of action.

7

THE THIN FOREST

As ZETA RAN, it struck her that the trees of this forest were almost entirely devoid of low branches. Instead, they held their scrubby tops high overhead. It was like no other forest she could remember — dry and cool, with sparse undergrowth. A thick mat of brown needle-leaves covered the ground. Sweet sap filled her nose with a fresh, tangy aroma. What sort of forest was this?

> **Temperate coniferous: a biome characterized by evergreen trees. This specific forest's predominant species is pine. It is called The Thin Forest by its inhabitants.**

This concept came with a flood of ideas and images. She now understood what sort of weather she could expect in the forest and what animals lived there. She felt as if she had spent a year in a forest such as this, while a moment ago it was absolutely foreign.

What a wonderful thought-giver this was! This had to be some sort of helpful spirit that had latched onto her mind now that she wandered The Realm of the Gods.

Zeta ran with light feet and Penelope-pooch followed. Her stealthy retreat was ruined by the crunch of the dry needles underfoot, so she traded stealth for speed. She dodged past trees and jumped over logs, bounding through the forest with the speed and agility of a deer.

Escape the evil spirits and their traps!

Seek the safety of the tribe!

Defy the cursed Gravan!

She clutched the stolen stick-sling tightly — her spoils.

It was great fun, just like hunting for bro-critter again. Her eyes fluttered, and the forest turned into the thicket. This was where she would find Charra!

Zeta cried out as she crashed to the ground.

She tumbled through the needles and low underbrush. Once she settled to a stop, a hot pain registered in her shin and her favored arm.

"What just happened?" She asked the moss covering the dirt below her head. She lifted herself. Sweat stung her eye. She rubbed it clear, then pulled back a reddened forearm. No, not sweat — that was blood. She probed her forehead, finding the sensitive spot, pressing it to stop the bleeding.

Zeta's heart pounded in a new panic. It wasn't the blood that bothered her — it was that her mind had...slipped. It was as if she had left her body, then snapped back again. She had been in Talmid's Stinking Thicket, for just a moment.

A woman's voice spoke in her mind, saying, *"Zeta fell. She is hurt."*

The voice seemed familiar. She looked around, seeing nobody, then looked at Penelope-pooch. Was that *her?* She thought the words, *"Pen, did you just talk in my mind?"*

The pooch barked as the woman's voice in her head exclaimed, *"Yes!"*

Zeta squealed with delight. She kneeled and scratched Penelope-pooch behind the ears. Penelope-pooch wagged her tail and licked Zeta's bloodied face with a gentle, timid lap of a mother kissing a wound. This had to be something magical that the spirits had done to them, like what they did to her eyes! Or maybe it's just how things work in The Realm of the Gods. Either way, it was a miracle, and she was grateful for it.

There were so many things she wanted to say to Penelope-pooch, but that would have to wait. And she'd worry about the mind-slip later. For now, they would run.

<hr />

THEY RAN until the sky turned indigo.

On the few occasions when she heard foreign-tongued voices in the distance, Zeta skirted around them.

There had been plenty of trickling streams to drink from, which they did every time they passed one, but it would be nice to have something to eat. She remembered catching a whiff of burning wood and cooking meat wafting through the forest during her escape run, but that was a long way back. She wouldn't want to approach a strange tribe's camp, anyway.

She sat on a rock and pulled the stick holder off her shoulder, tipping it until a red fruit rolled into her palm. She held it up and examined it.

"Thought-giver, what sort of fruit is this? Is it safe to eat?"

You are holding a domesticated apple. It is safe for you to eat.

Her mind filled with ideas about what apple trees look like, what varieties of size, color, flavor, and consistency that domesticated apples can be found in, and how they are used in recipes and cooking.

So many strange ideas! She would save her questions about what it means to be "domesticated" for another day.

The apple's skin was smooth, shiny, and thin. It had been torn in a few places, showing a bit of browned flesh underneath. She closed her eyes and pressed her nose against the fruit to savor its aroma, breathing in deeply. Marvelous, flowery sweetness came as an explosion of scent. Her eyes rolled back in her head as her mind tumbled backwards into a dizzying emptiness, surrounded by aromatic enchantment.

Opening her eyes, a flower-laden tree stood before her.

"Do this tree grow a fruit, pa?" Zeta asked, pointing with one hand and holding onto Wilhelm-pa's ear with the other.

Wilhelm-pa lifted her from off his shoulders, placing her on the ground. "Yes, I think I remember a tree like this growing large, green fruit which was sweet and tart. It was good to eat, but you'd get a tummy-ache if you eat too many!"

"I'm gonna wait here. It gonna grow me fruit!"

Her pa laughed, "We can't do that, my little fruit bat. We're only passing through here. Tomorrow we continue walking."

"No! I don't wanna walk! I don't wanna leave the tree — it smells so good!" Zeta ran towards the tree and pulled down one of the low-hanging branches to press her face into the fragrant white flowers. A sharp stinging pain erupted on her cheek, coupled with a frantic buzzing.

Zeta threw down the apple, gasping and swatting at her cheek, scrambling backwards through the pine needles. The world spun around her as she came crashing back into reality.

The living memory echoed in her mind, the white flowers still etched into her eyes. The pain of the sting was gone, but the distinct sensation of having just been stung persisted. Her heart pounded. She sat in a daze for a moment, trying very hard to get a firm grasp on where she was and why she was there. Was she a child? She looked down at her body, relieved to see that she was a maturing young woman, but confused over how easily she had accepted that she had been a child again.

Zeta knew the fragrant white-blossomed fruit tree and bee sting on her cheek to be one of her earliest memories, even though she had just relived them. She could think back to them now, without reliving them, just like she could any other memory. Or could she? None of her other memories came to mind quite so easily. She wanted to think harder about them, but she feared that digging one up would send her diving back to slate-space.

Riding on Wilhelm-pa's shoulders while holding onto his ears had been her favorite way to get around until she grew too big for it. What she had just experienced had been an often-remembered, bittersweet memory of her pa. Not because of the bee sting, but because she would lose him someday.

Flower-covered trees would always remind her of him.

That, and the crack of thunder in the night. Night-thunder?

Penelope-pooch caught her attention just before she slipped again. The pooch whimpered as she thought-spoke, *"I am hungry and confused about you throwing your food."*

"I'm sorry, Pen. I just got...mixed up for a second."

"I want to hunt. I can hear an animal nearby. May I kill and eat it?"

Zeta looked over to her pooch and met her brown eyes. What a strange thing this was, to have Penelope-pooch talking in her head. And now, asking for permission to hunt? Zeta replied with an inner voice of her own. *"Yes, you can hunt the animal. I will stay here and be still."*

"Good, thank you," Penelope-pooch sent. She sniffed the air, rotated her ears, then padded off into the dark.

Zeta found the apple she had thrown, brushed the dirt off, and took a bite without any more fanciful sniffing. It could have easily been the most delicious fruit she had ever eaten, but she was careful not to let it pull her back into a living memory.

ZETA WATCHED Penelope-pooch hunt as she ate her apple. She could spot the pooch prowling through the forest, despite the darkness. Seeing in the dark was amazingly easy to do by focusing her eyes in a certain way. She imagined this was how a jungle cat sees the night. As she swept her eyes over the forest, she realized that she could see bright little hints where animals and birds hid in their nests and burrows. How easy hunting would be, now!

A glowing form darted through the trees in the distance, as swift as a bird. Zeta was startled, but soon realized that it had been Penelope-pooch closing in on her kill. She was *so* fast!

There was an animal cry, a thrashing, then silence.

"Penelope-pooch, are you okay?" Zeta thought, unsure whether the thought would carry across the forest.

"Yes, I am fast and I killed a raccoon. I will bring it to you."

Sure to her word, the pooch came trotting between the trees, proudly carrying her prize. She dropped the creature to the ground, then began pulling at its skin as she held it down with a paw.

"You can eat it, too," Penelope-pooch thought.

"No, thanks! It's all yours, girl!"

Zeta certainly wasn't hungry enough to eat raw meat, and she was in no mood to build a fire — she'd stick with the apples.

Once Penelope-pooch had eaten her fill, they walked some distance from the animal's carcass, looking for a place to bed down for the night. Zeta found a nice hollow, partially concealed by a large rock on one side and a tree on the other. She gathered a few armfuls of pine needles into a pile to make a bed. She considered going back for the raccoon to make a pillow out of it, but worried that its scent would attract scavengers.

The prickly bed wasn't the most comfortable, but it was better than the dirt. Penelope-pooch sighed as they curled up together for the night.

Zeta tried to remember whether she had ever slept alone, without a tribe of snoring elds and cooing babes spread out all around her. She was afraid of slipping into a memory so she didn't think *too* hard about it, but it certainly seemed like this was the first time.

It wasn't so bad.

As they lay, Zeta listened to the calming sounds of the sleeping forest. She looked through the gaps in the treetops to see if there were any familiar star patterns. Yes, there was the tortoise. And there, the crooked staff. Strange. It was a mild night, like summer, but those were winter stars. Zeta let it pass. Of all the strange things she had seen that day, this was the least interesting.

After letting her mind drift for a while, Zeta became aware of a sensation pulling at her, like the feeling of remembering that she forgot to do something. But what? She focused on the sensation, then discovered that in the back of her mind, waiting patiently for her attention, was Genevieve. The woman wanted to say something.

Zeta liked Genevieve more than Oraxis. The woman seemed warm. This didn't mean that she could trust her — the two were conspirators with the same sinister intentions. One of the oldest tricks of the elds was to set one eld against you while another stood in support of you, though they both worked towards the same goal.

No, if she opened her mind to hearing Genevieve's thought-speech then she would be falling for a trick. She decided that she shouldn't do it.

With that, the nagging sensation faded away, and her mind was clear. Zeta enjoyed learning how to control her new powers of mind and body. Her favorite power had to be that she could talk to Penelope-pooch. She tried it out again.

"Good night, Pen."

"Yes, the night is good. We will sleep now. I love you, Zeta."

The crooked staff star pattern twisted and blurred as her eyes welled with tears. She rolled over and hugged her guardian spirit tightly. Penelope, the Golden Goddess of Pooches. She always knew that Penelope-pooch loved her, but to hear the words filled her with overwhelming joy.

As much as she hated being all alone in this strange place, having Penelope-pooch with her made it okay. They were changed, with faster bodies and sharper senses. They were heroes of legend. Together, they could do anything.

8

KARN'S WISDOM

The only thing worse than being overcome by a torrent of emotion is the adrenaline hangover that follows. Jamji was exhausted. She wanted nothing more than to hide under a boulder and sleep for the next month. Pepper would bring her fresh meat. He would snuggle up into a big crescent and she would sleep against his belly.

No, better yet, she'd get an offworlder to court her with delicacies. After tonight's performance, every Proliferan on the planet would flood her public message queue with requests for a private audience. The Proliferans always had the best food.

Oh, but the Guardians had what she *really* wanted. They'd see her feats of mental and physical ability for what they really were. The Students of Sun Tzu appreciated the beauty of power. Their sponsored martial arts training programs and biotech enhancements had already made her dance so much more deadly. Soon, with the help of the Guardians, she would hone her body and mind to perfection.

The backwater Genesisians, on the other hand, disgusted her. Jamji's lips tightened. These Luddite caveman wanna-be's were so full of themselves, strutting around wearing the mantle of the beast, as if that was all the camouflage they needed from intellect-hunting aliens. It's a joke! You terraformed the planet, people! The whole ruse is so mind-blowingly transparent.

Even the planet's name disgusted her. Genesis? Ooh, clever! The oldest sci-fi trope for a first extraterrestrial colony's name, made real, courtesy of an Anglocentric, homogenized, Westernized, post-Judeo-Christian society on the verge of destruction.

And to top it all off, those self-absorbed ancients, Oraxis and Genevieve, built themselves a log cabin complete with a potbelly stove! Hypocrites!

Jamji punched the stone floor, fracturing a knuckle bone. Pain shot through her hand and up her arm, yet the tears that welled in her eyes were not a response to physical pain, but to the anger.

"Hmph," a gruff voice said from the entrance, "what a quake. I should look up the seismic readings on that one." Karn the Beastmaster stepped into the room, looking around warily, his gaze passing over Jamji. She had remained in active invisibility mode as she stewed, and the few passers-by who poked their heads into the dressing room looking for her had been fooled.

"I'd say the epicenter," Karn said, rounding towards Jamji, "is right there!" He pointed at the wall next to her.

Some people might take one look at Karn and assume that such a towering barbarian-lookin' guy would be a hard-ass. Nope. The man was as kind-hearted as they come. That's the only reason Jamji didn't send him tumbling back out of the room with a flying kick to the head.

"Go away," Jamji grumbled from between gritted teeth. She opened and closed her hand, reveling in the numb burning of her rapidly healing bone. Pain really wasn't a problem, if you had control over it.

"Ooh, hey now. What was that?" Karn bent his knees, spread his arms with hands downward as if to stabilize himself, and looked about with mock fear. "An aftershock? These tremors, they sound *dangerous*," he whispered loudly.

Karn dragged the joke out for way too long. His lips were frozen in an "ooh" expression. His eyes bugged, scanning the ceiling and walls fearfully. After thirty seconds of glaring at his comically absurd pose, Jamji let out a loud nasal snort of a laugh which defied her every attempt to stifle it. Tears of laughter replaced tears of anger. All the while Karn just kept on with the awful "man expecting an earthquake" gag.

Once her laughter subsided, he broke character and smiled down at her. "There, now I think the quake has passed, eh?" She had switched back out of active invisibility mode and was again glowing in her default aquamarine wavelength.

"Karn, you're a putz."

"Thank you, my dear," Karn said with a bow, extending his hand to help her up.

"That's not a compliment. Look it up," Jamji said, accepting his hand and standing.

"I'm certain the word is the vilest slander, but when it passes through lips as lovely as yours, it takes on the sweetest of meanings."

Jamji reached up and patted the burly man's black-bearded cheek. "Shakespeare, eat your heart out."

"More slander?" Karn asked, arching an eyebrow.

"No, a sarcastic compliment."

"A gruesome one, to be sure."

Jamji laughed. "I suppose it is when you think about it." She sighed and wiped her eyes. "Karn, why did you track me down?"

"Oh, I wanted to see if you had heard anything about what happened with Oraxis and Genevieve."

Jamji's mood immediately soured again. "No, and I don't care. They can go to hell."

Jamji crossed her arms, but Karn dared to put a hand on her shoulder. He might lose it in a moment.

"You think they crossed you? Ah, your heart broke when they left." Karn's gruff voice was sincere. "Did they leave before your dance, love?"

"They left *during* my dance," Jamji spat.

Karn had a sudden sense of urgency and a look of concern. "During your dance? They were running like gazelle to their gondola, and they called Zephyr in with so much of a rush that he about blew the trees over when he landed. Put it together. What does that mean?!"

"It means that they're inconsiderate, selfish, reckless jerks who always have some fire burning that they have to go put out! It means they never have time to pay any attention to what anyone else does! It means the world revolves around Oraxis and Genevieve Telson, king and queen of the goddamn universe!"

"It means they need you!" Karn shouted, shocking Jamji into silence. This had to have been the first time he had ever yelled at her. "It means they're in trouble and they need your help, girl! You're blinded by these tears! You think they would do anything like run out during your dance if they didn't need to? You're hiding in here, sulking like a child, while they're out there struggling with a real problem."

"They didn't ask me for help," Jamji said uncertainly. She never read Genevieve's message. Maybe they *had* asked for her help.

"Come, now, you know they're too proud to ask you for it. As much as they love Nod, you know they can feel everyone's eyes on them. A thousand eyes just waiting for them to fail so they can tear down the ancient Earthlings. But you? You're family, you and they. Not by blood, but by spirit, and you know that, child. When you see someone you love is in trouble, *you* be the one to speak up. You tell them you're there for them and you *figure out* a way to help." Karn's face was flushed red. Spit bubbles formed at the corners of his mouth. "And you don't flop around on the floor throwing a blasted tantrum!"

If Jamji followed her gut at this moment, she may have hurt Karn, either physically or mentally. She needed a time out.

———

Jᴀᴍᴊɪ ᴄʀᴀɴᴋᴇᴅ up her neural firing rate, sending Karn into imperceptibly slow motion. She wasn't going to let him stand there waiting while she worked out what to do next.

Maybe he was right about them needing her help. She needed to read Genevieve's message, so she made the request to retrieve the message out of her rejected queue. This would send Genevieve a notice that her previously rejected message was now being re-requested. Normally, the sender would need to acknowledge the receiver's request before it would be fulfilled, but Genevieve had marked it for automatic retrieval permission. Either the message was important enough to add the precaution, or Jamji's reputation for rejecting and then re-requesting messages preceded her.

The message apologetically explained why they had left in the middle of her performance. They had taken in a new beta — a girl named Zeta. This much Jamji already knew. The Beta Bootstrapping Protocol had been prematurely terminated. This meant that the beta had either died or had torn her mind free of the protocol. In either case, they had to run back and see what happened.

During their departure they had received a response from Zeta, Genevieve explained, which ruled out death. This also meant that she had miraculously broken out of bootstrapping on her second day.

This was arguably a worse fate. Bootstrapping was a sensitive and imperfect process. Failure at any of its crucial stages could lead to irrevocable CCDC — catastrophic cognitive dissociative collapse. A best-case scenario for improper bootstrapping was a long and stressful acclimation period. The worst-case scenario? Unmentionable. Oraxis and Genevieve needed to find the beta before some reckless Noddite ruined their chances of saving her mind.

One thing that Genevieve didn't do in her message was deign to ask for Jamji's help. Karn had said that they were too proud to ask for help. He was sure right about that.

Could she actually find it in her heart to reach out to *them* to offer help? After what they had done to her?

Then she thought about Zeta. She hadn't met the girl, but soon enough the new beta would be adopted into the Telson family. In a way, their departure was really just a matter of them setting aside the desires of the older child for the needs of the younger.

This was an epiphany — she was the big sis with a scraped knee who sulked at the attention her wailing sis-kin babe received. She warmed up to this imagery and decided that she would indeed help Oraxis and Genevieve with their crisis.

She wouldn't do it for their sake, though — she would do it for Zeta.

Jamji returned to her normal neural rate. In the time it had taken for her to read the message and come up with her decision, Karn had taken a breath and started to say something, which Jamji no longer needed to hear.

In a flash of motion, she covered his mouth. Karn flinched and reflexively grabbed her arm, almost matching her inhuman speed with his own. It took him a moment to realize that she wasn't attacking him and that she was smiling gently. He furrowed his thick black eyebrows in confusion.

"You're right. I'll help them, so stop your lecture or you'll talk me out of it," Jamji said. She felt his mouth shift into a broad smile under her hand. He let go of her arm and slapped his hand on her shoulder, so she pulled him into a hug.

"Is Pepper ready? I've got to run."

"Aye, your boy's full o' pride an' puppy chow. I've taken off his gold caps and sent him to play in the grazing grounds."

"Thanks, Karn," Jamji said as she made for the exit.

"Say!" Karn said, before she could escape, "when you get to Oraxis and Genevieve's cabin, let me know if they need anything from me. Tell 'em I'll do anything they'd ask if they'd let me have a flight with Zephyr."

"Will do!" Jamji shouted as she turned and sprinted down the corridor.

JAMJI HAPHAZARDLY BOUNDED down the winding stairwell, skipping four steps at a time. She crossed the antechamber in seconds, dodging between set pieces and startled stagehands. She ran out of the large opening which led to the grazing grounds. It had grown dark, with just a faint blue tinge in the sky. Patches of flickering orange light danced in the field, casting wild shadows — the torches of some early-to-bed types who didn't care to stay for the later performances.

Among the animals was an unmistakable sight — a massive doglike form strobing psychedelically in the darkness and charging towards her. Jamji didn't break her stride as she grinned widely and sprinted towards the pooch. She was a glowing aquamarine streak.

Pepper's hyperactive, anthropolinguistic stream-of-consciousness was pouring into her mind. *"It's you! It's you! I'm running to meet you and lick you because I love you so much!"*

She responded through the mind link, *"I see you, Pep, and I love you!"*

They closed the distance in seconds. Pepper leapt at her in a pounce, and Jamji jumped to intercept him at the pinnacle of his leap. Their bodies collided midair, and she wrapped her arms around his neck. His greater mass hammered her backward. They slammed into the ground, but she maintained the bear hug. Pepper thrashed his head ferociously, flinging her to the ground. She laughed and skidded across the grass.

Next came the licking. The beast repeatedly licked the laughing Jamji, lifting her up or rolling her across the ground.

"Okay, Pep! That was fun, but it's time to stop. We need to run very quickly to the Telson cabin."

Without missing a beat, the dog jumped, turning to the south, landing in a crouch. *"Jump on my back and I will run there very fast!"* His psychedelic strobe stopped, and he went back to a dull gray glow. He was ready for business.

Jamji mounted the dog's back and scratched behind his ears. She pulled her hands back, pushing the razor-sharp polymer claws out from her fingertips. She hesitated for a heartbeat before driving her claws into the thick flesh on the scruff of his neck and tightening her grasp on his thick skin. They had coordinated this riding routine many years ago, including the automatic dulling of the nerves and shunting of blood away from her grasping points. He would heal minutes after she released him, and he wouldn't feel anything but the general sense that he was being grasped.

Crude? Maybe, but there simply wasn't a better way to make sure she wasn't tossed from his back as he bounded and sprang at breakneck speed. They had tried straps and other riding gear, but they always became cumbersome and took too much time to get situated. She sure as heck wasn't going to burden him with a saddle.

Jamji squeezed her legs around Pepper-pooch's torso and sent the thought-command, *"Ok, Pep. Now run!"*

Jamji arrived at the cabin and pulled the door skins aside. Oraxis and Genevieve were standing in the dim, lantern-lit cabin, embracing each other. Oraxis's head rested against Genevieve's.

"Catch you at a bad time?" She asked, flatly.

They jumped, startled by her sudden appearance, and separated.

Genevieve's eyes were wet with tears. "Oh, hi, Jamji." Her voice wavered with emotion. "We saw that you had read my message, but I'll say it again. I'm *so* sorry we had to leave during your dance. You know that we'd been looking forward to it for months, and you've been working on it for so long. The part that we saw was so beautiful, Jamji! We're so proud of you!"

Jamji leaned against the doorframe with her arms crossed, her nose flared as her anger began to simmer. "Whatever. I read your message so I'm here to help *Zeta*. Tell me what you need me to do." The extra emphasis on "Zeta" was important — she was there for her sis-kin, not for them.

Oraxis said, "She ran away, so if you want to help, you could track her down. I was preparing to take Zephyr out for an aerial search, but using Pepper to follow her scent trail would be much more effective. She'll be with her dog, which should make it even easier."

Jamji sighed. "Alright, track her down, drag her back. No problem." She pulled open the door flap to leave.

"Jamji," Genevieve blurted, "hang on. Drag her back? This is a sensitive situation..."

Oraxis nodded. "Just find her, then send us a message detailing her condition and location. Unless she's in immediate danger, we should let her sleep through the night. In the morning Genevieve and I will approach and get her to come back to the cabin. It would be preferable if you didn't reveal yourself."

Jamji crossed her arms. "Oh? You're afraid I'll scare the kid?"

"She's never seen anything like you before," Genevieve pleaded.

"So, I'm a monster now?"

"Jamji, you're an absolutely breathtaking person. You're more beautiful than words can describe."

Jamji altered her skin's chromatites to project the image of a rotting corpse, complete with maggots crawling out of holes in the putrid skin. Her eyes were empty sockets. She pulled her lips back in a skeletal smile and said, "Are you sure about that?"

Genevieve breathed a laugh. "Yes, even when you put on a spooky Halloween costume. But maybe if you could switch over to a natural skin tone, put on some clothes, wear a wig..."

A wig?! "Ugh. No." Jamji reverted to her aquamarine tone. "It's fine, I'll just go invisible." She turned and walked out.

Genevieve followed. "You'll need something to get her scent off of, won't you?"

Pepper-pooch would have already picked up Zeta's dog's scent from the territorial markings in the area, but Jamji humored her. "Yeah, almost forgot. Bring out her bed furs."

Oraxis emerged eight seconds later with a fur draped over his arm. He presented it to Pepper-pooch, who gave it a good sniff.

Jamji and Pepper-pooch switched to active invisibility. It wasn't *true* invisibility, of course, but a passable knockoff. One of its short-comings — edge effect — was particularly problematic when you're in motion, set against a noisy background. Edge effect could also betray your form when your observer passed from one of your perspective points to another. Hiding your infrared heat signature was even less effective and required an entire suite of other enhancements. Yes, Jamji had the first-gen anti-infrared bio-mods, but she had little faith in them. Hopefully, the girl hadn't figured out how to switch her vision over to the infrared spectrum.

"Thank you for your help, Jamji," Genevieve said.

Jamji displayed an invisible rude hand gesture. "Oh, no problem, anything for you guys," came her sarcastically sweet reply. She bounded away as Pepper-pooch began his hunt.

9

SPIRIT

SOMETHING WASN'T RIGHT.

Zeta had been sleeping somewhat restlessly, with tormented dreams. She was awake now, and from the corner of her eye she saw hair covering the ground beneath her. She lifted her head. It was the same hair mat that she had woken up on back in the log man-trap. What was it doing here?

She lifted herself from the mat, which seemed to stick to her skin. She scrambled to her feet, retreating from the odd fur. A similar mat of golden fur spread out underneath Penelope-pooch, exactly the color and texture of her fur. It struck Zeta that her mat's hair was also the same as her own.

Penelope-pooch lifted her head, perky ears twitching. She paid no heed to the mat beneath her.

What were those things?

The thought-giver could help!

Zeta whispered, "Thought-giver, what is that?" She pointed at the brown, hairy thing.

Placental Mat: a biosynthetic structure manufactured

by bioenhanced humans and their owned animal companions. It is produced via rapid external growth, incorporating the user's metabolic and genetic profiles into its manufacture. It can be produced manually upon request, or automatically upon entrance into stage one sleep. It draws electrical energy, water, and organic compounds from the underlying Worldnet Utility Service's mycelite network. It synthesizes these raw components into adenosine triphosphate and other metabolic products, then draws them into the user's circulatory system via dermal microtubules. The mat can supplement a variety of metabolic functions, such as removing toxins or regulating glucose.

Zeta's mind reeled as she was pummeled with concept after concept. Images of tiny animals swimming about and putting new animals together danced in her mind. Thoughts of tiny reeds piercing her skin, squirting fluids into her body. She imagined her skin extruding a second skin, covered with hair. Half of the words and ideas were absolutely alien, but at least the other half was understandable.

"Do you mean it's a part of me?"

Partially correct; it was not generated via your native DNA coding, nor is it an extension of your bodily self. Your enhanced cybernetic somatic systems, which are a feature of your default bioenhancements, created it. These systems did, however, incorporate your DNA into its manufacturing processes, which serves to complement the synthetic systems while preventing a deleterious immune response.

Zeta sat for a minute as more images flew by. She could not grasp onto any of them. Tiny spirals, images of her body as a ghost filled with colorful spiderwebs. She was not absorbing whatever the thought-giver was trying to say. She tried to form an intelligent question.

"What?"

To repeat, you are partially correct. It was not generated via your native DNA coding, nor is it an—

"Stop! Ok, I didn't understand the first time and I'm not going to understand the second time."

Please specify points for clarification.

Where to start? Penelope-pooch laid her head on the mat and sighed. Zeta wanted to tell her to get away from it, but what the thought-giver seemed to be saying is that the mat was safe. It was supposed to be helpful. It was feeding her through her skin, or something like that.

After a moment she found the nerve to approach the placental mat and try to pick it up. It held fast to the ground. She pulled harder, lifting a corner. Its roots held it to the forest floor, like a plant, though they crumbled and seemed to turn into liquid as they separated from the mat and soaked into the ground.

Zeta considered the mat for a moment longer. She decided on a simple yes-or-no question. "Thought-giver, is it safe for me to sleep on this thing?"

Yes; sleeping upon your placental mat is its primary method of—

"Ok, that's all I need to know about it. Thanks," Zeta said. Then, after a moment of consideration, she added, "Good night, thought-giver."

The thought-giver did not return the sentiment. Maybe she had offended it.

The sound of a snort came from the forest nearby.

Zeta knew it wasn't her imagination, since Penelope-pooch's head popped up and her ears stood erect. The pooch stood slowly and sniffed the air, letting out a low growl, sending a thought, *"Be careful, Zeta. There is something in the woods that made a sound like a hog."*

Zeta kept her eyes on the empty forest as she kneeled and picked up the stick-sling. She didn't know how to use it yet, but she could try.

"If it was a hog, then we should hunt it," Zeta thought to Penelope-pooch. She had gone to sleep hungry, so she should still be hungry now. She wasn't, but hunger has a way of coming and going. She would surely be ravenous in the morning, and could make a hog last for a month. Especially since it would just be her and Penelope-pooch eating it.

Hogs were dangerous creatures, but she had confidence in her new body.

"Yes, let us hunt," Penelope-pooch thought back to her, prowling forward, sniffing the air.

SNEAKING through this forest was tricky. There were rocks and patches of dirt where no pine needles lay, so she tried stepping on them rather than the crunchy needles. The crickets helped to mask their sound a bit, but also masked the sound of their quarry.

They had gone a stone's throw or two from their camp when Penelope-pooch took interest in a tree. She sniffed around it, at its base, and looked up into its branches. Zeta also looked up.

"Hogs don't climb trees, Pen."

"I smell a human at this tree," came the pooch's reply.

"Human?"

She noticed a scattering of flecks of bark at the base of the tree.

Looking more closely at the bark of the tree, she saw scratches gouged in it, leading all the way up to the high branches. A human didn't do that.

"*I think a jungle cat climbed this tree,*" Zeta thought at Penelope-pooch, backing away from the tree. She did not turn her back to it, but pivoted her head to scan the forest all around.

"*No, it is a human. I will bark at it to scare it down!*"

"*No! Do not bark!*"

Penelope-pooch obeyed, circling and sniffing the tree. How could Penelope-pooch be so certain? Was her nose really so keen? Well, if there was a person up there, they were doing a *very* good job at hiding. Zeta's vision was keen, and she could even make her eyes focus so closely on the upper branches that it was as if she had climbed the tree and looked at them from an arm's length. No man or beast could be spotted among the pine's branches.

As she scanned, she noticed that a star behind the tree jumped.

Strange.

Zeta blinked and concentrated her vision on the star. She moved to one side, and it jumped in one direction, moved to another side, and it jumped back again, ever so slightly. It reminded her of how something very close to her face could be made to look like it was jumping back and forth by shutting one eye and then the other. What would do that?

Spending a few more moments rocking back and forth to see how that spot of the tree changed, she made out the vague outline of a form. As she watched, the form moved. It was a slight shifting of the branches, a slight distortion of the bark and pine needles. One of the branches underneath it had bobbed during the shifting.

It was a spirit!

It was watching her!

Her scalp tightened as a chill crept over her body. The hair on her forearms stood up. She wanted to run, but she didn't dare pull her gaze away from the spirit. Her eye's grasp on it was already slippery. If she even blinked, she would lose it among the branches and stars.

Zeta pulled a stick from the leather holder and placed its feathered end against the string of the stick-sling. Her eyes remained fixed on the spot high in the tree where the spirit watched. She pulled the string back, aiming the rock-tipped end of the stick at the spot. She held it close to her face, as she had seen the Red-Painted beast-men from across the plains do. Though she had no practice with a proper stick-sling, she could hope that luck was on her side.

It was not. Letting go of the string, it slapped her face. The sting brought water to her eyes. The stick tumbled feebly into the forest.

A woman chuckled. The spirit was laughing at her?!

"Be gone!" Zeta yelled. She dropped the stick-sling and scanned the forest floor. She found a large rock, picked it up, then threw it the mocking spirit. Astoundingly, the rock soared upwards as rapidly as if it had been flung from a sling. Her aim was true! It reached the spirit's perch.

The rock burst in mid-air.

Zeta flinched, covering her head as rock fragments peppered the nearby trees in a hailstorm. Birds sounded alarm and took flight. Pebbles rained down all around her as Zeta ran behind a nearby tree, Penelope-pooch close at her heels.

"Run, Zeta, danger!" the pooch urged in the back of Zeta's mind.

From the spirit's perch emerged a glowing form. It had the blue-green color of a precious stone or the shiny feathers of a beautiful bird. It looked like a woman, but with a smooth, hairless head. Its gentle glow reminded her of a lightning bug.

The spirit spread its arms, leaned forward, and fell.

"No!" Zeta put her hand to her mouth. It was too beautiful to die! She watched in horror as the glowing woman-spirit fell down between the branches, never striking a single limb in her fall, tumbling head-down and rolling forward in the air to fall feet-first.

Zeta hid her eyes as the thud of the woman-spirit struck the ground next to the tree.

"Alright, kid," the woman-spirit said, "you want me to go, I'll go."

Zeta opened her eyes again to see the woman-spirit glowing before her, unharmed, rising from a crouching position. She had landed on her feet! The woman-spirit assessed Zeta with blue-green, glowing eyes. It turned and walked away in a graceful glide, feet silent even on the pine needles underfoot.

She didn't want it to leave. She could learn things from this beautiful spirit. "Why were you hiding in this tree, spirit?" She called out.

The woman-spirit stopped, turned around, and crossed her glowing arms beneath her bosom. "Make up your mind, do you want to talk to me or do you want me to 'be gone'?"

"Let's talk," Zeta said.

The woman-spirit started walking back. Zeta tried not to stare at her naked form, peculiar in its smoothness. Why didn't she have nipples? And how did she pee? Of course, spirits probably didn't need to pee, and nipples were for suckling babes. Spirits probably grew their babes up out of magical eggs or plucked them from the stars. The woman-spirit returned to the tree and leaned against it.

"I was hiding in the tree," the glowing form said, "because I was watching you and I didn't want you to see me."

"Why were you watching me?"

"Because I was sent to find you."

"By who?" Zeta demanded.

"The Telsons."

"The Telsons? Who is that?"

The spirit seemed exhausted by her questions. "Your bootstrappers? You know, Oraxis and Genevieve? They want you to go back to their cabin and finish your bootstrapping."

Of course. She knew better than to trust the woman-spirit. "I'm not going back to their slate-space mind-trap or their log man-trap. Now, I'm done with you. Begone, or I'll...make you leave! By force!"

She picked the stick-sling back up, pulled a stick out, and prepared for the attack. This time she wouldn't let it slap her cheek.

A sinister smile came to the woman-spirit's face. She said, "Oh, *really?* By force, you say?" Her blue-green glow intensified. It turned white, forcing Zeta to squint at its brilliance. Then, it dulled to a deep crimson glow, the color of blood. She stepped slowly towards Zeta as black cat-claws emerged from the tips of her fingers. Zeta immediately regretted challenging the spirit.

No, not a spirit — this thing was a demon.

She stood her ground and held her bowstring tight. She hoped that the pounding of her heart was not visible through the skins which covered her chest.

"*Run, Zeta!*" Penelope-pooch pleaded, even as she barked ferociously at the demon which approached them.

"*We must face such demons in this strange land. We are changed. We are strong. We will not let them hold their power over us or we will spend our lives always running away. Be brave!*" Saying this was for Zeta's own benefit as much as it was for Penelope-pooch. The pooch growled through exposed fangs.

"Listen, *Zeta,*" the crimson woman-demon said. If snakes could talk, this would be their tone. She stood just a few paces away, now. Close enough for Zeta to release the stick into her heart. Close enough to be gutted by the demon's claws. "I know you're confused. I know you're running away, but you don't know where to go. I know you're scared, and that you have *no idea* what you're up against. And yet, you have the audacity to stand up to me, and threaten me with a weapon you don't even know how to use."

At that, the stick-sling slipped from Zeta's grasp and flew into the forest. It had happened so quickly, Zeta barely even realized that the demon had moved. The stick-sling bounced off two trees before tumbling to the ground in the distance.

"As if a bow and arrow could protect you from *me?*" The demon-woman said, stepping closer, bringing her face to within inches of Zeta's. She raised a hand and spread her fingers to display her shiny black claws. "Did you know that you just threatened the deadliest person you've ever met?"

Zeta trembled. This demon-woman would surely kill her in an instant. Her resolve broke, and she whimpered a plea, "Please don't hurt me, demon-woman!"

The demon-woman backed up, switching back to her previous blue-green beauty. Her claws disappeared into her fingers. She spoke again in a casual tone. "Alright, don't cry, I wasn't going to hurt you."

Zeta's heart pounded in her ears. She breathed rapidly, still trembling.

The demon-woman said, "Okay, I'm sorry, maybe I laid it on a little thick. It's just...you can't just go around challenging people like that. Not in this world." The spirit sighed, stepping forward and delicately placing her hands on the outsides of Zeta's arms. Zeta jumped at the contact.

The spirit-woman spoke gently. "I was just trying to teach you a lesson, okay? So, pay attention now — here's the take-away. I'm going to tell you something that a wise man said a long time ago. Are you ready?"

Zeta swallowed, finding her voice, squeaking out, "Ready."

"If you know your enemy and you know yourself, then you won't need to fear the result of any fight. If you know yourself but not your enemy, then for every fight you win, you'll also lose one. But," she jabbed a finger into the air, paused, and then continued, "if you don't know either yourself or your enemy? You'll lose. Every. Time."

Zeta let the idea sink in for a bit, then nodded. "I understand."

"Good. Bonus points if you can figure out where I got it from. The point is, you don't know anything about me, and you don't even know what *you're* capable of yet, so trying to threaten me was just reckless. Anyways, now that we have the pecking order sorted out, I should introduce myself. My name's Jamji, please-ta-meecha. I am a *human.* Not a spirit, not a demon, just a woman like you, thrown head-first into this messed up world, trying to figure out where to go and what to do. I look...different...because I've got some fancy biotech enhancements. Absolute black carbon-lattice-reinforced dermal tissue with variable-depth chromatites and photoreceptites, head-to-toe. You could do the same, if you wanted. Eventually. You gotta get used to what's going on with *that* body first, though." Jamji pointed at her.

An echo of a memory came to mind, of Yephanie-ma telling her about her changing body. "Like starting my monthly bleed?"

Jamji snorted out a laugh. Penelope-pooch barked.

"That snort!" Zeta pointed, eyes wide. "That was you laughing? We thought it was a hog!"

Jamji began laughing uncontrollably, and Zeta couldn't help but join in. The woman's laughter was hearty and contagious, and funny in its own right because of her occasional snorting.

───────

Zeta's laughter subsided before Jamji's. She asked, "Why did you laugh when you were hiding in the tree?"

"Oh, you were so cute," laughed Jamji, "talking to the 'thought-giver'. You told it 'good night'!" Her laughter erupted with new vigor. "Sweet dreams, robot voice in my head!"

Zeta laughed, but didn't get the joke.

"Anyways, you really need to be careful about asking the 'thought-giver' about stuff. There are a lot of things you're just not ready to know yet. The wrong bit of info could send you down some deep rabbit holes."

Zeta hadn't considered that the thought-giver might be danger-ous. "I shouldn't ask the thought-giver questions?"

"Yeah, you really shouldn't. Just ask me, and I'll explain anything you want to know. But what *I* want to know is when are you going to introduce me to this adorable little pooch?" She kneeled and held her hand out.

"That's Penelope-pooch," Zeta said.

Penelope-pooch kept her distance. She thought-spoke, *"This stranger makes me nervous."*

"It's okay, Pen, I think she's a friend."

Penelope-pooch approached Jamji and sniffed her hand, then stepped closer and allowed herself to be petted.

Jamji babe-talked, "Aww, Penelope-poochie-woochie! Whosha pwetty wil-poochie? Youwa! Oh, yeshua! Yousha gonbe good fwens wit wil Pep!" She switched back to a normal tone, saying, "Have you figured out how to talk to her mind yet?"

"Yes, ever since I...woke up."

"They can't *really* talk, ya' know. There are these tiny things called neurites that read your pooch's thoughts, her emotions, intentions, stuff like that. Then, there's another...thing...that translates them into speech in your head. When you talk to her, the same thing happens in reverse. It's fun talking to them, even if they're not really talking. They're not always the best conversationalists, though. My Pepper-pooch talks like a toddler on a permanent sugar rush. Want to meet him?"

"Sure, is he here?"

"Yeah, he's been hiding out in the forest for a while, staying downwind. You'll need to comfort Penelope-pooch when she sees him. He's pretty much a monster. Takes some getting used to."

Zeta remembered the black wolf-pooches. "Is he well-behaved? Could he attack?"

Jamji laughed, "Oh, he's an angel. Besides, owned animals can't attack unless their master lets them."

"If you think that, then you haven't met a wolf-pooch," Zeta scoffed.

"No, I mean in Nod — in these lands — the rules for animals are different. Wild animals can't attack humans or owned animals unless it's for self-defense, and owned animals can't attack *anything* unless they get permission from their owner."

Zeta doubted this, though she remembered Penelope-pooch asking for permission to hunt the raccoon. "Okay, where is Pepper-pooch?"

Jamji smiled and pointed into the darkness of the Thin Forest. Zeta looked, but saw nothing but trees.

Then came the thudding.

The sound of its approach was that of a stampeding bison. Her breath caught as she got her first glimpse of it. What started off as a ghostly gray figure darting between the trees became a nightmare bearing down upon them within a few heartbeats. The beast glowed dimly, detailing the contours of his hairless, muscled body. His movement was distinctly pooch-like, but his speed and size were inconceivable.

She tripped during her instinctive backward retreat, falling on her bottom.

Penelope-pooch barked ferociously. Zeta didn't have the wherewithal to do anything other than stare with wide eyes, fixated on the creature closing in on her. It skidded to a stop just paces away, followed by a wave of heat like wind blown over a campfire.

Zeta had never seen anything like it. It looked like the most dangerous predator she had ever seen.

Yet, its tail wagged, and tongue lolled.

Zeta snapped out of her transfixed stare. Penelope-pooch was having a fit, trying to drive the beast away with the fury of her barks. Zeta tried to calm her, though she struggled to find calm herself. Her heart pounded.

Jamji walked up to the beast-pooch and petted him. "That's my boy! My lil' Pep! Whossha wittle Pep?"

The beast-pooch licked Jamji with a massive tongue that ran up the side of her body. The tongue glowed, though less brightly than its skin. Zeta imagined him snatching Jamji up and gobbling her down in two bites.

"That's a pooch?!" was all Zeta could think to say.

"Sure enough," Jamji said, "I mean, I fixed him up, obviously. When he was born he was a tiny little snake-biter."

Zeta laughed, "You have to be kidding me!"

Jamji laughed with her. "Yep, he was a cute little morsel. Penelope-pooch would have had him for lunch if she could catch him."

"She'd do no such thing! My cousin, Brit, has a snake-biter and Pen loves to play with him." Zeta closed her eyes and shook her head at herself.

Brit?

Where is Brit, anyway? When was the last time she saw that clever Brit or little Whisker-pooch? Didn't they go off with another tribe? She should ask Yephanie-ma.

"Ma?"

"Yes, Zeta?" Yephanie-ma suckled that squealing little monkey-babe, Charra.

"Where'd Brit go? I want her to see this huge pooch I just met."

Yephanie-ma stared silently at Zeta for a moment, then dissolved into blackness.

Zeta floated in nothingness.

All at once she was overcome with an unspeakable sense of loss. She was lost, confused, trapped between two worlds.

10

BOOTSTRAPPING

"*I can't do this,*" Jamji sent.

"*Send your coordinates,*" Oraxis replied, "*we'll take Zephyr. We can be there in minutes.*"

"*It's fine, O. Jamji can handle it. We'll talk her through it,*" Genevieve replied.

"*This is such a load of crap. You guys completely screwed this up and now I'm cleaning up your mess.*" Jamji held the unconscious girl and patted her cheek.

"Come on," Jamji said aloud, "snap out of it, Zeta. Come on back to the real world." She didn't let her fury find its way into her voice.

"*You know what,*" Jamji sent, "*never mind. I shouldn't have bothered calling you. I'm looking up the protocol procedures myself. Obviously, if you knew what you were doing, you wouldn't have screwed it up the first time.*"

"*Jamji,*" Oraxis interjected, "*we're grateful for your help, but you're in over your head. Beta Bootstrapping certification takes a year. You're not learning everything there is to know in five minutes. Let us help.*"

"*No,*" she sent. Simple. Flat. Final. She shut them off. She could imagine the vein bulging on Oraxis' temple. They'd send another request and she would decline it.

Three seconds passed.

Incoming urgent conversation request from Oraxis and Genevieve Telson.

Declined.

Let them stew for a while. They deserved it. She queried WoQS for information on how bootstrappers tapped into a beta's slate-space. Neurite chain, direct link through the cranium, seems simple enough. She could do that. She imagined extending her mind out of her fingertips and connecting it to Zeta's.

It wasn't working.

Why wouldn't that work? She went back to WoQS for more information. No, that definitely should work. She cut to the chase and performed a direct query. *"WoQS, why can't I tap into Zeta's slate-space to perform a Beta Bootstrapping Protocol intervention?"*

Zeta of the Scorpion Tail Tribe's Beta Bootstrapping Protocol has been terminated. She is now protected by The Third Principal. As such, her slate-space interface cannot be tapped without her express, informed consent.

Jamji cursed. She was tempted to reopen the channel to Oraxis and Genevieve. No, not yet. She looked around, as if searching for an idea. She noticed Penelope-pooch staring at Zeta with the rapt attention of a dog listening to their master speak. Was Zeta talking to her dog? If she was, that meant she probably wasn't in a replay, but was stuck in slate-space. Jamji could try to talk to her through WorMS. She sent a conversation request.

"Jamji?" Zeta replied, her voice echoing within Jamji's mind. Her body remained dormant in Jamji's arms, her eyes closed.

"Zeta! Yes, I'm right here!"

"Jamji, I'm scared. What happened? Why am I back in slate-space?"

"It's okay, don't be scared. You just slipped, that's all. That's what you get for skipping past all the important lessons. You don't know how to control your double-mind yet."

"What do I do? I want out, Jamji!"

"Hey, you got out once before, right?"

"Yes, but that time Penelope-pooch helped me."

What on Genesis? Jamji looked over at the dog, then back to Zeta's slack face. She beckoned to the dog. "Penelope-pooch, come. Come see Zeta! Can you wake Zeta up, girl?"

Penelope-pooch stepped closer, nuzzled Zeta's arm, and licked her face.

Jamji sent, *"Do you feel her now, Zeta? She's right here."*

Zeta's eyes fluttered. She furrowed her brow. Her arm lifted with the unsteady wobble of a marionette, then flopped onto Penelope-pooch's back. Her hand closed on the dog's fur. A moment later her eyes snapped open, rolled around wildly, then focused on Jamji. She smiled, sat up, and wrapped her arms around Jamji's shoulders.

"Good job, sis-kin," Jamji said, hugging the girl back.

"Sis-kin?" Zeta pulled back to look at Jamji in the eyes.

"Yeah, didn't you know? We're family!"

Zeta stood up and brushed off the pine needles, saying, "I don't know about that. I know who my family is, and nobody I ever knew had blue skin and could turn invisible."

"We are," Jamji said, "distant family, but family none the less. My tribe splintered off from yours before you were born. If I could show you what I looked like before I changed my appearance, I think you'd see the resemblance. Also, I speak in your tongue, right?"

"I hadn't thought of that," Zeta said. "The faraway tribes all have strange tongues, but our kin tribes speak normally. Travelers might pick up some of our words here and there, but you speak too well to be a traveler. But there are words you use that I've never heard. Like, what was it you called the stick-sling?"

"Oh, it's called a bow. The sticks it shoots are called arrows." Jamji sent Pepper-pooch the thought-command to go fetch the bow. "I'm surprised they managed to keep those *forbidden words* out of your ears your entire life." She wiggled her fingers as she said "forbidden words" to mock the superstitious neoprims.

"Bow and arrow...I think I *have* heard those words, but don't know where from. I'm...having a hard time remembering things about my life."

Pepper-pooch returned with the bow, which Jamji took from his mouth. She wouldn't offer it back to Zeta. Not yet, at least. "Well, we're gonna have to fix that, huh?"

"Fix my memories? How would you do that?"

"We go back to Oraxis and Genevieve's cabin. You called it a 'log man-trap'? It's just a cabin — the place where they live. Think of it as a really strong tent or lean-to. You know what those are, right?"

"Of course," Zeta scoffed.

"Hey, I can't take anything for granted with neoprims. It's been a few years, and I lost track of what traditions your tribe had. Anyways, we're going back to their cabin and they're gonna finish your beta bootstrapping stuff. They'll have you go through some more replays, show you how the world works, and teach you all about your double-mind."

Zeta looked anxious. She said, "I don't think I like that plan. I really just want to go back to my tribe."

"Okay, which way are they?" It was a mean mind game to play, but Jamji knew she would have to be a bit manipulative if she was going to get Zeta back with the program.

"I...don't know. I don't remember how I got here, so I don't know the way back."

"Well, what I can promise you is that if you'll go back with me,

and listen to Oraxis and Genevieve, your replays will fix your brain
and your memory'll come back. They call it *assisted narrative reconstruction*, and it's a way to remind yourself of who you are. Don't
worry, it'll all come back to you, and you'll figure out how you got
here. Then, it's just a matter of retracing your steps to get back to
your homeland, right?"

"I guess so. I just," Zeta wrung her hands and seemed like she
was ready to cry, "I think something bad happened to my bro-kin. I
don't know if it's too late to go back and do anything about it."

Oof. What do you say to that? Genevieve had a way of taking the
edge off hard situations like this. What would she say?

Replace doubt with action.

Jamji considered for a moment. "Well, if there's still a chance that
you could go back and do anything, you had better hurry up, right?"

"Yeah," Zeta said, uncertainly.

"You'll need a good weapon to protect yourself on the journey."
She handed the bow back to Zeta. "And a sis-kin with a monster-
pooch to keep you company and protect you along the way."

Jamji held out her hand towards Pepper-pooch as she sent him
the thought-command to bark. He let out a roar of a bark, which
echoed through the forest.

Zeta jumped. She broke out into nervous laughter, saying, "Oh,
that scared me! Did you make him do that?!"

Jamji smiled, saying, "Yeah, just showing off. So what do you
say?"

Zeta looked meaningfully at the bow in her hands, then glazed
over as if slipping back into slate-space. Jamji took a quick step
forward, preparing to catch her again. Zeta snapped back out of it,
blinking her eyes and shaking her head. She looked up at Jamji.
"Okay, let's do it. Let's go now."

"I love your enthusiasm, but to be honest, I've had a long day and
I need to recharge. Don't underestimate the power of sleep. We'll get
up at Surya's first light and be on our way."

IN THE MORNING they began the long jog back to the Telson cabin.

To make small talk, Jamji said, "Oraxis'll want that bow back. But you know what? *Don't* give it to him. He failed at your first run through bootstrapping, so I figure the least he owes you is that bow, as consolation. He can get another one."

Zeta said, "He won't like that. I'll get a slap."

"Nah," Jamji said, "men here don't abuse girls and women like they do in your lands. I promise he'd never hurt you. He'll just call you a *cuss* or something. When he does, show him your middle finger, like this." Jamji demonstrated.

"What does that mean?" Zeta asked.

"It's an insult called 'flipping the bird'."

Zeta laughed, "It stands for a bird?"

Jamji said, "Nope! I don't know why they call it that." She almost recommended that Zeta should do a WoQS query to learn more about it, but decided against encouraging her to start a WoQS info crawl. One topic leads to another, and there was some very dangerous information she could learn that would blow her mind. Instead she said, "It's basically the same as this one." She held up her index finger and twisted it upwards.

"Oh, wow," Zeta said. "Flipping the bird is a *dirty* insult, then. Good to know."

By mid-morning they needed to rest and get a drink. Zeta drank deeply from the trickling creek, right next to Pepper-pooch, who lapped up liters of water at a time. Jamji was surprised at how quickly Zeta and Penelope-pooch had grown accustomed to the massive dog's company. Early in the morning the dogs had played chase, and Zeta had scratched Pepper-pooch's tummy when they returned. Jamji assumed that Penelope-pooch had given her good vibes about him.

The girl has good taste in animals. Unlike Oraxis, with his big bird. As often as he had pinged her for updates, she wouldn't be surprised if he was literally hovering over them right now.

Worrywart. Who can blame him, though?

"They're good people, you know," Jamji said, "Oraxis and Genevieve, I mean."

"What makes you say that?" Zeta wiped the water from her chin and patted Pepper-pooch's haunch.

"Oh, I was just thinking about them, and I think you got the wrong impression about them when you were in bootstrapping. I've known 'em for a really long time now. They might be..." Jamji grappled for the right adjective, "*flawed*, but their hearts are in the right place. They want to help you, and I don't want you to go into this with the wrong idea about them, okay?"

"Sure, I can give them a second chance. Ready to run?"

This girl had her eyes on the prize. Jamji appreciated that.

They ran for another few hours before they crested the last hill and approached the cabin. Zephyr was in his nest. He shifted to peer at them over its edge. This drew Zeta's attention to the treetop. She let out a yelp when she saw the oversized bird.

"That's Oraxis's golden eagle, Zephyr. They use him to fly places when they don't have time to walk." Jamji considered that to be discouraging proof that even if you lived for a thousand years, you still wouldn't have enough time.

Oraxis and Genevieve emerged from behind the skins that served as their cabin door.

"Is that them?" Zeta whispered.

Jamji was taken aback. She hadn't even seen their faces yet? She really *had* broken out early. "Yeah, that's them."

They hadn't changed a bit since Jamji's own bootstrapping. Both of them had the light skin of Earth's Caucasians. Oraxis had a bushy auburn beard, trimmed with a pair of grey streaks descending from the corners of his mouth. His long, copper-colored hair was tied back with a leather thong, revealing a deep hairline. He had a lean build and an average man's height.

Genevieve appeared to be more than a few years younger than Oraxis. The front strands of her blond hair were dyed purple with what Jamji assumed was a berry extract pigment. She was a few centimeters shorter than the average woman. She was thin, but not frail.

As usual, their attire was pushing against the boundaries of what was considered appropriate for a Noddite. They wore dyed leather jerkins and fur cloaks, but Genevieve's had a collar which was split down to her sternum and pulled tight by a woven leather cord. It was enough cleavage to catch the eye, but not so much that she would cause a scandal.

The dogs ran towards the couple, tails wagging. Pepper-pooch bounced and patted the ground in excitement at seeing them again. Penelope-pooch licked their hands, happy to be reacquainted with the familiar couple. Dogs had a way of smoothing over otherwise uncomfortable social situations. Once Jamji and Zeta reached them, they joined in on the dog petting.

Genevieve was the first to talk, saying, "I'm so glad you came back, Zeta."

"Jamji says finishing bootstrapping is the only way I'm going to remember how I got here. I just want to go back to my tribe."

"I completely understand," Genevieve said, standing up and stepping towards the cabin. "Would you like to come inside? You must be hungry after all that running, and we have some hot stew ready to eat."

Food bribery was the oldest trick in the book, but Zeta took the bait. She seemed nervous about entering the log cabin, but worked up the nerve and stepped inside. Oraxis turned to follow them, but Jamji tapped his arm to stop him. She requested a private channel.

He accepted, and she sent, *"I'm pretty sure you have Penelope-pooch to thank for helping Zeta break out of bootstrapping."*

"Her dog? What are you talking about?"

"Last night, when she slipped into slate-space, I think she used her mind-link with Penelope-pooch to get back to the real world again. It's like she used it as a lifeline."

Oraxis took on an irritated expression and fell silent. Jamji assumed that he was arguing with Genevieve on their private channel. She waited with a smirk on her face and her arms crossed.

Once he returned to her channel, Oraxis sent, *"That is an interesting theory. Once she's out on her own, we'll be spending a good deal of time researching Zeta's case to see where the protocol failed. Seeing your replay of her slip would be invaluable. If you can get Zeta's permission, please share it with our bootstrapping community group. I'd also like to invite you to stay with us for the next month or two while we work on Zeta. I know you're eager to get to the Guardian Embassy, so I'll understand if you have to decline."*

Jamji considered the invitation. Sticking around would mean putting her life on hold. She had already said her goodbyes to so many people. To delay the faction transfer application process could be construed as a lack of commitment to her goal.

And what was the point in staying, anyway? Normally, someone going through bootstrapping was essentially in a coma most of the time, though Zeta had already broken that norm. Oraxis wasn't inviting her because he wanted her company — it was a purely strategic invitation, but it was for Zeta's benefit. Zeta and Jamji seemed to have formed a sisterly bond already. The girl would need a sis-kin to talk to, to blow off steam between double-mind lessons or trips down replay lane.

On top of all that, Jamji would hate to miss the moment when Zeta flips Oraxis off.

She mindspoke, *"Yeah, I should stay, since you'll probably lose her again."*

GETTING Zeta settled in the cabin meant stuffing her with stew and dancing around uncomfortable conversation topics. They weren't going to rush her back into replays just yet.

By the time Surya's light faded, Jamji had decided that it was time to get her personal affairs in order. She excused herself, then went outside to lie with Pepper-pooch.

She was here for Zeta, and she would stick around as long as she had to. That could take a while. That was a problem.

She sent a meeting request to the Genesis Faction ambassador to the Guardians. His response came minutes later, saying he was available immediately. The man himself — not a delegate? Jamji gave a fist pump, then disconnected from her body. She entered slate-space, immediately queuing up a generic private meeting room venue construct and inviting her guest.

She was in a plain, white room. A rectangular table sat in the middle of the room, with chairs on opposite ends. Jamji sat across from the ambassador. The clean-shaven man had a modest, modern haircut, bushy eyebrows, a large nose, and a stylish brown jumpsuit.

"Thank you for your time, Eld Marco-Epsilon Rhind," Jamji said.

Three seconds of silence went by as Jamji's transmission passed to Soma Station and the response started being received.

Marco-Epsilon steepled his fingers and leaned back in his seat. "Any time, Jamji, any time at all. How's your family?"

Jamji doubted he really cared, but small talk was important to establish the veneer of familiarity. "Good. They're bootstrapping a new beta, actually. She's...a special case. That's kinda why I wanted to talk to you. She broke out of bootstrapping early, and now she's having trouble with her double-mind."

The Eld's inner eyebrows lifted in a sympathetic gesture as he listened and nodded. After a pause, he said, "That's a shame. Is she showing signs of cognitive dissociation?"

"I don't think so. But I'm not an expert in these things. I just know that having me around is helping, so I've decided to stay until her Beta Ceremony. We obviously can't schedule it yet, though. That's why I reached out to you. I know my transfer application said that I would be at the Embassy by the twelfth month, but this sets my timeline back. I don't know how much. I figured I should tell you about it, in case anyone asks you what's taking me so long. I don't want them to think it's because I got cold feet. I'm not a flake."

Marco-Epsilon sat in silence for three seconds, then erupted into a chortle. "Jamji, you worry too much! Everyone knows you're committed to this, and I don't expect a few more months to make any difference to the Guardian recruiters. But, if you're asking me to pass the word along to the Station Captain's office, then by all means, I'll do that for you. Is that all you needed?" His bushy eyebrows lifted.

"Thank you, yes, that's all," Jamji said. She seriously needed to stop staring at his eyebrows.

Over three seconds passed this time. The Eld seemed to be considering her. Did he suspect her of brow-gazing? Jamji stifled a sudden urge to laugh, masking it by shifting in her seat and scratching her cheek to cover her mouth.

"Jamji," Marco-Epsilon said, leaning forward and speaking softly, "I've read your transfer application essay. Your grievances with the Genesis Faction principals are legitimate. You put a lot of consideration into your arguments, and they are sound. You also indicate a strong desire to fight in protection of Genesis, for the sake of humanity. You love your Telson family, Jamji. You wouldn't be staying with them right now if you didn't. I personally review every faction transfer application. I have to say that yours is unique, in that you cite no grievances against your adopted family."

Jamji crossed her arms and waited for Eld-Epsilon-Eyebrow to finish.

"Jamji, I must ask, where do your *true* loyalties lie? With humanity? With your family? Your mind may be set on striking out on your own, but where does your *heart* belong?"

"With the Guard." She said, flatly.

Three seconds later, Marco-Epsilon furrowed his eyebrows dramatically and said, "You don't even *know* the Guard Faction, Jamji. It's just an offworld faction that you agree with. You're in love with the idea of joining them, but you can't honestly say that you're *loyal* to them. Jamji, I'm talking about family and tribe. I'm talking about *true* loyalties. You love your home world and your Noddite family. If the Guardians ever plotted a course that put your loved ones at risk, then you, my dear, would be in quite a tight spot."

He paused, as if expecting a response. She was *so* done with this guy. "Eld Marco-Epsilon? Can I ask...what are you getting at?"

Three seconds, then a chortle. "So straightforward! I like that about you, Jamji. Unfortunately, politicians don't have that luxury, so I'm going to change the subject and see if you can follow. You're a sharp one, I'm sure you'll catch on."

Jamji raised an eyebrow of her own. This was interesting.

He said, "You slipped a quote from The Art of War into your essay. I take that to imply that you're an aspiring Student of Sun Tzu. Since you're familiar with the work, I suggest you contemplate the implications of the final section. And remember, you can contact me anytime. Goodbye, Jamji."

He faded away, having closed the channel.

The final section? "The Use of Spies?!" Jamji shouted to herself in the construct.

Her mind raced.

What a slimebag! Was he really suggesting that she would want to be a *spy*? That she would infiltrate the Guard on behalf of Genesis? That she would give Guardian secrets to *him*?!

She had a right mind to report the ambassador to Guardian authorities right then and there. They'd kick him out an airlock!

Wait.

She crumpled, putting her head in her hands. "Eld Marco-Epsilon Rhind, you son of a bitch," she grumbled to herself.

This was complicated.

Here's the thing: maybe *he's* the spy — a double-agent, acting on behalf of the Guard, and he's just testing her to see if she'll leak Guardian secrets to him. Or maybe this was a test to see if she would be reactionary or if she would let the information simmer and settle until the proper moment. He didn't know her that well, so why would he think she would be a spy for him? So maybe he's a triple-agent. Maybe the Guard thinks he's their inside man, but in reality he's loyal to Genesis after all, and only letting them know about *certain* turncoats, or misrepresenting reported information, or building a spy network of his own.

"Spies cannot be usefully employed without a certain intuitive acuteness of mental discernment," Sun Tzu had said. You had to, "Be subtle! Be subtle!"

Subtlety had never been Jamji's strong suit, but she would play this game the right way. Her gut told her it was a test. Marco-Epsilon lives in the offworlder moon base, Soma Station. They must pamper him, treat him well. That's exactly what Sun Tzu says to do with converted spies. So they use him to ferret out any potential traitors among the applicants.

Once she took a minute to work the puzzle out, everything seemed to fall into place. It's so obvious! But what was her move?

She'd wait. That was all she could do — wait until they accepted her, then talk to her commanding officer in private. Whoever they assigned her to would be aware of the ambassador's gambit, and they'd commend her on her discernment and discretion. Then, if she was wrong, the Guard could react however it wanted.

Sun Tzu's "divine manipulation of the threads" sure sucks when you're the thread.

11

CENTIPEDE

THEY TRIED to get Zeta to settle in and relax on her first night, with little luck. There was an anxious energy about her that only faded during the fleeting moments when she let her guard down. Her single-minded focus on returning to her tribe was hard to deflect, but they avoided talk of slate-space or replays. Finding anything to talk about that wouldn't trigger Zeta's slipping or clue her into untimely information had been tricky, but they managed.

Dogs were a safe subject, at least.

Zeta was borderline claustrophobic, as many neoprims are, so they had gone outside and built a fire. They slept on the sand circle surrounding the fire pit, with Oraxis and Genevieve taking shifts staying awake. They weren't letting Zeta slip through their fingers again.

In the morning, they had a simple breakfast of dried fruit and nuts. Zeta marveled at the disappearing placental mats. They steamed as they dissolved, disappearing into the ground as an army of mycelites broke them down. Genevieve didn't care for the musky smell, which was somewhere between boiled meat, body odor, and dirt.

Genevieve and Oraxis had been tossing around ideas about the next steps in Zeta's bootstrapping and had settled on an approach. Getting Jamji to agree to the plan was another bit of work, but she relented.

"Jamji," Genevieve said, "has Zeta heard the story of how you decided what color to glow in?"

"Why, no, Genevieve," Jamji said, mocking a conversational tone, "she has not! Zeta, would you be interested in hearing the story of why I choose to glow in such a pleasing hue?"

"Could you at least try to pretend this wasn't scripted?" Genevieve mindspoke to Jamji.

"Sure," Zeta said, "that sounds interesting."

"Well, when I was a little girl, I looked just like any other person."

Jamji paused for a beat, to see if Zeta would take the bait. Zeta was petting Penelope-pooch. She idly scratched the hair on the side of the dog's neck, silently waiting for Jamji to continue.

"I'll bet Zeta'd like to have seen what you looked like," Oraxis prompted.

"Yeah," Zeta said, absently.

"Hey, here's an idea," Genevieve said, "Maybe we should *show* her the story, instead of just telling it."

"Yes, that's a great idea, Genevieve." Jamji turned to Zeta. "Okay, here's how it works: I'm going to go into slate-space and bring to mind a specific memory from my childhood. That'll put me into the replay. It'll be like I'm living it all over again, but I'll know that I'm not, because a part of my mind'll stay separated from the experience. From there, I'll invite the rest of you to join as external observers. You'll be able to experience my replay, as if you'd been there with me. When we're done, we'll all come back to our bodies. How's that sound, Zeta?"

Zeta sat up, looking nervous. "Are you sure I won't get stuck in slate-space?"

Oraxis said, "You'll only learn how to control going into and out of slate-space with experience. It takes practice."

"Penelope-pooch is here, right?" Genevieve offered, taking a spot in the sand next to Zeta. "If you get stuck, we'll just have her pull you out again."

Zeta looked to the dog laying by her side. "Okay," she said. "It will be good practice."

They all took their places in the sand. You could enter slate-space while standing, but it was safest to do it while sitting or laying down. When you disconnect from your body, it goes on autopilot, so if you're doing something like tending a fire or walking, you can end up hurting yourself.

Experience replay observer invite received from Jamji Telson.

Genevieve waited a moment, watching Zeta close her brown eyes, furrowing her brow slightly. After a few seconds, Zeta's face relaxed.

She mindspoke to Jamji, *"Is she in?"*

"Yep."

Genevieve laid her head down. She accepted the invite, slipping through slate-space, emerging into the replay.

IT WAS NIGHTTIME. Jamji's tribe was spread out in a meadow, surrounded by a thick forest. A dozen fires burned. It was an especially dark night, without Soma's glow. Only a semicircle of Varuna's somber blue graced the star-strewn darkness overhead.

The melancholy sounds of an eld woman's faint singing drifted on the night air. Now rising, now falling, ever soft and wonderful. It was a song about the night, borrowed from a foreign tongue. Before them, the form of a young child danced in the firelight, spinning slowly, lifting her arms, dropping them, swaying like grass in the night breeze.

The girl's skin was a dark tan shade, very much like Zeta's, though her eyes were a lighter shade of brown. The child was naked, having no mature bodily features to hide. Her untamed hair was decorated with beads and braids.

Genevieve stood to young Jamji's side. Seeing the replay from this third-person perspective was based on inference from Jamji's original experience, so she was *technically* in a construct. Same difference — splitting hairs was Oraxis's department.

She could see the semi-transparent forms of Zeta and Oraxis next to her. Zeta was looking around with wide eyes, walking about and examining the replay. She looked down at her ghostly hand, turning it over, then up to her face to look at Genevieve through it.

"I'm a specter," Zeta whispered, full of wonder.

Oraxis laughed, but it made Genevieve go cold. Why did she have to use *that* word?

Genevieve shook it off. "No, we're just made see-through to distinguish between the people in the replay and the people observing it. We don't see Jamji because she's living it from her original perspective. She could've opted to join us as observers, but it's preferable to be inside yourself, if that makes sense."

"Be quiet and listen," came the disembodied voice of Jamji. "You missed what Jenna-eld-ma said. I'll rewind it."

The replay jumped back a few seconds, making Zeta flinch.

"Jamji," the eld woman said softly after finishing her song, "Do you know why we call these the Starry Woods?"

"No, eld-ma," the child Jamji said, plopping onto the eld's lap, eliciting a grunt from the woman.

"It's because this is where stars are born. Have you seen the star-babes among the trees and leaves?"

"Is they the, the...lightnings bugs?" Jamji asked, meeting her eld-ma's gaze from a hand's distance.

"No, lightning bugs are made by lightning. I'm talking about the crawling stars."

"I want to see them!" Jamji exclaimed, scrambling back to her feet.

Jenna-eld-ma laughed. She leaned over and nudged another eld laying on a skin in the trampled grass nearby. The man snorted, then grumbled, "I'm sleeping."

Jenna-eld-ma nudged him again. "Wake up and come with me to show Jamji the crawling stars."

"They're no good to eat," The eld said, never opening his eyes.

"I didn't say we were going to eat them," she jabbed her finger into the man's side, causing him to jerk up and grab her hand, pushing it away. "We just want to look for them."

"Look in wet leaves," the eld said.

"You're coming with us to protect us from wolves and bears. Get up, Natch!"

"Natch-eld-pa loved his sleep," came Jamji's adult voice.

The grumbling old man got up and grabbed a pair of spears. He held one out for Jenna. "Alright, let's get it over with, then."

Young Jamji jumped up and down, brimming with joy. She whisked to a spot nearby, picked up a small spear, then ran to the stretching man. She hugged him around the waist, making him double over as she said, "Thank you, Natch-eld-pa!"

"Shh!" Came an angry hiss from the sleeping tribe nearby. Jamji stuck her tongue out at the shusher, then hoisted her spear and led the way to the tree line.

Genevieve and her fellow observers followed the trio into the forest. They walked in silence, crunching on the leaves. After a few minutes, Natch stopped and tapped Jamji's shoulder. He kneeled and pointed at the ground nearby.

At first it was difficult to make out the crawling stars, but after a few moments of letting her eyes adjust, it was easy to spot them. Hundreds of tiny glowing lines speckled the leaves of the forest floor. Their tone was a dim version of Jamji's hue.

"Wow," young Jamji whispered. She kneeled, picking up a leaf. A many-legged bug crawled along its edge. "Do they bite?"

Natch stood and stretched his back. "No, just don't put it in your mouth. They'll poison you. I's in the Starry Woods as a boy. My friend thought he's bein' clever, pickin' the bugs out the leaves, collectin' as many as he could find. They're easy to spot, glowin' like they do. He took 'em back to camp, cooked 'em up, gobbled 'em down, vomited, an' died."

Young Jamji gasped, dropping the leaf.

Jenna huffed a laugh, then whispered, "Stars are for looking at, not eating. It's okay, Jamji, you can touch it."

Jamji looked up to Natch, who nodded. She picked the leaf back up and coaxed the crawler into her palm. She poked at it, then oohed as its glow intensified. It curled into a tight, glowing spiral in her palm.

"It's so beautiful. Will it grow up and fly into the sky to be a star?"

"That's right," Jenna whispered.

"That's pretty much all there is to it," Jamji narrated. "We were out of the Starry Woods by that winter and we never returned. But, while we were there, every night I would make Natch-eld-pa take me out to see the crawling stars."

"Were they really star-babes?" Zeta asked.

"Nah," Jamji said. "They're called Motyxia — a name I wouldn't find out until much later. They're just plain old glowing bugs. You might as well get used to learning that everything you thought was magic is a fraud."

Oraxis looked up, addressing Jamji's omnipresence. "Just because we've come to a better understanding of reality doesn't mean it's any less amazing."

"I agree," Genevieve said, watching young Jamji marvel at the bug. "And I think it's wonderful that Jamji still cherishes this moment in her life so much that she glows in the same beautiful tone as these centipedes."

"Millipedes," Oraxis corrected.

Genevieve drew in a deep breath, then let it out slowly. That man just can't let imprecision slide. It's like a compulsion!

"Speaking of centipedes," she said, cheerily changing the subject, "there's another bit of magic I'd like to show Zeta. It's a place we can go in our minds, called a construct."

"Don't you think it's a bit early for that?" Oraxis mindspoke, privately.

"She's ready. It'll be good double-mind control practice."

GENEVIEVE LEFT JAMJI'S REPLAY, returning to slate-space. She started putting together an ad hoc construct by loading a popular grassland venue. She set the climate to mild, sky to overcast, time of day to late afternoon, and ordered all fauna to be removed.

Next, she pulled down the specs for the classic arcade game, Centipede, plopping the machine down right there in the grass. She overrode the realism thresholds, letting it run without a power supply.

She sent an invite to Oraxis, Jamji, and Zeta.

Nobody joined.

"What's the holdup?" She mindspoke to Oraxis.

He replied, "I'm back in my body. I want to make sure she makes the transition. I don't know what Jamji and her are doing. Probably talking. Give them a minute."

One minute passed, then another. Genevieve busied herself by trying out the game. She ran through her lives pretty quickly. Wow, she didn't remember the game being so *hard*. She tweaked the settings to make it run at half-speed, then removed all the extra opponents like spiders, then tweaked it so that the mushrooms got destroyed with one hit. The numeric point tally had to go, too, being replaced with tick marks.

Genevieve was so engrossed with her game modifications that she didn't notice Jamji and Zeta's acceptance of the construct invite.

"What is that?!" Zeta marveled, circling the arcade machine.

Oraxis appeared next. He chuckled as he surveyed her creation. "Welcome to the Savanna Arcade."

Zeta went so far as to sniff the machine during her examination. She said, "Is it a painted tree? It glows like there's a fire inside, but this part," she held her hand to the screen, "it's warm, but clear and smooth like ice. And the lights! Like embers come to life! Is this real? Am I...here?"

Here came the tricky questions. It was interesting how she had taken so easily to Jamji's replay, but that this arcade machine was just too much.

Genevieve said, "It's sort of real, and sort of not. And you're sort of here and sort of not. Your real body is laying in the sand back at The Thin Forest, alongside the rest of us. Penelope-pooch is there with you. But your *mind* is here. You're controlling an imaginary body, created in this place by your double-mind."

"Double-mind? I've heard you say that before, but I don't understand it. Jamji, can I ask the thought-giver what that is?"

Jamji smirked, as if to rub it in that Zeta deferred to her wisdom. "Nah," Jamji said, "it's pretty complicated. Let's just say that your mind has been improved so that you can do things like live through past experiences or connect to constructs — fantasy worlds — like this one."

"Right," Oraxis said, "it's not important for her to understand how everything works right now. Let's just call it magic."

Genevieve added, "A construct is imagination made real. I created this place with my mind."

Zeta marveled at her surroundings, then focused on the arcade machine. "So *you* made this glowing, painted thing? What's it for?"

"I'm so glad you asked!" Genevieve said, putting her hands to the controls. She hit the single player game start button, then started tapping the fire button and spinning the roller ball. "This is a game called Centipede. The forms moving on the screen — this smooth part in front of me — are supposed to represent an attacking giant centipede and a defending warrior."

She shot a mindspeech message to Oraxis, *"So help me God, if you tell me it's technically a magic-shooting gnome and not a warrior, I'm booting you."*

"I didn't say anything!" Oraxis replied, taken aback. *"I don't care what your little blob of pixels represents."*

She continued speaking to Zeta. "Oh, and these things are mushrooms. They just get in the way. The goal of the game is to kill the centipede before it can get to the bottom of the screen and kill the warrior. You're the warrior, this little guy down here that's moving around. You move him by spinning this ball and you make him shoot arrows at the centipede by hitting this button."

"The warrior uses a bow and arrows," Zeta marveled. "The arrows...glow. It's like he attacks using the light of Surya."

Zeta watched as Genevieve played through a few rounds, blasting mushrooms and breaking the descending centipede into pieces. She would stare at Genevieve's hands on the controls, then at the figures on the screen. Genevieve eventually let her guy get killed.

Zeta reflexively reached for the screen, as if to save the disintegrating pixel-warrior from his fate, pressing her fingers against the glass. "What happened? Where did your warrior go?"

"The centipede touched him, so he died."

Zeta looked at the screen, still touching the glass where the warrior had been. She met Genevieve's eyes and spoke with somber sincerity as she said, "I'm sorry your warrior was killed, Genevieve."

Genevieve laughed, "Don't worry about it, it's just a game! See, he comes back if we hit this button. We can play it as many times as we want."

Zeta observed silently for another minute before she asked, "Can I try?"

———————

GENEVIEVE STEPPED ASIDE and let Zeta take her place. Zeta ran her hands over the controls. She gave the buttons timid taps, then rolled the roller ball in a small circle, watching it spin smoothly. She seemed transfixed by the plastic texture.

Looking from her hands to the screen, she proved her understanding of how the movement of the roller ball resulted in the movement of the warrior. Her movements were clumsy and timid at first. For a while she forgot that she was supposed to keep hitting the button to keep firing arrows, but after a few minutes she started gaining skill and confidence.

"You're good at this," Oraxis said, watching over Zeta's shoulder.

He was being charitable, though she wasn't bad for a neoprim. At least she wasn't hiding from the arcade machine and throwing rocks at it. Her adaptability was really quite remarkable.

At least thirty minutes passed before Jamji said, "Okay, my turn."

"I'm sorry," Zeta said, stepping back and shaking her hands out. "It's just so much fun! I should share."

"No sweat," Jamji said. She stepped up to the machine, cracking her knuckles. "Alright, Genevieve, take the training wheels off."

Genevieve reverted the game to its original difficulty settings. Jamji slammed the game start button, then started blasting centipedes, spiders, mushrooms, fleas, and scorpions with expert efficiency.

Oraxis was finding a spot to lay down in the grass. He muttered, "Overclocking is for cheaters, kids."

"Says you," Jamji said.

Eventually, Genevieve had to double the game speed, then double it again, just to give Jamji a challenge. She reduced the number of extra lives to one. This earned a growl from Jamji, to which Genevieve replied, "I don't think you really want to play Centipede for the rest of the day."

Jamji's right hand was a blur as it spun the roller ball. Zeta gawked and laughed. She seemed torn between watching the light show of the screen or the superhuman speed of Jamji's hand. When Jamji's warrior finally died, she cursed and gave the side of the game a solid whack.

Zeta jumped back, startled. She laughed and shook her head, saying, "Jamji, I don't know how you could even see what you were doing, there was so much stuff going on."

"I can think pretty fast."

"And move fast, too! Your hand was like a bumblebee's wings."

"Since this is a construct with a loose realism constraint," Genevieve said, "we aren't limited to what our bodies are capable of. You can be as fast as your mind can imagine."

"Even so," Jamji said, "I can move *almost* that fast in real life."

"It did seem too fast to be real," Zeta said, nodding. "I think I understand; a construct is like a dream. But it feels real. The things you imagine come true, but the place where you are isn't a real place. You said we're still laying in the sand by the campfire, right?"

"That's right!" Genevieve exclaimed.

"But a replay is like living a part of your life again. It *was* real, but it's in the past now so you can't do anything to change it."

"You're a sharp girl," Oraxis said. "Both constructs and replays are very important tools. Once you have better control of your double-mind you'll be able to conjure slate-space at will and decide which constructs or replays to experience. You'll even be able to make constructs of your own."

"Will I ever be able to remember how I got here?" Zeta asked.

"Yes," Oraxis said before Genevieve could come up with an honest, if indirect, response. "In time you *will* find the replay that shows you how you got here."

"How do I do that?" Zeta asked, her mounting anxiety showing. "I need to find that replay. I need to find my tribe! I've been gone for so long. They might not even be in the thicket anymore."

"It's okay, Zeta," Genevieve said, placing a hand on Zeta's arm.

"We'll teach you everything you need to know. First, you need practice at going into and out of slate-space."

Zeta went backwards a step, pulling away from Genevieve's touch. She set her jaw, piercing Genevieve with her glare, then dissolved from view, leaving the construct.

Jamji laughed. "Yeah, I think she's getting the hang of it!"

12

REPLAY

ZETA'S EYES POPPED OPEN. Her vision spun for just a moment as she scrambled to her feet, shaking the sand out of her hair. Penelope-pooch bounded around her, sending happy thoughts about waking up and playing, but Zeta silenced the pooch's voice. Oraxis, Genevieve, and Jamji joined her in the real world, opening their eyes and sitting up.

"Very good," Oraxis said, "you got out with no trouble at all. I'd say with a bit more practice—"

"I don't need more practice! Tell me how to find my tribe."

She cursed herself for letting Jamji's replay and Genevieve's construct distract her. They had been avoiding any talk about how to get back or how she got here, and she was done with it.

Running away again would be pointless — these people held the answers. So why were they just sitting and looking at each other instead of telling her what she wanted to know?! It was like they were conspiring, using their silent speech to talk about her.

"You won't tell me how I got here, or why I'm here, or how to get back. Does my tribe know where I am?" Zeta remembered wanting to run away. If she had, and then later ran across these people and they poisoned her, that could explain how she got here and why her mind was behaving so strangely. It all made sense!

She furrowed her brow and made her accusation. "I think you abducted me."

"What?! No!" Genevieve squeaked.

Oraxis threw his hands in the air, then ran them through his hair as he shook his head.

"We didn't abduct you," Jamji chuckled. "Listen, Zeta, the truth is that Oraxis and Genevieve picked you up from a place in the middle of the Great Ocean, called—"

"Jamji! That's enough!" Oraxis barked.

"Let her talk!" Zeta shouted. It was the closest thing to an answer that Zeta had gotten yet.

"Jamji," Genevieve pleaded.

They were all on their feet now, and Jamji was putting her hands up in surrender. "Fine, I'll shut up. Do it your way, since that's working *so* well."

"Oraxis, Genevieve," Zeta said. They turned to her. She gave them the offensive hand gesture that Jamji had taught her. "Let Jamji talk."

Jamji snorted a laugh. Oraxis turned red, a vein pulsing at his temple. Genevieve looked like she would cry, but she didn't say a word.

"Okay," Jamji said calmly, "well, have you seen that huge basket under *yonder* tree?"

She was pointing at the tree, topped by the unsettlingly massive bird's nest. In the tree's shadow was the largest woven basket that Zeta had ever seen. She had noticed it earlier, but wasn't sure what to make of it.

Zeta nodded.

"That's the basket Oraxis and Genevieve brought you here in. Zephyr, the giant bird that lives up there, carries it for them. They picked you up from an island in the middle of the ocean. You had been under the island, in a sort of deep sleep. They took you and Penelope-pooch here so they could bootstrap you — wake you up."

Jamji's explanation made absolutely no sense. "How did I fall asleep under an island? Who brought me there?"

There was a long pause as Jamji seemed to struggle to find the words. Finally, she said, "There's only one person who knows what happened leading up to you showing up there, and that's you."

Zeta shook her head. "But I *don't* know. I can't remember anything after—"

Charra.

She couldn't say it.

She wouldn't even *think* it.

"I can't remember," she choked out.

Genevieve said, "Replaying your past experiences is the only way to find out how you got to the Land of Nod."

The Land of Nod. Somehow, Zeta had gotten herself there, so if replays could show her how she got there, then they could show her how to get back again. Maybe it wasn't too late.

ZETA LAID BACK DOWN in the sand.

"You're doing it now?" Genevieve asked, nervously.

Zeta nodded, trying to swallow the hard lump in her throat. "Will you all be with me? Like we did with Jamji's replay?"

"I'm afraid not," Oraxis said. "Until you're familiar with the content of a replayed experience, you can't give observer consent. What you're going to do is close your eyes and disconnect from your body. That will put you into slate-space. From there, you're going to bring to mind your past. Even if it's painful, you need to focus on your memories, letting them come however they will. To get your mind working, you need to seek and experience the defining moments of your life. It can take a long time."

Genevieve kneeled by Zeta's side. "Acceptance is the only way you can heal your mind and memory through replays. Accept your past and relive the moment as if it were the present. If any of it becomes too difficult and you want to get out, all you have to do is break the replay."

"Break it?"

"That's right," Genevieve said, brushing Zeta's hair off her forehead. "The easiest way to break a replay is to force yourself to do or say something that never happened. Say my name, for example, or Oraxis's."

"Do be careful," Oraxis said, "not to change it, or create a new reality. It's possible to build a construct directly from a replayed experience. Usually the replay will collapse, but if you're good at improvisational construction, you can jump right from your replay into a construct. If you reject your experiences and replace them with constructs, you can end up trapped in a fantasy world. You're looking for the truth, right?"

Zeta nodded, closing her eyes and taking a deep breath.

Oraxis continued, softly. "Then allow only what is true, and accept each moment until it reveals your full narrative. Relax and let your double-mind lead the way. Release your body, abandon your senses."

Oraxis's voice echoed into the distance as the sensations of her body faded. She was in slate-space. This was it — it was time.

In her last memory, Charra had given her a magical bow. His voice echoed now through the emptiness, "You can kill them wolf-pooches with this! Use the light of Surya, it's everywhere!"

The glowing green eyes of wolf-pooches appeared in the darkness. They danced from side to side, hiding behind giant mushrooms. Their bodies were long, segmented, glowing a sickly shade of green as they twisted downward toward her. She raised her bow and started shooting at them, sending shaft after shaft of Surya's light into their sides, breaking them into pieces.

As quickly as the imagery had formed, she shook it away — it wasn't real! Slate-space emptied. It seemed to go rigid around her.

She had to try again. Minutes passed as she tried to open up her mind and summon a replay. Every time the emptiness seemed to loosen up, it snapped tight again. She was doing it wrong.

"Acceptance," Genevieve had said.

"Allow only what is true," Oraxis had said.

It felt like she was trying to cast a spell on herself. She had to revive a memory, summon a ghost, command a specter of her past to possess her body and overtake her mind. Magic was everywhere in this world, she knew.

It had been the magic of the Red-Painted murderers that had stolen the Golden Grasslands from her people. Dark magic, stick-slings, and the Night-Thunder Spirit.

"Their dark magic is powerful because they drink the blood of their enemies."

"You're a fool." Zeta shook her head. Vihaan believed everything.

"That's what Porom said. In his birth tribe there was an eld even older than Talmid. He knew all about the Red-Painted ones, and Porom told me all about them."

Zeta shook her head again. Fool.

They crouched together in the scrubby grass at the peak of a hill. The receding forms of the strongest men of their tribe looked like ants now. Soon, they would disappear into the dangerous valley.

A black line shot down from the sky like a spear cast down from Surya, plummeting directly towards the distant men. Just before striking the ground it stopped, pooling into a form like a tiny black slug, hovering above the scurrying ants of the distant men.

"Vihaan! Do you see—" Thunder clapped. Zeta flinched, covering her head. When she looked up again, she saw that a tongue of black was lowering from the hovering form. It picked up the flailing form of a man, pulling him into its belly.

"It ate that man!" Vihaan squealed.

Zeta's skin had gone numb. She froze in shock.

The black blob turned back into a spear, rising and disappearing into the cloud-speckled sky. After a few rapid heartbeats, another rumble of thunder echoed across the lands.

She was being pulled by the arm. She gasped, yanking her arm back and spinning around, twisting her ankle as she fell to the ground. Vihaan was pulling her up again, pleading for her to rise. He squeaked out, "Run, Zeta!"

As she rose to her feet, pain shot through her ankle. Vihaan bounded down the hill. She took a few steps before falling again. The pain was too much — she couldn't run!

"Vihaan! Don't leave me!"

"Come on!" Vihaan shouted back to her. He ran back up the hill, then saw that she was hurt. "Lean on me. Go as fast as you can."

As she stumbled down the hill with her arm over Vihaan's shoulder, some small part of herself — a separate, present mind — remembered now that what she had just seen would haunt her for the rest of her life.

"A BLACK SLUG that flies like a spear?!" Ala-eld laughed. "You two snuck away to watch the raid party cross the fields. A black *bug* flew by and spooked you. You've turned the bug into a boogie-monster to avoid punishment. Bethay, Yephanie, if you don't give your kids a slap for this, then I will."

"You have to believe me!" Zeta squealed, tears streaming down her cheeks.

"My Vihaan has never told a lie in his life, Ala-eld," Bethay-sisma said, pulling her boy away from the eld's grasp. "And sneaking away to watch his pa leave for a dangerous raid doesn't warrant a slap."

Zeta looked to Yephanie-ma, who spoke no words in her defense. Yephanie-ma had told her not to leave camp today, and Zeta had promised that she would not.

A distant call broke the brief silence of the camp — the "hoo-whoop" of one of their tribesmen signaling their approach. The pooches burst into a round of excited barking.

The entire tribe rose and looked nervously towards the sparse trees between the camp and the fields. Zeta hoped it would be Wilhelm-pa, but the flame of hope died when the man-boy Leopald and his bro-pa, Meck, came jogging into camp, gasping for air and ignoring the pack of pooches wagging their tails in greeting.

"What is it?"

"What happened?"

"Where are the others?"

The camp filled with questions as the men passed through the crowd of worried women and kids. They approached the eld-fire.

Chief Talmid said nothing as he looked from one man to the other, awaiting an explanation. Someone had brought them bladders of water, which they drank eagerly.

Leopald was the first to speak. "We...we were attacked."

Gasps and more questions rose from the women. Chief Talmid raised his hand towards the onlookers, quieting them, then looked back to Leopald.

Leopald spoke between gasping breaths, "It was summoned...by the Red-Painted tribe, using blood-magic. An evil spirit! It was..." he looked to Meck.

Meck just stood and panted. He eyed the treetops as if he expected the spirit to return.

"It was the Night-Thunder Spirit," Leopald said.

Chief Talmid clicked his tongue, skeptically. "Night-Thunder Spirit? Speak plainly, Leopald, what did you see? What happened?"

"That is as plainly as I can describe the thing, Chief Talmid! You saw it, Meck-bro-pa, tell them!" Leopald grabbed his bro-pa's arm, shaking him.

Meck yanked his arm from Leopald's clutch. He met Chief Talmid's eyes, then spoke in a strained croak. "It was past midday. We were cresting the rise just before the valley. Thunder cracked, though the clouds were white and thin. That's when the spirit appeared." Meck looked up and raised his hands, gesturing at the air overhead as he searched for the words. "It was...the *purest* black. Surya could not touch the depths of its darkness. A great, solid cloud. Writhing, swimming in the sky."

"We saw it, too!" Zeta shouted from behind them.

"Locusts!" Ala-eld spat, "It was just a cloud of locusts, you fools!"

Meck rounded on his eld, "I know what locusts look like!"

"It ate Wilhelm!" Leopald wailed.

Zeta squeaked. Her throat constricted as she pressed her hands against her mouth.

The man it had pulled into its belly was Wilhelm-pa?

It wasn't real!

Was this real?

No, it may have been real in the past, but this experience was a living memory — a replay. She just had to break it.

Zeta forced her hands off of her mouth. She said, "Genevieve."

The replay dissolved, returning her to slate-space.

———

She remembered it all now. The men in the raiding party had talked about the incident later and agreed that they all saw the same thing — the Night-Thunder Spirit had extended a black tongue from its belly, lifting Wilhelm-pa from the ground and swallowing him whole.

His death was the stuff of legends, retold over campfires to scare little boys into staying close to camp. She had nightmares about it all her life.

Some nights, her mind would play tricks with the shadows. Creeping tongues of black would reach for her.

But the thing that scared her the most was the sound of thunder. Whenever a thunderclap would split the skies, Zeta's heart would race. Her breath would come in shallow gasps. She *hated* thunder.

They all knew who had called the Night-Thunder Spirit down

upon them — the same tribe that killed her bro-pa. Wilhelm-pa's death had been a legend, but Jebbam-bro-pa's death had been a disgrace. An afterthought. Zeta wasn't sure which one upset her more.

The raiding party had sent Leopald and Meck back to tell the elds about the Night-Thunder Spirit, but decided that Wilhelm would not have wanted them to retreat. They thought they would make their Red-Painted enemies suffer for calling the spirit down upon them, but that's not how the fight had gone. The Red-Painted tribe's warriors waited in ambush, and their Gravan-cursed stick-slings had driven the raiding party away before they even got to the enemy camp.

Most of the men had made it back to camp. But not Jebbam-bro-pa.

Zeta felt herself slipping back into a replay. She allowed it, finding herself standing in knee-high grass.

In the distance before her was the body of Jebbam-bro-pa. He was laying face-down in the field, feather-tipped sticks poking from his back and hyenas feasting on his fresh meat. Many of the pack lifted their heads, grunting and laughing at the approaching humans. Their faces were painted red with his blood, marking them as familiars of the Red-Painted tribe.

"Make them stop, ma!"

"Zeta, look away," Yephanie-ma said, breathlessly. Her ma's hand pressed Zeta's face into her tight, round belly.

"It's not right!" Bethay-sis-ma cried. "We have to bury him!"

Vihaan wailed on his knees in the grass.

Illonia spoke excitedly, "There, in that grove, did you see them this time? Two man-boys wearing that vile red paint! There! They just ran off."

"We're going back, *now*," Shaman Mora-eld commanded. "I'm not asking you — I'm *telling* you. I'll not feed these beasts any more of our people by challenging them or by allowing the enemy to bait us!"

Zeta dared to take another peek at the body of her bro-pa, the bloodied faces of the mocking beasts, the feather-tipped sticks poking above the grass.

Bethay-sis-ma sobbed, collapsing in the golden grass next to Vihaan and pulling the boy into her arms. "You're leaving my Jebbam to be eaten like an animal. His spirit will roam the world!"

"What do *you* know of spirits, child?" Shaman Mora-eld spat, only slightly gentler than her usual tone. "The surest way to set his spirit wandering would be for you or Vihaan to die uselessly, trying to gather up some scraps of meat to put in the ground. The spirit isn't the body, child. Now, come!"

Yephanie-ma was turning, guiding Zeta by the shoulder. "Okay, Zeta-babe, we found him like we said we would. Let's go back to camp."

Zeta's head felt feverish as she limped back. Seeing where she was stepping was hard to do since her eyes kept watering so much.

"That's because you're crying," her present mind thought, agitated.

She became aware of her separate, present mind which observed her experience. When she thought about it, she could remember that there was a place called The Thin Forest where she was lying on a circle of sand. She knew that Genevieve and Oraxis, Jamji and Penelope-pooch were looking after her motionless body. But when she stopped focusing on it, she slipped easily back into the mind of her younger self.

She watched herself return to the tribe. She watched the elds debate, deciding that they couldn't hunt the Golden Grasslands with the red-painted tribe living in the valley. Their blood-magic was strong. Their ancestor spirits were pure evil, and more powerful than anything that the elds had ever heard of.

Murderous darkness had filled Zeta's mind that evening, as her tribe bundled their packs and debated which way to start walking at first light. All she could think of was killing the murderers all by herself.

They would never expect a girl-child to sneak through their camp and stab their necks!

She needed sharp sticks — lots of them.

But what about the evil spirits?

Zeta wandered the camp, silently searching for a solution, wiping her eyes and nose with the back of her hand.

Then she spotted it — Mileo—eld-pa's angry duppy mask! It dangled from a strap on his pack, which was slung over a low limb. The mask scared her when she was younger.

It still frightens you now, girl-child.

The mask sneered at her, bearing its pointed teeth in the moon-light. Zeta took a breath, then approached it. She gently picked at the knot on the strap, then pulled the mask loose and tucked it under her tunic. She looked around for anyone watching, then padded with silent feet behind a tree. She waited, then peeked back at the camp. Nobody had seen her! She retreated further from the camp, hiding behind another tree. Tree by tree, Zeta snuck to the edge of the open fields.

She pulled the angry duppy mask out. It mocked her with its glare. Did she have what it took to kill a man? That didn't matter, because the red-painted murderers were *not* men — they were blood-thirsty beasts. She pulled the mask to her face and tried to tie the cords behind her head.

Zeta's present mind waited impatiently for the fumbling, awkward child hands of her past self to figure out how to tie a simple knot. After much too long she finally got a slip-knot tied, pulling the knot tight before looping another simple knot to hold it in place.

She unrolled a bundle of leather, revealing her gathered sticks and a few sharp stones. She sat against a tree and set to work at sharp-ening their ends.

TEARS CAME and went as she worked, sniffling and sobbing behind the mask. Her pa was dead. Dead and gone, eaten by a spirit! She would become a shaman. She would kill evil spirits. She would be a huntress! She would hunt down every Gravan-cursed Red-Painted beast-man and make them into hyena food!

Voices came from between the trees.

Zeta frantically straightened the disordered pile of sticks on the leather and rolled them into a bundle. Without looking back, she ran into the grasses. Her injured ankle was shooting with pain, but she didn't have time to slow down.

"Zeta!" A man shouted from far behind.

She could make it if she could just get to the next grove of trees!

The scuffle that approached from behind was too fast to be a man. Something collided with her back, sending her toppling, spilling her sticks and knocking her mask askew. There was a bark, and then the pooch was jumping around her and nipping at her arms and legs. A second pooch came bounding through the grasses and joined the first. Zeta glimpsed the golden fur of Penelope-pup.

"Go away, pooches! I don't want to play," Zeta panted, trying to straighten her mask. She lifted her head and growled at the pooches, raising a hand as if she had claws. The pooches backed away, barking and growling.

She tried to gather her leather bundle and sticks, but they were everywhere. The pounding of grass marked a man's approach. Just as Zeta gave up on the sticks and ran, a hand clutched her arm.

"No! Leave me alone!"

Fighting him was useless. Bakkra was one of the stronger men of the tribe. She would have scratched him, but her bitten nails were too short. She couldn't bite him because of the mask, so she ended up being carried like a felled foal, slung over his shoulder. Bakkra gave the "hoo-whoop" that marked his return to camp. He cursed her under his breath the entire way back. Once they arrived, he threw her to the ground near a fire.

"I found her trying to run across the open field. She had a bundle of sharpened sticks."

Yephanie-ma was crying nearby. Zeta scrambled to her feet and looked around, finding that she was face-to-face with Chief Talmid.

"What have you found, Bakkra? This creature is not Zeta," Chief Talmid said.

The mask was pulled from her face, violently. "Of course it is! Look!"

"Bakkra wasn't the smartest man," Zeta thought in her present mind.

Chief Talmid grabbed her chin, turning her head from side to side. She scowled at the eld, heat flushing her face. He said, "I'm not so sure, Bakkra. If this isn't the face of an angry duppy, I don't know what is."

Several elds laughed. Zeta sneered at them.

"Zeta," said Chief Talmid, "it was noble of you to want to avenge your pa and bro-pa, and brave of you to try to do it alone. You're not the only one who wants to stay here and fight these people. But fighting is not what we've decided to do, because we want to live more than we want to kill."

"I don't," Zeta growled.

Chief Talmid considered her, then turned and pointed at Yephanie-ma. "A babe will be born soon. Wilhelm's babe. Your pa will not be here to look after this babe, to protect it and teach it our ways." He turned back to Zeta, paused for a heartbeat, then raised his hands. He turned his face up to the sky, addressing the air above the fire. He intoned, "I call out to you, Wilhelm of the Scorpion Tail Tribe!"

The tribe sprung into action, preparing to open their camp to the realm of the spirits.

Shaman Mora-eld began warbling in a spirit-song, softening the barrier between the spirit realm and the realm of the living.

The other elds rattled necklaces of tooth and bone, warding off any unwelcome spirits which may try to cross into their world.

Porom thumped a heartbeat rhythm on his drum, signaling to the spirits that this was the realm of the *living*, and not a place for the dead to linger. Zeta's own heart pounded, racing at a beat much faster than Porom's drum.

Mileo-eld-pa hobbled towards her with amazing speed. She retreated a few steps as the eld dug his knob-knuckled hand into a pouch. He pulled it out, then opened his palm and blew a puff of powder over the fire. A cloud of colorful sparks erupted, dancing upwards through the treetops, crackling as they burned. He snatched up his angry duppy mask from the ground, then retreated to the opposite side of the fire, crouching like a frog. He tied the mask onto his face, then began jerking his head around. The angry duppy glared at the darkness of the night, then cast a menacing sneer at her, sending a chill down her spine. This display, Zeta knew, would frighten away any spirts bold enough to ignore the rattling bones or heartbeat drums.

Chief Talmid chanted in the eerie tone reserved for speaking to ancestor spirits. "Wilhelm, my kin, my beloved tribemate! Do not linger in this world for fear that your babe will be in peril. I now charge Zeta, your blood-kin, for whom Soma shed tears of joy on her naming day, with the protection of your babe!"

Zeta felt the skin of her neck and scalp pull tight at the haunting sounds all around her. Countless unseen ancestral faces seemed to watch from the shadows between the tree branches. A fresh round of tears pooled in her eyes as the weight of the charge fell upon her.

Zeta looked over at Yephanie-ma. Her ma's lip quivered as she stroked her swollen belly, tears streaming down her face. Beside her, Vihaan was clutching onto Bethay-sis-ma, hiding his face against her bosom like a frightened babe.

Chief Talmid's voice commanded, "Zeta, do you accept this charge?"

Zeta turned her face back to Chief Talmid, nodding vigorously. She pressed her palms to her eyes to clear them.

Shaman Mora-eld shouted, "Say the words, child! Tell your pa-spirit! Your ancestors are here to witness your vow!"

Porom's heartbeat drumming intensified. Bones rattled. Elds hummed. Her tribal ancestors watched from above. Her skin was cold, numb.

She took a breath and looked up to the night sky between the treetops. The bright tiger-eye twin stars shone, looking down upon her to witness her vow. The stars danced in her watery eyes. "I'll protect the babe for you, Wilhelm-pa! I'll protect my blood-kin. I'll stay here and make sure nothing bad happens to Yephanie-ma, too. I vow it!"

Blackness flooded her world, washing her tribe away.

Zeta slipped back through slate-space, reconnecting to her body.

She opened her eyes. The chirping of the crickets was the only sound. Above her, between the treetops of the Thin Forest, glared the tiger-eye stars.

She had made a vow. She was supposed to have protected Charra.

Maybe it wasn't too late.

13

CREATION STORY

A MONTH PASSED, day by day. Every few days, Zeta would take on another replay session, followed by the emotional backlash accompanying the relived experiences. When she would cry at night, Genevieve would stay outside and lay with her. When she would ask tough questions about why things were the way they were, Oraxis would explain it as best he could with the limited information he could share.

He brought her through a set of strategically curated educational constructs — fully immersive experiences where he'd conjure representations of the topics he taught. Within these, WoQS filled in the meanings of the concepts, monitoring Zeta's comprehension level and prompting Oraxis to elaborate or repeat as needed.

Zeta came to understand how the tribes, collectively called either *neoprims* or *Edenites*, lived in The Land of Eden — the place where she had lived with her tribe. She learned that advanced people, called *Noddites*, lived in The Land of Nod — the place where she was now. She learned that these lands existed on opposite sides of the planet, called *Genesis*. That is, once she wrapped her mind around the concept of a planet.

Before long, Zeta figured out that this meant she was as far away from her people as a person could be.

It hit her, *hard*.

But then she learned that there were ways to travel so quickly that she could be back with her people within days, if she only knew where they were. This hope encouraged her to press on.

Zeta gained proficiency at entering and exiting slate-space. Sometimes she would talk about her replayed experiences with Genevieve, sometimes Jamji, but never Oraxis. He presumed she never had a close relationship with her father, so he didn't blame her for remaining distant. Oraxis conceded that he wasn't the best listener, anyway.

Jamji and Zeta grew inseparable. While it was nice for Zeta to have a trusted friend, it was problematic when Jamji bucked against Oraxis and Genevieve's ideas. They had a bit of a scare the night Jamji snuck off with Zeta for a snipe hunt without telling Oraxis or Genevieve. They had declined all WorMS messages and conversation requests and didn't return until Surya rose the next morning.

Jamji was also teaching Zeta how to use a bow. *His* bow, that is. Once, when Oraxis had tried to remind Zeta that the bow was his, she had the audacity to flip him off. He called her a cuss, and Jamji snort-laughed until she cried. Even Genevieve was tickled. His bow was too big for her, with a heavy draw which she struggled with. Oraxis put in a request for his bowyer to make one better suited to her height and build. It would make a nice Beta Ceremony gift.

On the night of the thirty-third day, Oraxis and Genevieve took Zeta for a hike. Jamji was away, wishing an old friend goodbye. She wouldn't give any details, but Oraxis was certain she was visiting poor Paulie-boy, tormenting him with yet another final fling.

They planned on being gone for the night and camping at the

lakeside. When Surya was low in the sky, Genevieve and Zeta gathered wood and kindling while Oraxis built a rock circle.

Once the wood was arranged, Oraxis poked his finger into the kindling, using WUtils to create a static discharge between the ground and his fingertip. This instantly caught the kindling on fire. He blew on the small flames, feeding them kindling until they had a crackling fire. Acrid smoke billowed from the fire as the dry pine needles burned.

"Ta-da! It's not magic — it's WUtils!" He said in his best infomercial impression, standing and gesturing to the fire.

"Any technology sufficiently gimmicky," Genevieve said, shaking her head.

Gazing into the flames, Zeta also shook her head and said, "There is magic in this world. I know you say it's not magic. I know you can explain how it works, like you always do, but it still seems like magic to me."

"You'll come to understand soon enough," Oraxis said, sitting on the pebbles of the lakeside, "that there is no such thing as magic, spirits, gods—"

Zeta laughed. "If you believe that, then you haven't seen the things I have seen. Besides, without gods, humans wouldn't even exist."

Oraxis nodded. "I'm familiar with your tribe's creation story. Surya planted the seeds of the first man and woman in the grasslands, and so on. That's still the story your elds tell, right?"

"Yeah." Zeta seemed surprised he would know that.

Oraxis grunted. "So far as creation stories go, it's a fine one. But that's all it is — a *story*, passed on from generation to generation."

"And your tribe's story isn't?"

"That's right. But it's not just my tribe — all modern humans accept the same common theory. And it's based on *evidence*: hard facts, truth, reality. No gods required. If you want to figure out what's true, you use science."

"Science?"

"Do a WoQS lookup on the word."

Zeta nodded, closed her eyes, and zoned out for a minute. When she returned, she furrowed her brow at Oraxis. "Science doesn't seem so special to me. It's just people learning how the world works."

"It's special because it's a way of asking and answering questions which transcends our intuitions. It compensates for our human fallacies and biases. It's rigorous, self-correcting, and denies no inconvenient evidence. It acknowledges ignorance, even while working to abolish it."

"WoQS said nothing about how science came up with your creation story. I still don't know where you think humans came from."

"Just show her," Genevieve mindspoke.

"You don't think it's too soon?" Oraxis replied.

"Nah. Let's do it — Earth data dump time. Dibs on narrator."

"Okay," Oraxis said to Zeta, "do you want to know where humans came from?"

Zeta smirked. "Sure."

"Alright, meet me in slate-space. I've got a construct that'll blow your mind. We're going to start right here, then go back to the dawn of the universe, then work our way back to the present. Don't worry if you don't understand everything. You can replay this experience any time you'd like and flesh out the details using WoQS."

Oraxis laid down. Zeta and Genevieve were doing the same. He disconnected from his body, loading the construct. He modified it slightly so their initial setting would be the lakeside camp, then sent Genevieve and Zeta an invite.

ZETA STOOD as the lone observer at the lakeside. Instead of dusk, it was now nighttime, and the sky was filled with stars, made subtly more luminous than normal.

Genevieve's disembodied voice began, "Zeta, you were born on this planet; Genesis. Oraxis and I may call this planet our home, but it is not the planet where we were born. Nor is it the planet where humans came from."

Zeta lifted from the lakeside, then soared into the sky. She gasped as the ground below shot away. In seconds, they were in near-Genesis orbit.

"This is what Genesis looks like from above, when you go so high that you leave the planet," Genevieve said. "But in space, there is no up or down, no above or below. But there is near and far. Next, we will go *very* far from home."

Genesis zipped away as they shot into the blackness of space, leaving Surya behind as a fading star. They traveled at an impossible speed. The closer stars slid by in the distance, but the greater starscape remained mostly fixed.

"We are now traveling in the cold, empty space between the stars. That one, shining right in front of us, is our destination. We call it 'Sol', or 'the sun'." Oraxis made Sol glimmer for a moment, then dimmed it again.

After compressing a five hundred light year trek into one minute, they approached the sun. Oraxis brought them soaring past the outer planets. They settled into a near-Earth orbital view, basking in the warmth of the sun.

"This is Earth as it looked when Oraxis and I were born, many years ago. It's the planet where all the plants, animals, and people of Genesis originally came from."

The Earth's dark side was illuminated with clusters of light, like a miniature starscape. An orbiter sailed by, its solar panels extended. A moment later, their perspective plunged to the planet. The ground rushed up toward them, then slowed to a stop as they descended into Times Square.

People and buildings were everywhere. Vehicles hummed by on elevated rails over the dense crowd, flowing down the street like a river. Holographic billboards advertised the latest immersive experience. Zeta turned in circles, taking in the alien landscape with wide-eyed wonder.

"This," Genevieve said, "is a city. These things around you may look magical, but they were all made by humans. We could do miraculous things, Zeta. In fact, we still can. There are people on other planets living in underground versions of cities, like this, right now. Exciting, right? So, how did we get to this point? Let's go all the way back to the beginning of time."

And so began their hour-long course in the brief history of the universe, starting with the Big Bang. Zeta never lost interest as they explained the formation of star systems and planets, and then the dawn of life and process of evolution. Seeing how humans had turned from hairy primates to not—quite-as-hairy hominids actually made Zeta laugh.

"I always told Charra he was a monkey-boy!" Zeta had joked.

They walked her through the basics of human history, from the Paleolithic age to the twentieth century. Seeing how people could go from tribes to cities was simple enough. As was showing the transition from primitive tools to simple modern ones like hammers and plows.

They got stuck for a bit trying to explain how science came about and how it was used to learn about things like atoms and electromagnetism. At a certain point they had to brush past her confusion, for the sake of getting to the true reason for the lesson — the reason they were on Genesis.

GENEVIEVE NARRATED, "Our understanding of the universe and our applications of technology kept growing, until we figured out how to send words and images through the air, over great distances, using things called *radio waves*."

Oraxis illustrated the concept using stylized blue waves radiating from the surface of the planet. He showed a person talking in one place, and then the same image appearing in another place. He followed one of the blue waves out into space.

"Something we didn't realize when we started sending those messages through the air was that they were also leaking out into space."

They continued following the blue wave. It grew faint until it was barely visible. They followed it through the cold interstellar space until they stopped, abruptly. A mass as large as a mountain loomed before them. It was grey, with golden veins webbing its surface. The wave disappeared into the mass.

"Something else we didn't realize was that there were monsters out there, between the stars."

The mass stirred.

"Sleeping."

The mass began to sprout tentacles. Its surface came alive with the dark forms of millions of crawling black bugs.

"Waiting."

More waves from Earth struck the mass. It started advancing towards them.

"Listening."

As it was almost upon them, a dozen slitted eyes as big as boulders shot open, circling a gaping hole filled with pointed teeth. Zeta screamed and hid her face in her hands.

Oraxis had taken more than a few artistic liberties with his interpretation of The Monster from the Stars, but it got the idea across. Nobody knew what The Monster looked like, so it may as well have been a many-eyed, tentacled nightmare.

"The Monster from the Stars had caught our scent; it followed the trail left by our radio waves, leading it straight to Earth. But, thankfully, not right away."

Their perspective returned to Earth. They sat among the audience at the Apollo 11 launch.

Genevieve said, "If it had shown up right when we started using radio waves, then it would have easily consumed us all, and that would have been the end of humanity. Lucky for us, space is an enormous place, and The Monster was *very* far away, so it took a long time for our messages to reach it. It took an even longer time for The Monster to follow the messages back across space to reach us. In that span of time, we learned how to go to space ourselves."

Fire burst from the bottom of the shuttle and it rose into the air. They followed it as it rose, shedding fuel containers, reducing to the coupled moon lander and orbiter. Their time-compressed journey followed the spacecraft until it landed on the moon. Neil's famous flubbed line played within the construct.

Genevieve continued, "The next several hundred years were a golden age for humanity. Granted, we had our difficulties. The other plants and animals of Earth certainly suffered, but as far as humans were concerned, we were doing great. Using science, we learned how to do all sorts of wonderful things. For example, we could essentially craft life out of stone." The construct transitioned to the interior of a modest dining room. They watched as a robotic servant glided into the room, laying a plate of steaming food in front of a child.

"We conquered death, learning how to stop ourselves from aging. We learned how to improve and enhance our bodies and minds. It was an *amazing* time to be alive, Zeta. Today, we call this The Revelry Era." Oraxis showed towering, muscled men fighting in an arena. In the crowd, every woman was a goddess of impossible dimensions, surrounded with glowing holograms or shimmering with colorful skin.

They jumped to a town center, circa 2390. Trees and hanging gardens were grown in harmony with the terra-cotta architecture. Ivy climbed the sides of most of the buildings, and birds flitted between them. The polarized city dome overhead cast the sky above it a rich shade of blue, punctuated by sparse clouds.

Zeta stood next to younger versions of Oraxis and Genevieve. Oraxis's younger self was almost unidentifiable, since he didn't have a beard. Their hair was cut and styled in an old Earth fashion, and their outfits were absurd — bands of striped fabric, colored with hues of blues and greens. The fabric wrapped and draped over their bodies, revealing as much skin as they covered. The young Oraxis and Genevieve talked and laughed, oblivious to Zeta.

"Is that you guys?!" Zeta asked, half-laughing. "Is this a replay?"

Genevieve spoke fondly, saying, "Yes, that's us. It's not a replay, though. It's just a reconstruction of what we looked like. This was before anybody could store experiences for replay. Hey, Oraxis, don't shave your beard, okay?"

Oraxis laughed. He had grown the beard when they had arrived at Genesis and started living as primitives, and she had hated it then. It's funny how tastes change.

Genevieve sang, "There we are, just as happy as could be. Blissfully ignorant that *everything* was about to change."

A KLAXON SOUNDED. Zeta jumped, as did the young Oraxis and Genevieve. The holoboards around the town center came to life, displaying identical messages of black text over a red background.

Worldwide Emergency Broadcast

The message vanished, being replaced by a stately woman in a conservative band-suit. She said, "Hello. Please remain calm." Oraxis could remember his heart skipping a beat at the broadcast's opening statement. Even now, so many years later, his anxiety began to build. What better way to incite panic than to open with a line like that?

The woman continued with a borderline robotic tone. "We have received an extraterrestrial message. The message was recorded and decoded simultaneously at multiple, independent radio monitoring stations around the Earth and Moon, just minutes ago. Triangulation algorithms confirm the origin of the broadcast as a point in interstellar space, twenty light years away, in the direction of the Aquarius constellation. The message was received on twelve distinct bandwidths. Each bandwidth contained the same basic message, as spoken in a different language. We will now broadcast the English band of the transmission."

The woman cast her eyes down as a high-pitched, warbling whine and heavy static played through the town center speakers. A guttural voice proclaimed, "I am The Monster From the Stars. I will consume you in eighty years."

Seeing the broadcast again gave Oraxis chills. The surrounding crowd stood and stared with equal parts dread and skepticism. Young Genevieve watched the broadcast with wide eyes and a white-knuckled grasp on young Oraxis's arm, who glared at the billboard with a clenched jaw.

Zeta asked, "That was the big monster that heard the radio waves?"

"Yes," Genevieve said.

"So...it was going to eat everybody?"

Genevieve took an unsteady breath, then said, "We think it wanted to consume our *ideas* — the things we learned using science. That may seem strange, but today we know that basic forms of life are pretty common across the universe, so they probably get ignored by aliens like The Monster. There's nothing it can gain from them. Intelligent beings, like humans, are rare. The Monster waits and watches for signs of intelligent life, like radio waves. Then, it rushes to the planet to steal their ideas, tools, and ways of thinking. After that, it wipes them out so that other monsters can't have what it took."

"We think," Oraxis chimed in, "*maybe*. We have numerous theories as to The Monster's motives and strategy."

"Why did it tell you it was coming?" Zeta asked. "If it was hunting you, then why would it reveal itself?"

"That's a good question," Genevieve said. "Nobody really knows. Personally, I think it just wanted to shake us up and get us to develop stronger weapons to prepare for the fight. Then, when it showed up to wipe the floor with us, we'd have even nicer things for it to take than if it hadn't sent the warning. Some think it was a form of mercy, giving us the chance to run away and save ourselves before it got there."

It impressed Oraxis that Zeta thought to ask about The Monster's motives. He had his own pet theories about the message, but they were way too complicated to explain to Zeta.

"So," Zeta said, "you thought everyone was going to die?"

Genevieve said, "It seemed likely. We weren't giving up that easy, though. Some people built powerful weapons and bunkered down to defend Earth and fight The Monster. But not Oraxis and I — we joined many others who stored their minds in special vessels called *aposynchronic orbs*. This was how we escaped to Genesis before The Monster got to Earth."

Young Oraxis and Genevieve morphed into floating metallic orbs with perfectly smooth, reflective surfaces. They shot into the sky. The construct followed the orbs as they wove their way between orbital construction platforms and into the belly of a matte-black starship — a behemoth shaped like a donut — the Genesis colony's interstellar gas-jet torus carrier, The Ark.

A swarm of other orbs joined them, lifting from the Earth and into the open belly of the starship. The black space donut disconnected from the construction platform, then crawled across the solar system. Earth reduced to a pale blue dot behind them.

The form of Jupiter grew larger until it filled their field of view. The carrier aimed for the planet's horizon, descending into the upper atmosphere of the gas giant. A rapidly swirling bubble formed around the carrier as it lowered into the atmosphere. A flaming, spiraling tail of superheated gas began spewing from the carrier's donut hole — Jupiter's atmosphere, electromagnetically funneled through the center of the torus to build thrust. After zipping around Jupiter several times, the starship angled away from the planet and shot off into interstellar space.

Their view returned to Earth. A looming darkness blotted out the star field behind the planet. Waves of black bugs swept over the Earth. Tendrils of grey flesh webbed with gold filaments wrapped around the planet. Genevieve said, "Sometimes running away is the smartest thing to do. This period in human history — our retreat from Earth — is called The Exodus."

They left Earth and returned to The Ark, soaring silently through interstellar space. It was barely visible — a shadow in the dark. "The Genesis colony was founded by people who believed that reverting to a primitive state was humanity's best chance at survival, now that we knew there were malevolent aliens — monsters looking for signs of advanced intelligence — laying in wait between the stars. It wasn't an easy choice to make, but as our reasoning goes, humans had lived like that for a *very* long time on Earth without catching the attention of any aliens. We hoped it would work again on Genesis. These newly primitive humans are what we call *neoprims*."

The colony ship reached the Surya system, plunging into the upper atmosphere of the blue and white swirled gas giant, Shiva. Brilliant fire burned around the carrier as it shed speed. After several slowing orbits, it broke free of Shiva and crossed the system, falling into an orbit around the green, blue, and white Earthlike planet, Genesis. Their view descended through the clouds and returned to the lakeshore where they had started, though there were no trees. The ground was rocky and dappled with lichen. Dense green moss grew along the lakeside.

"We came to this planet because it was already seeded with life. Most planets are horrible places to live, but not Genesis. We think what happened was that a long time ago, a large rock from space struck the Earth and kicked some tiny Earth critters into space. They landed here, where they grew until they spread around the entire planet. We didn't have to do much to prepare the planet to be a suitable place for the humans and animals of Earth to live, so we moved in!"

THE SCENE TRANSITIONED to the present day. The campfire and surrounding forest reappeared.

Genevieve concluded, "So, that's where we came from, how we got here, and why we're living like we do. The idea is that if aliens look at our planet, all they'll see is basic, unintelligent life. With any luck, they'll leave us alone."

With that, Oraxis ended the construct. He opened his eyes, sitting up. Zeta was doing the same. Night had fallen while they were in the construct, and their fire now burned low.

Oraxis picked up a bundle of sticks to put it on the fire as he said, "So, that's *our* creation story. That should give you an idea as to our purpose, here in Nod. We're here to watch over the neoprims, and to keep an eye out for hostile aliens."

"Or hostile humans," Genevieve added, privately.

Zeta stared at the growing fire for several minutes, then laid back and looked up at the sky. Shadows from the firelight danced across her face. She was furrowing her brow, trying to make sense of the universe, seeing the stars above with a new set of eyes.

She raised her arm, pointing up. "Is that one Sol?"

Oraxis said, "You actually can't see Sol from Genesis. Not without special tools."

She let her arm drop. "It's still out there? The Monster from the Stars?"

Genevieve said, "Yes, but—"

"Can it see us?"

"We don't think so," Genevieve said.

"What about radio waves? Are we sending those out into space?"

"No," Genevieve said.

Oraxis started, "Well—", but Genevieve shot him a glare, shutting him up. Zeta lifted her head to look at Oraxis, then Genevieve, then laid her head back down and returned to examining the stars. The silence was filled only by the chirping of crickets and the gentle lap of the lake against the shore.

What Oraxis had almost said was that a form of radio communication, tightbeam, was still sent to and received from other human colonies, occasionally. And interplanetary signals are constantly being sent within the Surya system, though they're supposed to be so narrowly focused that they're entirely absorbed by the receiver relay stations.

In hindsight, he shouldn't have muddied the waters. The general consensus is that the probability of a distant observer detecting a tightbeam burst or a wayward interplanetary signal is negligible. They're patterned to blend in with cosmic background radiation, though that doesn't help if the receiver is close enough to the source to detect the intensity spike.

Skeptics, like Oraxis, argue that classifying tightbeams as safe and undetectable was a foolhardy bit of motivated reasoning. The Specters proved that point well enough.

"How long before we tell her about the Specters?" Oraxis mind-spoke to Genevieve.

"She's got to process what we've given her, first. We'll bring it up when the time is right. I just hope she doesn't stumble upon it through a WoQS query."

Oraxis sighed, wishing for the thousandth time that there was a way to restrict a beta's access to WoQS. He had written a bill and campaigned for it on three different occasions, but could never get The Council of Ten to put it on a ballot. "Information wants to be free," they would say. As if quoting an old hacker mantra was some sort of sagely wisdom.

Xavier and Pip had plunged into the Bibliotheca database head-first, consuming information ravenously. Carff and Jamji had been only casual users. Susie-Q, of course, never even had the chance. Zeta didn't seem to go overboard with her queries, so maybe they'd have some time before the uncomfortable and complicated topic of Specters came up.

AFTER A LONG WHILE, Zeta spoke again, shaking her head. "That story was the strangest thing I've ever heard."

Genevieve laughed. "It's not just a story, Zeta. It's the truth — it's what really happened."

Zeta closed her eyes. "The universe started as a speck. The planet humans came from was called Earth and started as a fireball. Tiny animals crawled around on it before they turned into monkeys, and then into humans. The humans lived normal lives for a while, then they learned about science, and that made it possible to do unimaginable things like living forever and flying between the stars. But then, The Monster from the Stars came to take our ideas, so we had to run and make a new home on Genesis. And all of this happened without gods or magic."

"Correct." Oraxis said.

"We're on this planet," Zeta said, sitting up, "and we're not doing any of the amazing things we learned how to do on Earth, because we're *hiding?!*"

"That's right," Genevieve said.

Zeta fell silent for another minute, then abruptly got to her feet. She spoke with an urgent tone. "Sometimes hiding can work and the predator will pass right by you, but sometimes it *doesn't.* The neoprims don't even know they're supposed to be hiding! They could learn how to use science and build the things that make radio waves and send a call out to The Monster From the Stars on accident."

Zeta paced as she talked. "And even if they don't, what if there're other monsters that find us some other way? If there's one, then there's got to be more! You need to have some people around who know the truth, and can use science to defend the planet. To run or to *fight!* That's a Noddite's job, isn't it? That's why you gave me this double-mind and why you're teaching me these things. You want me to help to watch over the neoprims!" The campfire's flames danced in Zeta's eyes. Her face was set with pure determination.

"Would it upset you if I said that were true?" Genevieve asked.

"Upset me?" Zeta scoffed. "It would mean there's actually a good reason why all this is happening to me. I've been chosen to be a protector. That's always been my destiny. And if science can make it so a person doesn't die, then I can..." Zeta trailed off.

"Don't be mistaken," Oraxis cautioned, "about what science is capable of. It can't change the past. If someone you know has died, they're gone."

Zeta eased herself back down, hugging her legs.

Oraxis continued, "It is true that you have been chosen to be a protector of the neoprims. You're the only one in your tribe that was given the gifts you now have. Only one person per tribe every three generations gets chosen."

After another long silence, Genevieve spoke. "It's a lot to absorb, so let's just call it a night and get some sleep."

"*I'll take first shift,*" Oraxis mindspoke to Genevieve.

Genevieve replied, "*I was thinking the same thing — after all that, she's liable to sneak away in the night.*"

And the vigil began.

14

TRUTH

Zeta dreamed of Earth — of the creation of her people at that far-away place. She imagined the first humans being birthed out of foreign soil under Surya's glowing sister, Sol. In her dream, babes were born as monkeys who would only shed their fur as they aged. She made fun of Charra's patchy fuzz until Penelope-pooch told her to be kind because her bro-kin was dead now. A swarm of black wolf-pooches descended from the stars, snapping at her face and startling Zeta awake.

"Oh, Zeta, it's okay!" Genevieve said, rushing to her side.

Zeta sat up, heart pounding. She looked around, finding Penelope pooch sniffing at something that washed up on the beach nearby.

"*Penelope-pooch,*" Zeta asked using her mind, "*what do you remember about Charra?*"

"*Charra is our kin,*" Penelope-pooch sent, lifting her head to look at Zeta. "*Is he here?*" She sniffed the air.

"*Is he okay, Pen?*"

"*He is our kin, but he is not here.*"

Zeta shook her head and laid back down on her placental mat.

She knew that the pooch had no stored experiences of her own. Besides, pooches don't think the same way people do.

"Bad dream?" Genevieve asked, laying on the pebbles of the lakeshore.

Zeta nodded.

"Sometimes dreams are our mind's way of working through the things that we're worried about. They have a way of stirring up the ghosts haunting the back of our minds."

Zeta knew what she had been avoiding. There was one experience she never returned to. The one she wouldn't mention to Genevieve or Jamji, or even to herself.

They ate a breakfast of baked fish with sweet roots, seasoned with some of Genevieve's aromatic herbs. The rest of the day was consumed by their silent trek back to the cabin. Zeta dwelled on her dream, and the unthinkable replay.

Soon after arriving at the cabin, Jamji returned.

"Seriously?!" Jamji whined. "You gave her the Earth data dump without me? I was gone for *one* day!"

"Jamji," Genevieve pleaded.

"I know what it is," Jamji said, jumping off Pepper-pooch's back, "you just didn't want my colorful commentary ruining your mood. Did you leave out Googolplex again?"

Oraxis greeted Pepper-pooch, scratching behind his ear. "Googolplex isn't integral to the narrative we convey with that construct, *Pip-Tau.*"

"Oh, come on, I'm not as bad as Pip-Tau. I just think you leave out too much. I *know* you didn't talk about the S-word."

"Jamji!" Genevieve barked.

"I figured as much," Jamji said, giving Zeta a greeting hug.

"You can tell me about those things yourself," Zeta mindspoke to her.

"I can't wait!" Jamji replied. *"Tonight?"*

"Not tonight. I have a replay I need to get through."

After a few more pleasantries, Zeta excused herself and laid down on the sand circle. Genevieve followed her, kneeled next to her, and brushed her cheek like a ma to her babe.

"This one might take a while," Zeta said, trying not to let her tone reveal the dread in her heart.

"You take as much time as you need, Zeta," Genevieve said. "We'll be right here."

Zeta smiled slightly, then closed her eyes. She slipped easily into slate-space. She sat alone in the void for a long time, gathering her wits. Maybe she should start with a pleasant experience?

No, she had experienced enough of those. What she needed was to face the truth, and the pain that would follow. She needed to pick up where she had broken the unmentionable replay.

Slate-space softened as her double-mind prepared. Conjuring the replay felt like sliding down a muddy river bank into a raging river. Her mind reeled as it simultaneously rejected her reality and accepted it.

Charra's bundled form was before her, held like a babe. Her heart pounded, sending bolts of light into her vision. She was paralyzed, forced to watch as Rod-non-pa revealed the pallid, mangled face of her dead bro-kin.

Her body was out of her control. It fell backward, then was caught by someone. She wrestled free from their grasp, collapsing to the ground. The pain of her impact shot through her arm, then resonated throughout her body. It took the breath from her lungs, stunning her mind. She found herself twisting on the cold ground, contorted in raging sobs.

It wasn't real!

It was real.

Something inside of Zeta died, taking with it the idea that there was anything false about what was happening, or anything that could be done to stop it or undo it. It *had* happened, it *was* happening.

She could retreat! Say Genevieve's name and break the replay!

She took a deep breath and shouted the only name which could come to her lips.

"Charra!"

CHARRA WAS DEAD.

This truth was a cold plunge into icy, black waters. It numbed the limbs, pierced the mind with its icy pain.

Zeta lived this truth, in all its unreality.

If she tried, she could still sense her present self as a separate mind. She was not the one living through the experience. She was a ghost, haunting her own past. But, when she wasn't thinking about it, she was a single mind, living through the worst day of her life.

Yes, this was worse than losing Wilhelm-pa to the Night-Thunder Spirit, worse than finding Jebbam-bro-pa laid out as a meal for hyenas. Charra was just a child. He was her ward.

Yephanie-ma had been brought away when the old man and red-speckled man-boy arrived at their camp. She had been inconsolable. Once she returned she pulled Charra's body from Rod-non-pa's arms and rocked him like a babe, wailing and rambling incoherent pleas to the gods.

Zeta's minutes of raging grief were followed by hours of para-lyzing depression and absolute exhaustion.

Charra had been her reason for staying, for living. Even before he was born, the spirit of Wilhelm-pa had bound him to her. That vow, now broken, released her spirit from her body. It wandered the world already, and the body it left behind held no love, no life.

Zeta slipped in and out of consciousness, each time returning to a sudden and renewed awareness. Each awakening came with an upheaval of a fresh round of pain — her heart ached, her throat was raw and dry, and her injured arm pulsed.

As Eve-eld-ma held her, Zeta's present mind disconnected from the experience. She was as powerful as a goddess now. With her strength, speed, and knowledge, she could avenge Charra. She could have her skin changed, like Jamji's, and return to The Land of Eden as an invisible spirit of vengeance. She would find the red-speckled man-boy and end him, then end his entire tribe.

As if her past self sensed her present thoughts, she croaked, "I curse the red-speckled man-boy. I curse his wolf-pooches. My vow is broken. Wilhelm-pa's spirit will return. He will possess me and give me the strength of a man and I will kill them all."

Eve-eld-ma pulled Zeta's head back from her shoulder to look at her face. "You will do no such thing. That foreign tribe will break camp and leave the thicket to us, and we will never see them again. They said as much — the forest is ours. They only wish we could have crossed paths more peacefully."

Zeta's memories within the memory went back through the events leading up to Charra's death, asking what she should have done differently. She kept going back to that red-speckled man-boy, being dragged by his wild wolf-pooch through the dirt. He was the one to blame, and he had no right to leave the thicket with his breath still in his lungs.

The day dragged on, with the mood of the camp remaining grim. Penelope-pooch slept most of the day, and would only drink water when Zeta woke her. Zeta slept, too. She was exhausted. She just wanted to die. But not before the red-speckled man-boy.

Zeta watched Soma creep up from behind the treetops, half-full. "Weep for Charra, Soma," she whispered. The silent watcher simply hovered in the inky blue. Zeta waited her whole life to see Soma's tears falling, just like Yephanie-ma said they did on her naming day. The glowing tears had streaked slowly across the sky, and a pair of pale-skinned travelers had retrieved the tears for use in weaving powerful magic. If Soma wouldn't weep for her tonight, Zeta would forsake her.

Her present self wondered if Soma's tears could bring Charra back to life. The people of Earth had traveled to their moon, walked on it like it was a planet. Could she visit Soma, to gather the tears herself? Was that the true purpose of her journey to The Land of Nod? This was a thin hope, fleeting and fanciful, but it was better than nothing.

She turned her head to see the men finish digging a hole. The ground in the thicket was all hard-packed clay, roots and rocks, so it wasn't as deep as the hole would have been in the grasslands.

The tribe gathered. Eve-eld-ma helped Zeta to stand and walk to the grave. Inside the hole lay Charra's body, flanked by the tattered remains of Gorgon-pup and Chimera-pup. Apparently someone in the tribe cared enough to go back and look for the pups, but hadn't beaten the forest scavengers to the bodies.

Zeta couldn't bear to watch as they packed clods of mud atop the pups and her bro-kin. Instead, she stared at Rod-non-pa. Her vision pulsed at its edges with every heartbeat. His jaw clenched as he wrapped his arms around Yephanie-ma and watched the burial. Zeta knew he felt her glare cutting into him.

Chief Talmid said some empty words about how sad it was, and how it was all an unfortunate accident. A misunderstanding. Wrong place, wrong time, reckless kids and poorly trained pooches. The tribes had made peace, and the foreigners would be gone soon. Zeta wanted to knock the last of the eld's teeth out with a rock.

They chanted, wishing Charra's spirit safe travels. The tribe took turns putting stones on the grave, then returned to their fires to eat or sleep. They would go on about their lives now. Other than herself and Yephanie-ma, nobody had lost anything when Charra died.

Nobody cared.

Night fell. Zeta lay glaring at the cold stars and Soma's vacant glow. Hate burned in her heart as her upper arm throbbed with a deep pain.

She had no sensation below her elbow. The elds wrapped the arm up with leather straps, to hold healing herbs and maggots against it. She suspected that they just didn't want to look at the ruined, ragged flesh. Her arm was as dead as her bro-kin. It would become diseased and kill her soon. Nobody had the courage to say so, but everyone knew that injuries this bad were followed by a stinking rot, a fever, and death.

She wished she had died by bleeding out, like Charra, instead of going through the pain behind and ahead of her.

A fitful and nightmare-filled sleep eventually overtook her.

THE SKY WAS a cold blue of early dawn, and Rod-non-pa was kneeling beside her with a tortoiseshell of water. She considered tossing it across the camp in defiance, but her thirst would not allow it — her mouth and throat were painfully dry.

She curled her nose as she choked down the sour water. It had probably stewed in a bladder for days — nothing like the fresh water of the spring pool. She needed clean water. She could wash her wound in it — heal herself with its purity.

Her present self thought, *"You will be healed someday, Zeta. You will be whole again."*

Rod-non-pa's voice was soft and hoarse. "Why did you look at me instead of at Charra when he was being buried?"

Zeta spoke in the whispers of a snake's hiss. "Because it's your fault, as much as mine. Because you swore to Yephanie-ma that you would protect her children, even though they were not your own. That was a lie you told so that she would let you put your seed in her."

Surely he wouldn't strike her in this condition.

Rod-non-pa tightened his lips and leaned in closer. "No, it was the truth. I protect and feed you as my own kin."

"Then where were you? Tending to *your* babe. And what are you going to do about Charra being killed? Nothing. You're glad he's gone. One less mouth to feed. You're glad I'm going to die soon, too.

Then it'll just be precious little Hareshnid, like you've always planned."

"That's. Not. True." Rod-non-pa spoke through clenched teeth. He clutched Zeta's shoulder. When she winced and yelped, he released her, recoiling.

Penelope-pooch growled at the man as she struggled to her feet nearby.

Zeta laughed sardonically. "I'm surprised you didn't choke me to death as I slept. I'll bet you put poison in that foul water!" She wasn't whispering anymore. Let the tribe hear her accusation.

"That's not true!" He looked around at the few who had taken interest in their quarrel. He went back to a whisper, softer than before, leaning in. "Zeta, I mourn for Charra, and I want you to live. How can I prove to you that I *do* think of you as my blood-kin?"

Zeta looked into his glassy brown eyes, then whispered, "You find that red-speckled man-boy, and you put a spear through him."

"Zeta, I...can't kill a boy in cold blood. It wouldn't be right."

"Then kill his wolf-pooches. Kill every last one of the beasts."

Rod-non-pa nodded. "That I will do, Zeta. I swear it."

ROD-NON-PA AGREED to carry Zeta to the spring pool for clean water. If she could wash her arm in the pool, it might heal. The elds say cold water has healing properties.

As Zeta gathered empty water skins, Chief Talmid caught her by her good arm. Brushing the chief off would be an insult that even she wouldn't dare, though she was tempted. Zeta's present self thought, *"Get your bony claw off me, old man."*

The wrinkled eld smiled sadly, then brushed her hair away from her face. The gentleness behind his hazel eyes turned her into a meek child again. She cast her gaze to the ground, but he put his finger below her chin and lifted it again.

His voice was high-pitched, yet firm. "I've seen this look in your eyes before, Zeta, after your pa was consumed by the Night-Thunder Spirit. His bro-kin thought to avenge him and died at the hands of the Red-Painted tribe. While the rest of the tribe prepared to leave, you were sharpening enough sticks to end the lives of every one of our enemies. All the men and pooches went out searching for you. When Bakkra found you, then took off that silly mask, the face beneath it filled me with fear.

"You have that look now, Zeta, and it frightens me even worse than before. Hate and loss don't mix well. They make a poison called vengeance. It will turn your heart black, and can spread through a tribe like a disease. Set aside the Night-Thunder Spirit and stick-slings. It was vengeance that killed your pa and bro-pa."

She had heard the story too many times. They had started out by trying to trade and make friends with the Red-Painted tribe, but one tribe had offended the other. Food was stolen. A woman was made to spread her legs. Depending on who told the story, the offenses came in a different order, from different sides, but the story always ended the same.

Our tribe had planned a raid. Our enemies had summoned their evil guardian, the Night-Thunder Spirit. Our brave men continued with the raid even after the spirit's attack, but the Red-Painted sinners against Gravan drove our men off with their stick-slings, killing Jebbam-bro-pa and a tribesman named Randall.

"I don't want vengeance," Zeta lied. "I just want some clean water to drink, and to wash my arm."

Chief Talmid smiled with more gum than tooth and nodded his head. "That is a good idea. Just remember, Zeta, violence brings violence. Blood thirsts for blood. Someone has to be the first to stop. Sometimes that means running away or letting a death go unavenged. If it saves a tribe, that's how it must be."

Zeta couldn't stomach the advice, but she didn't argue. She nodded. The chief seemed satisfied, so Zeta retreated from him.

Rod-non-pa whistled for his two male pooches, which he only ever called the strange word, "dogs". One was the chestnut-brown sire of Gorgon-pup and Chimera-pup, so Zeta had taken to calling him pa-pooch. That made the other one bro-pa-pooch. Penelope-pooch also joined them, albeit with less energy than the other pooches. Across Rod-non-pa's broad back was a spear loop, holding several of his skillfully crafted spears. He also discretely tucked a sling and a rock pouch under his fur mantle. He looked over his shoulder, and Zeta met his eye. She gave him the slightest nod. She had no love for the man, but she couldn't help but admire his deadly accuracy with a sling.

When he offered to carry Zeta, she told him that it would be good for her health to walk. Her present mind thought, *"No, you just want his hands to be free so he can be ready to fight wolf-pooches."*

THEY DIDN'T SAY a word to each other on the walk to the spring pool. They passed a tree, smeared with dried blood. It was either hers or Charra's. Rod-non-pa looked back to her as they passed the smear, but there wasn't anything to be said.

Emerging from the trees near the pool, Zeta's heart jumped into her throat. There he was — the red-speckled man-boy! He sat on the other side of the pool with a stick-sling in his hand. Three black wolf-pooches laid near him. Two young men with auburn hair and tan skin sparred with blunt sticks behind him on the rocky shore.

Rod-non-pa sprung into action, pulling his sling from his belt and loading it with a rock. His pooches started growling, taking on the aggressive demeanor of their master.

One of the young men shouted, "Non-aggresio! Compartos aguos, my friend!" The man-boy stood. The black wolf-pooches raised their hackles and wrinkled their snouts, exposing their long fangs.

Rod-non-pa shouted back, "Non-aggresio conti, my friend, pero nesso morta du lobos!"

Rod-non-pa spoke their foreign tongue? Zeta had no idea what they were saying, but she didn't care. This would be her only chance to take vengeance. She slipped one of Rod-non-pa's spears from the straps on his back with her uninjured hand. It was her odd hand, so it felt awkward, but it would be good enough to stab the red boy.

The young men were talking to each other when Rod-non-pa shouted again, "Su brohito roho usar una arco, my friend? Est verbotten de Gravan!"

"Est arco de-hi-ha, my friend! Vete ackee und de ascio!" The foreigner shouted back, grabbing the stick-sling from the red boy's hands. The wild-eyed man-boy used his free hands to grab the fur on the scruff of the wolf-pooches' necks. The other young man slapped the man-boy across the face and grabbed his arm, jerking it back to make him to release the wolf-pooch.

Zeta was certain that the stick-sling was the one which Charra had found. Now he was dead, and it was in their enemy's hands. Surely, this was Gravan's curse. Zeta vowed she would never touch a stick-sling again.

Rod-non-pa's sling hummed through the air, spinning overhead. He shouted one more time, "I'll sola mente mortar su lobos. Vass-ee-day ah-hora or *bleed*!"

"No!" the red-speckled man-boy squeaked. The spinning sling's whirling rose to a higher pitch and then silenced as Rod-non-pa released the stone, sending it across the pool in a flash. It struck one of the snarling wolf-pooches squarely on the head. With a yelp, it stumbled backwards.

The battle had begun!

———

THE FOREIGNERS YELLED and held their blunt sticks high, sprinting around the pool. Rod-pa pulled out a spear as he let out a thunderous roar of a battle call, charging around to meet the foreigners.

Zeta screamed, "ay, ay, ay!" and followed him, her own spear held high.

The pooches sprinted ahead of them, darting in front of Rod-pa as the two surviving wolf-pooches rushed to meet them.

Zeta's gaze was fixed on the red-speckled boy, who had stopped to pry a stone up from the muddy shore.

Before the pooches clashed with the wolf-pooches, the foreigners both pulled rocks from their pouches and chucked them. One struck bro-pa-pooch in the side, but didn't phase him. The sound of snarling beasts erupted as the larger wolf-pooches crashed into the pooches, quickly gaining the advantage. One had already clamped its jaws on pa-pooch's throat. It thrashed its head violently.

A moment later the men clashed. Rod-pa tackled the one who had done the yelling, then jabbed his spear sideways at the other, who knocked it aside using his blunt stick.

Zeta reached the fight. She thrust her spear at the standing man. In a swirl of the man's stick, the spear was knocked from her hands. The stick continued its spin and struck her head, sending a bolt of color into her eyes. The world whirled about her.

When she regained her senses, she found that she was lying on her back. Rod-pa was roaring and slamming the head of one of the men into the rocks as the other crawled towards a spear. Pa-pooch was laying down, as was one of the wolf-pooches. Penelope-pooch and bro-pa-pooch were a blur of gold and brown, battling the black wolf-pooch.

From the corner of Zeta's vision, a large rock tumbled through the air towards the pooches. Zeta watched it land with a solid crack against the side of Penelope-pooch's head, sending her to the ground in a lifeless heap.

"No!"

She couldn't take this! This wasn't happening! Her present self wanted desperately to change the replay. The name "Genevieve" was at the tip of her tongue. She looked over to see the red-speckled man-boy leaning down to pick up another rock. Her past self had gotten to her feet. She shouted, "You killed my pooch!"

Her present self resigned to let the replay continue. She had to accept this truth or she would never find her way back to her tribe.

She stood, her vision clouded with rage and fatigue, and began a careful approach towards the boy, ready to dodge his rock. He backed away. His eyes bugged as he held back his arm, stone in hand, threatening to throw it. His pale gaze shot towards the fighting pooches and men, then surveyed his surroundings as if searching for an escape. She had him cornered on the slate outcropping overhanging the deep end of the spring pool. He would either have to swim across or go through her. And he would *not* get through her.

He pleaded in his nonsense tongue, "Pour favor, no puedo nadar be-in. Stop, please!"

She did not stop, but continued her wary approach.

He rambled, "Pa-so adras. Pour favor, no key-erro me hurt you. No key-erro nada de dees sucedeera. Low see-ento neena bonita. Low see-ento much!"

She couldn't stand to hear another nonsense word. Zeta lifted her good arm up to protect her face as she charged. The red-speckled boy threw the rock, glancing the top of her head, sending her vision spinning. She felt her body collide with his, and then she was falling.

She plunged into the frigid water, her chest striking something hard — an elbow or knee of the man-boy, knocking the air out of her. She breathed in water, tried to cough, but choked.

Everything was spinning, swirling, frigid and dark. The red boy was clutching at her, clawing at her injured arm, sending shooting pain through her body.

She had to get to the surface, but which way was up?! The only thing she could see in the shadowy waters was the horrified grimace of the red-speckled man-boy. His red hair drifted and danced, waving like flames in the water as they sank together.

She coughed, gagged, choked. Her lungs burned, her throat constricted.

She could hear her heartbeat pounding in her ears, see it pulsing in her eyes.

Her skin was numb.

The boy's eyes were wide, staring straight through her, pale blue irises surrounded by white — a fish's vacant eyes, atop a fish's gasping, gaping maw.

Her vision brightened, filling with images. She had visions of the grasslands, Yephanie-ma suckling Charra, a rabbit on a skewer, her pa standing in a field, the sky, the crescent Soma.

Surya shone brilliantly through a hole in the trees. She floated upwards, lifting into the beam of light. Fading embers swirled.

Then...

Nothing.

She was nothing.

Time became meaningless.

The weight of an eternity passed in a heartbeat.

Her mind stirred in an empty place. She was alone, without a body. Her present self realized that she was back in slate-space, yet she was still in the replay.

Her past self said, "Hello?", then realized that she was a "she". Two forms slipped into the slate-space replay.

Zeta was reliving her first memory of slate-space, rather than returning to the *true* slate-space where the replay existed. She didn't need to experience any more — she knew everything that had happened from this point on.

This memory was the beginning of her life in The Land of Nod. She took control of her past self, breaking the replay by saying, "Oraxis, Genevieve, I'm done. I want out."

The slate-space replay faded seamlessly into what she knew to be the true slate-space where her current mind drifted. Though it was indistinguishable, she could sense the difference. She pulled herself out of slate-space, opening her eyes.

SHE WAS BACK in The Thin Forest. She sat up to find Oraxis sitting on a log nearby, watching her.

"Welcome back," he said.

Zeta lifted her arms, finding them both to be intact. She laid back down on the soft placental mat under her. The shock of her experience still reverberated in her mind.

She had *died*. Of that, she was certain.

The thought made the hair on her neck stand up. Her face went numb as a chill swept over her.

Her lungs had been filled with water. She had drowned in the spring pool. She started breathing heavily, feeling like she couldn't get enough air.

She *died!*

The tribal ancestors had punished her for breaking her vow and allowing Charra to be killed.

But then, she wasn't dead. Here she was, alive, in a new place. She still didn't know how she had gotten there. What had Jamji said about an island in the ocean?

What did that mean?

Zeta knew several stories about where a person went after they died. Her memory was still imperfect, so she didn't know where she had heard them, but she could think of at least four or five different stories of the afterlife. One told of judgment, with the reward of eternal bliss for being good, eternal torment for being evil. One told of a river where your mind was wiped clean and you drifted as an empty husk. The Happy Hunting Grounds was what her tribe believed. It was a land beneath The Realm of the Gods.

Is that what the Land of Nod was?

Cynical people didn't believe in any of it. They said that when you died, you simply ceased to be. Zeta always worried that the cynics were right — the afterlife was a story that people told themselves to find consolation in the death of a loved one. People like Chief Talmid, who would rather move on and accept a death instead of doing something about it.

She couldn't tell whether this afterlife was a place of judgment, of mind-cleansing, or of hunting. Maybe it was all of them. Certainly, the living could never fully understand the dead.

It didn't *look* how The Happy Hunting Grounds were supposed to look. There were no rolling plains as far as the eye could see. There were no herds of bison, grazing lazily under eternally blue skies. Wilhelm-pa, Jebbam-bro-pa, and Charra didn't greet her to share their cooked meats.

But Penelope-pooch *was* here.

Maybe the fields were beyond the forest? Maybe her ancestors were off on a hunt? Jamji had said that she was kin, so maybe she was an ancestor who died long before Zeta was born. They could have sent her to guide Zeta to the rest of her tribal ancestors, waiting in the rolling plains.

If Jamji was her ancestor, then she had witnessed that vow! She could be testing Zeta now to see if she deserved to join in the hunt!

A tiny ember of hope glowed in her heart. She might be with Charra again, soon.

Penelope-pooch came over and laid her head on Zeta's belly. Zeta pushed her fingers into the pooch's golden fur. Her guardian spirit, the golden hunter, her eternal companion. Without Penelope-pooch, she would truly be alone among these strangers. Did Penelope-pooch remember being killed by the man-boy? Did she remember Gorgon-pup, Chimera-pup, or pa-pooch? Would they be here?

"Zeta, are you okay?" Genevieve asked, approaching from the cabin.

She had nothing to say to the woman. She reached out with her mind to Jamji.

Jamji's voice rang in Zeta's mind, *"Zeta, you're back! What's up?"*

"I just...returned. From the replay of...my death."

Jamji took on a solemn tone. *"I'm close by. I'll be there in three minutes."*

Putting it into words and telling Jamji about it made her death real. It was like springing a trap, wrapping an invisible cord around her throat, constricting it. Tears welled in her eyes, clouding her view of the trees above.

She didn't want to die! She erupted into wailing sobs. She didn't want Charra or Penelope-pooch to die! Yephanie-ma and Rod-pa would have lost two children within as many days.

It wasn't right! It wasn't fair!

She got to her feet, stumbling away from the campfire, wailing, pulling at her leather tunic.

Oraxis and Genevieve followed in her shadow. Genevieve wept. She laid a hand on Zeta, but Zeta cast her off, falling to her knees. Only Penelope-pooch was allowed to comfort her, whimpering and licking her salty tears.

By the time Jamji arrived, Zeta was mumbling a rant of curses between sobs. "Curse Gravan. Curse Surya, Soma, and Varuna. Curse Anansi. Curse The Land of Nod, The Thin Forest, slate-space. Curse Oraxis and Genevieve! Curse death!"

Jamji ran to Zeta and fell to her knees, putting her arms around her. Zeta took Jamji's face into her hands.

"Jamji, bring me to them!"

A tear rolled down Jamji's cheek, glimmering in the light of her glowing skin. But she didn't speak.

"Bring me to the rolling fields — The Happy Hunting Grounds! I have a bow — I'm ready to hunt. My bro-kin, my pa, they're waiting for me!"

Jamji shook her head, barely able to squeak out the words, "They're not."

"They are! We just have to find them!"

"Zeta, they're gone. This isn't the afterlife, sis — it's just another messed-up life that you have to go through, riding on the same old rock as you were on before."

Zeta couldn't speak. Nothing made sense.

Oraxis said, "Be careful, Jamji. She's at her breaking point. We have to take this easy."

Genevieve placed her hand on Zeta's back, stroking it. With an unsteady voice, she said, "Tonight we'll just cry, okay? We'll mourn Zeta. Simple as that — no more questions, and no more answers, okay?"

And that was what they did.

15

MORNING AFTER

ZETA FINALLY WOKE up at 8:10. Who sleeps until 8:10? It was fine — the kid had been through a lot. At least she had slept.

Still, Jamji was certain that the breakfast which she had helped to prepare would be a dried-out disaster after sitting in warming pots for almost two hours.

Zeta pulled herself from the placental mat, stood, and stretched. Penelope-pooch danced circles around her. Pepper-pooch pawed at the ground nearby, hopping back and forth, brimming with excitement.

"Zeta wakes so I will lick her and she will pet me! She stood up! Zeta looked at me and now I will lick her," Pepper-pooch sent.

"Give her some room, Pep," Jamji thought-commanded.

"We'll bring the food to the table," Genevieve said. "Jamji, please stay with her."

Jamji approached Pepper-pooch, then scratched him behind the ears, silently watching Zeta. After greeting Penelope-pooch, Zeta approached Pepper-pooch, holding her hand out.

"Thanks for making him stop jumping," Zeta croaked in a morning voice.

Pepper pooch sniffed her hand. When he licked her, his massive tongue moistened her entire forearm. She didn't seem to mind, smiling slightly as Pepper-pooch blessed her with his scratchy kisses.

"It smells good, have you been cooking?" Zeta asked.

"Yep," Jamji said. "I know you're not feeling hungry, since your placental mat has been feeding you all night, but your stomach is empty so there'll be plenty of room for food. And, once you taste this stuff, you're gonna wanna gorge yourself. Trust me. C'mon."

She led Zeta to the stone table at the side of the cabin where the food was being laid out. Jamji pulled the lid from the skillet holding the bacon, leaning forward to take a deep whiff of its incredible aroma.

Zeta asked, "What is all this?"

Oraxis placed a glass pitcher and an iron kettle on the table. He rubbed his hands together, then pointed at the foods. "Bacon, eggs, pancakes, maple syrup, fruit compote, toast, orange juice, and coffee."

Genevieve returned from putting away the pot lids. She sat on the stone bench as she said, "It's a Telson tradition to cook a grand slam, all-American breakfast, the morning after."

Nobody had to ask, "the morning after *what*?"

Zeta picked up a pancake, gave it a sniff, and took a bite. Her eyes widened as she hummed, "mmm!"

"Divine, right? Try it with the syrup," Jamji said, pulling the stoneware bowl in front of Zeta.

Zeta dipped the pancake in the syrup and took another bite. "Oh, sweet Surya!" she exclaimed, her mouth full. She closed her eyes and made delighted grunting sounds as she savored the pancake.

Jamji laughed, then grabbed a handful of bacon. She shoved a piece in her mouth, then tossed a piece to Penelope-pooch. The rest went to Pepper-pooch.

Zeta squealed through a mouthful of food, "Pen loves it!" She picked up another piece of bacon, tossing it to her dog.

"Take it easy," Oraxis said, "leave some for the humans. Thank you, Gen."

Genevieve spooned a helping of scrambled eggs onto Oraxis's plate. Jamji and Zeta gathered their own helpings. Zeta had acclimated to the tradition of eating off a plate a while ago. The wooden utensils to the side of her plate, however, went unused.

"Food of the gods," Zeta said, between ecstatic bites.

Oraxis said, "Most Americans weren't gods."

"Yeah, just the Mormons," Genevieve laughed.

Zeta shrugged off the inside joke, returning to her food.

Eating real, honest-to-goodness food was one thing which Jamji would miss about living on Genesis once she moved to Soma station. Almost all offworlder nutrition came from overnight placental mat feeding, with the occasional snack of synth-slop for a quick midday refueling. Sure, if you wanted to indulge your senses you could load a feast construct and fool yourself into thinking you're having the most marvelous meal in history. Or you could replay the experience of your favorite meal, but it's not the same.

Zeta turned her head and sprayed a mouthful of something out onto the ground. "Ack! What is that?!" She pushed her mug away.

"Coffee," Genevieve laughed. "Sorry, I should have warned you. It's an acquired taste."

"Drink the orange juice," Oraxis said, "you'll like that."

They ate until their stomachs were ready to burst. The pooches made short work of the leftovers, licking the pots and plates clean. Zeta was a sticky mess of syrup and bacon grease. Genevieve went into the cabin, coming out with a stack of warm, wet washcloths. She handed one to Oraxis and one to Jamji, then took it upon herself to clean Zeta's face and hands.

"Thank you for sharing that meal with me," Zeta said, smiling mildly up at Genevieve. "Where do you find such delicious food?"

"Wal-Mart," Jamji said, wiping her hands clean.

After a round of chuckles, then a few beats of silence, Genevieve spoke in a gentle tone. "Zeta, do you think you're ready to talk, now? We can go back inside. Maybe lay in the hammock?" She had been cleaning Zeta's hands and now held them with care.

Zeta's mood darkened. "I...I don't know..."

Jamji stood and stepped away from the table as she said, "Not everyone likes to lie around all day, Gen. Want to take a walk, Zeta?"

Zeta nodded.

———

THEY WALKED in silence for a while. Oraxis and Genevieve brought their walking sticks, while Zeta brought her bow and arrows. The dogs ran ahead of them, returning from time to time to check in on their masters.

Jamji noticed that Oraxis was matching Zeta's pace, preparing to strike up an uncomfortable conversation. He cleared his throat. "Zeta, I'd like to explain how it came to be that you're alive again."

"Nothing ruins a pleasant walk like too much talking," Jamji said, from behind them.

"Zeta," Genevieve said, "if you don't want to hear about it yet, we can wait."

"No," Zeta said, "I need to know. I want to understand."

"Good," Oraxis said. "Before I start, I want to clarify that there is no such thing as an afterlife."

Zeta scoffed. "Okay, sure."

Oraxis cleared his throat again. "Not long after you were born, Genevieve and I visited your tribe."

Zeta looked from Oraxis to Genevieve. "You saw me when I was a babe?"

"We did!" Genevieve said. "And you were a precious little thing!"

"You met Yephanie-ma and Wilhelm-pa?"

"Well," Genevieve said, looking at Oraxis, "we aren't supposed to talk about the people we met or the things we saw."

Oraxis continued, "What's important to know is that Genevieve did something special to your alpha that day. *Alpha* is what we call our first life, and *beta* is what we call our second life; the one you are living now. We call what Genevieve did *alpha seeding*. She put a small version of a double-mind in your head. Once you were old enough to talk, your memories started being collected inside of an orb, far away, under the ocean. It also collected the way you think and speak, along with the directions on how to make your entire body. The orb storing all your past experiences is still under The Great Ocean, right now."

Jamji decided that some levity was in order. She caught up and walked beside Zeta. She gestured with wiggling fingers, saying, "Syn-Cen!"

Zeta humored her with a confused laugh.

"Yes," Oraxis said, perturbed, "the place I'm talking about is the Synthetic Intelligence Central Processing Facility, which we shorten to Syn-Cen. That's the place under the island in the ocean that Jamji had told you about. There's a floating island above Syn-Cen, but the place where our orbs are kept is in the ground under the water. It's also a place where a being named Cain lives."

"A *being*?" Zeta asked.

Oraxis sighed, "It'll take a while to explain synthetic intelligences, so I'll use a metaphor and say Cain is a spirit."

"A *spirit*? He's not a *god*?" Jamji said with mock surprise.

"Jamji!" Oraxis barked. "If you're going to keep interrupting—"

"Hey!" Jamji said, stepping in front of Oraxis and turning to face the man down. "The Pips *do* call Cain a synth-god. Lots of people do. If either of the Pips were telling the story, they'd call him a god, so I think that's what you should call him. They're better storytellers than you, by a long shot."

Genevieve said, "Okay, Zeta knows it's just a metaphor anyways, so we can call Cain a god."

"Fine," Oraxis grumbled. Jamji smirked and turned back around, leading them in resuming their walk.

Oraxis said, "A *god* named Cain lives in Syn-Cen. All of your life, he gathered the information about you — the story of Zeta — and he saved it inside a *magical* relic, called an aposynchronic orb. Then, after you...died..."

Jamji glanced back at Zeta to read her reaction. Her sober gaze was fixed on the path in front of her feet.

Oraxis continued, "You were resurrected at Syn-Cen. Your body was made anew, and your mind was put back together. Your new body and mind were made better than your first one. I'm sure you have noticed that your body is stronger and faster than before. And your new double-mind gives you the ability to do things like communicate with the Worldnet, or use slate-space. When you summon a replay, your double-mind is accessing your orb."

"I did die, then," Zeta said, flatly.

"You did," Oraxis said, softly.

"But you resurrected me at Syn-Cen."

"Not us," Oraxis corrected. "It's an automated process — you could say Cain did it. After that, Genevieve and I picked you up from there and brought you here."

"Why didn't you take me back to my tribe?"

Oraxis was silent, so Genevieve took the question. He was probably tossing her the hot potato since she was the compassionate one. Genevieve said, "Zeta, this second life is a magnificent gift. You're essentially immortal, now. If you were to slip and fall and break your head open on a rock, you'd be resurrected at Syn-Cen again within a matter of months, as good as new. Your new mind and body can do superhuman things. Very few Edenites receive these gifts. They are special, but they come at a great price. It means leaving your past life behind and devoting yourself to the greater good of Genesis. You guessed as much after we showed you the Earth construct."

"Are you saying I can't go back? Ever?"

"No, you can't," Genevieve said, "I'm sorry, Zeta."

Zeta slowed to a stop. "But there *are* ways to travel there! You know the way, or else you wouldn't have been able to get there and put the alpha seed thing in my head."

Genevieve made a move to hold Zeta's hand, but Zeta dodged

her. Genevieve said, "It's a tragedy, I know. It breaks my heart that you died so young, leaving your kin and tribe with so much heartache. But the Zeta that lived in Eden died in Eden. You are, in many ways, a different person than she was. This mindset is one way that many betas cope with their situation. You share the memories with that other version of yourself, but you are a new person, in a new place, with a new purpose."

Tears rolled down Zeta's cheeks. "There has to be a way to tell them I'm okay. Yephanie-ma's lost so much, Genevieve." Zeta reached for Genevieve's hand now, squeezing it pleadingly. "If I can't go back, can't you just...tell her I'm okay?"

Now Genevieve wept, pulling Zeta into an embrace. "The best we can do is keep this planet safe for your tribe and your ancestors. That's your purpose, now, Zeta."

Jamji sniffed, turning away to watch the pooches racing through the forest nearby. It turned her stomach to listen to Oraxis and Genevieve dance around the truth, and for Zeta to be in so much pain. It all came down to the fundamentals. At its core, the Genesis Faction Charter was an unethical, backwards atrocity. All the other factions knew it, and it was about time someone took the keys.

AFTER A GOOD DEAL MORE CRYING, they were walking back to the cabin.

Zeta broke the silence. "Why couldn't all the neoprims have orbs?"

Jamji spun around to walk backwards for a moment, pointing at Zeta. "That's a *damned* good question, sis-kin!" She smirked at Oraxis as she awaited an answer.

"Jamji, please!" Oraxis exclaimed, then addressed Zeta gently. "It was a tough decision we had to make long ago when our people first came to Genesis. We saw the value of converting neoprims into advanced humans, since they would have lived the life that they were then working to preserve, but if we resurrected too many people, we'd have way too many Noddites. Remember, the objective of Genesis is to emulate primitive life, for the preservation of the human species. Crowding the planet with too many advanced people introduces more risk of leading The Monster from the Stars to our doorstep. Remember, Noddites don't die, so if we had brought back every neoprim since the colony was founded, Nod would overflow with people in just a few hundred years."

As Oraxis spoke, Genevieve lectured Jamji via mindspeak. *"Jamji, I appreciate you helping us with Zeta's bootstrapping, but if you're going to turn into an anti-Genesis propagandist, then it's time for you to leave."*

"Fine. Zeta's smart, I'm sure she'll figure out for herself that the Genesis Faction is a joke."

"Jamji, I told you last year I was done fighting with you about the factions, so I'd appreciate it if you wouldn't stir the argument back up again."

"Ok, 'shut up Jamji', I hear you."

They walked in silence again.

Jamji counted six minutes and forty-two seconds before Zeta declared, "I'm going to live *forever*."

"Sort of," Oraxis said. "Forever is a very long time. If something happens to Syn-Cen and our orbs are destroyed, you and the rest of us could not be resurrected again. Our last death would be our True and Final Death."

Jamji offered, "You can also lose your orb if your resurrection goes wrong. Like, if your brain rejects the double-mind or if you can't stop breaking your replays."

"Yes," Genevieve rushed to interject, "but the risk of that is behind you, now. Getting your double-mind working right is a tricky bit of business that goes wrong sometimes. When it does, it can destroy the mind beyond repair. That's what bootstrapping is meant to prevent, so when you broke out early, we had quite a scare. We're still not sure how it happened, but we think it has something to do with your connection to Penelope-pooch."

Zeta looked around until she caught sight of her dog, sniffing around between the trees, followed by the massive, gray-glowing Pepper-pooch. "How is it that Penelope-pooch is alive, too?"

Jamji said, "Any animal you spent a lot of time with, and you consider your own, gets to be stored in your orb. The nanites in your brain crawled into hers when she was a pup sleeping on your bed furs. That's how I got to keep Pepper-pooch. It doesn't save their experiences, but it saves their mind and body right alongside yours. When you got resurrected, she got brought back, too."

Zeta stopped walking again. She whispered, "Penelope-pooch died right before I did. I..." She choked, then swallowed hard. "I hope they buried her with me."

Zeta broke down as another round of sobs overtook her. This was a lot for her to absorb. Jamji and Genevieve both put their arms around her and helped her to walk the rest of the way back to the cabin.

Oraxis and Genevieve spent the rest of the day busying themselves with simple tasks as Jamji watched over Zeta. Pepper-pooch curled up like a giant grey croissant by the campfire, with Zeta and Penelope-pooch cradled in the nook formed by his body. As he fell asleep, a huge, black-furred placental mat grew beneath him.

Zeta used mindspeech to talk to Jamji a few times, asking clarifying questions about Syn-Cen, Cain, and the alpha seeding. Jamji behaved herself, giving simple, unbiased answers.

Part of Jamji itched to leave. Now that Zeta had experienced her death replay, there wasn't much else left for Jamji to help with. Zeta would be fine on her own, now.

Maybe.

Looking over at the girl's bloodshot eyes, peeking over Pepper-pooch's foreleg at the flickering fire, Jamji resigned to stay for a *little* while longer.

16

PURPOSE

Another month passed.

The pain was fading, but the longing for her tribe and family stayed with Zeta like a splinter under her skin.

She distracted herself with educational constructs, bow lessons with Jamji, and walks through the Thin Forest. Genevieve had taken her into a few constructs to show her these acted-out stories called "movies" that people used to watch. They were pretty weird — first you'd be looking at one thing, then in a blink you were looking at another thing. Then it's suddenly a different day? Really hard to follow.

Math was easier. After a few lessons, Zeta understood how to use numbers. She never had the occasion to count higher than ten as an alpha, but now she juggled huge numbers with ease. It helped that the synthetic half of her double-mind did most of the work. She learned about numbering years and began to get a sense of the time-lines of Earth's history.

They were inside the cabin, staying warm and out of the rain, on the afternoon when Zeta decided to replay the Earth data dump. When she returned to her body, Oraxis and Genevieve were laying together in the hammock. Zeta was laying in her usual bedding spot near Jamji, who was either sleeping or doing something in slate-space.

It occurred to Zeta that she could do WoQS cross-references against the Earth data dump, to see how old Oraxis and Genevieve were. They said they were alive when The Monster sent The Message, so...

"You're three thousand years old?!"

Oraxis gave his correction in a half-asleep slur, "Three thousand four hundred eighty-one. And that's *Earth* years. Those are shorter than Genesis years."

Genevieve lifted her head from Oraxis's chest and smiled to Zeta, saying, "The polite thing to say after throwing out a big number like that for a woman's age is to tell her that she doesn't look a day over twenty."

Oraxis cleared his throat, then spoke without opening his eyes. "We don't usually count the years we didn't experience. We spent most of those years as inanimate data — aposynchronic orbs on the colony ship. Interstellar travel is a time-consuming affair. But it's still correct to say we're old. I've lived through nine hundred fifty-six Earth years, myself."

"Old? Speak for yourself," said Genevieve, tugging Oraxis's beard. "I'm only nine hundred fifty-four."

"What's it like to live for that long? Aren't you...weary?" Zeta asked.

Oraxis chuckled.

Genevieve said, "Well, you know what it's like to live for a year. Do you remember everything that happened every year of your life?"

Zeta said, "I'm still piecing some of my memories together, but I know what you mean. You only remember the important parts."

"Do you think you would feel more weary if you lived for another year?"

"Of course not! But it's different when you're young. By the time people are old, they start talking about being ready to die."

Genevieve laughed. "That's more a product of their body's degrading physical state than it is of their eagerness to live. You're as old as you feel. Our enhanced bodies and brains keep us feeling young, so as far as I'm concerned, we're young. It's not like all that time behind you is some sort of weight you have to carry every moment. It's all just history."

"Can you remember everything from all those years?" Zeta asked.

"Not even close," said Oraxis, with his eyes still closed. "We have the same fallible meat for brains as anyone else. If I couldn't look it up in my log, I wouldn't be able to tell you what I had for breakfast yesterday. Granted, we have years of experiences stored in our aposynchronic orbs, but that's different. Also, there's a limit to their capacity, so we have to be selective about what gets saved in full detail and what's just transcribed to descriptive text."

Zeta said, "Text — written words. I've learned about text. That means you could *read* your own life's story?"

"Sure," Genevieve said, "but who wants to go back and read a transcript of their life? Boring! The point of the transcript is so you can do searches for things that have happened. Like how many times your old man has called you a nag. Let's see..." She closed her eyes for a moment.

Oraxis groaned.

Genevieve opened her eyes. "Seven hundred sixty. But who's counting?"

Oraxis grumbled something.

Genevieve leaned in and kissed his cheek. "Make that seven hundred sixty-one. You'll also live for a very long time, Zeta, so my advice is this: learn to live in the *present*. Every day has its own joys and sadnesses, challenges and victories. Cherish the parts of your past that are worth cherishing, and for the parts that aren't? Leave them behind. Sure, learn from your mistakes so you don't repeat them, but don't let the past weigh you down."

Zeta nodded.

"Most importantly," Genevieve continued, "find a purpose that gives you goals to work towards and problems to solve. Once you've got a purpose, you'll never grow weary of waking up and embracing every day, no matter how old you get."

ZETA TRIED to take Genevieve's advice to heart, but every night the spring pool loomed at the edge of her mind. She tried to remind herself to live in the present, but how could she move on when her family and tribe were just a replay away? What's worse, they were half a world away, oblivious to her existence. She was dead to them.

She needed to find her purpose in this second life.

Sure, protecting the neoprims from The Monster from the Stars was important, but when she thought about facing The Monster, all she could imagine was being swallowed whole, along with the rest of the planet. She was a fool for thinking she could do anything useful. Practicing shooting her bow only made things worse. How was a pathetic little arrow going to do anything against a planet-conquering alien?

After missing the target for the fourth shot in a row, Zeta let out a primal shout, stomped to the tree, pulled an arrow out of the bark, and stabbed it into the center of the target.

"Bullseye," Jamji said flatly.

"It's pointless! Why are we even bothering with these sticks and stones, anyway? What are these going to do against *them*?" She pointed up.

Jamji shrugged. "It's good to know how to use all kinds of weapons. You build your coordination and focus, gain confidence in your power. Mainly, it's just fun to shoot a bow. Satisfies a primal urge to kill from a distance, maybe? I don't know."

"Well, if it's supposed to help my confidence, it's failing! I feel...so small." Zeta looked at the bow in her hand, "I want to protect the neoprims, Jamji, but I don't know what I can do."

Jamji walked towards Zeta. "Some people — cultural influencers we call them — travel throughout Eden, manipulating the neoprims. They try to guide their way of life, their way of thinking. They think they can make life in Eden better, but it's not working. If nothing else, they have to keep the neoprims from advancing their tech level by doing things like growing crops or using Gravan-cursed weapons like that." Jamji pointed to the bow.

Zeta looked to the bow, then back to Jamji. "You know about Gravan?"

Jamji laughed. "I lived with your ancestors, Zeta. I heard the same age-old lies you did. Gravan and his curse were stories made up by the founders of Genesis — Oraxis and Genevieve's people — to scare the neoprims away from anything more advanced than sticks and stones."

Zeta looked at the bow again. Her whole life, she had believed that bows were forbidden and powerful weapons. Her fearful elds never even taught her their proper name, calling them "stick-slings" instead. But it was just a stick and a string, and the gods didn't care one way or the other about it. If there even were gods.

"Other people spend all their time studying the sciences. Doing experiments, implementing their results. Ecology, biology, geology, climatology. If it ends in *ology*, it's something you could devote a life of study into and still only scratch the surface. I mean, there's nothing wrong with any of that, and Genesis certainly needs the help. The ecosystem's an absolute mess. You can't just dump all the plants and animals out of The Ark like Noah and expect them to thrive, but that's basically what they did."

Jamji had lost Zeta's interest — she was imagining The Monster again. "Jamji, don't they know...what if they do all this work to make Genesis better, only to lose it to an alien? How are they going to protect the neoprims if The Monster returns?"

"Well, to be honest, if you're interested in fighting off aliens, I'm afraid you're on the wrong team. If any of the factions are gonna save humanity from being exterminated, it's gonna be the Guard. You've heard about 'em, right?"

"Yeah, one of the five factions. They're the ones that like to fight."

Jamji smirked. "You could put it that way, but it's not that simple. The way I'd put it is that they understand that you can't expect to stay alive in a hostile environment by hiding in a bush, like the Genesissies are trying to do. The Guard's goal is simple: protect humanity. If we can learn to be stronger, faster, and smarter than our alien enemies, we can defeat them. Someday, the Guard's gonna face off with The Monster From the Stars, and they're gonna *win*."

Zeta liked the sound of the Guard Faction. They were actually *doing* something.

Jamji continued, "Easier said than done, though. From the limited information we have, The Monster seems to be the ultimate intellect-predator. Every time it conquers a planet, it gets stronger. That includes what it gained from consuming Earth. It knows everything about humans now. We can be sure it'll use that knowledge against us."

Jamji pulled an arrow from the target. She held her hand out, requesting the bow. Zeta handed it over. Jamji nocked the arrow, aimed diagonally upwards, and released. A satisfying *shick* was followed by a thud and a squeak from above. She jogged a few yards away, then bounded up a tree with the grace of a jungle cat. She dropped back to the ground, walked back to Zeta, and held the arrow up, presenting a skewered squirrel. "You can't hide from a super-predator like a scared little animal. The Monster caught our scent once. It will sniff us out again. It knows we're smart, and it still wants what we've got. It's just a matter of time."

She pushed the arrow through the squirrel, pulling the shaft all the way through the animal rather than going against the arrowhead's barbs. She threw the kill, overhand, into the forest. Pepper-pooch appeared between the distant trees, catching the morsel and swallowing it whole. She wiped her hand down the shaft of the arrow, cleaning off most of the blood, then handed it back to Zeta, along with the bow.

JAMJI WIPED her bloodied hand off on the bark of the tree as she said, "You know what the other factions are doing to save humanity? The Clanculi actually had a pretty good plan — run and hide, then run some more. Don't tell anybody where you went and don't leave a trace. It's a hell of a lot smarter than this hiding-in-plain-sight thing that Genesis is trying. I'd predict that the Clanculi will survive, maybe even longer than the rest of us. That's assuming they don't split into factions and kill each other off. But so what if they make it? Imagining that another faction is hiding out somewhere on the other side of the galaxy doesn't do us a lot of good, does it?"

Zeta opened her mouth to answer, but Jamji continued.

"The Proliferans think reproducing like bunnies in the spring is the thing to do. It's a viable strategy — you see animals do it all the time. By that, I mean produce so many offspring that predators can't possibly eat 'em all. A few slip between the cracks at the babe-feast and survive to make swarms of their own. If feeding your kin to monsters is your idea of survival, then, sure, Prolifera may be the faction for you!"

Jamji checked over her shoulders, obviously for show, since there was nobody around for kilometers. She continued, quieter than before. "But the worst are the Astri. Don't get me wrong — they've adapted to life in space better than any other faction, and they're deeply integrated with their technology. I admire that about them. As you know, I'm a bit of a cyborg myself. But they took their reinvention way too far. Yes, they've got a good shot at going the distance, but we're talking about saving *humanity*, right? *Humans?* The Astri gave up on the whole 'being human' thing a long time ago, so even if they survive longer than the rest of us, it won't be *humans* that survived. Does that even count?"

Zeta shrugged. "It doesn't seem like it."

Jamji pointed at the southern sky. "The largest Astrus Faction colony in a ten light-year radius is *right there*, orbiting our planet, attached to us by a cable. They don't even have *bodies*, Zeta! One hundred thousand brains hooked together and combined into one! It's called a hive mind, and it's damn creepy! Forget about The Monster. Mark my words: the alien invasion that Genesis needs to worry about is the Astri, riding down on the backs of Specters."

Zeta had a hard time understanding what Jamji was suggesting. "You mean like, ghosts?"

"No, Zeta. *Specters,*" Jamji said, leaning forward and emphasizing the word as if it was supposed to mean something different when she said it that way. "You don't know about Specters?"

"Of course I do! The elds would tell scary stories about—"

"Freaking *seriously?!*" Jamji shouted at the air. She turned and punched a tree, knocking off a chunk of bark. She instantly calmed as she turned to Zeta, grabbing her by the arms. "Zeta, we're not going back to the cabin tonight. If Oraxis and Genevieve aren't gonna teach you what's important, then I will."

Pepper-pooch had trotted to join them. Jamji sprung into the air, flipping and landing on his back. She said, "We're gonna get some distance and then settle in for the night. Call for Penelope-pooch and run southwest. Pepper-pooch'll follow you. I'm heading to slate-space for a minute."

Zeta nodded once. *"Pen? Are you close?"*

"I'm drinking water from a creek close to you. I could hear you talking and I smell Pepper-pooch."

"Come to me. We're going for a run."

She heard the incoming scuttle of Penelope-pooch dodging through underbrush and crunching over pine needles. Once the golden streak that was her pooch was in sight, Zeta turned to the southwest, clutching the bow in her hand as she broke into a run.

Whatever this was about, she trusted Jamji's judgement. She'd follow her sis-kin anywhere.

17

SPECTERS

"No!" Pip-Tau shouted.

"Why not? I think it works great!" Pip-Rho chirped, returning to her battle with the typewriter.

The ancient typewriter's strikers were a blur as they attacked the paper, hammering words into existence with the rapid-fire intensity of a machine gun. The "ding-shick" of the margin bell and carriage return formed a rhythmic back-beat to her creation. Once it was completed, the paper flitted into the air and settled into a pile to her left. A fresh page fed itself into the typewriter, replacing the finished one with the seamless efficiency of a relay runner.

The white porcelain cherub that was Pip-Tau's avatar floated to the completed pile. "This is all one chapter? This is way too long for one chapter." She snatched up the page, smearing the wet ink. Her solid black eyes scanned the text for less than a second before she crumpled it up and threw it at Pip-Rho. "Do you even know how novels work? You can't add another P.O.V. character this far into it!"

Pip-Rho didn't bother lifting her solid white eyes from the type-writer, letting the paper wad ricochet harmlessly off the head of her glossy, black cherub avatar — Pip-Tau's negative image. The paper unfurled in the air, smoothing out and drifting back to the pile, settling into place just in time to be covered by another completed page.

Pip-Rho said, "This coming from the queen of the Deus *Lex Machina*." She punctuated the insult with an aggressive whack of the carriage return arm.

"What?!" A swarm of notecards covered with illegible scribbles lifted from the floor, organizing themselves into a complex formation in the air. Glowing lines appeared, linking circled words in an intricate web. "Lex underpins the *entire* story!"

Pip-Rho rolled her eyes, though lacking pupils reduced the effect. Ask Pip-Tau who was really behind the Kennedy assassination and she'll come up with a plot involving Lex sending an Arnold Schwarzenegger robot back in time.

Their novel, tentatively titled "Black and White", was already approaching three hundred thousand words, and they hadn't even agreed on the climax yet. Pip-Rho doubted that anyone besides Genevieve would read a historic fantasy novel featuring a virtual universe of 1950s black and white T.V. shows, brought to life by Googolplex.

In Pip-Rho's idea for the climax, the characters would outsmart the synth-god and send it into a crash loop by presenting it with a to-be-determined moral duality paradox.

Pip-Tau agreed that it would be awesome if Andy Taylor delivered the killing blow, using some clever bit of homespun wisdom. They also agreed that Andy and Lex should be alone. They would meet in the Gunsmoke universe — Main Street, Dodge City, high noon.

But Andy wouldn't be wearing a gun! Gasp!

It writes itself, really.

Minor problem: he wasn't one of the original P.O.V. characters, and they were writing in first person. They sure as hell weren't making Lex, their enigmatic antagonist, a P.O.V.. They could go back and inject earlier Andy chapters, but that would bloat their word count even more. Another one of the existing P.O.V.'s could watch the showdown from side-stage, but then it would lose its teeth.

Simple solution: introduce a new P.O.V. when it's time for the showdown. They already had four, so what's one more? Maybe even two more? What if Barney Fife showed up for the essential "high tower surprise"?

Pip-Rho didn't see the problem. They had been flaunting conventions since their much-debated "intro to the prelude" — a fourth-wall-breaking monologue by Rod Serling.

The antique phone on the wall of their quaint grayscale cabin in the Monochrome Woods rang as Pip-Rho received a WorMS message.

Incoming conversation request from Jamji Telson.

"Alright, you keep chewing on it," Pip-Rho said, drifting across the room to the phone, "Jamji's calling."

"Jamji! Patch me in!"

"Sorry, Tau, private convo."

The suspended notecards drifted to the floor as Pip-Tau sank to the couch. "What am I, chopped liver?"

"What can I say, I'm her favorite," Pip-Rho laughed, picking up the receiver, accepting the conversation request.

———

"AHOY-HOY," Pip-Rho mindspoke to Jamji. She stayed silent in the construct, keeping the conversation private.

Jamji paused. *"What?"*

"It's an old-timey hello. What's up, sis? Wanna join our construct?"

"No," Jamji said, *"I mean, no offense, but—"*

"Fine, you wouldn't fit in here, anyway. No color."

"Rho, I've got a problem. You're the solution."

"*I'm listening.*"

"*You've heard Oraxis and Genevieve are bootstrapping a new beta?*"

"*Yeah, Zeta-Beta! We're super excited to meet her! Can't wait!*"

"*Well, your wait is over.*"

"Oh?" Pip-Rho looked over at Pip-Tau, then back to the phone. "*You're introducing me to her? Jamji-sis, do O-pa and Gen-ma know what you're up to?*"

"*Nope.*"

"*Did you kidnap her?*"

"*No! Seriously, Rho?*"

"*They don't let anyone meet their betas until the ceremony, so how is it you're running around with her behind their backs? I call shenanigans. Show your cards.*"

"*Rho, they asked me for help! Eighty-nine days ago, on her second day as a beta, Zeta broke out of the protocol early and ran away—*"

"*Shut up! She broke out?!*" Pip-Rho already liked this kid.

"*Yeah, so they had me track her down, then asked me to stick around and help. We didn't want to tell you guys about it since you'd—*"

"*Jealously hold it against all of you forever?*"

"*Basically.*"

"*Well, you were right. I sincerely hate the lot of you now, but you've got a shot at redemption if this is good. Don't worry, I won't tell goody-Tau-shoes. She'd run and tattle to ma and pa if she found out what we're up to. So, what're we up to?*"

Jamji caught Pip-Rho up on Zeta's unique bootstrapping experience, with all its ups and downs. Jamji dwelled on the things she thought Oraxis and Genevieve should have done differently. Pip-Rho considered the uncharitable critique a bit naïve. Was Jamji really a good judge of proper bootstrapping technique? She had never done it herself, never received training, probably never even watched a training video about it. Not that Pip-Rho wanted to argue about it — she just put the thoughts onto the pile of things to consider.

What Jamji had contacted Pip-Rho about was that today she found out Zeta hadn't learned about the Specters. Little Zeta-Beta had received a proper Earth data dump, complete with The Monster. These days she was being trained in handling her double-mind and other Noddite 101 stuff.

But nothing about Specters.

"When did they teach you about Specters?" Pip-Rho asked Jamji, via mindspeak.

"Around the same time as The Monster. You?"

"Stumbled on the topic in WoQS, then looked up a construct about 'em on Bibliotheca. Watched it in slate-space, all by myself. Scared me shitless," Pip-Rho laughed. *"I avoided going outside at night for a month after that."*

"See, that's what we're trying to avoid. Nobody should have to stumble onto the Specters."

Pip-Rho smelled what Jamji was cooking. *"So, we're teaching her about them tonight? She'll still be scared."*

"But at least she won't be alone. And I can't imagine a single person in the universe better suited to host a Specter data dump construct than you."

"I was wondering when you'd finally get to the flattery."

"Please, Rho!"

"Begging, too? Alright, fine, let's do this."

Pip-Tau literally flipped when Pip-Rho refused to tell her what Jamji called about. When Pip-Rho subsequently ducked out of the Black and White writing construct, slipping back to slate-space, Pip-Tau started spamming her. Pip-Rho told WorMS to silence the pest's notifications for the next 10 hours, then set to work.

She could have improvised the data dump, but she had some time to prep, so she pulled together some materials. An hour later, she got the message that Jamji had settled down for the night with Zeta. She wrapped up her edits and loaded the construct, sending invites to Jamji and Zeta.

The construct's initial setting was a rolling plain. A herd of Zebras grazed nearby, under the bright midday light of Surya. A family of giraffes graced the view in the distance.

Zeta accepted the invite. She popped into existence, followed by Jamji. The girl was as cute as a button!

"Well, Jamji," Pip-Rho said, nudging her. "You gonna introduce me, or..."

"Oh," Jamji said, "Zeta, this is Pip-Rho, our sis-kin I was talking about."

Pip-Rho gave a floating curtsey. Zeta gave her jet black porcelain cherub-woman avatar an assessing look, saying, "Hi. Are you really like that in real life?"

"Nah," Pip-Rho said, laughing, "I'm really a brain encased by a huge alien tumor inside an invisible, giant, metal egg in space."

Zeta laughed. She probably thought it was a joke. "Well, whatever you really look like, the way you look in this construct is beautiful. You remind me of a polished stone, come to life."

The girl has good taste.

"Well," Pip-Rho said, "I think *you're* freaking adorable! Can I hug you?"

"Okay..."

As she squeezed her new sis-kin, she had to repress the sudden urge to cry. What was that about? Maybe she was lamenting Zeta's impending transition from blissful ignorance to fearful knowledge, or some such sap.

"Zeta," Pip-Rho said, pulling back from the hug and looking into her eyes, "this is going to be pretty intense. Before we start, you should know that even though the Specters are scary, they're nothing like The Monster From the Stars. They're a problem, yes, but we're getting closer to solving it every day. We can do this. Hey! You can even help!"

Zeta gave her a nod, looking at Jamji and nodding again. A hint of a smile came to her lips.

Pip-Rho mindspoke to Jamji, *"Are you guys whispering to each other?"*

"Maybe," Jamji replied.

Jealousy washed over Pip-Rho. *"You'd better not be making fun of me."*

"We're not," Jamji mindspoke. *"Can we get on with this?"*

"Fine."

Pip-Rho rose slightly, her tiny wings fluttering, as she gestured to the landscape around them with open arms. "This is the scene of the first confirmed Specter sighting, a little over three hundred years ago."

Zeta took in the scene, making a full circle. "This is on Genesis, right?"

"Yes, in the area we call Berm's Savanna."

"It must be far from where I lived. I've never seen animals like this before. I like the black and white stripes on those big deer."

"Zose're zebra, Zeta." Pip-Rho laughed at herself. Jamji humored her with a snort and a shake of the head.

"Zebra," Zeta said, trying out the word.

The thunderclap of a sonic boom made Zeta jump, throwing her hands up as if to cover her head. A thin, black line descended from the sky, coming to an abrupt stop and pooling into an undulating, amorphous ink blot in the sky. Looking at a Specter was like looking at a hole in space. They were absolute black — zero reflectivity.

It hovered over the zebra herd, sending the animals into a panicked dash. They brayed as they ran, kicking up a cloud of dust. The Specter tracked the herd, keeping them in its shadow for just a few seconds. Next, a black tendril descended from the alien's under-side, plucking a single specimen out of the mass. The zebra kicked the air as the tendril lifted it, swiftly engulfing and absorbing the victim into its black void.

The Specter thinned into a black line as it retreated at supersonic speed. Another sonic boom rocked Berm's Savanna in its wake.

Pip-Rho shook her fist at the alien, shouting, "Bring back that zebra!"

She looked over to Zeta, to see if her comic relief had helped soften the frightfulness of the scene. Nope, the girl looked to be in shock. Her breathing was shallow, and she staggered a bit.

Pip-Rho held Zeta's arm and stroked her back. "You okay, Zeta-sis?"

Zeta gaped at the sky where the Specter had disappeared, eyes wide, chest heaving.

"Wow," Jamji mindspoke to Pip-Rho, *"that shook her to the core. You think this was a mistake?"*

"Did she react like this after seeing Oraxis's version of *The Monster?*"

"Dunno, wasn't there."

Zeta looked at the Zebras. They were settling down again. A few started grazing.

"That black thing that took the Zebra was a Specter," Jamji said. "They're aliens, sort of like The Monster from the Stars, only they live in our system. There are a lot of things we don't know about them, but we're sure they're not as dangerous as The Monster. Or, if they are, they haven't shown it yet."

Zeta fell to her knees in the grass. "They eat humans, too."

Strange — that was a statement, not a question.

"How'd you know that?" Jamji asked.

"They ate my pa," Zeta said, half-dazed. "We called it a Night-Thunder Spirit."

Pip-Rho met Jamji's eyes. Well, this was *not* going the way she had expected! They sat in silence for a moment. Pip-Rho wasn't sure whether to continue or let her come to terms with what she just saw and save the rest for another day.

Zeta resolved the conflict by looking up at Pip-Rho and asking, "How much do you know about these aliens?"

Pip-Rho shrugged. "Not as much as I'd like to, but more than anybody else."

"I want you to teach me about them, Pip-Rho," Zeta stood, taking on the eager intensity of a person getting their first drink of water in days. "Teach me everything."

Pip-Rho didn't miss a beat. "Okay, let's talk motive. Why did it eat that Zebra? At first they only snatched up animals. Why? Well, *I* think they were sampling Genesis life, trying to figure out if the animals we brought to the planet were intelligent. We're sure this wasn't the first abduction, since random sonic booms — that thunderclap you heard — had been detected since we got to Genesis. We just never knew what was making them until this video was caught. So, of course, everyone freaked out about it. A lot of people said we should have just run away and found a different planet to call home. Maybe one a little less alien-infested? The thing is, the Specters weren't causing a lot of problems. At least, not at first..."

Pip-Rho cut the scene to Flint Ochaway's Lagoon. Jamji and Zeta stood in warm, knee-deep water as Pip-Rho hovered above it. A pair of dark-skinned neoprims stood in their midst, sporting immodest loincloths. An attractive young man — the world-famous Flint Ochaway — tossed a net into the water. It splashed immediately in front of them. A mother carried her baby on the shore, shouting in a foreign tongue to someone in the distance.

Pip-Rho said, "For years the Specters would show up out of nowhere, randomly pick up an animal, and zip away. Until one day..."

A thunderclap ripped through the air. Zeta flinched, as did the neoprims in the construct. The Specter spread out above them, blotting out Surya's light. The water of the lagoon churned and spiraled unnaturally, flowing around their legs and clouding with silt.

Flint abandoned his net, shouting and pointing at the hole in the sky. He crashed through the water in retreat. Zeta was crouching, eyes wide. Primal fear burned in her eyes and posture. Pip-Rho could practically hear her instincts imploring her to run, despite her conscious awareness that this was just a construct.

Adding to the girl's unease would be that she was also feeling the Specter Shadow Effect — an uneasy lifting sensation, the sudden onset of nausea, and a buzzing or tingling sensation in the skin. Pip-Rho had designed the construct to place them directly underneath the Specter for this reason. Zeta's hair lifted slightly in the exotic gravitational field. The water being kicked up by Flint Ochaway's retreat wobbled in the air for a bit too long, falling behind him in slow motion.

Flint's shouts were silenced as the Specter's tendril slurped him up into its black belly. A concussive pressure accompanied an ear-splitting whip-crack. The surface of the lagoon burst upward as if a mortar had exploded below the surface, spraying them with saltwater.

As fast as it had come, the Specter was gone. The woman on the shore screamed, running through the palm trees and underbrush, clutching her wailing baby. Her tribemates followed closely, in a panicked retreat from their fishing spots in the lagoon.

Moments passed in an unsettling calm as the lagoon's churning subsided and the shouts grew distant. Zeta trembled in her post-adrenaline hangover, chest heaving, staring at the sky. "Where—?" Her voice cracked. She tried again, "Where do they come from?"

Jamji went to Zeta and put an arm around her shoulder.

Pip-Rho said, "If you mean, like, their origin story? We can only guess. If you mean, specifically where do they hang out? They live in space, kinda drifting around. Though they favor the area around Varuna."

Zeta looked at the sky, blinking as the settling saltwater mist wafted into her eyes.

"That man was the first human abducted, that we know of," Pip-Rho said.

"Flint Ochaway," Jamji said.

"We had a Noddite observer in his tribe that heard about the incident and created this reproduction. After Flint, they acquired a *strong* preference for humans," Pip-Rho said. "After a few more neoprim abductions, they finally abducted a Noddite."

The construct cut to a serene lake, just before dawn. Zeta and Jamji got to stand on the surface this time, a-la Jesus. Fog clung to the water's surface, obscuring their feet. A black-bearded, light-skinned man in a rowboat was staring at his bobber as it floated lazily in the water. His eyelids fluttered closed as he nodded off. A moment later his bobber twitched, sending rings across the water's surface.

A sonic boom shattered the serene scene. The fisherman's arms and legs flew into the air as his eyes bugged open. His boat lurched wildly. His bamboo fishing pole ricochetted off the side of the boat and landed in the water as the inky form of a Specter pooled overhead.

The man glanced up, then barked, "Shit!" He didn't waste a second before he dove overboard. The Specter's tendril reached into the water, pulling the man out and into the air by his legs. "Dammit! Let go of me, you mother—"

Boom! The Specter disappeared into the indigo sky, having bagged the catch of the day.

"Freaking hilarious! Gets me every time!" Jamji mindspoke to Pip-Rho, laughter in her voice. She had the good taste not to allow her avatar to reflect her mental state. She solemnly stated, "That was Sleepy Sloan, the Foulmouthed Fisherman, our first Noddite abduction."

Poor guy never lived his abduction down. Pip-Rho always wondered why he never embellished the story. If she was in Sloan's shoes, she would have said she was reeling in the biggest bass you'd ever seen. The twitch on his bobber was as much artistic liberty as she allowed herself.

"You can meet him, if you want," Pip-Rho said. "He's still around. Since he was synching to his orb, he could tell us what it was like to get abducted. He described it as being dunked in ice water. Then he blacked out. Sudden acceleration can do that."

For Zeta's sake, she opted to leave out the part where he woke up again, just in time to feel his skin being burned off.

Pip-Rho announced, "Next up, the Specter space menace!"

———————

THE SCENE CUT TO SPACE, somewhere between Genesis and Soma. Varuna, the small, icy moon, floated as a blue orb in the distance. Pip-Rho, Zeta, and Jamji floated near each other.

A patch of stars directly in front of them shifted like a bubble being blown — thinning in the middle while condensing at the edges, then snapped back to their proper positions. A silent, bright flash flared just below them.

Thousands of tiny flecks of debris spread from the impact. A small fireball belched from the split ship as it rotated towards them, revealing that its insides were a honeycomb of gray and white. Some of the debris was moving — tiny human forms, arms and legs flailing.

The Specter's amoeboid mass swam through the wreckage. In its wake, bits of debris flew in every direction. Specters are absolute black — perfectly non-reflective — so tracking them in the visible spectrum against the blackness of space was more a matter of watching for the blinking out of stars than actually *seeing* anything, which sucks for demonstration purposes. Pip-Rho remedied this by painting the space backdrop a charcoal hue, casting the Specter as a black-on-black silhouette. Enhanced optics systems could spot them against cosmic background radiation, so she didn't consider this cheating.

A bright line swept across the surface of the Specter, creating a tiny puff of vapor. The vapor briefly illuminated a filament of light from the otherwise-invisible laser beam, originating from the forward section of the ship. A lightning-fast tendril darted out from the Specter, destroying the laser turret.

Multiple tentacles sprouted from the alien's mass. Each one would engulf a chunk of debris — or a human — then flick it away before receding and being replaced by another. In its frenzied search, it hurled bodies by the dozen into the void of space. Seconds later, the alien retreated like a spear cast into the darkness.

"Fifteen seconds," Pip-Rho said. "That's about as long as the average Specter attack takes."

"I don't understand what I just saw," Zeta said.

"Okay, I'll recap." The scene rewound in fast motion. When it got back to the beginning, Pip-Rho drew a yellow circle around a patch of the star field. "Right there is a shuttle, taking people from Genesis to Soma. You can't see it because it's running active invisibility. *Everything* we put in space has to be invisible. Here, I'll show you its outline."

A green wire frame shuttle appeared.

She circled another patch of stars. "Right there, very far away, a Specter is coming towards us. You'll see the stars bulge out when they're coming or going. That's called gravitational lensing." She'd save the lesson on exotic gravitational fields for another day.

The stars bulged, then the Specter lanced the wire frame shuttle, splitting it in two.

"Now it's rummaging through the wreckage, looking for a Noddite. That's another funny thing — they prefer Noddites over offworlders."

Pip-Rho made the laser being fired from the shuttle's nose an artificially red, glowing beam. She narrated, "At this part, the people piloting the shuttle tried to fight off the Specter using their sad little debris deflection laser. Specter smash!"

The Specter took out the laser turret, then resumed rummaging.

"It strikes like lightning," Zeta marveled.

"Yep! They're fast and tough. They brutalize Guardian warships almost as easily as they did this shuttle. This was the attack that got my attention, since I'm one of those poor souls that you just saw get launched. Specters toss you so fast, either your brain smashes against your skull and turns to mush, or your spine snaps. It's pretty much insta-kill. R.I.P., Pip-Pi!

"After my resurrection I became obsessed with figuring out what they were all about, and I came up with some wild ideas. So what did I do? I got out there and said, hey, aliens! Come and get me!"

The scene cut to interplanetary space. The small form of a human came into view, wearing a form-fitting white jumpsuit. A pair of blue flames shot from the soles of her large metallic boots. On her back was a gray reactor pack, and over her face was a golden visor.

And she was dancing.

"That's me! Just a lone Pip, cruising the system, listening to The Beatles and The Stones."

"You brought beetles and stones with you?" Zeta asked, as innocent as can be.

Jamji snort-laughed.

Pip-Rho said, "That's, um, not bugs and rocks. It's music from Earth. Genevieve'll get you into it someday."

"Yeah," Jamji laughed, "but if you say you like The Rolling Stones even a *fraction* as much as The Beatles, she'll disown you."

The dancing Pip-Rho angled her thruster boots in opposite directions, sending herself into a rapid corkscrew.

Pip-Rho said, "I spent a lot of time out there, so I had to keep myself entertained. I didn't have to eat or drink because the suit recaptures water and that reactor pack can power a placental mat. That's the thing on my back. Oh, and you're gonna to love this — you know what they call it? A ZETA reactor! No joke, it stands for Zero Energy Thermonuclear Assembly. This version doesn't pump out a ton of power, but it can run for years without refueling."

"I'll be honest," Zeta said, "I can barely keep up with what you're talking about, but I guess it's funny that it has my name."

"Sorry, I geeked out. It's okay to be confused. You'll understand it more as you build on your understanding of the universe. This gives you source material to go back to later. Now, back to the action!"

THE STARS in front of Pip-Rho bulged. A black mass spread out in front of her. She barely had time to gawk before the Specter consumed her. The black fluid enveloped her, stripping away her jumpsuit, ZETA reactor, and thruster boots. It formed back into a thin stream as it darted away, disappearing into a bulge of stars.

"It swallowed you," Zeta said. "They resurrected you again, right? At Syn-Cen?"

"You are correct!" Pip-Rho said. "I was pretty experienced at dying and being resurrected by this point, as you can tell by my name."

After a pause, Zeta said, "I don't know what you mean."

"You know, the Greek progression?"

"I don't think she's learned about that yet," Jamji said. She turned to Zeta, floating beside her in space. "So, ya' know how they call your first life your alpha, and this one your beta? Those are the first two letters of the Greek alphabet, which we use as a numbering system. Some people, like Pip-Rho, like to keep track of their resurrections by renaming themselves every time they're brought back. It's like a philosophy — treating every one of your lives as if you're a new and different person."

"Which you are!" Pip-Rho squeaked. "I wish everyone would do it! Jamji'd be Jamji-Epsilon, and you'd be Zeta-Beta. The way the Greek progression goes is: alpha, beta, gamma, delta, epsilon, zeta..." Pip-Rho paused.

Zeta took the bait. "That's my name..."

"Yep! Your name is the sixth Greek letter. Weird, huh?" Pip-Rho and Pip-Tau had their own pet theories as to how that had happened. The Telsons' sixth alpha seedling named after the sixth Greek letter? Shenanigans!

"It seems like my name is everywhere," Zeta said.

Pip-Rho laughed, then continued, "After zeta comes eta, theta, iota, kappa, lambda, mu, nu, xi, omicron, pi, then rho — the seventeenth letter, which tells you how many all-too-short lives I've lived. After that comes sigma and tau. You'll meet Pip-Tau later. Finally, there's upsilon, phi, chi, psi, and omega."

"What happens when you run out of letters?" Zeta asked.

Jamji beat Pip-Rho to the mic, quipping, "That's when it's time to seriously reconsider your life choices."

"Yeah," Pip-Rho laughed. "So, let's meet Pip-Sigma!"

The starscape vanished, dropping them into a void filled with a thousand floating bits of data. Graphs, text, videos, and formulas hovered before them. At the center of the data was a red, glowing orb.

"Pip-Sigma's avatar was kind of boring. She's that red ball."

"I'm confused," Zeta said, shaking her head. "You said rho comes before sigma, and you're Rho, and this is Sigma. But we just saw you get killed by a Specter."

"Abducted, not killed. It'll make sense in a bit," Pip-Rho said, assuringly. "Before I left on my mission, I had a small beacon implanted in my brain which would emit a quick radio burst, just once a year, at a certain date and time, on a certain frequency. It would have been nice if the beacon could have transmitted more often, but you're not allowed to use radio waves willy-nilly like the good ol' days on Earth, what with the aliens and all. Pip-Sigma hoped to use the beacon to figure out where the Specter had taken me. A year after the abduction, she received the first beacon signal."

A map of the Surya system floated before them, with a red circle drawn between Shiva and Genesis. The scene flashed back to space, showing a distant wire-frame outline of a personal transport pod using active invisibility.

Pip-Rho narrated, "Even using the fastest transport she could get, it had taken way too long to get to the origin of the beacon. Nothing was there. Then, the next year, it was the same thing. Beacon blip, run out to investigate, nothing there. Everyone told her that the beacon was just floating around in the dark, following some weird orbital pattern, but its change in position every year was *impossible*. Something was moving it. This went on for *six years*, until, finally..."

Pip-Sigma's personal transport was in a deceleration burn, its plasma thruster spewing a blue torch towards Varuna's icy blue disk. A tiny black dot was silhouetted against the moon's surface, growing larger as they approached. It resolved into an oblong shape, as large as a whale. It was black and bulbous, with deep red accents. Flecks of white peppered its surface.

The transport slowed until it matched the form's orbital trajectory. A door slid open down the middle of the pod, and the spacesuit-clad form of Pip-Sigma emerged.

"You said the beacon was supposed to lead Pip-Sigma to you," Zeta said. "Are you inside of that huge black thing?"

"No," Pip-Rho said, gravely. "I *am* that thing."

———

THEIR VIEW ZOOMED in on the mass before them. White flecks resolved into the forms of bones. The red patches were pulsating with purple veins. Pip-Rho watched as Zeta's expression shifted from wonder to horror. Their view moved closer, following Pip-Sigma, until they were a meter from the massive form. An eye flicked open on its blackened, fleshy surface.

Zeta yelped. "That's you?! Pip-Rho, is this what happens when people are taken by Specters?!"

"That's me, alright, in all my horrifying glory. We're certain that this is *not* what happens to most people taken by Specters. From what we've learned about the process of abduction, they normally dissolve their victims, leaving nothing behind."

She hoped that her matter-of-fact delivery would soften the blow, but it looked like Zeta realized that this meant her father had suffered a gruesome death. Zeta covered her mouth as tears formed in her eyes.

"This is a lot to take in," Jamji said, floating towards Zeta to put an arm around her. "Do you need a break?"

Zeta shook Jamji off, backing away. "No! The Night-Thunder

Spirit haunted me my whole life, and Pip-Rho has answers! I need to know everything."

Pip-Rho considered her options on how to proceed, then cut to a tribal campground at nighttime. "The reason I survived while everyone else abducted seemed to have died is complicated, but this is where it all started. I was born a little...different."

A woman moaned in pain nearby, surrounded by a group of other women. The women's faces were painted with white dots and blue patterns. The men and children sat on the other side of camp, speaking softly and wearing the telltale expressions of nervous expectation that always accompanied a woman giving birth.

Pip-Rho narrated, "Lynn-ma and Obba-pa had been trying for a long time to have a babe. For years, they were cursed with stillbirths, miscarriages, and heartache. Until..."

A baby cried. Obba-pa ran across the camp, elbowing through the women. His deep brown eyes were wild with expectation. An older woman handed a pelt-wrapped bundle to him, slowly, with sad eyes. Obba-pa's shaking hand pulled the wrap open, revealing the wiggling baby in his arms. The baby's form was tiny and frail, like a newly hatched bird.

"So...small," he whispered, beaming at the babe with tears rolling down his cheeks. The baby let out a weak cry. Obba-pa laugh-cried. "Lynn, it's a girl — such a little *pip* of a girl! Feed her, Lynn! She's so small, she must be hungry."

He put the baby on Lynn-ma's belly, pulling the woman's breast out from underneath her furs, then pressed Pip's face against it.

A woman placed her hand on Obba-pa's shoulder, speaking in a consoling tone. "Such a weak babe will not live through a cycle of Soma, Obba-kin."

He stood and rounded on the woman. His wild eyes flicked back and forth, from one of the eld's eyes to the other, challenging them each in turn. "Woman, you know *nothing*! This babe will feed and grow and live for longer than any of you!"

Pip-Rho said, "I sure would live longer than any of them, but not in that life. Not that I didn't try. And I definitely wouldn't have made it long if it wasn't for Obba-pa's stubborn refusal to give up on me. I did feed and grow, but not like a regular babe. I'm sure you haven't studied genetics yet, but once you do, look up chromosomal abnormalities. Without high-tech genetic manipulation, there's not much you can do about them but make the best of the life you get."

———

THE SCENE TRANSITIONED to the inside of the Telson cabin. Genevieve kneeled over the frail form of a girl — Pip-Beta — weeping and caressing her cheek.

Pip-Beta was lying on a placental mat covered in short, tight curls of deep brown hair, matching the puff of hair atop the girl's head. Her skin was darker than most Northern Grasslanders, a reflection Obba-pa's mocha tone. Having very little muscle tone or fat gave her an emaciated appearance, though she was well-fed. Her eyes bulged and were set apart on her face. Her forehead was small, and her jaw jutted slightly.

"Not long after my beta resurrection, I died again. My brain was just fine, but the standard beta bioenhancements weren't compatible with my body. If I was born in any other faction, they'd have just fixed my genes, but that's against Genesis's First Principal. So, after a few more brief lives, deaths, and resurrections, a cross-factional team of cyberneticists finally came up with a nanite suite that would work for my special situation. Do you know about nanites?"

"Yes," Zeta said. "They're like small animals — too small to see. And humans made them."

"Close enough. So, on account of my chromosomal abnormality and our constant experimentation with genetic and cellular repair nanites, my nanite suite was exponentially *awesomer* than the average Noddites. So awesome, in fact, that they were able to fight off the Specter disintegration. Here's a fun animation I made to symbolize what happened between my body and the Specter's when I was abducted."

The cabin was replaced by a white void. An army of evil, black Specter cells charged towards them from one side, looking like ravenous beasts. Rho's opposing army of grey, robotic nanite warriors stood their ground on the other side, protecting a rear guard of chubby, red, organic cells. The nanite warriors locked shields and set their pikes against the ground. The Specter army crashed through the fortifications. Metal and blood flew in every direction. At first, the Specter cells carved through Rho's forces with ease, but soon the rear ranks of Rho's army expanded. They surged forward, pushing back the invading Specter forces, reclaiming their lost ground. The nanites started consuming the fallen Specter remains, as well as those of the fallen organic and robotic forces. The nanite and bio forces multiplied, building a wall of fleshy organic matter, latticed with metal. As quickly as the Specter army could carve through it, the wall would grow. After several minutes of back-and-forth waves of combat, both sides showed signs of weariness. Yet, neither side would yield their ground.

"It's a stalemate!" Pip-Rho announced. "Neither my bioenhanced body nor the Specter trying to consume it can gain an advantage. They both run out of energy before they can get the upper hand, and since my nanites learned how to feed off the Specter's energy resources, everything they do to replenish themselves ends up leading towards mutually assured destruction. I should mention, the experience is one of constant, unimaginable torture."

They returned to the scene of Pip-Sigma, inspecting the massive Pip-Rho tumor. Pip-Sigma pulled a device from the side of her pack and began scanning the monstrosity hovering in space before her. A geyser of black fluid sprayed from the top of the form. Pip-Sigma flinched, retreated several meters, then slowly returned.

Pip-Rho continued her matter-of-factly narration. "Luckily, the one organ declared out-of-bounds by both sides of the battle was my brain. Our best guess is that the Specters break down the body first, then take their time picking the brain apart, neuron by neuron. Funny thing is, my brain works better than ever now. I can ramp up my neural firing rate to record-breaking speeds, with *no* Humming-bird Effect. It takes energy, but the Specter cells supply all I need. Just give me a drink of water every so often and I'm good-to-go. That water-for-energy requirement is why we think Varuna is the Specters' favorite place to hang out."

———

"I KNOW I look like a hot mess, but at this moment I was *ecstatic*. My beautiful little clone, Pip-Sigma, had finally rescued me. I was so happy, I wanted to hug her." Her tone darkened. "I'm...not proud of this next part."

Tendrils of black fluid sprouted from the sides of Pip-Rho's form, enveloping Pip-Sigma's waist and one shoulder. She was pulled against the side of the nightmare that was Pip-Rho, pressing into it. The blackened flesh began to envelop Pip-Sigma as she struggled to push away. A blinding, blue-white explosion swallowed the scene.

Pip-Rho said, "She blew the ZETA reactor. Self-destruct thought-command. It *hurt*, but I don't hold it against her — it was the right move. Luckily, my brain wasn't damaged."

The blackness of space returned as wisps of plasma dissipated, revealing a massive, fleshy hole in the monstrosity's side. It writhed and pulsed in angry shades of purple, red, and black. Bits of flesh and undulating orbs of dark fluid littered the surrounding space.

Pip-Rho's tone was morose. "I know it's hard to sympathize with an alien-infested tumor, but after Pip-Sigma blew up, I *truly* wanted to die. The pain, the thirst, and the knowledge that I had just destroyed my only hope of salvation were too much to bear.

"Luckily, Pip-Sigma had opened a short-range link to Genesis as soon as she got within a kilometer of the beacon. They saw the whole thing. So what did they do? Sat on their thumbs! Maybe they'd have sent a drone to investigate after a few days, but by then I'd be gone. I had a Specter companion that had been dragging me around and keeping me alive those six years, and it would return soon. Well, the Genesis Faction might have failed me, but the Astri saved the day. Thank you, XT-Prime!"

A swarm of Astri drones descended on the scene like metallic locusts. They strung a web of cable around the injured mass, then sped off with their prize. A few drones stayed behind, zipping around with blue jets of plasma, gathering bits of floating flesh and debris. The scene transitioned in a time lapse. An observation drone floated idly around the blue moon. In a blink, a Specter lanced through it, turning the drone into a cloud of metallic debris. The Specter extended strands of its fluid form, picking through the wreckage for a moment, then disappeared into the stars.

"It came back for you," Zeta said.

"Yep! I couldn't move like them, so my companion would go down and soak up water to bring back for me. Sweet, isn't it? By the time it returned, I was almost all the way back to Genesis. The Astri brought me to within a few kilometers of their station atop Jacob's Ladder. Then they built my egg."

A cluster of drones worked to shove Pip-Rho's tumorous mass into the open end of an enormous metallic egg. Lasers carved off any jutting chunks of bone and flesh which wouldn't fit through the opening. Other drones hovered nearby, shooting barbed cables into the floating tidbits and drawing them in, like frogs at a fly feast.

"Ugh," Zeta moaned, "are they eating you?"

"Nah, just collecting samples. The Astri *love* slicing off samples of my juicy hybrid human-nanite-Specter flesh."

"So gross," Jamji said.

———

THE SCENE WENT into a time lapse. The bots finished cramming Pip-Rho into the egg, then brought the cap into position. Brilliant welding torches sealed it, then they covered the exterior in absolute black invisibility paneling. The panels switched to active invisibility mode, broadcasting the image of the stars behind. She gave the egg a wire frame overlay so they could watch it get hauled to the similarly invisible Astri Hive Station on the Jacob's Ladder cable. They attached the egg to a long cable extending from the rotating station.

"There's another twist in my strange story. Since Genesis had already declared me dead, and since Pip-Sigma had just self-destructed, Cain automatically resurrected the next Pip. Enter Pip-Tau, the latest in a long line of adorable Pips!"

Pip-Rho showed the form of Pip-Tau laying in a resurrection recovery bed, in a white-walled room. Instead of being resurrected as a scrawny child, like Pip-Beta, Pip-Tau was a tiny woman.

"Wait," Zeta said, "they resurrected you? You're a human again?"

"No, keep up, sis! That's not me, that's Pip-*Tau*. I'm Pip-*Rho*. The monster in the egg, remember? All of that happened about 90 years ago, and that's where I still am, today."

Zeta blinked, shaking her head. "It happened *that* long ago? That's longer than a lifetime! You're *still* up there?! You're still a big... blob thing?"

"As gross as ever!"

"Then how are you...talking to us?"

Pip-Rho cut back to space again and zoomed in on her egg, turning off its active invisibility. "See that panel on the side where the cable connects? That's my utility panel: water, sewer, power and data. My neurites built a bridge from the panel to my brain, and data lines running down the cable connect my egg to the Astri station. From there, we connect to Syn-Cen via the ladder data pipe. But my orb isn't down there — it's up in the Astri Hive Station. It's a copy of Pip-Sigma's orb, excluding everything recorded since after I left Genesis on my Specter-baiting mission."

"You have two orbs?" Zeta asked.

"No, I have mine, and Pip-Tau has hers. We're not the same person anymore. There are rules against orb cloning, of course, but the Astri and Genesisians made an exception for me, on account of my *unique* circumstances."

"What would happen if you died? Would they resurrect you like you are now? Or like a human?" Zeta was so full of wonderful questions.

"I'd be a human again. Now, I know what you're thinking — why not just have them throw my egg into Surya and resurrect me to put an end to this tortured existence? Well, it's not as simple as that. My body's a goldmine of Specter research that the Astri aren't giving up — I'm their prize guinea pig. Nope, the only way I'll get resurrected is if everything left of my human mind got destroyed by the Specter cells — not likely, given the homeostasis I've reached with them — or we defeat the Specters, in which case the Astri won't need my body anymore."

"Or if you get liberated by the Guard," Jamji mindspoke.

Oh, sweet Jamji. Pip-Rho was certain that the Guardian researchers would subject her to tortures undreamed of by the Astri. No need to fight about it, though.

Pip-Rho returned them to Berm's Savanna. Her white-eyed, black porcelain cherub floated before Zeta, giving a bow. "That's the end of our lesson, today. Now, don't tell Gen-ma and O-pa — Genevieve and Oraxis. If they find out that Jamji introduced you to us and that we taught you all about Specters, they'll flip!" She performed an aerial backflip.

"That's the end?" Zeta almost whined. "But I need to know more! Genevieve said for me to find my purpose in this second life, and now I've found it. A Specter killed my pa." Zeta paused to take a few breaths. Her eyes glistened and nostrils flared as she continued, "They still threaten the neoprims and Noddites and they need to be stopped!" She turned to the sky and screamed, "Gods, spirits, ancestors, hear my vow! I will defeat the Specters! I will avenge Wilhelm-pa and set Pip-Rho free!"

Pip-Rho had Zeta's proclamation echo through the hills. The

grazing herd of Zebra retreated, barking in fear. She added a distant rumble of thunder.

Jamji let out a whoop. She pounded a fist to her chest three times, then put a hand on Zeta's shoulder, looking her in the eye. They locked gazes, prolonging the potent moment.

Pip-Rho wanted to pinch Zeta's flushed cheeks. She admired her enthusiasm, but the girl was as ignorant as they come. Zeta would have to devote decades of her life to mastering the maths and studying the sciences before she would be ready to contribute to the Pips' cause in any meaningful way. There had to be something she could start Zeta on which would set her on her path without saddling her with boring old schoolwork. Something fun, yet constructive.

Constructive? Yeah, that's the ticket!

"Thank you, Zeta," Pip-Rho said, "for vowing to set me free. I vow, in return, to guide you in this new purpose. So, if you want to play ball with the big kids, first you've got to learn how to use the equipment. You know how to manipulate slate-space yet? How good are you at freestyle construct creation?"

Zeta was a deer in the headlights.

Pip-Rho bailed her out. "That'll be your first step — learning how to master your double-mind. It's one of the most powerful weapons in your fight against the Specters. You need to be able to build scenarios, run simulations, explore what-if's. Constructs are the best tool for the job. And learning how to make them is a *blast*. You two go get a good night's sleep. Digest what you've learned today. Tomorrow, we start double-mind training!"

18

CONSTRUCTS

"Welcome back." Pip-Tau's avatar sat in a leather chair inside the darkened cabin. A beam of moonlight through the window illuminated her crossed legs, but her face and torso remained in the shadows.

"Thanks. Why'd you put out all the lights?" Pip-Rho asked.

The glowing tip of a cigarette came to Pip-Tau's mouth. Its glow intensified, faintly illuminating the solid black eyes set within her glossy, ghost-white face. The cigarette returned to the arm of the chair as a billow of smoke illuminated the moonbeams.

"You're smoking, now?" Pip-Rho laughed.

"What's it to you?" Pip-Tau asked, cooly.

Pip-Rho shrugged. "It's a classic look and all — fits in with the construct's setting, which is nice. I just don't think it's worth the risk. We've got to think about our rating with the Motion Picture Association. You know, when they make the movie of our lives."

Pip-Tau snuffed out the cigarette, leaning into the moonlight. "Tell me about Zeta."

"Zeta? The new Telson beta? Why should I know anything about her?"

Pip-Tau spoke just above a whisper. "Because you just met her, *Rho.*"

"No, I didn't! I was just hanging out with Jamji, helping her with a personal problem."

"You're a terrible liar."

"Look," Pip-Rho said, raising her hands in front of her, "I don't know where you got that idea."

"Jamji calls, you leave. I ask Gen-ma if she knows about what Jamji has been up to ever since she went dark on us. Gen-ma confesses that she's helping with Zeta's bootstrapping. Turns out, Jamji and Zeta didn't come home tonight. Gen-ma's worried sick, of course."

"That doesn't mean—"

"I asked *Jamji*, Rho!" Pip-Tau barked. "She told me what you guys were up to! As bad as you are at lying, she's even worse at keeping secrets."

Pip-Rho sighed, "Did you tell Gen-ma?"

"Ah-ha! *That's* a confession!" Pip-Tau flew across the room to jab her finger into Pip-Rho's chest.

Pip-Rho swatted her hand away, "Oh, come off it! Jamji already spilled the beans, so—"

"No she didn't! I lied! Ha! I'm *so* much better at lying than you are!"

"You little *imp!*" Pip-Rho pushed Pip-Tau so hard that she tumbled backward through the air, knocking over the smoking chair. "You didn't talk to Jamji?!"

Pip-Tau dusted herself off, righting the chair. "Oh, I tried, but she wouldn't talk. Alright, now I'm in on the caper. Gimme the deets, sis."

AFTER THE DEETS were given and apologies were exchanged, Pip-Rho agreed to let Pip-Tau take the lead in Zeta's "Double-Mind 101" class. They caught a few hours of sleep, then sent a construct invite at first light.

An hour later, Zeta accepted. What a sleepy-head!

Pip-Tau conjured a one-room schoolhouse, then opened the construct for Pip-Rho, Jamji, and Zeta to join.

Zeta was just as adorable as Pip-Rho had claimed. The girl looked around, taking in the surroundings, smiling slightly. It was like seeing a baby smile for the first time. The urge to squeeze Zeta until she popped washed over her. Instead, Pip-Tau introduced herself.

"Hi, Zeta, I'm Pip-Tau!"

"Hi. Pip-Rho told me about you. You were the version of Pip that was resurrected after Pip-Sigma self-destructed."

"That's a pretty *clinical* way to put it, but yeah, sounds like you got my origin story. Something you might not know about me is that I'm considered the top construct-slinger in the Genesis Faction."

"Not as good as me," Pip-Rho mumbled from the back of the classroom. Jamji snickered. Pip-Tau teleported the braggart into the corner of the room, placing a conical dunce cap on her head. Pip-Tau was the only one with creator privileges, so there was nothing Pip-Rho could do about it.

Pip-Tau addressed Zeta. "Since Pip-Rho and her alien-buffed brain aren't part of the Genesis Faction, my statement was *technically* correct — the best kind of correct! Jamji! Name that reference!"

Jamji shrugged, "I got nothin'."

Pip-Tau clicked her tongue in a tsk. She addressed Zeta. "If Jamji had performed the appropriate WoQS search on my obscure cultural reference, she could've easily found its origin. Instead, she gets to clap erasers."

Jamji scoffed, but complied. She got up, grabbed a pair of erasers, and went outside.

"Do you think you can do the search, Zeta?"

Zeta shifted in her seat. "I don't understand what you want me to do."

"That's ok. Knowing what questions to ask and how to ask them isn't something that comes naturally. Our double-minds and the systems they unlock are unimaginably powerful tools, but they're useless if you don't learn how to leverage them. What is a double-mind, anyway? How does it work?"

Pip-Tau pointed to the chalkboard, where a lifelike baby drawn in chalk appeared. "Set aside the double-mind for a moment. What about your natural, human brain? It's a remarkable thing! It has lots of parts that do lots of stuff, but it all pretty much works together as one thing." The baby's brain could now be seen through its skull. "Your brain is where your thoughts and feelings come from, where your ideas hatch, and where your body is told what to do. Your brain creates your mind and the entirety of your experiences. You are your brain. Got it?"

Zeta nodded. Pip-Tau gave her a thumbs up as the chalk drawing of a baby came to life behind her, doing a goofy little dance. Zeta laughed as Pip-Tau turned to look at the chalkboard, turning the chalk baby inanimate again.

"Why did you laugh?" Pip-Tau asked.

"The babe drawing danced," Zeta said, chuckling.

"So?" Pip-Tau said flatly. "Why is that funny?"

"I don't know," Zeta said, sobering up. "I'm sorry if I upset you."

"I'm not upset, but I wonder if you can describe why you laughed."

"Well, it was a dancing babe drawing. You don't see that every day."

"Ah, you're on the right track! It's almost like your human mind had some reflexive, instinctive response to an unexpected, non-threatening event. But then, when you had to put the reasons for your response into *words*, they weren't easy to come by. You weren't confident that your explanation was sufficient, but if I kept pressing you for it, you'd come up with answers, and the more you explained it, the more confidence you'd have in your reasons. You'd believe whatever you said to be true, because you would convince *yourself* of it as you were convincing *me* of it. This is all because your human mind has two complimentary aspects: the *essence* and the *storyteller*."

The baby drawing underwent a rapid growth spurt, turning into a cartoon rendition of Zeta. The animation then divided into two Zetas.

"People also call those two systems the upper and lower mind. The *storyteller* is the upper mind. Its job is to observe, interpret, describe, and make plans. It's how you make sense of the world. It tells stories about what it notices going on in the world around it, just as much as it tells stories about the feelings and drives going on within the lower mind — the *essence*. The stories it comes up with don't always have to be true, they just have to sound right."

As Pip-Tau talked, one of the Zetas on the chalkboard acted out the storyteller's role, watching the other version of Zeta and mouthing words as if to narrate. The other Zeta acted out a range of emotional caricatures, reacting to such stimuli as spiders walking by, meat cooking on a skewer, and anger at an enemy.

"Your *essence* is where your true motives lie. It's your deep, inner mind, full of instincts, desires, habits, and feelings. When you act without thinking, that's your lower mind. When you make a plan or you exert mental control over your desires, that's your upper mind."

The walls of the schoolhouse vanished, revealing an endless, rolling plain. Jamji was laying in the grass. She scrambled to pick up the erasers laying nearby and started hitting them against each other. Slacker.

"As a demonstration," Pip-Tau announced, "I shall be eaten by a T-Rex."

———

WITH AN AUDIBLE "POP", a Tyrannosaurus Rex appeared in the grass behind her. Zeta bolted from her seat, running to the back of the classroom, ducking behind the last row of desks.

"Back on Earth, before humans even existed, enormous animals like this roamed the—" Pip-Tau's lecture was cut short as the T-Rex lunged its great head downward, slamming its teeth around her torso. It threw its head back, crunching Pip-Tau into ceramic rubble as it gobbled her down.

Observing from an omniscient vantage point, Pip-Tau watched Zeta cry out in terror, bolting across the plains. The T-Rex dutifully roared a roar that Spielberg would have been proud of, then crashed through the desks as it charged after its fleeing student.

"This is a little dark for you," Pip-Rho mindspoke.

"You must be rubbing off on me," Pip-Tau replied. *"Hey, it's a lesson she won't forget."*

Jamji ran beside Zeta, keeping her company in her mindless flight. Pip-Rho knocked off her dunce cap as she flew in pursuit of the T-Rex. She mounted its back, trying to ride it.

No, ma'am, this beast can't be tamed.

The T-Rex's head turned around an unnatural 180 degrees. It opened its mouth and shot a massive chameleon tongue out at the black porcelain rider. In a flash, Pip-Rho was in the monster's mouth, being chewed to bits and swallowed into its bottomless belly.

"What the heck was that?!" Pip-Rho squealed via mindspeak.

"T-Rex 2.0."

"That's the worst! Does your T-Rex 2.0 shoot lasers from its eyes?"

"Sure!"

Red laser beams shot from the T-Rex's eyes, vaporizing Jamji into a cloud of aquamarine powder. Zeta screamed, turning with wild eyes to catch a glimpse of her monstrous pursuer.

After another few seconds of mindless flight, Zeta stumbled to a stop. She turned to face T-Rex 2.0. "This isn't real!" She screamed at the monster.

T-Rex 2.0 pounded to a stop, lowering its Volkswagen-Beetle-sized head down to meet Zeta's glare, eye-to-laser-eye. Its mouth opened wide. At the back of its throat sat the black-eyed, white-faced porcelain head of Pip-Tau. Zeta's chest heaved. Pip-Tau could practically taste the girl's fear as she stood her ground against the phantasm.

"It's not real?" Pip-Tau's head asked.

"No! You made it! This is a construct, and you made this monster up. You're not dead, and neither is Pip-Rho or Jamji. If it ate me, I'd just disconnect from slate-space and I'd be back in the forest, in the *real* world. Penelope-pooch would be there, and I'd be fine."

As she talked her way through it, Zeta's fear visibly dissolved. She stood confidently, challenging Pip-Tau's talking head.

Pip-Tau beamed, emerging from the T-Rex's mouth and flying to Zeta, wrapping her in a hug as she laughed, "You got it, sis! Your essence — your instinct — told you to run, right? You had no time to think! But once you started thinking, your storyteller put it all together and figured out what's up. That was the perfect example of your upper and lower mind at work."

Pip-Tau flew back to the T-Rex, plunging down its throat. Her disembodied voice said, "Now, it's double-mind time! I'm giving you complete creative control over the construct. Come up with a way to defeat the monster!"

Pip-Tau modified the construct's parameters, granting Zeta creative control. She had T-Rex 2.0 roar at Zeta, causing the girl to jump.

But this time, Zeta didn't run.

A bow appeared in Zeta's left hand. Her right hand reached into the air, plucking a shaft of light into existence. She nocked, drew, and released the light-arrow with practiced, fluid motions. White light pierced the heart of the monster. Glowing cracks formed in its skin, as if it were a shell that had been shattered by the light arrow. The light from within the cracks grew in intensity, culminating in a brilliant explosion.

The light faded, revealing the floating black and white cherubs of Pip-Rho and Pip-Tau. Jamji stood next to Zeta with a hand on her shoulder.

"How did you do that?!" Pip-Tau marveled.

"Please," Pip-Rho mindspoke, *"that was all you."*

"Okay, I gave him the cinematic death, but Zeta did come up with the light arrow on her own."

"Really?"

"All her!"

"Nice. Didn't take her any time at all."

"I don't know," Zeta said, looking at the bow in her hand. "I just sort of wanted it to happen and so it did."

"Zeta, what you just did demonstrated incredible double-mind control! You're a natural! Have you done this before?"

Zeta dropped her eyes for a moment, then looked up and shook her head.

"Okay, so let's break down how that worked! For you to conjure that light arrow, your human bio-mind, the inner mind, had to command your synth-mind, the outer mind, to manipulate the construct." Translucent figures came into being, showing a brain surrounded by a shell, with moving dashed lines representing information flow. "Your outer synth-mind interfaced with the Worldnet, where the construct is hosted. The brilliance of the entire system is that it's just as intuitive as the brain you were born with! Much like your inner-upper storyteller-mind naturally interprets your inner-lower essence-mind, your outer-upper synth-mind *interface* naturally translates your inner mind's intentions to your outer-lower synth-mind *engine*. Your *local* processing seamlessly integrates with the *remote* Worldnet services — WoQS, WorMS, WUtils, orb access, and aposynchrony. It's cybernetic perfection!"

Pip-Tau had continued building graphics as she went. They now filled the air behind her in an elegant representation of the complex systems. She took a moment to admire their beauty. She had a poster with these graphics on the wall of her dorm room at Syn-Cen.

Jamji raised her hand.

"Yes, Jamji?" Pip-Tau said, without turning away from the marvelous systems diagram.

"I'm confused."

Pip-Rho broke out into laughter.

"Seriously!" Pip-Tau squealed. "I mean, I get it if Zeta's confused. It's a lot to take in all at once. But you, Jamji? You're kidding, right?"

"No, seriously. This whole thing?" She gestured to the graphics. "It's a mess. No-one needs to know that stuff to know how to manipulate a construct."

Pip-Tau was speechless.

Jamji turned to Zeta. "Like you said, sis, when you're in control of a construct, you just have to *want* stuff to happen and it happens."

Pip-Rho held her belly as she laughed, tumbling through the air.

Pip-Tau was about to bring back T-Rex 2.0 when Zeta said, "I'm going to study this." She was pointing at the graphics. "If it'll help me fight the Specters, then I'll learn what it means."

"Atta girl!" Pip-Tau cheered.

THEY SPENT the rest of the day practicing construct manipulation. Zeta was a natural! She was almost as good as Pip-Gamma had been when she was learning about constructs for the first time. O-pa had marveled at her innate ability. A part of her felt guilty for robbing him of the privilege of going through these lessons with Zeta himself.

It takes a tribe to raise a child, they say. So, why should beta bootstrapping be such an isolated experience? Most other bootstrappers introduce their beta to the family within a few days. Was it because the Telson family was just too much to handle?

Nah, Susie-Q was the real reason. O-pa and Gen-ma had blamed themselves for her breakdown, thinking they had subjected her to too much too fast. But every beta is different. After six of them, you'd think they would have figured that out by now.

What caused Susie-Q's CCDC was anyone's guess. Neurite integration had a long way to go, back in that first generation. Pip-Tau was certain that it was more of a physical failure than a product of the protocol.

Oh, well! Some people insist on blaming themselves for things that're out of their control. Pip-Tau didn't do anything wrong by meeting Zeta and showing her how to control constructs.

Right?

As the day came to a close, the weight of guilt piled on until Pip-Tau finally cracked. She broached the subject as subtly as she could. "I had a marvelous time teaching you today, Zeta. I think O-pa and Gen-ma'll be proud to see—"

"Whoa, whoa, whoa!" Pip-Rho shouted, dismounting her velociraptor. "We're *not* telling them anything about this!"

"They'll kill me," Jamji said. "Or at least tell me to take a hike."

"What's the problem?" Zeta asked, commanding the dinosaurs to disappear. Penelope-pooch transformed from a monster-mutt back into a normal dog. The animal had taken to participation in constructs almost as naturally as Zeta had taken to manipulating them.

Jamji answered, "Oraxis and Genevieve can be kinda protective of their betas. They're not gonna be happy if we tell 'em what we've been up to out in the forest these last couple days."

A tiny Pepper-pooch hopped through the grass, yipping around Jamji's ankles, trying to entice her back to playing.

"And, as usual," Pip-Rho spat, "goodie-Tau-shoes has to run and tell ma and pa."

Pip-Tau flew up to Rho, meeting her negative image face-to-face. "Like we're supposed to just pretend we've never met Zeta when we see her at her beta ceremony? It's a joke!"

"You're a joke!" Pip-Rho squealed. "You said you wanted in on the caper and now you're gonna sing like a canary?!"

"I'll show you a canary!" Pip-Tau blinked a skyscraper-sized yellow canary into existence. It leaned down, twitching its head to assess Pip-Rho, then tried to peck her out of existence.

"Weak!" came Pip-Rho's booming voice from behind the canary-monster. Mechagodzilla appeared, shooting an energy beam out of its chest, striking the yellow nightmare between the eyes and exploding its head into a cloud of feathers.

Oh, it's on!

The feathers transformed into a swarm of titanium-eating bird spirits, impervious to physical or energy attacks. They descended upon Mechagodzilla, quickly disintegrating layer after layer of his armor. The movie monster tried shooting them with missiles out of his fingers, to no effect.

"Cheat!" Pip-Rho whined.

"Stop!" Zeta commanded. She banished the towering monsters and the feather swarm from the construct. "I don't care if Pip-Tau tells them what we've been doing! In fact, I'm just going to tell them myself! Genevieve said I needed to find a purpose," Zeta said, lowering her voice, "something to live for. Something that gives me a reason to wake up in the morning. Pip-Rho, *you* gave me that purpose when you taught me about Specters. And Jamji, you knew exactly what I needed, just like a good bootstrapper should. Pip-Tau, you explained my double-mind and trained me in construct manipulation, and you made it fun. They'll be proud of what we've done."

"She don't know them very well, do she?" Pip-Rho mindspoke, in the voice of Bugs Bunny. "Fine," she said aloud, "tell them."

Jamji said, "Alright, we'll talk to them when we get back."

Zeta nodded.

Confessing would have suited Pip-Tau much better. But, whatever. It's fine. Zeta can tell them.

It's *fine!*

Grr...

19

A LIFETIME AGO

THEIR RETURN TRIP was made in silence. As Zeta ran, she thought about what her future would hold. She was definitely ready to have her Beta Ceremony. Not because she was excited about meeting a bunch of strangers, but because it would mark the end of her boot-strapping and she would be free to follow her own path. Oraxis and Genevieve wouldn't be burdened with her anymore.

She daydreamed about the sorts of things she would learn from Pip-Tau and Pip-Rho. Specters, double-minds, ZETA reactors? Their knowledge was incredible, and their goals were the same as hers. The way Jamji talked about her reasons for joining the Guardians, it seemed like she would also be on a quest to fight the Specters. Maybe they would fight them together!

But, before she could fully commit herself to her future, Zeta had to do something about her nagging urge to give a proper goodbye to her past. She accepted the truth of Charra's death — there was nothing to do about that. She even accepted her own death. Her tribe would have buried her months ago. They might have even moved on from Talmid's Stinking Thicket by now.

Rod-pa survived the fight. She was sure of that — he was getting the best of those stick-swinging man-boys before she fell into the spring pool. He would have comforted Yephanie-ma as she mourned.

Hareshnid might even be able to walk by now. The babe had embodied her hatred for Rod-non-pa for so long that Zeta had all but forgotten that the boy was her half-blood bro-kin.

And Vihaan? He had always been so kind. They shared a tragic past, but they never talked about it. She remembered hearing him crying at night. She had pulled the furs over her head and shed private tears of her own instead of sharing them with him. What was the last thing she said to him? Did she thank him for bringing her water?

She shook her head at herself. She knew she couldn't go back. That life was over. And how would that look, giving a "hoo-whoop" and jogging into camp? They'd put on their angry duppy masks and try to scare off her wandering sprit!

Ideas blossomed in Zeta's mind as she ran behind Jamji's glowing form.

Maybe there *was* a way...

They were entering familiar territory. If she was going to ask this favor, she better do it now.

"Jamji," Zeta huffed between panting breaths.

"Yeah?" Jamji asked, without turning around.

"Stop for a second," Zeta said.

Jamji slowed, stopped, and turned around. She was smiling. "You're afraid they'll be mad at you. Look—"

"No," Zeta interrupted, "it's not that. Jamji, you've done so much for me. You've broken all the rules. Oraxis and Genevieve tried to do things their way, but you always knew what I actually needed."

"Well," Jamji gave an embarrassed laugh, "I tried."

"And you're itching to go join the Guardians. I've already kept you from following your dreams for too long, so I'll understand if you tell me no."

Jamji leaned her back against a tree, watching Zeta with her piercing, glowing eyes and waiting for the question.

Penelope-pooch trotted to her side as she mindspoke, *"We are close to Oraxis and Genevieve. They will see us and be happy!"*

Zeta quieted the pooch's voice in her head so she could think.

"Jamji, I know I can't go back and join my tribe, that's not what I want."

"Okay..."

"I just think if I could see them again..."

"That's kinda what replays are good for, sis."

"No, I mean *really* see them, in real life. I was thinking that I could have my skin changed to be like yours. I'd be invisible, and if you'd show me how to find them again, maybe I could just—"

"You died, Zeta," Jamji said, delicately.

"I know, and I accept that. I just want to say goodbye." Tears pooled in her eyes.

Jamji approached, putting a hand on the side of Zeta's arm. "You can't, Zeta. It's simply not possible. Trust me, I wanted the same thing when I was a new beta. I begged for it until I finally learned—"

"If I could just see them...all I want to do is *see* them! I could whisper my goodbyes. They'd never even know I was there."

Jamji sighed. "You want to replace your skin with dermal chromatites and travel halfway around the planet so you can stalk your tribe and whisper to yourself?"

"No, I'd be whispering to them, they just wouldn't be close enough to hear it."

Jamji huffed a laugh. "But what if they did hear you? The wind can carry a voice."

Zeta dropped to a whisper, closing her eyes, smiling gently. "No, I'd be quiet, like this. Goodbye, Yephanie-ma. I love you, and I'm sorry for breaking your heart. Goodbye Hareshnid-bro, sweet babe. I'm sorry for calling you a squealing little piglet."

Jamji laughed again. She whispered, "Careful, I think they can hear you."

Zeta whispered even quieter. "Goodbye Rod-pa. I'm sorry I didn't accept you as my pa and I made you mad so often. Thank you for fighting for me. Even if it was for my bloodthirsty vengeance. Goodbye, Chief Talmid. I'm sorry I didn't listen when you said—"

Zeta was jarred as Jamji grabbed her by both arms. "Say that name again," Jamji commanded. She almost seemed angry.

"Chief Talmid?" Zeta asked.

"How *old* was Chief Talmid?" Jamji commanded, squeezing Zeta's arms tighter.

"Jamji, you're hurting me," Zeta gasped, trying to pull from the stronger woman's grasp.

Jamji shook her, screaming, "How old was Chief Talmid, Zeta?!"

"Old!" Zeta barked. "He was the oldest man in the tribe! Jamji, what's wrong with you?!"

Jamji released her, then started pacing, shifting her skin's glow to red. She turned to a tree and swiped at it, raking it with her cat-claws, sending splinters and chunks of bark flying. She rounded on Zeta, her eyes burning red like embers, and growled, "Tell me about Chief Talmid. Old men like to talk about their ancestors. Tell me what he said about his parents."

Zeta's mind was a blank. Fear and confusion clouded her senses. She barely caught herself from slipping into slate-space. A replay was pulling at her. Instead, she closed her eyes and breathed. She didn't want a replay. There was no time for that. Whatever was upsetting Jamji about Chief Talmid, Zeta knew it had to be important. She'd never seen her this mad.

She remembered that she could perform a search through her life transcript. The speaker had to be Chief Talmid. The subject had to be his ma, his pa, his ancestors, his upbringing.

The results were almost instantaneous. Zeta scanned them, absorbing the key bits, refreshing her memory. She kept her eyes closed, reading the results in her mind as she summarized. "He was raised by his two sis-ma's. His ma died when he was born. She — she died birthing him. His pa was from another tribe and left with a broken heart when his ma died. I...he never told me their names. He always told me to cherish my ma and be glad she survived three births. His eld-ma was—"

The rapid sound of crunching pine needles marked Jamji's departure. Zeta opened her eyes. Jamji was gone.

"Jamji! Jamji, where did you go?! What's wrong?!"

Pepper-pooch bounded past her, a wave of heat rolling by in his wake. He was headed towards the Telson cabin.

Zeta broke into a sprint, following the grey-glowing monster-pooch.

ZETA HEARD Jamji shouting in the distance. Once she caught sight of the cabin, she found Oraxis and Genevieve standing in the clearing, being berated by a crimson Jamji.

"Don't give me that crap!" Jamji screamed. "You should have told me! I know you met him when you seeded Zeta! You had no right to keep it from me! You and your damn protocols, your pointless traditions! I'm done with it!"

"Jamji! Jamji, please," Genevieve cried.

Oraxis stood with his arms crossed and jaw clenched. A vein bulged on his temple.

Zeta kept her distance. Whatever this was, it was obviously between Jamji and the Telsons.

Jamji dodged Genevieve's attempts to put a calming hand on her. "Don't touch me! I'm so done with you two. You are the *worst* boot-strappers on the planet! Freaking clueless!"

Oraxis spoke through tight lips, looking like he wanted to shout. "Jamji, you will calm down and listen. It would not have helped you to move on if—"

Jamji advanced on Oraxis, "Shut up, old man! You say another word and the next thing you see will be the ceiling of a resurrection chamber. Calm down? No! I'm not one of your Telson children anymore! I'm done!" She spat on the ground between them, then turned to Genevieve and spat at her feet.

As Jamji turned to walk away, Oraxis reached out to grab her arm. "Jamji—"

Jamji moved so fast that Zeta didn't realize what she had done until Oraxis bellowed in pain. She had grabbed the wrist of Oraxis's outstretched arm with one hand, then spun her body around and drove her other palm into his elbow. The crack of his elbow was like a snapped branch.

"Jamji!" Zeta and Genevieve chorused. Penelope-pooch erupted into angry barking.

Oraxis went to a knee, using his other hand to hold his broken arm, which now bent the wrong way.

"I told you not to touch me," Jamji growled, turning her back again and stomping in Zeta's direction.

Pepper-pooch sat next to Zeta. He hunched over and shivered, his tail between his legs. Jamji vaulted onto his back and turned invisible. Pepper-pooch also faded from view, though Zeta could feel him trembling through the ground under her feet.

"I'm sorry, Zeta," came Jamji's disembodied voice, "but I can't stay here anymore — I have to get off this planet. I'm joining the Guardians. Good luck with those two."

The sound of Pepper-pooch's heavy footfalls marked them bounding away. A second later they stopped, circled, and returned. Zeta heard the invisible Pepper-pooch panting and whimpering right in front of her. She could smell the sweet musk of his breath in the air.

Jamji spoke flatly. "Something they should have told you by now is that your alpha died a lifetime ago. Genesis Faction always waits a really long time between alpha deaths and beta resurrections. They say it's good for you to be fully separated from your tribe, in both time and distance, so you can focus on your duty to the faction. That babe bro-kin of yours — Hareshnid — he's an eld by now. That's if he was lucky enough to grow old. Most neoprims aren't. One or two of the other kids you knew might be elds now, too, but the rest of your tribe is dead. I'm sorry, Zeta. Goodbye."

Pepper-pooch bounded away again.

Zeta's legs were weak. She sat down. She found that she was sitting next to the sand circle around the cold bones of the campfire. Genevieve wailed, but she seemed so distant that she may as well have been on the other side of the planet.

The world was spinning. Zeta's breath rang in her muffled ears.

It wasn't real.

Zeta held her hand out to Penelope-pooch, earning a meager lick.

"Lay down with me, Pen," Zeta mindspoke. Penelope-pooch obeyed.

Zeta curled up in the sand. She held Penelope-pooch in her arms. Together, they slipped through slate-space.

PENELOPE-POOCH WAS LICKING HER FACE.

"My guardian spirit, my golden hunter, the goddess of pooches," Zeta sang, scratching the pooch behind the ears, "let's hunt bro-critter. Where's Charra, Pen? Go find him! Find Charra!"

Penelope-pooch took the lead, sniffing her way through the undergrowth. The fresh scents of the forest replaced that of the foul camp as they sped between the trees and dodged around hanging vines.

She would find Charra. He lives! Find him and hold him and take him safely back to camp instead of going to the spring pool. Her tribe awaited her safe return. Yet, her alpha defied her, reciting a headstrong mantra to herself.

Escape the stagnation.

Seek the waters of purification.

Defy the caution of the elds with their twisted walking sticks and twisted spines.

Before long she was charging down a muddy slope, shouting, "Ay, ay, ay, ay!"

The pups went yipping and barking off into the forest, and her silly little bro-kin ran away, squealing.

Zeta jogged to a stop, laughing, "Bro-critter, you scared little monkey-boy! Come back and pick up your sticks!"

She saw his bow, then went to pick it up. "I found your stick-sling, Charra! It's mine now!"

She looked down at the bow in her hands. They had no business playing with a Gravan-cursed tool of man-killing. This was where it had all started — where everything had gone wrong.

She grabbed both ends of the bent wood and drove it down, sending her knee upwards to meet it in the air, snapping the bow in half.

She had broken the replay.

The world began washing away. Darkness rushed in, enveloping the trees, swallowing her distant bro-kin.

"No!" Zeta pushed her hands out to her sides, holding the darkness at bay. She imagined the trees reappearing, just as they were.

And they did.

She could make trees and dirt and trickling streams without having to think twice about it. She knew the thicket so well, reproducing it would be easy. She'd pull in details from replays, if she needed to.

Zeta scanned the forest that she had conjured. It was too quiet. Birds should be chirping, monkeys chittering, leaves rustling.

And they were.

Charra should be standing beside that tree.

And he was.

Charra pouted and crossed his arms. Why was he just standing there? He would scream if she snapped his bow like that.

"Zeta!" Charra whined, stomping towards her. "You broked my bow!"

No, he doesn't know that word. Charra transported back to his spot by the tree.

"Zeta!" Charra whined, stomping towards her. "You broked my stick-sling!"

Zeta smiled. "You deserved it for running off like that. I'm telling Rod-pa about this Gravan-cursed thing right now."

"Zeta!" Tears were welling in Charra's eyes. "He's gonna give me a spank for that!"

"No," Zeta said, tears of joy filling her own eyes. "Rod-pa's gonna be nice to us from now on. I promise. Come on, let's go back to camp. Yephanie-ma's been worried sick about you."

"Hoo-whoop!" Zeta called, joyously. "Hoo-whoop!"

"Hoo-whoop! We're back!" Charra shouted.

Penelope-pooch bounced through the underbrush, followed by Gorgon-pup and Chimera-pup, yipping and barking. They met with the other pooches of the tribe, pouncing and wagging their tails.

"Zeta!" Came her ma's voice through the trees.

Zeta and Charra ran, and in a blink they were in her arms.

"You're back! You're alive!" Yephanie-ma cried.

"Of course we are!" Zeta laughed.

"Is it a feast day?" Charra asked, clapping with excitement. The smells of roasted meat and sweet roots filled the air.

"Yes!" Rod-pa boomed from his spot by the nearest fire. "Today, we celebrate the return of Zeta and Charra!"

The reunion celebration went on for the rest of the day and into the night. Laughter came almost as easily as tears. Vihaan sang a solemn song — a tribute to his Jebbam-pa. Mileo-eld-pa even put on his old angry duppy mask and did a spirit dance for them. Charra hid behind Zeta, afraid of the mask. She resisted the urge to tease him for it. He was just a babe-boy, after all. Let babes be babes.

"I want to hold Hareshnid," Zeta told Rod-pa. The sleeping babe was bundled in a sling across the man's broad chest.

He furrowed his brow skeptically. "You've never wanted to hold him before. What's gotten into you tonight? You seem...older."

Zeta shrugged. "I guess I am older now."

Rod-pa gave a laughing "humph" as he unlashed the bundle. He handed the babe over, careful not to wake him.

Zeta pulled the softened leather back to peek at Hareshnid's face. The firelight made the warm shadows dance across the babe's soft, almond skin.

He would be an eld someday. And she would be on the other side of the planet. But that day hasn't come yet.

Incoming conversation request from Genevieve Telson.

Every head in the tribe turned to look at Zeta, wearing expectant expressions. Even Hareshnid popped his eyes open to look up at her with a steady stare.

Her heart pounded.

"No," Zeta whispered. "Go away. You can't take this from me."

Conversation request declined.

The tribe returned to their merriment as if nothing had happened. Hareshnid's eyes were closed again.

How long could she hold this world together? What would happen to her tribe when she fell asleep?

Zeta handed Hareshnid back to Rod-pa. She walked to the edge of the firelight, stepping into the darkness of the trees. She reached out with a conversation request.

It was immediately accepted.

"Hey, sis-kin!" Pip-Tau's bubbly voice rang in her head. Zeta could feel her grasp on the world slipping. She already regretted this, but it was too late. Pip-Tau was saying, *"How's it going with Gen-ma*

and O-pa? Didja get a stern talking-to for running off with Jamji and playing school with the Pips?"

Zeta ignored the questions. *"Can my construct keep going without me?"*

Pip-Tau paused. *"You mean, like, can a construct you're hosting keep running after you disconnect? You can set up a persistent collaborative space, like for a club lounge or a gameworld, but it's not really practical for personal constructs. You can just save the state when you leave and pick up right where you left off—"*

"What if I go to sleep? Will it keep running or will I disconnect?"

"Oh! That's an easy parameter to set — Proliferans are known to spend years at a time in private constructs. You remember when we tweaked the realism restrictions on the monster war game? That was in the construct parameter interface. You pull back from the world, feel around for the settings for disconnect parameters, and set 'em so it doesn't kick you out when you fall asleep. Are you working on a construct right now? Wanna share?"

"No!" Zeta blurted. *"Sorry, it's something I need to do on my own. What if I'm not paying attention to the people in one part of the construct? Will they keep doing things so that when I go back and see them it's not like they were just sitting and waiting for me?"*

"Well, if a tree falls in your construct and you're not there to hear it, its sound isn't rendered. All that matters is you saw the tree standing and then later it wasn't. If Cain rendered every bit of unobserved content in your virtual universe in full fidelity, you'd take his servers down. But still, it's standard for artificials to have basic off-camera autonomy. What they do when you're not looking's based on your design. You can use sim templates from prefab archetypes, pull in personalities from your stored experiences, or design your own from scratch!"

Zeta had a hard time following, but she thought she had heard what she wanted to hear. *"If someone in my construct is someone from my life, then they'll act like that person would, on their own?"*

"Yeah, pretty much. It's not perfect, and you can direct their

actions to make them act out of character, but...Zeta, what sort of construct are you making?"

"Thanks, I have to go," Zeta said, closing the conversation.

She took a deep breath and turned around. She jumped when she saw the silhouette of Charra standing behind her, the campfires glowing behind him.

"Zeta!" He whined. "What is you doing in the trees? Is you running off?"

"Of course not," Zeta said, walking towards Charra. She turned him around and put an arm around his shoulders as they walked back to the tribal fires. "I'm not going anywhere."

20

TALMID

Jamji had to get off this damn planet, and she would not wait a month for a turn to take a ride through the tubes. No, they were running. She drove Pepper-pooch hard. He was strong — he could take it.

But could she? Keeping herself from being thrown from the bounding mount pushed the limits of her myofibrite-enhanced muscles. Surya was setting, and they were making great time. They'd be there in a week at this rate. She could do it.

Their course was straight, but in her mind she was running in circles. She had gone through the scenarios fifty times. The timing was right — after her Beta Pilgrimage to Syn-Cen to see her orb, Oraxis and Genevieve had left for Eden. They had used their privileged tracking data to find the Scorpion Tail tribe. They had seeded Zeta's alpha. This much was undisputed fact. Her only inference was that they had met Chief Talmid.

Of course they met him! You can't visit a tribe without meeting the chief. Was he a chief when Zeta was seeded? It didn't matter! When Jamji called them out, they hadn't denied it or pretended they didn't know. They practically admitted to it.

Yeah, they met Chief Talmid.

And how deluded could they be, thinking Zeta would never let his name slip? They drive the whole "don't talk about Eden" thing in so much, it's like they don't even care about our first lives. It's like they think healing means you've stopped talking about the past.

Of course they wouldn't want to talk about tribal life! They grew up on Earth — first generation Gilgamesh Era immortals. Sterile, genetically modified, pompous golden children. Packaged products of centuries of an Anglocentric, Westernized Earth. Oh, teach me about your magical world, my white-skinned gods! The enlightened ones are here to usher us lowly brown primitives into the ranks of the civilized!

She should have spit in their *faces*, not on the ground between them.

They don't know what it's like to die, knowing that there's no going back — that this is it — game over! The end, no take backs. They don't know what it's like to feel the world slipping away, *hoping* there's an afterlife, *terrified* at the deep suspicion that there's not.

They can never know what it's like to have your last words be "let me see my babe," and the last thing you hear be your mother's sobs and the silence that can only mean one thing — the babe was *dead*.

A sharp pain struck Jamji's chest. She winced, clutched at it, half-expected to find an arrow or a laser-rifle wound. What was this? She thought-commanded Pepper-pooch to stop. She slipped from his back, collapsing into a heap on the pebbly dirt. She curled up, clutching her heart with one hand, pounding the dirt with the other. Tears of anger, pain, and remorse trickled down her face.

Then came tears of joy. She gasped with a sudden elation, turning her face up to the dark clouds.

"He lived!" She shouted at the night. "Talmid lived!"

Racking sobs came over her. Her heart pounded in her ears. Minutes passed in choking, pained, overjoyed sobs.

Pepper-pooch licked her, whimpering timidly, scratching her back with his coarse tongue.

Some detached part of her mind managed to get a message through the maelstrom. *"You gave yourself a heart attack. You turned off your bioenhancement governors and pushed your body to the limit. Your brain chemistry is a stew of stress hormones, your blood pressure is off the charts, and you're dehydrated. Get it together, Jamji."*

Jamji issued the bio-overrides to flush the excess hormones and slow her heart. Her vision swam, closed in, threatening a blackout. She turned her governors back on and let her autonomic systems stabilize.

As her head cleared, she asked WoQS which way the nearest source of fresh water was, then dragged herself to her feet. She took shallow, shuttering breaths as she led Pepper-pooch to the pond. They both drank eagerly, then laid together in the scrubby grass.

THUNDER RUMBLED IN THE NORTH.

She needed to go back to the beginning.

The rapist who put Talmid inside of her had killed her. Murder via pregnancy, executed during childbirth. She had always believed — *known* — that the babe died, too. As a beta, she replayed that experience time after time, and could never hear the faintest cry. The only sounds had been the sobs of her kin as her life slipped away, her hemorrhaging uterus draining her life's blood out onto the flattened grass.

Her babe's death was intertwined with her own into a single, shared tragedy. She had accepted this truth as a cornerstone of her own alpha death narrative. Now, the narrative was changing.

She slipped into slate-space, summoning the replay of Talmid's quickening.

She laid on her back, on fresh furs. Jamji looked through her alpha's eyes, wondering up at the stars. A small, fluttering feeling came from inside. Was that her imagination?

Then it came again. Just a tiny tap, but unmistakable. It was the babe inside of her! She gasped, covering her mouth with a hand.

Conflicting emotions washed over her alpha, seeping into Jamji's present mind, pushing her hormonal buttons until her thought patterns matched those of the alpha in the replay. Here, inside of her body, lived a helpless babe whose father had been a monster. Did this make him a monster? This fluttering little butterfly, a monster?

She had hated the babe for so long.

At first she tried to deny that she was pregnant. The vomiting was on account of something she ate. The tummy bump was just gas, or a full belly. But when the bump grew too large to deny, she admitted the truth of it. But she didn't have to like it. She imagined dashing the unwanted babe's head against a rock as soon as it was born.

Now, that thought horrified her. *She* was the monster! How could she ever imagine such a thing?

The flutter came one more time that night. When it did, the stars twisted and stretched as tears pooled in her eyes. Acceptance, regret, forgiving the babe for his monster-pa's sin.

She remembered always thinking of the babe as a boy. She would name him after her dead eld-pa.

Talmid.

She retreated from the experience replay, swimming in the null value of slate-space for a full count of thirty seconds, steeling her resolve.

Then she summoned her death replay.

Jamji's alpha stood in knee-high grass, calling for help. Fluid leaked down her leg. Her belly tightened, sending a shock of unimaginable pain through her body.

"It's happening! Talmid is coming! Help me!" She cried.

Sure, she was a young mother, but she was strong. She had mentally prepared herself to be ready for the pain, ready for the struggle, ready for the babe. Her tribe's women ran to her as she went to her hands and knees.

She swore a silent oath in that moment, that she would raise this babe to be a good man. He would *never* be told of the monster that put him inside of her. She would teach him to treat women with gentle respect. She would do anything for him — she would die for him, if that was what it came to.

Jamji's current self darkened at the bitter irony of the idea. She certainly *would* be dying for his sake, and soon.

Jamji forced herself to relive the entire experience of childbirth. Hours passed in agony, waves of pained tension and exhausted release. Her tribe and kin painted their faces with glyphs of blue and white, as was their tradition. They tended to her. They showed her how to squat. They cleaned up the stinking mess that came with the pushing.

She gave the final push, her vision pounding as she screamed the breath out of her lungs. The women pulled the babe out of her. She collapsed to her side, looking for her babe. Her eld-ma held Talmid, rushing away.

White film and red clots had decorated his purple skin.

He had been silent. Still.

Too silent. Too still.

She only caught a glimpse before the world turned pale, sparkling, distant. She reached up with a hand, dripping with blood from the pool forming around her in the grass.

"Come...back. Let me...see my babe."

The sobbing women, the forms of silent men, the fading away, and the nothingness that followed marked her death.

———

JAMJI WAS BACK in a blank slate-space.

Jamji *was* a blank slate.

She began the process of rewriting her narrative.

The babe lived? Yes, Talmid lived, and so did she. They had lived on the same planet at the same time, on opposite sides. One planet composed of two worlds — Eden and Nod.

Jamji retreated from slate-space, finding that she was being rained on. Pepper-pooch's warm body curled around her in a protective crescent. His oversized placental mat all but engulfed her own. The cold rain couldn't touch their combined warmth, fueled by the mycelites pumping energy into their mats from underground. Steam wafted over her from a hot Pepper-pooch sigh.

Crying in the rain felt good.

For hours, she let the emotions work their way through her. The rain slowed to a drizzle. The night clouds brightened to a deep blue — a hint of dawn. At one point she almost slipped into sleep, but was startled back awake when she felt her uterus contract.

No, it was her imagination — a premature dream intruding on the twilight of her mind. Noddites don't get to have functional uteruses, anyway. Neither do Guardians, which is fine. She didn't need another babe.

Jamji's mind wandered. She thought about what Talmid's life must have been like. She remembered that her cousin was still suckling her own babe when Jamji's alpha died. The woman must have fed Talmid.

Jamji imagined her purple boy taking a deep breath, letting out a squealing cry, and turning a healthy brown. She imagined him as a headstrong adolescent, a noble man, then a wizened eld. He had earned respect. He was Chief! Her kin and tribe had raised her boy for her, and they had done well. Talmid became a good man without her.

The clouds were turning a lighter shade of blue, taking on pink highlights as Surya kissed them good morning. Surya's rise would bring Jamji's sleepless night of pain and mourning to a close. A sense of loss still weighed her heart down. But now, at least, one part of her tragic story had a happy ending.

She debated whether she should ask Zeta to tell her stories about Talmid, or share replays of him. That could be a mistake, since Zeta may not have liked him. She was the sort of girl that would buck against an eld. Jamji wouldn't want to poison her new fantasy. She was proud of her son — her Chief-babe!

Jamji chuckled, waking Pepper-pooch.

"You're awake and you're happy!" Pepper-pooch sent. His tail wagged, nervously.

She pushed herself up, giving the pooch a good scratch. *"I'm sorry I was mean yesterday, lil' Pep. I was sad, but now I'm happy."*

The pooch licked her with vigor. *"You are happy! I am happy and you are happy in the morning!"*

"Let's take it slower today, okay? Unless you want to race?"

"Let's race and run! You run fast, but I run faster! Catch me!"

The strobing monster-pooch scrambled to his feet, then dashed away faster than a creature his size should be able to move.

"You're running the wrong way, silly boy!" Jamji laughed, bounding to her feet and sprinting after him.

"I NEED to submit a revised application essay," Jamji told the bushy eyebrows. Eld Marco-Epsilon Rhind was remarkably easy to get a meeting with. Council members should be too busy for spur-of-the-moment requests like this, but here he was.

"Oh?" Watching the three-second-delayed reaction play out on his forehead was like seeing twin black caterpillars leaping in surprise.

Jamji stifled a laugh. Focus!

"Yeah. My original essay only cited disagreements with the Genesis colony charter and principals, but this new version adds a section regarding my disdain for my beta bootstrappers. I've always had problems with the standard practices of bootstrappers, in general, but mine *really* messed up. Not just with me, but with all their betas."

The eld sitting across from her had picked up a simulated piece of paper and was scanning through it now. "Oh, Jamji. Was this written in the heat of the moment? Did you have a fight with Oraxis and Genevieve?"

Jamji didn't wait for the eld to finish before she started, though it wouldn't interrupt him on account of the delay. "No, sir. It was written in thoughtful contemplation after their new beta leaked an important piece of info. It's all in the essay."

Marco nodded as he listened, continuing his reading. He furrowed his mighty brows as he cited the list of Telson bootstrapping failures. "Susanne: catastrophic cognitive dissociative collapse, termination of orb. Xavier: gender identity crisis, transfer to the Astrus Faction. Pip: multiple successive deaths, extreme risk-seeking behavior leading to Pip-Rho's current compromised state. Carff: failure to adapt to modern civilized sensibilities. Jamji: see Appendix B." He flipped to one of the back pages. "Oh, that's a list. That'll take a minute. Back to the essay. Zeta: premature bootstrapping protocol termination, failure to find purpose, uninformed of temporal situation. Temporal situation?"

An eyebrow raised as he looked up at her.

"They didn't tell her that her alpha died seventy Earth years ago." Jamji was getting in the habit of thinking in Earth years, the Guardian standard calendar. "She thought she could go spy on her tribe and whisper her goodbyes. I had to be the one to tell her they were long gone."

Marco clicked his tongue and shook his head. "Spy on her tribe? They could have at least ingrained in the beta that covert observation of fellow Genesisians, Noddite and Edenite alike, is treasonous."

Jamji wanted to facepalm. She had to go and use the word "spy" with this tool.

Marco smirked ever-so-slightly at his coyness, then put on a serious face. "It's a poor track record, indeed. I think I'll put a word in with the Bootstrapping Committee to look into the Telsons. This was excellent information, Jamji. Don't hesitate to contact me again in the future with any other information you might consider important."

He *had* to be working for the Guard. No, don't make assumptions. Stick with the plan. She would report him to her commanding officer once the Guard accepted her and let the proper chain of command call the shots.

In war, the general receives his commands from the sovereign.

Jamji would play his game and get this over with.

She feigned eagerness. "I *certainly* will, Eld Marco-Epsilon Rhind. Thank you for your time," slimebag.

"Any time, Jamji. I'll submit your essay just as soon as I'm able to fact-check it. The essay becomes public record, you see, once your transfer is accepted. It will bear my seal, and if I haven't confirmed the factuality of your specific accusations, I will have been derelict in my duties."

Fact-check?! What, like she would lie about this stuff? Whatever. Jamji nodded. "Of course."

She just hoped he would do it fast. Even at a leisurely pace, she would be at the embassy in a few weeks. The last thing she needed was to have to sit on the beach for a month while the bureaucratic wheels grind. It was worth it, though. The Guard deserved to know her true motivations, both philosophical and personal.

They exchanged final vacant pleasantries and disconnected. Jamji returned to her body, opening her eyes to Surya's midday glare. Pepper-pooch stood, excited at her return. She gave him a scratch, then headed south at a leisurely jog.

And she was at peace.

21

VASILIS

"Could you take the tent back down again?"

"The weather model says it's going to rain again tonight, Gen."

"I know, and you can put it back up before that. I just don't want her out there being cooped up in that musty skin-hut all day."

"She's disconnected — it's no difference to her. Look, taking the tent down and getting it back up again is a bit of a pain. If she comes back out of it, then—"

"*When* she comes back, O. It's not *if*, it's *when*." Her lip trembled as she spoke. She couldn't go ten minutes without crying these days.

Oraxis sighed. "I know, Gen. I'm sorry." He put an arm around Genevieve, who turned to press her forehead against his chest.

A day on Genesis was twenty hours long. Normally, that meant that the days flew by *way* too fast. But the past week had been the longest one-hundred—forty-plus hours that Genevieve could remember. Passing the hours by watching Zeta's face for any sign of waking made time stand still.

She would have been ecstatic if even Penelope-pooch would disconnect and return to the real world. Then they could try the face licking thing. When Genevieve had suggested finding another dog and coaxing it to lick Zeta's face, Oraxis shot her down.

"Does your elbow still hurt?" She asked.

Oraxis worked his elbow, bending and extending it. "Na."

"Then take down the tent."

"Okay." Oraxis kissed her forehead, then pushed through the furs and went outside.

Genevieve looked around the cabin for something that needed tending. It was better to be doing something than sitting around doing nothing. Their list of productive uses of time had been exhausted, so now it came down to busywork.

She could message the Pips again, but they were probably sick of her by now. Pip-Tau had felt awful and seemed certain that Zeta's retreat to the slate was her fault. Pip-Rho was optimistic, strangely enough. She seemed to think Zeta was in the midst of some sort of deep dive through all known Specter data. Hearing that Zeta's father had been abducted by a Specter was certainly a surprise. She hoped that Pip-Rho was right, but it was a stretch.

She could pick some flowers to decorate Zeta's mat. It would be like the scene from Snow White when she was poisoned, and the dwarves all stood vigil over her. What would her dwarf name be? Probably "Weepy".

"Gen, come outside. We've got company," Oraxis mindspoke.

"Company?!" Genevieve burst through the furs, ready to berate whoever was intruding on their bootstrapping boundaries. Anyone coming within a half kilometer of the cabin would have been warned by WorMS that there was a beta being bootstrapped here, and to take a detour. When she saw who it was, she was glad she held her tongue.

"Hail, Vasilis, welcome to our cabin," Oraxis shouted. Genevieve could tell his merry tone was forced. "What brings you to these parts of the Thin Forest?"

Vasilis Pilspa was on the Bootstrapper Council, so he was one of the few people who had every right to intrude on their boundary. Surprise inspections or pre-Beta-Ceremony audits were not unheard of. Zeta's current state could mean an automatic fail. The council would transfer her to another bootstrapper and revoke their certification.

This was *bad*.

Vasilis approached, showing his palms, then lowered a hand to clutch Oraxis's extended forearm. They exchanged pleasantries as Genevieve approached.

Vasilis's attire broke Noddite conventions: a cloth turban and thwab — an Arabic robe. Everybody deserves a few reasonable concessions. Genevieve would wear cloth herself if they hadn't already pushed their luck with the cabin. As rumor went, Vasilis became obsessed with the pre-Westernized Arabian culture as a beta after finding that a significant portion of his genetic makeup could be traced back to the region.

Genevieve eyed the cloth, suppressing her jealousy. Just one pair of blue jeans would be *all* she needed! That, and maybe a simple t-shirt. Or a sundress.

"I would never intrude on a bootstrapper at work," Vasilis said, "if the reason was not important." He even spoke in an Arabian accent. None of the neoprim tribal dialects confer such an accent when speaking Common, and nobody has spoken Arabic since before the Earth cultures homogenized, so the accent was fake. Or, to be generous, it was a historically accurate reproduction.

"Would you like to come into our cabin?" Genevieve offered.

Vasilis beamed at the cabin. "Yes, what a delight! Is Zeta within?"

"No," Genevieve said, uncertain whether to offer anything more.

"That is good. We should talk in private."

"What is this?" Genevieve asked Oraxis, via mindspeak.

"Your guess is as good as mine. Let him talk. Play your cards close to your chest. Just keep calm."

"WHAT?! How could she say these things?! I can't believe this! I just can't!" Genevieve shouted. She paced, trembling, rubbing the outsides of her arms.

"Vasilis," Oraxis said in a voice much too loud for the small cabin, "this is nothing but unfounded slander. I knew Jamji was mad, but this? I won't stand for it. Lies, exaggerations, half-truths." He took a deep breath, let it out, then put a pleading hand on Vasilis's shoulder. "You're a bootstrapper, Vasilis, you know how hard it is to find the right words, to find the right balance of comfort and challenge. We got her through it, and I *used* to think we did a fair job of it. She used to be at peace. Have you seen her dance? She was happy! But now she's just...*hateful*."

Genevieve wiped her face. "This hate for her faction, for us, it started with that Students of Sun Tzu crap! She got herself brainwashed by that glorified warmonger macho cult propaganda!"

"Genevieve!" Vasilis shouted, "Oraxis! Calm yourselves! Anyone who reads this can see that it is poison — the spiteful opinions of a headstrong traitor to Genesis. I only came to set the facts straight."

"Well, put a big red line through the entire thing," Genevieve spat.

"I have already parsed the document," Vasilis said, "and isolated the few factual claims from the sea of opinions. Of those, most simply don't constitute a failure on your part. Take this, for example."

Vasilis pointed to the floating hologram of the essay, displayed via micro holo-projector. He popped out a bubble containing, "Carff: failure to adapt to modern sensibilities."

"I doubt she could even define what modern sensibilities are. As for Carff, the man is as true of a Noddite as I have met. A cursory meta analysis of his records reveals him to be a highly productive member of our faction, with deep insights into applied philosophy and the human condition. As an observer and cultural influencer, his record is unmatched."

"Is he talking about our *Carff?"* Genevieve mindspoke to Oraxis.

Oraxis glanced at her, then turned to the hologram. "Okay, show us the claims and we'll refute them."

The document became a gray wall of text, with bits and pieces standing out in yellow highlight.

After glancing through the highlights for a second, Genevieve could tell that it would take a refutation ten times the length of Jamji's original essay to explain the context of the situations she listed.

"I just can't believe she would do this," Genevieve said, shaking her head and returning to pacing.

"Well, we know what set her off," Oraxis mindspoke.

"Of course I know. She thinks she knows better than we do about what we should have done with her. She thinks knowing about Talmid would've changed things for her. Oraxis, she'd have caught the next tube to Eden and spent years searching for him. And what if she found him? She has to know what damage that could've done!"

"But," Oraxis replied, *"twenty years after we saw him? Thirty years? We could've told her after he was unquestionably beyond the longest human lifespan."*

"And gotten the exact same reaction as we got last week! I can't believe you're on her side with this!"

"I didn't say I was on her side, Gen. Only that maybe getting my elbow snapped twenty years ago would've been preferable to this. She may not have gone down this dark path."

Vasilis cleared his throat. "It will take time for you to compose a response. You should cool down for a while, first. I will take my leave of you."

Genevieve mindspoke, *"He's not even going to ask about—"*

"But first," Vasilis said, handing the mini holo-projector to Oraxis, "I'd like to have a talk with Zeta."

Oraxis and Genevieve stared at each other.

"What do we do?" Genevieve mindspoke to Oraxis.

"The only thing we can do — we tell him the truth."

AFTER THE BEANS were thoroughly spilled, Genevieve did, at least, feel as if a burden had lifted. Confession is cathartic. What's more, now that the Bootstrapping Council knew about their problem, maybe they could help.

Oh, who was she kidding?! *"They're going to take her from us,"* Genevieve mindspoke to Oraxis.

"We'll see. I should've sent them a message days ago. It doesn't look good for him to have to stumble upon it like this. But, I don't think a week disconnected warrants reassignment."

"Not just reassignment, O. They'll take her to Syn-Cen and test her for CCDC." It was Susie-Q all over again. A lump formed in Genevieve's throat.

"If she was going to dissociate, she would have started down that path when she broke out early. She's been doing great. This," Oraxis looked over to the curled-up bundle laying next to a slowly breathing dog, *"is her last-ditch effort to return to her former life. The questions she asked Pip-Tau speak for themselves — she's making a fantasy world, but she's self-aware enough to know that it's a fiction. It's only a matter of time before she lets us in, or comes back out."*

They had taken down the tent and now sat in the wet sand encircling the muddy remains of campfire ashes. Vasilis kneeled in the sand with his eyes closed, having gone into slate-space to confer with his peers. He opened his eyes, took a breath, and addressed them.

"She's ignoring our messages. Not surprising, since we are strangers to her, but we felt that if she knew that there were other people in Nod who wished to meet her, she may consider reconnecting with reality. I assume you and the other Telsons have tried messaging her?"

"Yes," Genevieve said.

Thunder rolled in the distance.

"We haven't told Jamji," Oraxis said.

Genevieve shot him a glare. "Like she'd talk to us?"

"She'll talk to me," Vasilis said. "And, if not me, then Eld Marco-Epsilon Rhind."

Genevieve shook her head. "Jamji was the one who triggered Zeta's disconnect in the first place."

"She didn't do it on purpose," Oraxis said, softly.

"But she *did* do it."

As sick as it made her to ask Jamji for help *again*, after everything she said about them, Genevieve had to swallow her pride. "Okay, Vasilis. Talk to Jamji, see what she can do. I just hope she doesn't make matters worse."

Vasilis nodded, stood, and brushed the sand off his cream-colored cotton thwab. "If Zeta stays disconnected for another week, we'll need to talk about next steps."

They all knew what that meant.

Oraxis stood, extending a hand, "Thank you, Vasilis. I'm sorry we didn't come to the council with this problem sooner."

Vasilis held Oraxis by the forearm, putting his other hand on Oraxis's other arm in a gesture of consolation. He said, "I don't judge you poorly, Oraxis," he turned to look Genevieve in the eye, "nor you, Genevieve. You take undue personal ownership of the problems that your betas encounter. You see this as a failure on your part, and nobody rushes to broadcast their failures."

He let go of Oraxis, taking a few steps to leave, before continuing. "I've heard your story. Eternal mates, cursed with genetic sterility. They say bootstrapping satisfies paternal and maternal instincts. Do those you've bootstrapped call you mother and father?"

"The Pips do," Genevieve said, "and Xavier did, for a while, but not the others." For Susie-Q, it went without saying — their parent-child relationship had been genuine.

Vasilis said, "I was a father, as an alpha. I had four boys, one girl. The boys worshiped me, while the girl despised me. I don't know why I had such a hard time with her. I never even hit the child, which was rare for my tribe. So, when I seeded my first alpha, do you think I picked a boy or a girl?"

The first few drops of rain started falling as Genevieve considered the question. Oraxis was looking at her to answer. Would he pick a boy, because he had such luck with them as a father? Or a girl, to see if he could do a better job in this next life?

"Did you pick a girl?" Genevieve asked.

"Are you joking?!" Vasilis laughed. "Of course not! I'm terrible at giving girls or women any sort of guidance. I picked a boy, and continued picking boys every time I seeded an alpha. The more they looked like me, the more likely I was to pick them!"

Oraxis joined him with a chuckle. Genevieve could only manage a polite smile.

Vasilis quickly sobered. "Know your limits, and if you find you have taken on more than you can handle, reach out to your support network. That's what the Bootstrapping Council is here for."

Oraxis nodded. "We will readily seek your advice in the future. I'm afraid that Genevieve and I suffer from an abundance of pride."

Vasilis held his hands out to his sides, feeling the rain on his palms for a moment. He said, "In bootstrapping, as in parenting, every one of your charges comes to you with its own unique makeup, its own struggles. You must satisfy *their* needs, not your own. If you're seeding alphas to poise yourselves as the nucleus of a Telson family or to correct the mistakes of your past — your lost Susanne — then you're doing it for the wrong reasons. And if your fear of having the same thing that happened to Susanne happen to your other betas is preventing you from seeing what they truly need, then you are doing them a disservice. Overprotective parents can be as harmful as negligent ones."

The rain was coming down harder now. Oraxis said, "You're a wise man, Vasilis. Let's pitch the tent, then we can retreat to the cabin to talk some more."

Vasilis smiled up at the rain. "I appreciate the invitation, but I have intruded for long enough. Goodbye, Telsons." He started walking away as Oraxis scrambled to gather the sticks, ropes, and skins.

Genevieve hurried to help Oraxis, then stopped. She looked up at the calmly departing man. "Thank you for your wisdom, Vasilis Pilspa," she said, in all sincerity.

He kept walking, not turning back. A moment later he spoke, barely audible from across the clearing, in the falling rain. "If you heard my words and believed them to be wise, then you would let the rain fall upon her."

Oraxis stopped, with a pole in one hand and a rope in the other. He looked first at Vasilis, then Genevieve, then Zeta.

And the rain came pouring down.

THROUGHOUT THE STORMY evening and into the night, Oraxis laid beside Penelope-pooch while Genevieve laid beside Zeta. The cold rain pelted them, washing away Genevieve's tears as quickly as they came.

There was nothing quite so miserable as crying in the rain.

Just after midnight, lightning struck somewhere nearby, sending a clap of thunder through the air. Genevieve couldn't help but raise herself to one elbow and look at Zeta's face. The sound could have woken the dead, but it didn't make the disconnected girl stir.

Oraxis caught her peeking. He smirked and shook his head. "Let's just go inside, Gen." His auburn hair and beard were matted down like a drenched dog. She didn't want to think about what she looked like.

"But what if she—"

"If she comes out of it, she'll go inside, too."

"You don't know that."

"You're right, I don't." Oraxis grunted as he got to his feet.

Genevieve stayed down on the sand. Leaving Zeta alone out here was unthinkable.

"Come on, stop torturing yourself," Oraxis said. "I tell you what,

I'll have Zephyr watch her and tell us if she moves. He's a great sentry, eyes like an eagle."

"He *is* an eagle," Genevieve said, looking up at the tree topped with Zephyr's oversized nest. The giant eagle's head appeared, peering over the edge of the nest.

Genevieve put a hand on Zeta's cheek. Even in the cold rain, she was warm. Her placental mat would fuel her metabolism with as much ATP as it needed to keep her body temperature up, even in a blizzard. In her *mind*, Genevieve knew that Zeta would be fine. But her *heart* couldn't let go.

Slowly, reluctantly, Genevieve stood.

Together, they walked through the rain back to the cabin. Genevieve gave one final peek at Zeta through the furs covering the door. They took off their drenched leather tunics and hung them to dry. Oraxis fed the potbelly stove, stoking its fire until its warmth filled the cabin.

Together, they laid in their fur-pile bed. Genevieve wouldn't be able to fall asleep on her own, so she performed a bio-override, forcing sleep upon her troubled mind.

And in the morning, as she had been for the past week and a day, Zeta was still laying on her placental mat in the sand.

22

HAPPY HUNTING GROUNDS

THEY TRAVELED FOR A WEEK.

First, Zeta took them through the Starry Woods. Charra and the other children had marveled at the Motyxia — star babes — and Zeta had told them a story about a beautiful girl who played with the star babes so much that her skin had begun to glow.

A few days later, they passed through the Thin Forest. Oraxis and Genevieve weren't there, of course. Their cabin had tumbled down long ago, as she always knew it would. Now it was just a pile of logs. Zeta considered setting the cabin's remains on fire, but decided that there was no need to risk starting a forest fire.

As they departed from the clearing, Zeta noticed Penelope-pooch sniffing around at the sand circle. They couldn't exchange mind-speech in this construct, since she had set its parameters to disallow advanced technology. But she could still tell what her pooch was thinking — she wanted to go back.

Spread out in the sand were fragments of ancient bones. Most were too deteriorated to make out, but she spotted a fragment of a human skull and what looked like a pooch's jawbone.

Why would she create such things?

She blinked, and the bones were gone.

"That wasn't us," Zeta told Penelope-pooch. "We're alive — we all are. This is our reality now, and we're going to live here forever. Go play with your pups, girl."

Penelope-pooch whimpered, hesitated, then trotted away.

Incoming conversation request from Vasilis Pilspa.

Who? *"No, go away!"*

Conversation request declined.

Not a moment passed before the next intrusion.

Incoming conversation request from Tammie Mattau

Who are these people? *"I said go away! Leave me alone!"*

Conversation request declined, sender blocked.

"WorMS, block any strangers from sending me requests."

Privacy settings updated.

She had to get away from this place — it was haunted by Noddites. She rushed into the trees. Her tribe followed at a jog, like obedient pooches. In moments, the Thin Forest gave way to a grove of broad-leafed trees at the bottom of a valley. The murmur of a gentle river could be heard nearby.

"We camp here tonight," Zeta declared.

Without complaint or question, the tribe set to work at settling in.

Zeta paced to calm her nerves. Who were those people? What did they want from her? She just wanted to be left alone. Her tribemates could tell that she didn't want to talk, and kept to themselves as they built their small fires and laid out bedding furs.

That night, Zeta lay awake among her sleeping tribe. The snores of Elds, the rambling of the river, and the lullabies of toads should have soothed her to sleep. Instead, she watched Charra breathing through a slack mouth.

She tried not to let the darkness of the truth disturb the peace of the night. That's the problem with intrusive thoughts — as soon as you tell yourself not to think about something, there it is.

The first unwelcome thought was that the age when Charra died was not much younger than she had been when the Specter snatched Wilhelm-pa away.

Next came the sad knowledge that Wilhelm-pa had no place with her construct-tribe. Yephanie-ma had Rod-pa, now. This was the tribe as she had left it when she and Charra had taken their ill-fated trip to the spring pool.

A distant voice called, "Zeta."

She lifted her head. All was still.

She rose to her feet. A dense fog had rolled in, dampening the light of the camp's low fires.

She whispered, "Who's there?"

There was no response, but Zeta knew whose voice it had been. A chill went down her spine.

She stepped carefully over Charra, then made her way past the sleeping pooches. Penelope-pooch raised her head. She got to her feet and followed Zeta. They walked out of the grove and up the grassy slope of the valley.

A barren tree of twisting branches resolved before her, just upslope. Barren, save for a small scattering of brown-tinged white blossoms which clung to its branches. One of the drooping blossoms fell to the ground before her. She caught the faint smell of apple blossoms in the air, and her breath caught.

She knew this tree.

Zeta kneeled, picked up the fallen blossom, and brought it closer to her face. Resting within its browning pedals was the curled-up body of a dead honeybee.

Tears welled in her eyes. "I can't do this, Pen."

She looked over at her pooch, who was sniffing her way cautiously up the slope. She looked back at Zeta, letting out a faint, high-pitched whine.

Zeta laid the blossom gently on the ground and wiped her eyes, then rose and followed Penelope-pooch. They moved cautiously through the cold, wet grass until a glowing fire shone through the fog, upslope. Zeta's throat constricted and a fresh round of tears clouded her eyes as she approached the fire atop the crest of the valley.

The forms of two sitting men resolved from shadows into likenesses of Wilhelm-pa and Jebbam-bro-pa. They sat on the ground, looking into the fire, then turned to look up at her with welcoming expressions.

Penelope-pooch wagged her tail nervously, approaching Wilhelm-pa. She was sniffing, trying to see if she knew the man. Would she recognize him? She was a pup when he died. Her tail began wagging vigorously, and in a moment she was trying to pounce on him. Wilhelm-pa petted the pooch for a moment, then gestured with a palm down, calming her. She laid in the grass by his side, showing her belly. He rubbed it idly as he turned back to the fire.

Zeta knew that her lower mind had created this encounter. But, why? What did she want from these ghosts?

She didn't want them to speak, so they didn't. Zeta knelt by their fire, letting her silent tears flow. The three of them gazed into the crackling flames for several minutes as Zeta worked up the nerve to talk.

"I broke my vows," Zeta said, weakly. "All of them. That's why your spirits wander the world. I vowed to protect Charra, then led him to his death. I vowed to avenge you, and to free Pip-Rho, but I know now that it was a ridiculous idea. I can't fight aliens — evil spirits, I mean — I'm just a child. I don't know anything."

The ghosts sat in silence. Zeta met Wilhelm-pa's gaze. There was something warm there, in those chestnut brown eyes from long ago. Forgiveness? Consolation? She didn't deserve it.

"I'm done with making vows. All they do is make you disappointed in me. I can't control the world, and I can't conquer things that are so much bigger than I am."

Another minute of silence passed. She had said what she needed to say.

Zeta got back to her feet. "I'm sorry you can't be with the tribe. Next month I'll make a new construct and I'll be a little girl again and you'll both be there. Wilhelm-pa, you can put me on your shoulders and run as fast as you can. I promise you won't trip. And Jebbam-bro-pa, you can teach me how to throw a spear again. Okay?"

Neither ghost responded. They stared into the fire, as if contemplating its depths.

"Okay, I should go before someone wakes up and wonders where I ran off to. Your spirits are settled now — you're looking forward to living again, in the past."

Zeta decided that this encounter was just a vivid dream. She closed her eyes, placed herself back on the bed furs, and placed Penelope-pooch back with her sleeping pups. She opened her eyes again, then sat up with a start.

Yephanie-ma woke. "Shh, shh, shh, Zeta, it's okay. You were just dreaming."

Zeta laid back down, panting. She wiped her face, which was still wet with tears.

Her ma reached over and stroked her hair. "Just a dream, Zeta-babe. You can tell it to Shaman Mora-eld in the morning. She'll tell you what it means."

Zeta nodded and closed her eyes.

Yes, it was all just a dream.

IN THE MORNING the tribe climbed to the top of the hill and marveled at the beauty of the lands before them. Finally, they had found their way back to the Golden Grasslands. With all the recent rain, the grasses were actually not golden at all. They almost seemed to glow in a brilliant shade of green. Patches of flowers of every color decorated the rolling hills. Yephanie-ma gasped as they took in the view of their reclaimed lands for the first time.

Zeta hadn't seen bison since she was a young child, yet there they were, on the other side of the hill, just a spear's throw away. The beasts snorted as they grazed, eagerly fattening up on the lush greenery. They paid the humans in their midst no mind, as if they had never seen what hunters could do.

Charra and Jadon, another boy his age, chased the yipping Chimera-pup and Gorgon-pup all around the hilltop. The pups would let the boys get close before darting away again in a game of chase. Zeta might have joined in on the game, if she hadn't been taking care of Hareshnid.

Zeta came to a realization — these were the Happy Hunting Grounds, exactly as she had always imagined them. There would be no Red-Painted tribe, no stick-slings, no Night-Thunder Spirits, no hunger or pain. Nobody in the tribe suspected that Zeta had created this paradise for them. She wasn't entirely certain that she had created it herself.

Incoming conversation request from Jamji Telson.

"No," Zeta said, reflexively. A few people turned to look at her, then returned to what they were doing.

Conversation request declined.

Her heart pounded. She was torn — she wanted to see Jamji, but she didn't want to do what she knew Jamji would ask her to do. Maybe she wouldn't ask.

Zeta handed Hareshnid over to Yephanie-ma. She slipped away from the tribe, running down the hill and back into the shaded grove from where they had emerged.

She closed her eyes and reached out, asking for Jamji to join her world.

A heartbeat later, a twig snapped. Zeta opened her eyes to see a young woman stepping out from behind a tree. She wore a leather tunic, fringed with furs. Her hair was braided, with beads woven into the ends, and her skin tone matched that of Zeta's tribe. It took Zeta a moment to realize that the woman's face was Jamji's.

"I didn't recognize you at first," Zeta said.

Jamji stood beside the tree, looking down at her body. "Well, your construct's parameters don't allow for modern tech, so I had to revert to my tribal avatar."

"Sorry about that," Zeta said. "I just...I want the world to be simple. To be...real."

"Zeta—"

"I know what you're going to say, and I know — this isn't real. I'm not delusional. But I don't see what harm this is doing, me staying here. This is all I need to be happy."

Jamji was looking at her palm, turning it over to look at the back of her hand. "I'm glad you're happy," she said, then smiled up at Zeta, "and it's good to see you again. I'm on my way to the Guardian Embassy. They told me you've been disconnected ever since I left. I'm sorry that what I said about your tribe being gone upset you so much."

"I told you I'm happy, now."

"And I believe you!" Jamji stepped forward. "It's wonderful — you deserve some happiness. If this is what you need, then what's the harm? Seriously, you should stay here as long as you want. They can't force you to disconnect."

Was this a trick? "So, you're fine if I don't return to my body in Nod?"

"Sure, if this is your thing, go with it. Disconnecting from reality for a while can be good for you. I've met Proliferans who've spent more time in constructs than the real world. Usually they're collaborative social spaces, but being a hermit's fine, too."

A wave of relief washed over Zeta.

"So," Jamji said, "the next thing they're gonna do is in a few days they'll take you from the Telson cabin to Syn-Cen. Cain'll check you out, and if you pass, they'll tuck you in a tiny room and leave you alone. I was a little worried you wouldn't pass Cain's test, but it sounds like you can tell what's real and what's not."

Zeta had been sure that someone would end up dragging her, kicking and screaming, back into the real world. Hearing that she wouldn't be forced to do anything gave her a renewed sense of peace. She really could live here, with her tribe, for as long as she wanted. She ran to Jamji, wrapping her arms around her and squeezing her in a hug.

Zeta grabbed Jamji's hand. "Come on, I'll introduce you."

Jamji yanked her hand out of Zeta's. "You don't need to do that." She took a step backward. "This is your world, not mine."

Zeta vaguely remembered Jamji being angry about something to do with Talmid.

"Jamji," Zeta asked, "why did you ask me about Chief Talmid?"

———

THE TRIBE SPENT the day hunting, fishing, and settling in at the new camp in the valley. Zeta and Jamji went a short way upstream and made a small fire of their own, out of earshot from her tribe.

That was where Jamji told her story.

They shared tears. Zeta could never imagine what it must have been like for Jamji. When Zeta had offered to show her replays of Talmid, Jamji declined. She wasn't ready.

When the sky grew an inky black, they decided to call it a night. Jamji stayed with her, sleeping in the construct on a bed of furs. Zeta had let her bring the tiny, natural form of Pepper-pooch into the world. The pooch slept on Jamji's belly in a curled little bundle like a sleek, black-haired roly-poly.

In the morning, Zeta woke to find Jamji sitting on a log opposite Chief Talmid. The eld poked the fire with a stick, then smiled up at Jamji, showing more gums than teeth. Jamji seemed transfixed.

"I'm sorry," Zeta said, "I didn't know he would wander over. I can send him away—"

"I called him over," Jamji said. "We haven't talked, yet. The construct doesn't seem to want to decide what he would say without your input."

Zeta never actually told the people in the construct what to say, but she knew that for anything other than mundane conversation, they would only say the things she *expected* them to say.

"No," said Chief Talmid, "I just didn't want to wake Zeta. The girl does enjoy her sleep, after all. Now, come closer, Jamji-ma. My eyes aren't what they once were. Let me see you."

Jamji looked nervously to Zeta, then went to Talmid's side, kneeling on one knee. The eld put a hand to Jamji's chin, turning her head to one side and the other. The eld's eyes were glassy with tears. "You visited me in my dreams. Your back would be turned, or your face hidden in shadows. However hard I tried, I could never see what you looked like. Now I know why — I never dared to dream that my ma would be *this* beautiful."

Jamji teared up, reaching for her long-lost boy and squeezing him in an embrace. Zeta's heart went out to her sis-kin. A pang of guilt struck her as she wondered if she *made* Talmid say that or if he really would have said it.

The real Chief Talmid certainly wouldn't have said something mean, or cold. He wouldn't have been angry at Jamji for not being there when he was growing up, or disappointed that she didn't go back to Eden and find him.

That was all anyone in Zeta's construct seemed to do. They were simply happy to have Zeta back, and the only time anyone got upset was when she thought they should. It was always for some silly reason, and they were always apologetic afterwards.

"Tell me about yourself, Jamji-ma," Talmid said, "are you living a good life?"

"I am." Jamji sat on the log next to the eld, putting an arm around him and resting her head upon his. "Right now I'm preparing to go live with the Guardians."

"Guardians!" Talmid laughed, "What a noble name for a tribe! Better than *Scorpion Tail*, for certain. What do these people guard?"

"Humanity," Jamji said, "everybody."

"And what are they guarding everybody from?"

Jamji looked across at Zeta, giving her a wink. "Evil spirits, mostly."

Chief Talmid laughed. "Then they should be called the Guardian *Shamans!*"

"I'll make the suggestion," Jamji laughed. She smiled absently for a few moments, her arm around the eld. Then her smile faded. She stood, wiping her eyes. "I better get going."

Pepper-pooch got up, ran around the fire, and bounced in circles by Jamji's side.

"Don't leave," Zeta blurted, scrambling to her feet.

"Zeta," Jamji sighed, "this was nice, but we both know it's a fantasy. I'll honor Talmid's memory by moving on, living a good life, and doing something important. I wanna be someone he'd be proud of."

Zeta looked through the trees. She could see Rod-pa swinging Charra in circles as the boy laughed. Eve-eld-ma turned a spit over a fire, cooking a fresh kill. Yephanie-ma suckled Hareshnid. Chief Talmid was no longer at their fire — he was with the tribe through the trees, sitting with another eld, grinding an herb between a stone and a bowl.

"Do you think they'd be proud of me?" Zeta asked.

"You've been through a lot, and I think you've done great. Look, this thing you're doing, I think it's important for you. But I'll be honest — if it's all you ever do for the next hundred years, it's gonna get kinda old. And, no, it really wouldn't be anything to be proud of. That doesn't mean you have to disconnect, yet. Not if you're not ready."

How would she ever be ready? The longer she stayed here, the more comfortable she would get, and the more it would hurt to leave. But, yes, she had to leave someday. She was already growing impatient with the shallow personalities of her reconstructed kin in this false world.

"They say I have to have a Beta Ceremony before I can set out on my own," Zeta said.

Jamji shrugged. "Tell 'em you're not following their traditions, if you want. Nobody's gonna make you do it. Still, ceremonies are important. They mark beginnings, ends. When I get accepted into the Guard, if they don't hold a ceremony, I'm gonna be disappointed. Before I got wrapped up with your bootstrapping business, I gave my farewell tribute dance to the Genesis Faction. It was ceremonial, in its own way. Symbolic." She shrugged. "To me, at least."

Zeta was still watching the tribe from between the trees. They seemed happy enough without her. Though, if she wanted them to, they would switch in an instant to wailing, pulling at their garments and crying her name. They were put here by her, for her. They were her creation, her servants, her playthings. Was this any way to honor them?

"Thank you, Jamji," Zeta said. "I know what I need to do."

———

THEY STOOD in the knee-high grasses on the hilltop of The Happy Hunting Grounds. The grove where her tribe had made camp was nearby. Jamji and Zeta stood alone, along with their pooches, in the wide open space.

Zeta closed her eyes and sent her invites.

Oraxis and Genevieve appeared simultaneously, no less than five seconds later. Genevieve started to run towards Zeta, but slowed to a stop when she noticed that the woman by Zeta's side was Jamji. She probably hadn't recognized her.

Zeta could sense the tension between them. She walked to meet Genevieve. "I'm sorry for disconnecting like that. I know you were scared for me."

"I'm sorry we didn't tell you about the time difference sooner," Genevieve said. "Can I hug you?" Her bottom lip trembled as she said this, and her eyes glistened.

"Of course," Zeta said, opening her arms. Genevieve rushed in for the hug and squeezed her tightly.

Oraxis approached. "This is beautiful," he said, gesturing to the scenery. "Thank you for inviting us. It's good to see you again, even if it's not in the real world."

"Thanks," Zeta said, releasing Genevieve. "I designed the scenery based on a place my tribe lived once. It wasn't this green, and there weren't as many flowers, but I kind of wanted this to be a special place. I wanted it to be perfect — The Happy Hunting Grounds."

Two little women appeared nearby. They were absolutely identical, all the way down to their stain-painted leather vests and hooded fur capes. Zeta had no idea which one was Pip-Tau and which was Pip-Rho.

"What gives?!" One of them squealed.

"Yeah, this tech cap setting is killing me," said the other.

They looked at each other, then broke out laughing.

"Hey, you shop at the Caveman Emporium, too?"

"This was the last neoprim avatar I'd used. I guess that means it's the last you'd used, too, eh?"

"Has it been that long?"

"Yep!"

"Okay, we need to look different. I get black hair, you get white hair. Deal?"

"Like I'm an old lady or something? No!"

"You *are* old!"

"I am not!"

"Fine, I get black hair, you get a white floral wreath."

"Oh, and you should have a black floral wreath!"

"Zeta's got the reality setting maxed and, sorry, there's no such thing as black flowers."

"Sure there are! They're really dark purple, but close enough."

"Deep purple? Not my jam." The Pip's hair shifted from dark brown to jet black. That must have been Pip-Rho.

"Fine." The other Pip reached down and picked up a wreath of woven white flowers. She placed it on her puff of curly brown hair. They both smiled up at Zeta.

"You two are adorable," Zeta said.

"We know!" Pip-Rho sang, wading through the grass. The three exchanged hugs.

"I guess this is everybody I know, now," Zeta said, looking at the five Telsons around her.

"You'll meet more people soon," Oraxis said.

"Would you like to meet the other two Telsons?" Genevieve asked.

Zeta considered it for a moment before saying, "I guess they're my ancestors, right? You always pick someone from the Scorpion Tail Tribe?"

Oraxis said, "As close as possible, yes. Tribes split apart, join with others. It's safe to say that their gene lines are close to yours."

Genevieve elbowed Oraxis in the ribs, then said, "Yes, they're from your tribe. You're running the construct, so you'll have to invite them if that's what you want to do. Their names are XT-Prime of the Astrus Faction and Carff Telson."

Zeta nodded once, then closed her eyes and sent the invites.

Genevieve said, "It might take a minute for them to—"

An eld appeared in front of Zeta, giving a delighted cackle of a laugh that made Zeta jump.

"Hoo-whoop!" The eld called, cupping his hands around his mouth. "Hail, Zeta of the Scorpion Tail Tribe!"

"Zeta, meet Carff," Oraxis chuckled.

Carff was dressed like a shaman, a necklace of fangs tied around his neck. Pouches and bladders hung from his belt. His wrinkled, leather-toned cheeks were painted with white lines. One of his eyes was milky white, and long brown and white feathers decorated his shoulders.

Zeta recalled Oraxis saying that even though Noddites could allow themselves to grow older, or even younger, most preferred to stay near the age they were when their alpha died. Pip-Alpha had died as a child, and even though the Pips were women now, they still overflowed with youthful energy. Zeta guessed that Carff's alpha had lived a *very* long life.

"Oraxis," Carff whistled, taking short, hobbling steps towards Zeta, "you didn't tell me she was *perfect*! Just look at her!"

Zeta looked up at Jamji, who stood with arms crossed, leaning on one leg. She smirked as she shook her head at the eld's odd behavior.

"It's good to meet you, Carff," Zeta said.

Another man appeared. He was tall and lean, wearing only a loinskin. His body was completely hairless. Seeing a beardless, bald man was strange. It also made it difficult to place his age. Zeta wondered if he actually looked like this in real life.

The man assessed the construct, then silently nodded to each of the Telsons, in turn, before turning to face Zeta. He glided towards her with the grace of a jungle cat, never dropping his gaze. It was unsettling.

"Hello, Zeta," he said, closing his eyes and bowing his head and shoulders forward. His voice was soft, gentle, and higher pitched than Zeta would have expected.

Zeta gave an awkward bow of her own. "Hello."

Genevieve went to the man and placed a hand on his back. "Zeta, this is XT-Prime. He's not a Genesisian anymore, but we still include him as part of the family."

"It's good to meet you," Zeta said. She looked to Jamji again, remembering what she had said about the Astri, wondering how she would react to the man's presence.

Jamji's arms were still crossed, but now she glared darkly. Zeta couldn't let her sis-kin's attitude affect her judgement of the man — she seemed to judge everyone more harshly than they deserved.

Zeta stepped away from the group, Penelope-pooch trotting by her side. She turned and took a moment to meet the eyes of each of the seven faces before her. They waited patiently for whatever she had in mind to say or do.

With as much significance as she could put behind it, Zeta spread her arms and intoned, "Welcome to my Alpha Ceremony."

23

TWO CEREMONIES

"I KNOW we aren't supposed to talk about our alpha's life and tribe with anyone besides our bootstrappers," Zeta started.

"I think we can relax that rule," Genevieve said. "We're all family here."

"We're reconsidering a lot of our practices," Oraxis said. "You can share anything you want."

Oraxis could feel the surprised glances of his past betas.

Zeta gave a nod. "This was my tribe." She gestured to a grove of trees at the bottom of the valley. From between the trees, people began to emerge. First, there came men carrying spears, accompanied by sniffing, trotting dogs. Next came the women, carrying babies or wearing packs upon their backs. Kids walked at their parents' sides, or held the hands of elds. Oraxis counted seventy-eight heads. Their numbers had diminished slightly in the time between Zeta's alpha seeding and her death.

Zeta said, "We called ourselves The Scorpion Tail Tribe. I guess it was your people, too?"

"In my time," XT-Prime said, "we were called The People of the Scorpion's Stinger."

Pip-Tau laughed. "Weird! Yeah, that changed by my alpha's time. We were The Scorpion's Stinging Tail Tribe."

"You old timers," Carff whistled through his missing teeth. "What a mouthful! We were The Scorpion Tail Tribe, and that name stuck! Right, Zeta?"

Zeta smiled at Carff. "It did, yes. In The Scorpion Tail tribe, we have traditional ceremonies for lots of things, as I'm sure you did in your time. The elds said we're following the ways of our ancestors, all the way back to the beginning of time. I guess that means we've had the traditions since humans came to Genesis from Earth." She looked to Oraxis for confirmation.

He smiled and gave her a nod. Genesis's colonization seemed like yesterday. It really wasn't long ago, relative to geological time scales — the first generation of neoprims emerged from their synthetic wombs only six hundred and six Earth years ago. Oraxis's throat tightened as he reminisced about their little hatchling — their little Susie-Q.

Zeta continued, "We have ceremonies for when someone's born, when someone dies. When we pick out a new place to camp, we cast out evil spirits and invite friendly spirits to warm themselves at our fires. When we cross paths with other tribes and some of our people go with them, we have a ceremony to say goodbye. If someone joins our tribe, we have a ceremony to welcome them."

The tribe was climbing the slope of the valley's side, closing the distance between the grove and the Telsons. They could hear the chatter of small talk, the yips and huffs of puppies at play.

"I never had a chance to say goodbye," Zeta said. "So, that's what my Alpha Ceremony is for. It's a funeral for my past self, and a goodbye ceremony for my tribe."

She choked up a bit at this, then turned from the Telsons to face the approaching ghosts of her past.

Genevieve walked to her side, putting an arm around Zeta's shoulder. "I think this Alpha Ceremony is a wonderful idea," she said.

THEY WAITED in silence until the first men of the tribe began walking between them. The men gave the Telsons passing glances, but mostly ignored them.

"Their faces," Carff marveled. "It's like they're my own kin. By Surya, that young'n could be one of my boys!"

Pip-Rho and Pip-Tau held each other, tearing up as they looked from face to passing face. The women, children, and elds were now passing between them. A few paused to give a smile or a nod, but for the most part they paid the Telsons no mind.

The woman that Oraxis recognized as Yephanie was walking towards Zeta, holding a baby. Zeta ran down the hill and wrapped her arms around the two, shaking with sobs.

Oraxis wasn't the sentimental type, and it always seemed like Genevieve did enough crying for the both of them, but this was too much. He let the tears pool in his eyes, unblinking. They trickled down his cheek, soaking into his beard.

A man that Oraxis didn't recognize came to Yephanie's side, putting a hand on Zeta's shoulder and patting it. Zeta went to him and gave him a brief hug before releasing him. She stepped backwards from them, then squeezed her eyes shut. Her lip trembled and her chest heaved as she stood apart from the two adults and their baby.

Genevieve glanced back at Oraxis with a concerned expression.

Yephanie and the man faced forward and started walking again, wearing solemn expressions.

Genevieve gasped, covering her mouth. *"Oh, Oraxis, did you see that? That had to be the hardest thing she's ever done,"* Genevieve sent via mindspeech.

"Goodbye can be the hardest word," Oraxis replied.

"Not just goodbye, O! She just told them to keep moving on, to live their own lives, without her. She has to move on without them, and they have to do the same."

As the man passed by Oraxis, he looked him straight in the eye. The man glanced over his shoulder at Zeta, then back at Oraxis. He gave the slightest of nods, as if to say, "Now, she's in your hands. Take care of her."

Oraxis bowed his head to the man in a gesture which said, "I will." Fresh tears stung his eyes.

Chief Talmid was approaching Zeta, now. They looked into each other's eyes for a few seconds before Zeta gave him a slight bow. The eld moved on, ascending the slope with a great deal of help from his walking stick. At the hilltop, he eyed Genevieve, Oraxis, and then Jamji.

Oraxis watched as the reproduction of Chief Talmid approached Jamji. Until now, she had been standing with a closed posture, arms crossed, eyes wet with wiped tears. She stepped forward and opened her arms, pulling the eld into a gentle hug. Her chin rested on his head and her eyes closed tightly as she held him.

Meanwhile, Zeta was meeting the somber gaze of tribe member after tribe member, saying her silent goodbyes.

A full minute later, Jamji let go of Talmid. She tried to step aside to let him pass, but he reached for her hand. She was surprised, but didn't resist as the eld silently led her forward.

ORAXIS AND GENEVIEVE exchanged a curious glance. Chief Talmid was leading Jamji towards them.

Jamji seemed to have caught on, too. The three of them looked over at Zeta, suspecting her of orchestrating the eld's actions, but she had her back to them, hugging a boy about her age.

"*This is some bold autonomy,*" Oraxis sent Genevieve.

"*He's doing what Chief Talmid would have done,*" Genevieve replied. "*Zeta's been training these artificials for the last week.*"

Jamji stopped a few meters away, not letting Talmid pull her any further. Talmid gestured for Genevieve and Oraxis to come to him, to close the distance.

"I know what you're trying to do," Jamji said.

Oraxis and Genevieve approached Jamji. Talmid patted her on the cheek, then departed in a steady hobble.

"We're sorry we didn't tell you," Genevieve said, softly.

"We're still learning," Oraxis said, "about how best to bootstrap betas."

Jamji's arms crossed again. She glanced at Zeta, who was now looking in their direction. She returned her glare to Oraxis and Genevieve. "So, you admit you screwed up? With me? With them?" She gestured to the other Telsons. "With Zeta?"

"We did the best we could, Jamji," Genevieve whispered. "Now, this Alpha Ceremony is important to Zeta. Let's not fight."

"Chief Talmid would have said for you to forgive them," Zeta said.

"Would he?" Jamji said, sarcastically.

"Yes, he would have," Zeta said, growing heated. "He was wise, and he always stepped in when people would fight. Jamji, your boy was a peace-loving man."

Carff piped in, "Forgiveness is tough to swallow, but it settles the stomach."

"It has been said," XT-Prime added, "that the primary beneficiary of forgiveness is the giver, not the receiver."

Jamji seemed to grow more agitated. She shot a glare at the Pips. "Anything you two have to add?"

Pip-Rho stepped forward and jabbed a finger at Oraxis. She growled, "I say you break his *other* elbow!"

"Rho!" Pip-Tau squealed, back-handing her clone's arm.

Pip-Rho stood with eyes bugged and a snarl on her lips, with a stare that dared Jamji to do it.

Then, inexplicably, Jamji snorted. She was laughing?

The tension melted as the rest of the Telsons came to realize that

Pip-Rho had masterfully executed a surgical strike at Jamji's funny bone.

"Alright," Jamji said, taking a breath and turning to Oraxis and Genevieve, "Fine! My boy was a wise man, what can I say. You're forgiven, go now in peace and all that crap."

"Thank you, Jamji," Genevieve said. She seemed to know better than to try for a hug.

Jamji looked towards Zeta. "Sorry I ruined your Alpha Ceremony."

Zeta wiped her eyes. "Well, I think it was over, anyway." The tribe had all passed by, now. Most of them had made it to the bottom of the other side of the hill and were crossing the dip between the rolling hills.

Zeta and the Telsons stood in silence for a long while, watching the tribe recede into the distance, until they disappeared between the flowery hills.

"*O, look,*" Genevieve sent.

Oraxis followed Genevieve's gaze back towards the grove in the valley. Between the trees stood a handful of small figures. The low tech level of the construct disallowed enhanced optics, so Oraxis squinted to see. It looked like Zeta, standing with a boy on one side and a pair of men on the other. Three dogs sat by their sides.

As Oraxis watched, the figures turned away, disappearing into the shadows between the trees. Her alpha's life had now been laid to rest.

"That was a beautiful ceremony," Genevieve told Zeta, returning to her side.

Zeta was watching the grove. "Thanks. Can we have my Beta Ceremony, now?"

Oraxis winced, involuntarily. He responded as calmly as he could manage. "Now?"

"We'll send the invites tonight," Genevieve said, "but we do need to let people know at least a few days ahead of time so they can work it into their schedule."

"Hoo-hoo!" Carff called out. "Two ceremonies in one week!"

To Oraxis, it seemed premature. She hadn't even reconnected with her body yet, and she was ready to dive into a crowd of strangers? But if it was what she wanted, then so be it.

ZETA RECONNECTED to her body in the real world.

The next morning, Oraxis and Genevieve cooked another traditional Earth-style day-after breakfast for her.

Then they set to work. The next three days were a flurry of activity in preparation for Zeta's Beta Ceremony and, more importantly, her reception party.

Genevieve was in charge of the guest list, venue, and program. She spent most of her time "hand delivering" messages. This consisted of non-stop WorMS conversations with friends, acquaintances, and VIP's. The only way to get a large group of far-flung people together on such short notice was to host it in a construct, so Genevieve delegated the venue design duties to the Pips.

Oraxis took on the task of preparing Zeta. The cultural norms of civilized, large societies can be hard to reconcile with neoprim sensibilities. Everyone at the ceremony would have lived as a neoprim at some point, so there was leeway in their expectations, but for many of the faction's elds that life ended hundreds of years ago.

On the morning of the ceremony, Genevieve sent Oraxis the confirmed RSVP's. He sat with Zeta in the Zen rock garden and briefed her on the "who's who" of the attendees, using a mini-holographic projector to show their public profile images.

After an hour of this, Zeta told him, "You don't need to tell me about these people before you introduce me to them. All these names, the things you say they do. Nanobiology? Theoretical mathematics? It's just...I'm not going to remember any of it. It doesn't matter, anyway — if I run across them again someday, I'll just look up their profile. And if I want to know what a Neoanthropologist does, I'll just ask WoQS."

Oraxis threw up his hands, running them through his hair. "Okay," he said, "just remember, when someone asks what discipline you've taken an interest in, you say *Xenobiology*."

Zeta looked at him skeptically, then glazed over in the far-away expression of one performing a WoQS query. When she returned, she grinned and said, "You're right! I'm going to take on the Specters, so, yeah, that makes me a Xenobiologist."

It felt like telling a toddler who had slammed her hand down on the keys of a piano that she was a pianist now. It was fine, he shouldn't discourage her, but there was a certain sensitive subject she should be warned against.

"When you talk about your goals, it's best not to talk about the Specters, specifically."

"Why shouldn't I talk about the Specters?"

"It's complicated. Let's just say, there are people who don't think we need to worry about them. They consider it an offworlder problem. Even the people who do think something should be done don't like to talk about them. If you talk about taking them on, you're bound to raise some hackles."

Zeta scoffed.

There was no point in arguing with her — he knew how poorly that would go.

This would be an interesting party.

"Well, it's about time to start. Are you ready?" Genevieve asked Zeta.

Zeta nodded. She seemed nervous, but excited. She turned and started towards her bedding furs at the corner of the cabin.

"Before we begin," Oraxis said, "I have something for you."

Zeta stopped and turned towards him. Penelope-pooch had

continued walking, laying down on the hard-packed floor beside Zeta's bed.

He pulled a leather-wrapped bundle from behind the wardrobe. As he approached Zeta, he unwrapped the bow. It was a recurve bow, with tips that curled away from the holder. The thickest part of the bow, near the contoured handle, was carved with twisting patterns. The glow of Zeta's smile as he handed over the custom bow warmed his heart.

"It's beautiful," she whispered. She ran her finger along the intricate carvings, then settled her hand into the grip and gave the string a test pull.

"Its draw should feel more natural to you than my bow."

"Ah-ha!" Zeta laughed. "You just wanted your bow back!"

"I—"

"I'm kidding, Oraxis. Thank you!" She stepped forward and pulled him into a hug. "Besides, I lost your bow."

Genevieve laughed.

Oraxis couldn't help but join in, giving a hearty chuckle. He had been wondering where she hid the thing. Somewhere deep in the Thin Forest, apparently.

"Don't worry about it," he said.

"I also have a gift for you," Genevieve said. She was holding a small glass vial woven into a leather sleeve. "It's perfume — a fragrant liquid. Put a few drops on your neck and wrists and you'll smell wonderful for the rest of the day."

Zeta accepted the vial, graciously. Genevieve showed her how to remove the stopper and shake out a drop onto her fingertip. They both applied a bit. Zeta put her perfumed finger to her nose, breathing deeply.

"Oh, Genevieve," she marveled. "This smell." She sniffed again. "It's wonderful — like nothing I have smelled before. I can't describe it."

"It's called Eau de Thin Forest," Genevieve said. "Fresh rain, sweet sap, undertones of pine and moss. It's all in there — the scents of your beta birthplace."

"*Where'd you get that?*" Oraxis mindspoke to Genevieve.

"*From Juliet de Turin, at last year's bazaar.*"

"Who?"

"*The Proliferan perfumer? Shows up at the bazaar every twenty years or so? You know, with the short, black hair?*"

"Four arms?"

"*What?! No, you're thinking about Jolette, the silk-weaver.*"

Oraxis clapped his hands, rubbing them together. "Alright! Let's see what the Pips came up with."

They went to their respective beds. He caught a whiff of Genevieve's perfume as they laid down together. It was *very* nice.

"*You know, the Proliferans mix pheromone activators into their perfumes,*" Oraxis mindspoke to Genevieve.

"*Not in the ones they gift to Noddites — that's against the tribute treaty. If you're having amorous stirrings, it's just the natural flames of your eternal love.*"

Oraxis humphed. "*Oh, good. I thought it was heartburn.*"

They slipped into slate-space, then joined the construct.

It was Zeta's Happy Hunting Grounds, but with the saturation level turned up several notches. Every color was richer, every flowery breeze a warm caress.

Zeta was speechless as she surveyed the construct.

"Welcome to your Beta Ceremony!" came a Pip's voice.

"Like it?" asked another Pip's voice. At first, Oraxis thought they were disembodied, then noticed the cherub avatars floating overhead. Carff and XT-Prime stood nearby, and Jamji sat in the grass a distance away. The head of Pepper-pooch's tiny yipping avatar popped up over the top of the grass as it bounded towards them.

Zeta said, "It's so beautiful! But where are all the people you said would be here?"

"Just over yonder hill," Pip-Rho said, making the hill adjacent to their own mound jiggle like gelatin. "They don't get to be here for the family ceremony. They're waiting for us to finish so they can throw you a reception party. That's where the fun really happens."

Genevieve stepped towards Zeta. "We know you don't like to draw things out, so this'll be a nice, short ceremony. It started with the giving of gifts. Next is the family invitation."

The Telsons gathered, standing before Zeta and Penelope-pooch. Jamji took her time joining the group, then stood in a strategically selected spot close to the Pips.

Oraxis cleared his throat and said, "Zeta of the Scorpion Tail Tribe, the death of your alpha has separated you from your tribe and family. If it is any comfort or consolation to you, we humbly invite you to join our Telson family. We would be honored if you would accept, but you are under no obligation—"

Zeta was already nodding, "Yes, of course I accept! I kind of already considered myself to be a Telson after Jamji started calling me sis-kin."

Pip-Tau laughed, "Well, give your O-pa an' Gen-ma a hug, already!"

Zeta went to them, joining in a group hug that the entire family took part in.

"I name you Zeta Telson," Genevieve intoned, playfully.

In a matter of seconds, Surya plummeted from the sky, plunging them into darkness. The stars shone brilliantly overhead, and Soma hung brightly above them, looking larger than life. The group hug broke apart as they watched the sky change. The sound of cheers drifted over the hill from the crowd awaiting their arrival.

Near the horizon, a bright spot bloomed.

"Zeta," Genevieve said. "Oraxis and I want to share this with you. You see, we were there on your naming day."

Oraxis and Genevieve had prepared this portion of the ceremony. They agreed that they could share the info, in the spirit of trying a new, more open-minded approach. It still felt wrong to talk about their visit to Zeta's tribe.

"In fact," Genevieve said, "I sort of gave Yephanie your name."

"I knew it!" Pip-Rho and Pip-Tau exclaimed in unison.

Genevieve continued, "I had been singing a counting song using the Greek alphabet, and you giggled in the most adorable way when I got to zeta. Your ma liked the sound of the word, so she chose it for your name."

The bright spot was crawling across the sky, glowing bright white, growing an orange tail of sparkling fragments.

"Soma's tears," Zeta whispered, covering her mouth. "Is this really what it looked like?"

"It is," Oraxis said. "We pulled this imagery directly from our stored experiences. It seemed appropriate that you should witness it for yourself on this, your second naming day, and know it for what it truly was."

"I recognize this incident," XT-Prime said. "The atmospheric reentry of Proliferan communications relay vessel, Lahaina, destroyed by Specters in Earth Standard Year fifty-five twenty-one. Correct?"

"Correct," Oraxis said. "Immediately after the Proliferans turned up the tightbeam transmitter they got attacked by a Specter. This is what your tribe saw when the destroyed vessel's wreckage fell down from space."

Zeta gaped as the fireball split into two parts, overhead. "Soma's tears. The Specters did that?"

Oraxis nodded, gravely. "Yes."

They watched in silence as the wreckage descended. A distant flash that faded to an orange glow marked its crash on the western horizon.

"This Specter attack happened on my naming day?! It's like I was fated to fight them," Zeta said, looking from face to face.

Genevieve, Carff, and the Pips were nodding, but Oraxis wasn't into the whole "fate" thing. He kept his mouth shut.

"Let Surya rise on the new Telson," Pip-Tau said. Soma zipped away and Surya peeked above the horizon in the east, casting brilliant hues across the sky.

"Okay," Genevieve said, "next we would normally go through the speeches, but we decided we'd just send them to your WorMS queue and let you read them on your own time. I trust everyone sent Zeta their Words of Wisdom message?" She looked around.

Carff took on a shifty expression.

"Carff..." Genevieve moaned.

"It'll be in your inbox by this time tomorrow," he told Zeta, nodding resolutely.

"To wrap up the ceremony," Genevieve said, "I just want to say that we're all deeply proud of you, Zeta. Your path may not have been a straight one, but it was inspiring to see you navigate it."

After another round of hugs was exchanged and a few more tears were shed, the Telson family made its way down their small hill and up the side of the larger hill beside them. Zeta walked in the lead, with Jamji by her side. When they reached the pinnacle, Zeta staggered. Jamji caught her as she covered her mouth, taken aback by the scene before her.

Oraxis and Genevieve reached the hilltop. They surveyed the party grounds, glowing with pride.

"Nice." Oraxis nodded. "How come nobody ever throws me a party like this?"

Nobody replied.

24

ROHITO

IT WAS OVERWHELMING.

Zeta could barely absorb everything she was seeing. She was overlooking the biggest crowd of people she had ever seen. The entire crowd was applauding, shouting cheers, calling her name.

To one side, stone tables were lined with a feast of meats, fruits, and unfamiliar foods. To another side, a raised square of ground glowed in alternating patterns of color. A shimmering orb hovered above the ground. Thumping music filled the air.

Dashing over distant hills were dinosaurs, like those they had ridden when she had learned how to build constructs. Laughing men and women held on tightly as the dinosaurs clashed in brief skirmishes.

"Introducing, Zeta Telson!" The Pips chorused. Their voices echoed through the hills like gods.

The crowd roared. Even the dinosaurs stopped what they were doing to turn towards her and clap their forelegs.

"A'right," Pip-Rho shouted, her voice filling the construct, "playground rules! This is a moderately bounded collaborative freestyle construct. Dino Rides to the north, Barker's Field to the west, Infinite

Eats to the south, and Disco Inferno to the east. Blink-transport is on, Babelfish auto-translate is active, and avatar properties are open as long as you keep your clothes on and don't be a *punk*. That means you, Q-Bert!"

Laughter rolled over the crowd.

"Final rule: you get *five* minutes of Zeta's time, *max!* See that little counter over your head? If that hits zero, your mouth seals shut!"

More laughter. Zeta was laughing now, too.

"She's serious about that," Pip-Tau told Zeta.

"Oh!" Zeta laughed.

"A'right, them's the rules. Party on, dudes!" Pip-Rho squealed. Powdery explosions flashed in the sky as colorful bands of light jumped from hill to hill, like great snakes swimming through the ground.

"Is this too much?" Genevieve asked Zeta, quietly.

"No," she said breathlessly, "it's just...amazing. I've never had so many people be so happy to see me. They don't even know me."

"But they know what you've been through," Pip-Rho said, turning back around to face her, "because they all had to do the same thing."

"Not the Earthlings," Jamji murmured.

Pip-Rho rounded on her. "Right, my mistake — all *they* had to do was kill themselves and leave half of their friends and family behind to get gobbled up by hungry-hungry *aliens*, trusting that a couple thousand years later their mysterious synthetic benefactor would do them a *solid* and resurrect them with their minds intact using some sketchy first-gen orb tech."

Zeta braced for Jamji's reaction to Pip-Rho's rant. She just rolled her eyes and crossed her arms.

Pip-Rho seemed disappointed she didn't get a rise out of Jamji. She sang, "B-T-Dubs, Paulie-boy's on the dance floor, if you want to say hi," then disappeared.

Jamji deflated. "You invited *him?* I hate you guys so much." She disappeared.

Pip-Tau was the next to vanish.

"What happened?" Zeta asked Genevieve. "Are they disconnecting?"

"Teleporting," XT-Prime said from just over her shoulder, making her jump. She turned to face him, glimpsing his effeminate face for an instant before he vanished.

"Party, Zeta!" Carff called from the bottom of the hill. "It's your day!"

"You should send Penelope to the dog park," Oraxis said, kneeling by Zeta's side to pet the golden pooch.

Zeta was confused.

Genevieve pointed at the hill to their left. "Barker's Field, see?" On the hillside was a pack of playing pooches, ranging in size from Pepper-pooch's real-world monster form to his miniature avatar.

"Do you want to go play with those pooches, Pen?" Zeta mindspoke.

Penelope-pooch replied, *"Yes, I see lots of pooches. I should see which of them is the strongest and smell their odors."*

"Gross. Have fun!" She imagined sending Penelope-pooch to the hill with the other pooches, and she was gone.

"Ready to go rub elbows?" Genevieve asked, taking her by the hand.

Rub elbows? Oraxis hadn't prepared her for that tradition.

"Not really," Zeta said, "but let's do it, anyway."

MEETING new people was fun for a while. But eventually, faces started blurring together. The odd avatars, the strange things these people were interested in, the nonsense questions they asked — it felt like her mind was turning into mush.

Most of them just wanted to talk about themselves. When they would ask questions, they were always the same. She recited her practiced answers, trying not to sound bored.

"What discipline strikes your fancy?"

"Xenobiology."

"Congratulations, you're done bootstrapping! What's next for Zeta Telson?"

"Studying Xenobiology."

"If you had to pick just one field of study—"

"Xenobiology."

Then, if they were bold, "Why Xenobiology?"

"I'm interested in Specters."

Then, if they were *really* bold, "Specters? Isn't that more of an *offworlder* problem?"

"I have my reasons," she would say.

The flippant dismissal of the Specter problem started getting to her. After a while, she started coming right out with it.

"So, tell me about your interests."

"Xenobiology. I want to take on the Specters."

Oraxis or Genevieve would try to redirect her or change the subject. It was infuriating.

"Maybe let's take a break," Genevieve said after a particularly awkward introduction to some eld lady that was supposed to be important.

Oraxis and Genevieve joined hands with her. They teleported to the infinite feast. Genevieve and Zeta sat on the stone bench as Oraxis stood by them, turning away people who thought it would be a good time to introduce themselves.

"I just don't get it," Zeta said, looking at the food.

"You eat as much as you want, and the construct makes more," Genevieve said. "You never get full, so it's not as satisfying as a real-world meal, but it's still fun. There's lots of tasty stuff here you'll want to try."

Zeta shook her head. "No, I mean these Noddite people — I don't get them. They think The Specters are someone else's problem. Don't they know about the abductions? Neoprims are being abducted and killed — torn apart, burned and dissolved, digested inside an alien.

They might have slowed down since they started attacking things in space, but they haven't stopped. Doesn't anyone care about that?"

Genevieve put her hand on Zeta's. "Yes, they do care, and so do we. But there's a difference between caring about it and knowing what to do about it. They feel helpless. That's why everyone is looking to the offworlders to take care of the problem for them."

"Not the Pips," Zeta said.

"And a lot of other people. You'll find your community, and you'll be welcomed."

She sighed. "Can I just be alone for a while? Like, disappear?"

"Of course. It's your party, you can turn invisible if you want to. Just...do come back, okay?"

"I will."

She rose from the table, then imagined herself becoming see-through, like Jamji could.

It worked!

She walked a few steps away, but Oraxis was still looking at where she had been standing. She looked around, almost bumping into someone. Their hand went right through her arm.

She hadn't only made herself invisible — she was a ghost! This lightened her spirits. Now she could actually relax for a bit.

———

ZETA TELEPORTED BACK to the hill where they had looked down at the party, before. She assessed the crowd, all supposedly gathered just for her. They seemed to be having plenty of fun without her. The Pips were easy to spot, as they were both surrounded by their own little swarm of people trying to get their attention.

Jamji was also easy to spot — the glowing lady on the back of the turquoise T-Rex, doing battle with a pack of purple velociraptors.

Zeta wondered where XT-Prime and Carff were. She scanned the crowd, then spotted the tall, hairless man talking to a young woman. They stood away from the crowd, down the hill from her. She teleported to him.

"So, it's like a flock of birds?" The young woman asked. She seemed out of place — younger than any of the Noddites. She could have been Zeta's age. Her avatar was as simple as Zeta's, too — just a round-faced, stout girl. Her skin tone was a natural brown, but her hair was darker and straighter than most neoprims. She wore thick leather pants, fur-topped boots, and a fluffy white fur mantle.

"Not quite," XT-Prime said, "but you are getting closer. Do you know of honeybees?"

The young woman paused, looking down. She looked up again after a long, awkward silence. "Yes, I do now. Are you saying the whole Astrus Faction is like one big beehive?"

"No, Alasie, not the *entire* faction. Each group of Astri is an isolated hive. The overarching faction could be likened to the honeybee *species*, with each hive colony acting as an independent unit, on its own volition."

"Who's the queen bee?" Alasie asked.

XT-Prime laughed merrily. "The closest thing to a queen would be our central consciousness. That's where the analogy breaks down. Also, it's important to remember, bees are bees, and Astri are humans. Humans are, by our nature, very socially complex."

Zeta started feeling guilty for listening in without being seen. She reappeared, then pretended to have just teleported there.

She waved. "Hi, XT-Prime."

"Ah, Zeta," XT-Prime hummed, "we were wondering when you'd show yourself again. Have you met Alasie?"

Wait, did they know she had been standing there?

"No," Zeta said, "I haven't met anyone my own age here, yet. It's good to meet you, Alasie."

"You deserve a private audience, Alasie," XT-Prime said, "so I will take my leave. If you would like to learn more about the Astrus Faction, it would be my pleasure to talk with you any time." He rocked his head and shoulders forward in a bow, closing his eyes and disappearing.

Zeta asked, "So, are you a new beta?"

"Yeah, uh," Alasie said, seeming to stumble over her words, "I finished bootstrapping six months ago. No, seven months ago. It's hard to keep track, right?" She seemed to search Zeta's face for something, then continued, "So, uh, I just finished my thing — my, uh, Beta Pilgrimage to Syn-Cen. My bootstrapper, Natasha-Zeta Herrington, have you met her? That's funny, her being a Zeta, right? It's her sixth life — no, seventh? I'm sorry, I'm rambling."

"It's fine," Zeta laughed.

Alasie laughed, which sounded more like a series of huffs.

Zeta waited for her to finish what she was saying for a moment, then realized she was done. "What were you saying about your bootstrapper?" Zeta offered.

"Oh!" Alasie put a hand to her forehead. "So she got an invite and said it would be nice if I could meet another beta, so here I am. She's over there, eating. Oh, uh, there's another beta here, too. He was a boy about our age that showed up late. You should meet him. I'm sure the boys all fall at your feet, right?"

She huff-laughed, anxiously.

"I don't know about that," Zeta said, feeling her face flushing. She had to change the subject. "So, does your family have a Beta Ceremony gift-giving tradition?"

"Oh, uh, there's not really a Herrington family yet — I was her first beta. But, yeah, I think everyone does the gifting thing. She got me a bag of this sweet food called candy and, *oh-Harama!* It's *good* stuff."

They laughed together. It was nice to finally meet someone she could relate to.

"I got a bow and some perfume," Zeta said.

"A bow — very nice, I like those. I don't know what perfume is. Hang on, let me ask WoQS." She looked at the ground for a few seconds, then back up to Zeta. "Perfume sounds great. What's it smell like?"

Zeta searched for the words, but knew they wouldn't do the scent justice. Could she use the construct? Maybe if she changed her avatar so that she was wearing the scent? She closed her eyes and concentrated for a moment. Her double-mind reached back in her experiences, but she was careful not to let herself slip into the replay of smelling the perfume at the cabin.

She caught a whiff of the scent, opening her eyes. "Hey, that worked," she laughed. "I'm wearing it now."

Alasie gawked. "Wait, you just changed your avatar so you're *wearing* the perfume, just now?"

Zeta nodded.

"Are you *serious?!* How under Surya did you know how to do that? I think I smell it! You put it on your neck, right?"

Before Zeta could reply, Alasie had rushed towards her, standing on her toes and putting her head next to Zeta's, inhaling deeply.

A tickle shot down Zeta's back, making her reflexively cock her head and jump backwards.

"Oh! That was *so* rude of me!" Alasie said, putting both hands on her head and stepping back. "I'm sorry, I just — I don't think before I do things. My mom always said that was my problem, and she was *right*, Zeta."

"Don't worry about it," Zeta laughed, nervously. "I'm wearing it on my wrists, too. Here." She held her wrist out, stepping towards Alasie.

Alasie held Zeta's hand and took a timid sniff. "It smells like...I don't know what. It's great, though."

"It's supposed to smell like rain and sap and moss." It sounded better the way Genevieve had said it.

"Well, I don't know about that, but it is a sweet smell. The boys will swoon over it."

Zeta laughed and shook her head, giving her wrist a sniff.

"You don't believe me? Here, I'm going to find that beta boy, you'll see. But don't blame me when he won't take his hands off of you." She laughed, then disappeared.

This Alasie was an interesting one.

A few people in the crowd downhill had noticed she was standing alone. They tried to catch her eye to see if they could have their turn to talk about themselves. Zeta pretended not to see them, turning her head to look up at the pooch-park.

"Okay, Zeta, meet Rohito!" Alasie said, reappearing.

Zeta turned back to look at the boy. Her smile disappeared.

Time stood still.

He had red hair.

No — it couldn't be.

His soulless blue eyes were wide with shock.

This wasn't real.

The red speckles covering his pale face were decorations painted upon a mask of horror.

Zeta stumbled backwards. The world went as pale as the face before her. Every sound was a ringing, thumping noise heard from underwater. Her skin was ice. Her heart had stopped.

This beta boy — this "Rohito" — was the red-speckled man-boy.

———

"It's her," Rohito slurred, mouth agape, in a daze.

Zeta turned away, pressing her palms against her eyes.

This wasn't real!

It wasn't real because this world — this wasn't real. This was a construct, and he was just a mistake — a corpse, dredged up from a stored experience, brought back to life by her own imagination. She dug deep and commanded him to disappear.

She pulled down her hands and looked again.

He was still there, pressing a fist against his mouth, muffling a chant, "It's her, it's her, it's her."

Alasie's confused voice intruded from some distant place. "Uh, yeah, it's *her*, who did you think we were meeting? What's going on with you two?"

Zeta reached out to Pip-Tau with an urgent conversation request. The white cherub appeared by her side in a heartbeat.

"Zeta, what's—"

"He's not real," Zeta said, hissing a whisper between her clenched teeth. She pointed at Rohito with one hand, pulling Pip-Tau close with the other. "There's something wrong with your construct. Make him go away."

"Zeta," Pip-Tau mindspoke, *"what are you talking about? We don't have any artificials here — these are all real people. That guy's a beta. Woodson family, I think. Why do you think he's not real?"*

"No!" Zeta shouted. She turned to the red-speckled man-boy. "You don't deserve to be a beta! Bro-killer! Murderer!"

Rohito wailed, turning and running down the hill. She heard him calling, "Ris-mama?! Ris-mama, I need you! Dante!"

Zeta chased after him, rage boiling in her veins. She shouted, "Come back and face me!"

"Zeta, *stop!*" Pip-Tau pleaded, flying by her side.

The red-speckled man-boy died long ago, drowned at the bottom of a spring pool. He was bones in the dirt. It was all he deserved. Zeta tried commanding the construct to put her bow in her hand, but it refused.

"Zeta!" Genevieve was running to intercept her. Oraxis appeared in her path, but she dodged past him.

The crowd parted as Rohito fled, pushing through people until he fell into the arms of a black-bearded man.

"It's her!" He squealed up at the confused man, "She's here to kill me! Her soul wanders the world!"

"You need to disconnect, Rohito," the man tried saying. "Let's go home, son. Disconnect!"

Rohito wailed incoherently.

"Not so tough without your bloodthirsty wolf-pooches, are you?!" Zeta taunted. She tried to lunge at him, to grab him away from the man and beat him, but some invisible force stopped her.

Zeta flinched as her world went black.

She looked around, finding that she was standing in an empty space, surrounded by blackness, but with solid ground beneath her feet. She had a physical form, so it wasn't slate-space.

"Send me back," Zeta growled at the emptiness.

She spun in a circle, finding that Pip-Rho floated behind her, a glossy black cherub with solid white eyes, wearing a sad expression.

"Send me back, Pip-Rho," Zeta said, as calmly as she could.

Pip-Rho shook her head. "You're in time out, sis. Oraxis and Genevieve are apologizing to the Woodsons and Tau's telling your guests to hang on while we get your head on straight."

Jamji blinked into existence with her hands on her hips. "Want to tell me what just happened?"

"That boy, that *Rohito*, his wolf-pooches killed my bro-kin. He brought them to the spring pool and set them loose on us. He's a murderer! I *died* killing him, and I'll do it again!"

"You killed Rohito Woodson's alpha?" Pip-Rho breathed.

"Here's the thing," Jamji said, calmly, "say Pip-Rho sends you back and unlocks the construct so you can feed the kid to a T-Rex. What good's that gonna do?"

Zeta shook her head. "It's not right! How does he get to be a beta? He has an orb? He's immortal, now? Even if I find him in real life and kill him, he'll come back!"

"And," Jamji added, "they'll erase your orb. Murder might not be as permanent in Nod as it is in Eden, but it's still taken pretty seriously. If people got to kill whoever they wanted, the resurrection queues would have a hell of a waiting list."

"It's not fair!" Zeta yelled, pacing.

Oraxis and Genevieve appeared, followed by Pip-Tau. A heartbeat later, XT-Prime and Carff appeared.

The Telson family stood in silence as Zeta paced, her mind

running faster than she could keep up. What was wrong with this world? Of all the people, why would *that* boy get alpha seeding?

"*If it'll make you feel any better,*" Jamji mindspoke, privately, "*I can track him down, go invisible, wait until he's alone, and make an 'accident' happen.*"

"*It wouldn't matter,*" Zeta replied. "*He'd just come back.*"

And he would *keep* coming back. Even after hundreds of years, *thousands* of years, they'd be stuck on this planet together. Zeta couldn't stand the idea of having to see his disgusting *face* every time there was a gathering of Noddites.

"Do you want to talk about it?" Genevieve asked.

Zeta shook her head.

Another moment passed in silence. Her nerves simmered down enough for Zeta to realize what she had do to.

"I think we might want to wind the party down," Oraxis said. "Pip-Tau, let's come up with something appropriately *vague* to tell the guests—"

"No," Zeta said. She stopped pacing and faced the family. "I'm sorry about that outburst, I just wasn't expecting to see that face again. I want to go back to the party and say something to everyone."

"You're pretty worked up. Are you sure you're ready?" Genevieve asked, moving to her side to rub her back.

Zeta nodded once.

———

JAMJI AND ZETA were the last of the Telsons to teleport back. They appeared alongside the other Telsons, atop the hill overlooking the party grounds.

"Can you make my voice loud, please?" Zeta asked the Pips.

Pip-Tau gave her a thumbs-up. "Done!"

Zeta surveyed the crowd. "I have some things I want to say," she announced. Her voice rang out loud, filling the construct with its uncertain tone. She cleared her throat and tried to stand tall, putting strength into her voice.

"First," she said, "I want to say thank you all for coming today. I'm glad I got to meet so many Noddites, to see what you were all about. I look forward to seeing some of you again, someday."

She scanned for Alasie, finding her standing at the foot of the hill, wearing a worried look. Zeta gave her a faint grin and a slight nod.

"I know you're wondering why I was yelling at Rohito Woodson. I shouldn't have done that — I was chasing the ghosts of my past. What happened between Rohito and I happened a lifetime ago. I put that past behind, but it seems like a part of it still haunts me," Zeta paused, then added, "like a *specter*."

Murmurs went through the crowd.

"That word makes you uncomfortable?" A hint of venom came to Zeta's voice. "Specter? I'm sorry, I know you don't like thinking about *Specters*, but I can't stop thinking about them."

"Zeta," Oraxis warned.

She stepped forward, putting him behind her. "A *Specter* destroyed a Proliferan ship and sent its wreckage flaming through the sky on *my* naming day. This was the sign that sealed my fate. A Specter abducted my *pa* when I was a child, right before my eyes. This was the tragedy that defined my life. Pip-Rho, my tribal ancestor, my Telson sis-kin, got turned into a giant tumor by a failed *Specter* abduction. This is the curse that I vow to break!"

Zeta glanced at Pip-Rho, who almost looked embarrassed at the attention. She turned back to the crowd, continuing her speech. "If you Noddites had taken the Specter problem seriously when they first showed up and figured out how to fight them instead of pretending they're not there, I might not have lost my pa. But, like you say, it's an offworlder problem," Zeta shrugged, "and I agree. That's why I'm applying for a transfer to the Guard Faction."

Shouts erupted from the crowd.

Jamji let out a "whoop!" and thumped her chest three times. She put a hand on Zeta's shoulder and they exchanged glances.

"Well done," Jamji mindspoke.

Zeta looked back at Pip-Tau and Pip-Rho, apologetically. Pip-Tau looked dejected, while Pip-Rho stuck her tongue out at Zeta, then smirked and winked one solid white eye. She would've loved to study under them, but the Guardians were the ones taking the Specter menace seriously.

Oraxis wore an unreadable expression. He wasn't angry, but certainly wasn't happy. Genevieve clutched his shoulder, covering her mouth with a hand, tears welling in her eyes.

Zeta looked back to the crowd. She looked for Alasie, but she was gone. A few people were trying to make their way up the hill to her, but they kept slipping backwards. That must have been the Pips' doing — holding the mob at bay. She caught bits and pieces of some pretty mean things being said about her.

"I'm done with these people," Zeta mindspoke to Jamji.

"Then, let's give 'em a farewell salute and we're out," Jamji replied, wearing a conspiratorial smile.

Zeta smiled back, then turned to the angry crowd. Jamji joined her in raising both hands, flipping the crowd two pairs of birds before disconnecting.

25

FLIGHT

THERE WASN'T MUCH LEFT to say.

After the party, Genevieve had tried to convince Zeta to sit on the idea for a while and make sure it wasn't made in haste, but the young woman's mind was set. She didn't even want to sleep on it. She insisted that Rohito had nothing to do with the decision — he was just the spark that lit the fire, as Zeta put it. The kindling had been piling up for a long time.

Now, Zeta waited in the gondola while Oraxis stood with his feet on the basket's rim, tying a thick rope to the handle. Zephyr clutched the other end of the rope in his enormous beak. The bird glared down at them with his dinner-plate eyes from the edge of his oversized nest. Oraxis insisted that his bird's permanently stern gaze was a false interpretation — misreading human facial expressions from the bird's natural features — but Genevieve was *convinced* that the bird secretly hated them.

Zeta gawked up at Zephyr. "I simply can't believe how big that bird is."

"Yeah," Genevieve said, "enhanced animals are a modern marvel of biotechnology. Did you know their anthropolinguistic and thought-control interfaces were all developed right here on Genesis? Our faction is capable of amazing things."

Zeta met Genevieve's eye. "I'm sure they are once they put their minds to it."

Oh, that was a jab.

Genevieve took a breath to reply when Oraxis cut her off via mindspeech. *"Gen, stop. Nothing you or I can say will change her mind. At least make this a pleasant goodbye."*

He was right. This was Genevieve's last chance to leave Zeta with a fond memory of her time with them.

Genevieve forced a smile. "I have a parting gift for you."

"That's nice of you, but I can't bring anything with me up to Soma Station, remember?" Zeta looked down and added, playfully, "Except Pen, my warrior-pooch companion!"

Genevieve held up a "wait, you'll see" index finger, then turned and jogged back to the cabin. Inside, she rushed to the mini-cellar, pulling open the wooden door covering the recess in the floor. She snatched up the gift, then turned to head back out.

Hanging on the wall above Zeta's bedding was her bow. The perfume flask hung by a cord from the same wooden peg. Genevieve paused for a moment to wait for the sudden rush of sorrow to pass.

By most measures, their bootstrapping had been a moderate success. But, to Genevieve, it felt like a failure. Most of all, she couldn't shake the feeling that they had failed to make a meaningful connection with Zeta. Bonds of love and trust had helped them to guide their prior betas through their bootstrapping period. For Carff, that bond had been with Oraxis, but for the others it had been Genevieve's role. Where did she go wrong with Zeta?

Well, obviously, Zeta bonded with Jamji instead of them. How would it have gone if they never reached out to her for help, that night that Zeta broke free of bootstrapping?

Genevieve shook it off. She could torture herself with what-if's later. She had a gift to give!

Oraxis stood in front of the gondola. "You almost missed the elevator."

Genevieve accepted his hand, sitting on the gondola's edge and swinging her legs inside. "Thank you, liftman."

Oraxis hopped in. "Going up!"

"Can we wait—"

They lifted off the ground. The gondola shifted and leaned with their uneven weight distribution. Zeta and Genevieve tumbled into each other, almost landing on Penelope-pooch.

"Have a seat, ladies," Oraxis laughed.

"Glad you're enjoying this," Genevieve mindspoke.

Oraxis looked up, watching Zephyr, beaming with pride at his bird's performance. The "elevator maneuver" involved the bird lifting the rope with his beak, grabbing it with one leg as he balanced on the other, then leaning down to bite a lower section of rope and repeating. He spread his wings for balance, blotting out much of the sky overhead.

It was always a terrifying ride, and Genevieve worried that either the bird or the rope would fail with the added weight of Zeta and Penelope — normally the only passengers were her and Oraxis.

Zeta should have been terrified, too. Instead, she bubbled with laughs and squeals as the gondola rocked, bounced, and lurched upwards. She must have tweaked her neurochemistry or something.

No, she was just resilient.

AFTER A NERVE-RACKING RIDE, they had lifted past the tree limbs and sat, swinging, in Zephyr's beak. The bird placed their basket down in his nest.

"Well, that was fun," Genevieve said, flatly.

"It was!" Zeta said. "Is that what flying is going to be like?"

What was this girl on? Even Penelope-pooch looked happy. That could only have been due to a stress inhibitor thought-command from Zeta.

"Nah," Oraxis said, "it'll be a smooth ride. But it will be cold and windy, and you'll be high enough to touch the clouds. You'll probably fly through a few of them, actually."

Genevieve and Zeta stood up together. When Zeta saw how high up they were, she gave the gondola's rim a firm two-hand grasp. She looked out over the treetops, beaming with a glow of adrenaline-fueled joy. Oraxis climbed onto the rim again and set to work untying the knot.

"Here's your farewell gift," Genevieve said, handing over the dried cacao pod. It was about the size of a large potato, with a chestnut brown shell. "Inside of it is a sweet treat called *chocolate*."

"Thank you," Zeta said, turning the pod over in her hands. "Do I...crack it open?"

"Oh!" Genevieve laughed. She reached for the pod, turning it so that the stem faced upwards. She twisted the top off, revealing the hollow interior. It was filled with small nuggets of the finest milk chocolate on Genesis.

Genevieve helped Zeta to shake a few chocolate bites out onto her hand. Zeta gave them a sniff. "Well, it smells good," she said.

Then she put one in her mouth.

Watching someone eat chocolate for the first time is one of the highlights of bootstrapping — even better than seeing them eat their first piece of bacon. Zeta closed her eyes, savoring the sweet flavor, making delighted sounds.

Zeta's reaction tickled Genevieve. Oraxis even stopped what he was doing for a minute to watch. Zeta opened her eyes and smiled, nodding.

She shook a few more pieces out into her hand, then gave one to Genevieve. "This is definitely the food of the gods. It should be shared." She handed a piece up to Oraxis.

"Oh, you ain't kiddin'," Oraxis laughed, popping it into his mouth. "Mmm-mmm! You can't recreate this rich flavor in a construct, Zeta. Nobody can — not even the Pips."

Genevieve let the chocolate melt in her mouth, savoring its fine flavor, making the moment last.

The chocolate-filled cacao pod had been gifted to her by Oraxis, on their anniversary. She had no idea how he had procured it, and it only made him laugh impishly when she would prod him to reveal his source. They had eaten some of it that night, but saved the rest for a special occasion. This fit the bill.

Zeta had another piece in her hand, looking down at Penelope-pooch. She started lowering her hand to give it to the dog, but Genevieve caught her arm.

"No, wait! Sorry, I should've told you — chocolate is poison to dogs."

"Poison?" She looked at the chocolate in her hand, "but it's safe for us?"

Genevieve shrugged. "Yeah, don't ask me why. I'm sure WoQS can explain it."

Zeta gave a nod, putting the piece into her mouth. She tried pressing the lid back on the cacao pod with her chocolate-smeared fingers. Genevieve showed her how it twisted on.

She warned Zeta about letting the pod get warm, since it would make a melty mess of her treats.

She warned Zeta about how cold it would get when they got high in the sky and reminded her to use the furs which sat in a cord-wrapped bundle on the floor of the gondola.

She warned Zeta that her placental mat couldn't form while she was in the sky — contact with the ground was needed, so they should take regular breaks to replenish their energy and give Zephyr a chance to hunt and rehydrate.

She reminded her to stay hydrated herself, and to share her waterskin with Penelope-pooch.

She warned Zeta not to get bold and try to lean out over the edge of the gondola when they were in the air, and to stay seated and hold tight onto the handles when they landed and took off.

She reminded Zeta that other Noddites she meets won't speak her tribe's tongue and that she would need to practice using her double-mind's translation function to get used to speaking the Common language. Or, at least remember to request WorMS conversations until her mouth got accustomed to forming words in Common.

As Genevieve racked her mind for more things to warn Zeta about, Oraxis went through the owned animal delegation procedure. He made sure Zeta was comfortable giving thought-commands to the bird, and that Zephyr was obeying appropriately.

"Anything else I need to know?" Zeta asked, sounding a bit impatient.

Genevieve had a laundry list of things, but she realized she should stop. Zeta was resourceful — she'd figure out what she needed to do as she went along.

"Nope, that's it!" Genevieve sang. "Give our love to Jamji when you meet up with her. Save her some chocolate."

Zeta smiled. "I can't *wait* to give her a piece of chocolate. I'll save some for the Guardians, too! Then they'll be sure to accept me!"

"We wish you the best of luck," Oraxis laughed. He was standing beside the gondola, now.

A lump was forming in Genevieve's throat. "It was an honor to bootstrap you, Zeta."

"Thanks," Zeta said, throwing her arms around Genevieve. "And thanks for making me a Telson. I love you guys. I'm sorry I caused so much trouble for you."

"We love you, too, Zeta," Genevieve said, squeezing her tightly. Tears began trickling down her cheeks. This could be the last time they'd see her in years.

She let the hug linger, savoring the moment for all it was worth.

But, just like a chocolate morsel, the sweet moment wasn't meant to last. Genevieve let go of Zeta so that Oraxis could lean over the gondola's edge to exchange his own hug with her before helping Genevieve to climb out.

They stepped back, careful where they placed their feet among the hard-packed bramble of sticks making up the base of the nest.

"Zeta Telson, you are cleared for take-off," Oraxis announced.

"I can go?" Zeta asked.

"Yes," Genevieve laughed, tearfully, "you can go, just give Zephyr the thought-command to take you to the Guardian Embassy."

A moment later, the black tip of Zephyr's yellow beak clamped onto the reinforced grasping point at the top of the gondola's handle.

"You may want to sit down," Oraxis said.

Zeta ducked beneath the edge of the gondola.

"Goodbye, Zeta!" Genevieve called out as the gondola lifted and swung around, dangling over the edge of the nest.

"Bye!" Zeta called back. A waving hand appeared over the edge of the gondola.

"Hold the handles!" Genevieve cried, reaching a hand out.

"She'll be fine," Oraxis laughed. "Bye, Zeta! Don't forget to send WorMS messages!"

Zephyr spread his broad wings, leaning down. Oraxis and Genevieve crouched, bracing for the gale-force blast.

The nest lurched as the massive golden eagle pushed off, leaping into the air with a whooshing of wind. Pine needles swirled, stinging Genevieve's face and skin. Dirt blew into her eyes. The thumping of his wings increased in tempo. Genevieve shielded her face, wincing as she watched Zeta's departure.

Zeta let out a yelp. Genevieve's heart dropped. She reached out with an urgent conversation request.

Zeta accepted.

"What's wrong? Are you okay?" Genevieve mindspoke, urgently.

"This is amazing!" Zeta replied.

"You're okay? I heard you scream..."

"I was just excited, Gen-ma! Alright, I have to comfort Penelope-pooch now. We'll talk later. Bye!"

The channel closed.

Zeta had called her Gen-ma...

Maybe they *had* made a connection.

Oraxis and Genevieve stood in the nest, watching the ascending form of Zephyr switch the basket from his beak to his feet.

To their right, Surya was setting, casting the sky in beautiful tones of pink. Genevieve was certain that Zeta would fly all night before taking a break.

Oraxis sighed. "Welp, that's that. Gone in three months. I was right."

"Right about what?"

"You said she'd stick around for a year. I said three months, so I pretty much nailed it."

"Yeah, good job helping drive her away so fast," Genevieve said, with enough humor in her sarcastic tone not to offend.

Oraxis chuckled.

They stood in silence with an arm around each other's backs until Zephyr disappeared into the southern sky.

"What do we do, now?" Genevieve rested her head against Oraxis's shoulder.

"I guess we could make plans to seed the next alpha." Oraxis looked down to watch her reaction.

"Um, no," Genevieve said, unamused. "I'm going to have to think hard about adding any more Telson troublemakers to the world. Which reminds me, we still have to finish our response to Jamji's accusations."

"Oh, sorry, I forgot to tell you — I ran across Vasilis Pilspa at Zeta's reception. He said Jamji revised her essay again. She took out all the ugly stuff about us. Her latest revision just rails against the practices of bootstrappers, in general."

Genevieve shook her head. After the stress she put them

through? Someday Jamji's snap decisions and unfiltered opinions would get her in trouble.

"We could make some social visits," Genevieve suggested. "There's always lots of gossip to catch up on after coming out of boot-strapping lockdown."

Oraxis groaned.

He was right — all anyone would want to talk about was how Zeta had burned down her own reception. Their family would be the prime topic of any gossip for the next week.

They sat and dangled their legs over the edge of the nest, watching Surya set.

Just as the upper sliver of Surya's glowing orb disappeared behind the distant trees, Oraxis started laughing. Genevieve looked at him, questioningly. His laughter intensified until he filled the forest with a bellow of a laugh that she hadn't heard from him in ages.

"You wanna tell me what's so funny?" Genevieve asked, leaning away from him and raising an eyebrow.

Oraxis gestured to Zephyr's nest behind them. "Get it?!"

Genevieve rolled her eyes and shook her head, frustrated. "Just tell me."

"We're empty nesters, Gen!"

Together they laughed.

And that night, in their empty cabin, together they cried.

ACKNOWLEDGMENTS

There's no telling what sort of hot mess *Neoprim* would have turned out to be if it were not for my beloved wife, Gabrielle. She read all the throwaway versions of my awkward first drafts, gave her honest feedback, and supported me every step of the way. Then she made the cover art and chapter headers. What a woman!

I'd also like to thank my kids, Zoë, Jude, Scout, and Briar, for being my inspiration. Honorable mentions go out to our dogs, Penny Lane and Sgt. Pepper. Ringo Starr and Eleanor Rigby, our newest two pooches, will have to wait until a future novel before they can find their spirits imbued into pooches with names suspiciously similar to their own.

To my beta readers, thank you for your feedback. Special thanks go to Jessica Walker and the Maddatu family.

Finally, I must pay tribute to my muse, Ourania, who compels me to gaze wistfully at the stars.